MW01248770

THE BEAUTIFUL CATASTROPHE OF WIND

A Novel

Roger E. Theodoredis

iUniverse, Inc.
New York   Bloomington

The Beautiful Catastrophe of Wind

iUniverse books may be ordered through booksellers or by contacting:

iUniverse
1663 Liberty Drive
Bloomington, IN 47403
www.iuniverse.com
1-800-Authors (1-800-288-4677)

Because of the dynamic nature of the Internet, any Web addresses or links contained in this book may have changed since publication and may no longer be valid. The views expressed in this work are solely those of the author and do not necessarily reflect the views of the publisher, and the publisher hereby disclaims any responsibility for them.

ISBN: 978-0-595-46569-9 (sc)
ISBN: 978-0-595-50590-6 (dj)
ISBN: 978-0-595-90865-3 (ebook)

Printed in the United States of America

iUniverse rev. date: 03/25/2009

To Fiona, on her birthday

I have always feared the sound of the wind beyond anything.

In my hell it would always blow a gale.

R. L. Stevenson

PART ONE

BLACK ROCK MESA

1.

"Black Rock," the bus driver said, almost to himself.

He slowed the bus but did not stop. Only a fool would actually stop here, and the driver was no fool. Years of experience had taught him to keep his momentum—first out of necessity, then out of habit.

"Black Rock," he said again, a nearly whispered afterthought.

There was a brief pause. The silence inside the bus was familiar; the driver had heard it before—every time he came to this place. He hunched his shoulders and punched the accelerator. The engine noisily built power in response to the pressure on the pedal, but before the steady roar overwhelmed the cabin, a voice rang out.

"Stop!"

Surprised, the driver looked up into his wide-view mirror. The distorted image of a small woman with jet-black hair moved toward the front of the bus. The driver eased off the accelerator and stepped on the brake, slowly bringing the bus to a stop. The normally satisfying hiss of air escaping from the hydraulic chamber this time left the driver unsettled. He leaned forward and clicked his small transistor radio off, then turned toward the woman, disbelieving.

"This is my stop," the woman repeated.

The driver's lips moved, but he said nothing. The woman appeared Asian, and his time in the army told him that she was at least partially Japanese. She stood defiantly in the aisle, dressed simply in rough cotton pants and a coat far too baggy for her small frame. She clutched a nylon bag, the long strap running up and disappearing under her jacket. From a glance, the driver knew the bag contained all of this woman's possessions. Her type rode buses to all corners, running from a lover or to a lover, from a family or to a family, from death or to death. The driver had spent hours trapped in his seat, listening to their endless stories, their eternal laments. Just another sad rider.

"You want to get off?" he asked. "Here?"

2

The woman looked at the driver's face. He had shaved poorly; strips of black beard lined his pale face. She waited until their eyes met before speaking.

"Here," she said.

The driver felt his face flush. Her voice marked her as something more than just another doomed rider, and her eyes shone with an unblinking fierceness. Unnerved and oddly embarrassed, he looked past the woman's demanding glare and down the aisle. Behind her, rows of curious faces stared at the two of them, relieved to have some small break in the monotony of the long ride. One elderly lady, the Asian woman's seatmate until only a few moments ago, narrowed her eyes to get a clear view of the scene. She had sat through four western states of the younger woman's irritating silence, and now she leaned forward eagerly to hear her former seatmate's words. Across the aisle from the now-empty seat, a silent teenage boy slowly realized that the miles of fantasies concerning this dark-haired woman were about to end.

The bus driver hesitated. "But I said 'Black Rock,' lady. This is Black Rock."

He looked at her uncertainly, as if he had something more to add.

"This is my stop," she repeated.

The force of her words made him turn back to the wheel; he gripped it tightly while staring straight ahead.

Finally, he spoke without turning. "We usually don't drop off people here."

She blinked once, slowly. The driver was suggesting that getting off the bus was out of the question. But staying on the bus was equally out of the question. For the duration of the trip, as she had sat in her aisle seat halfway back, she had thought she might go mad from the intruding noise. She had tried to create a boundary: shutting her eyes, hunching her shoulders, and tipping her chin toward her chest so severely that her seatmate, the portly old lady with white hair, wondered if she were in pain.

"You all right?" the elderly lady had asked. Her voice had sounded disinterested, even harsh. Miles ago, somewhere west of Sioux Falls, but still far to the east of Bear Creek, the lady would have been kinder. But hours of silence from her Asian seatmate had worked on her, and the younger woman had incurred the particular venom that strangers can evoke only when they fail to speak.

Later, in an aside to her family in Boise, the elderly lady would recount her impressions of her seatmate as she sipped coffee after dinner, the crumbs of bread and Dutch apple pie littering the checkered tablecloth.

"This strange young lady, real standoffish, you know? She looked to be Chinese or something. Black hair, dark skin, but pretty, the way those people can be. Younglike, but couldn't tell her age for sure—you know how you can't tell that either with them. Do you know she wouldn't say a civil word to me the whole trip? And you know how friendly I am, always with a question for a person. And when she got off that bus, I can tell you, all—excuse me for saying it—all hell broke loose. Bus driver cursed all the way to Boise about that woman. Some people are just trouble; you can tell right off."

The bus had been hurtling west, its awkward shape bludgeoning a great cavernous hole in the unseen wind, creating in the wake of its passage hysterical eddies of dust at the road's edge. If the noise had been solely the whistling sound of the bus rushing through the wind, perhaps the Asian woman could have managed, but the incessant questions of the lady next to her—which she had endured across parts of South and North Dakota, across Kansas and Colorado—these questions, she had thought, would kill her.

"You all right?" the lady repeated.

The Asian woman had remained mute, her eyes shut. The older lady *harrumphed* and drew her handbag closer to her chest more noisily than the task required. The women were separated only by a flimsy armrest; the seats creaked and lurched as the bulky woman moved, buffeting her seatmate—perhaps in the hope the movements would convince the smaller woman to vacate, opening the possibility for polite conversation with someone from America, rather than Vietnam, or China, or wherever.

The Asian woman looked away, across the aisle. A young man with bad complexion had been waiting for miles to make eye contact. He had been observing her: the long shiny black hair, her round face and brown skin, and he had imagined scenes with her in bus stations, in coffee shops, and in bedrooms. For miles he had watched her while listening to his headphones, the repetitive beat of the rap music and screams of the vocals too loud for such a small area. In return of her glance, he leered. Rather than scream obscenities, she leapt from her seat and strode forward without a glance back at her tormentors.

As she walked toward the front of the bus, the woman looked out at the town. It seemed clean and smooth. The road almost seemed polished, and the sidewalks were of worn wood raised in the old Western style. The three main buildings in town were clustered together. Strangely, each building seemed narrowed toward the westernmost edge, almost coming to a point like the bow of a ship; the group of structures gave the distinct impression of a fleet of ships huddling together for safety in a storm. On the streets and on the sidewalks she saw no animals, no activities, and, above all, no pedestrians. Though it was a windy day, the town looked peaceful and quiet—hopefully filled with people who kept to themselves and didn't feel the need to meddle in the business of others—a place a person could glide through without effort.

Based upon this impression and little else, the woman had pursed her lips and decided to stop here for a while, if only to escape the jagged edges inside the bus. She hoisted her small bag and stood on the bus steps, waiting for the driver to open the door. His hand reached out and carefully worked the silver handle.

"Be careful, now, miss. Stand clear."

Stubbornly, she held her ground. *Okay, don't listen to me*, the bus driver thought. *You don't know what you're in for, lady.* He inhaled sharply, as if he were about to plunge below the surface of an icy lake, and pulled the handle slightly—ever so slightly. The wind, which had been waiting for a foolish person to give it something to grapple with, instantaneously seized the door and blew it open so violently that bolts in the hinges stretched and popped as the door banged against the side of the bus. The heavy metal fluttered like a clothesline on a windy day.

The elderly seatmate frowned at the Asian woman, who stood stunned and disheveled in the doorway. Her long black hair blew in a thousand directions; her bag had unhitched from her shoulder and was being pulled by a delighted wind the way a fisherman pulls his rod when he has finally hooked the big one.

"Figures it would be her causing all the commotion," the elderly lady muttered.

The bus driver pushed the Asian woman to the side and stepped into the brutish wind. He cursed under his breath as he tried to pry the door closed. He curled his fingers around the side of the sharp metal and pulled until he thought his fingers would be cut off. Finally, he gave up and turned brusquely, only to find the woman standing uncertainly on the bottom step.

"Your stop, lady," he bristled.

With one arm latched firmly around her small bag, the woman attempted to brush the hair out of her eyes. This town, this place, had seemed so quiet from the bus window. Was it turning on her already, this quickly? No, she finally decided, it was just a bad wind. It would die down soon enough.

"You better get off. I'm turning the bus around to shut the door. And when it shuts, it ain't opening until we get to Bear Creek."

The woman didn't know where Bear Creek was, any more than she knew where Black Rock was, but her history on the bus had become too complicated for her to stay. She looked over the driver's shoulder at the elderly lady's judgmental scowl, then back at the bus driver.

He was a thin—impossibly thin—white man in his fifties, his hair short and graying at the temples. She saw his temper in his face, in his sharp nose, in his thin lips and scarred cheek. She saw him sitting in his seat for long hours, cursing silently at the traffic, the sun, the rain, even at the transistor radio propped up in front of his wheel. She saw him slicking back his hair in the men's room at countless stations.

"Lady…" He was sitting in his seat now, half pleading, half threatening her to get off the bus. Behind her, the elderly seatmate leaned forward, eager to see the confrontation. *Finally*, she thought, *she's gonna get her due.*

The Asian woman looked back at the bus driver and noticed the flecks of dandruff speckling his shoulders. For a brief moment she wondered how hair as oily as his could possibly produce so many white flakes. Then, just as she thought he was about to rise from his seat to physically force her from the bus, she noticed his nametag: Richard Sweeney.

"Fuck you, Dick," she said.

She smiled pleasantly at the elderly woman and the horny teenager, held her hair firmly in one hand, and stepped purposefully onto Black Rock's only street.

"Good riddance," the driver muttered.

He put the bus back into gear, executed a clumsy U-turn in order to allow the wind to help him close the door, then turned the bus once again and lurched gratefully away from Black Rock.

Unprepared for the savage wind, the Asian woman fell awkwardly to the ground the instant she stepped from the bus. Her bag, secured around her neck for protection from thieves in the bus, had soared out in front of her, causing her to move frighteningly fast across the road. She lost her balance, and the wind took over. To her astonishment, it refused to relent and dragged her away from the bus, down the smooth slate surface of the main street. She struggled to a sitting position, still moving down the street, then was knocked to her face again by a particularly savage gust.

In situations just short of being wildly out of hand, a person often finds sufficient thoughtfulness to narrate in an extraordinarily objective manner. This woman was no exception.

"This is crazy," she said.

To stop her awkward progress down the street, she spread her arms and legs wide on the street as if she were a skier seeking to stop a slide down a steep face. Her hand caught the side of a wooden platform that served as a sidewalk in the town, and she instinctively held fast. As she clung to the wood, she watched the bus drive away from the town.

Bastards, she thought, but not because they had chosen to leave her.

Another gust of wind—hard to call a *gust*, since it varied from the constant devilish wind only in the manner that a tornado differs from a background hurricane—tried to pull the woman loose from her precarious grasp. Her bag leapt into the air, and she struggled with her free hand to reel it back to the safety of her jacket. As she did so, she felt the pressure subside to the point at which she felt she could safely pull herself to a standing position.

The moment she was finally able to stand, she grabbed a wooden post to save herself from being dragged further down the street. She looked down and noticed that in reaching out to stop her slide, she had ripped her clothes and somehow gashed her hand. The hand throbbed ominously, and she watched as the blood running from the wound trickled to the end of her finger and was swept into the air by the wind. She needed to stop the bleeding and couldn't risk frivolous movements in this wind. She glanced around for shelter. A few feet away she saw a plate-glass window painted with the words, Shlomo & Sons General Store. She lunged for the door, wrestled it open, and collapsed onto the floor inside.

2.

The wind had carried many objects past the front window of Amos's store, random objects jettisoned by people and by the landscape itself, both by choice and by accident: pieces of wood, tumbleweeds, shredded bits of newspaper (from far-off locations, as most residents of Black Rock would not be foolhardy enough to even try to open a newspaper outside), and vegetation that had lost its fragile grip on the harsh mesa. Above all else, there was the black dust that found its way into every corner of Black Rock life, blown there by the incessant wind infiltrating every opening offered to it: a cracked door, an unsealed window, even a person's mouth left open an instant too long after finishing a sentence. Sometimes it was even a person that the wind blew past his window, and, if they were strangers unaccustomed to the ferocity of the wind, they lingered in his store for shelter—some for moments, some for years.

On this morning, the wind carried a young woman past Amos's window; a few minutes later she lunged through the door as if leaping from the peril of a violent sea into the safety of a lifeboat. Her legs were splayed outward, her knees bent, and she seemed unsure of her footing despite the relative calm inside Amos's store.

Amos knew every resident of Black Rock, but had this not been the case, he still would have known she was a stranger, as she did not immediately close the door behind her, but instead allowed the wind to carry its usual retinue of flotsam into his store. The wind then swirled up to the rafters, causing a raucous clattering above their heads. Startled by the noise, the woman squinted up at the ceiling, where she saw hundreds of walking canes, handmade of wood, metal, and bone, suspended from the rafters, wildly cavorting in the gusts blowing through the still-open door. She recoiled, fearing the canes would come crashing down on her head. Amos watched the disoriented woman as she calculated the risk. With years of knowledge built upon a lifetime in the hard wind, Amos knew the canes were secure. His father's canes had hung there for decades, through the birth of Black Rock, through the blunt and tragic death of the Quarry Town, and, above all, through the constancy of the wind. Amos knew that the canes were as likely to fall as the wind was to stop blowing. Neither had happened in his lifetime, nor, he expected, would they.

"My father's!" Amos shouted over the wind, gesturing at the canes as he walked past the woman to close the door. When he turned, he noticed she was bleeding from one hand and forearm.

"You okay, ma'am?"

She did not respond. Her eyes remained glued to the canes above her.

"Made most of 'em himself," Amos added, seeking to put her at ease. Her gaze darted over to Amos. She had heard men's stories and knew from experience when another was forthcoming. This tall man's father's story? Better his father's than his own, she knew. Unless he turned his father's story into his own. That would be worse.

"Old Shlomo used to say," Amos continued, "'Living in a tornado is hard, but it is not without its benefits.'"

3.

Amos spent his days behind the counter, serving the few townspeople who called Black Rock home, as well as the more transient men who worked the slate quarries. Amos sold all the necessities of life in Black Rock: foodstuffs, hardware, and hard liquor. While most small towns in the United States had a franchise of one sort or another, ready and willing to sell homogenous goods to homogenous customers, Black Rock's demographics had thus far not attracted any such consumer-based industries. There had been a rumor of a fast-food franchise several years ago, started by local blowhard Barney Tongate for some vague self-aggrandizing reason.

"I have it on unimpeachable authority," Tongate had confirmed to Amos one afternoon. He lowered his voice and looked suspiciously around the store, even though he knew they were alone. "I personally am of the opinion it will be a McDonald's-type establishment."

Amos was in the process of chiseling a mortise clean for the leg of a chair he was repairing for Old Man Proudfoot. Small slivers of oak and dried glue covered both the counter and his tools: a metal file, several chisels, and his most prized bamboo-handled Japanese saws.

Amos stopped carving and pointed the sharp chisel at Barney. "For Christ's sake, Barney. There aren't but fifty people in town at any one time. Who would they get to work?"

Milking the silence, Tongate helped himself to a handful of unshelled peanuts from the barrel in front of Amos's counter. He cracked one open with his teeth, spitting shells onto the floor. Being the only Black Rocker to leave for the nearest city on a regular basis, Tongate used the trips to inflate his worth to the others, doling out news and tips he had heard or created on the long drive into the city. He smiled an oily smile at Amos.

"Of those fifty people, how many you figure work in the quarry?" Tongate asked.

"Figure all of them, 'cept you, me, and Sis. Old Man Proudfoot. Luke. The rest are here for the slate." There was a pause. "You gonna pay for those peanuts?"

Unlike Proudfoot, who was prone to insult, Tongate was righteous enough to stand tall, make an ambiguous noise with his lips, throw some change on the counter, and walk out into the wind. Amos glanced at the change, mentally registering sixty-four cents. He sighed deeply and stared out at the wind, just as he did every day, wondering why he stayed, whether it was for Sis, or whether he thought the wind would blow something by his window that would tell him something huge, something which could make his terrible feeling of waiting—always waiting—disappear.

But nothing worth noticing ever blew by. Occasionally, newcomers would stop in, and he would enjoy their company. Usually, they were of the quarryman-to-be variety, and they'd quiz him about the easy money available in the Johnson quarry. Amos enjoyed taking liberties with the truth about Black Rock Mesa: talking about the quarries having started as gold mines, and telling them there were quarrymen who got rich suddenly after striking small veins of gold and pocketing them. Such talk amused Amos and, more importantly, kept the newcomers in town long enough for them to work a bit in the quarry and, more importantly still, to patronize his store.

But the Asian woman standing in front of him wasn't like other newcomers. For one, she clearly didn't like to talk, and Amos wasn't the kind of man to force anyone. She was blinking repeatedly, as if she were near tears, as she looked up at the canes.

"You okay, ma'am?" he repeated.

Amos kept his eyes on the disheveled woman, whose leaf-shaped eyes, like a bird's, darted about the store. They took in the two easy chairs by the door, the long counter like a bar, and between them shelves of dry goods, sacks of flour and animal feed, tent material, picks, axes, heavy shovels, canned vegetables, canned fruit, and other less recognizable items. She then looked down at her bag. People would wait until they became suspicious and insulted, but not forever. This man had waited longer than most.

"It's windy out," she finally volunteered.

Amos began laughing so hard she thought he might burst. His tall lanky form doubled over, and he slapped the counter in front of him, his face red, his breath wheezing.

"It is that, little lady. It is that for sure!"

She looked down at her bag again, concentrating hard. Weather was safe, safe to sound out a person until she got a feel for them. Weather got them talking, so she could just listen. But this shopkeeper was too patient to talk too much and inexplicably amused by the weather.

"I didn't mean …" she started.

"You're not from anywhere around here, are you?" It was more of a statement than a question. Not for the first time in her life, she felt the accusation: Outsider. Different. Alien.

"No. I'm not."

There was another long silence. She felt as if this man would wait all day to speak again. She looked up at him, a man of well over six feet. His hair was shaved close, so close she couldn't immediately tell what color it was. His eyes, gray-blue, were a cross between sky and slate. His windburnt skin wrapped tightly around his face, relaxing only in the deep crevices around his eyes and mouth.

She wondered whether she had made a foolish choice in stopping here. With this huge craggy man staring at her, she felt trapped. Of course, she could take the next bus, in a day or a week, but what if the door opened and the same driver was there waiting for her? What would he do to her? Even if the driver were harmless, she'd feel trapped, even more trapped than she had felt before getting off the bus.

The tears that she suddenly felt were controllable, but she let them come, because she knew they might be useful. As she moved her hands to her face, Amos realized her wound was still bleeding. She clearly needed some bandaging. Whether she liked it or not, he wasn't about to let her bleed all over his floor.

He opened the door behind the counter, and called, "Sis! Come on out here."

A minute or so later, behind Amos, a person emerged from a back room. It was a woman, dark-skinned, with short black hair, as short as a man's. She wore no jewelry of any kind, and her clothes were a man's clothes as well.

"Amos." With just one word her voice enchanted the Asian woman. It was as if the woman had sung to the man. He felt it too; she could see it in his smile. Amos nodded toward the new arrival. Sis's gaze followed Amos's nod; she then nodded back as if she had expected what she saw. She then came around the corner of the counter to the young woman, who watched, entranced. It seemed as if Sis were floating toward her.

"Come and sit," Sis said. The young woman nodded and followed, suddenly feeling warm for the first time since she had left Sioux Falls.

Sis shepherded the woman behind the counter. She nodded gently to Amos, who moved to one side. The silence was unsettling, punctuated as it was by the constant sound of the wind. It was almost as if this mismatched couple feared to speak in the face of the wind's power. She'd be damned if the wind would have any power over her. She glanced around for something to say, and noticed Amos's collection of Japanese saws.

"From Japan," she said.

"Huh?" Amos replied.

She pointed to the saws. Amos nodded.

"That's right," he said. "From Tokyo. That where you're from? Tokyo?"

Sis raised her eyebrows as the young woman nodded to Amos, and Tokyo realized, not for the first time in her life, that she had gained a new name for use in a new town.

4.

Amos's father, Shlomo, had arrived on the mesa nearly as accidentally as Tokyo, one of a few tenacious prospectors. Unlike the others, he had quickly determined that gold was unlikely to be found on the mesa. With a keen eye to what mattered, he quickly saw that prospectors were having an impossible time keeping track of their equipment in the unnatural wind. What the wind didn't take outright, it cleverly covered with dirt or slate dust, leaving cursing and stranded prospectors digging with their hands until they bled, or chasing heavy canvas tents across the mesa.

Shlomo began speculating, ordering more-than-needed numbers of extra-long tent anchors, shovels, and other equipment, and selling them to the prospectors. Golden dreams and hard manual labor having failed him, just as they had failed so many others, he began to harbor the belief that making a modest profit from the suffering of others might bring sustenance, if not wealth, and perhaps some of the freedom he had long desired.

"Goddammit, Joe," a prospector would say. "I lost me my shovel."

Shlomo would nod understandingly and look at the ground.

"I've got one I'm not using. I'd sell it to you."

"Ain't you gonna need it?"

"I've hurt my ankle. I can't make it up the mesa."

Shlomo had never actually hurt his ankle, but he didn't want to let on that he had lost his interest in digging on the barren mesa. He was right to assume the prospectors would have shunned him for trying to benefit from their toils. As cover for his story, Shlomo began using a cane and limping; eventually the canes became a sort of trademark, and Shlomo took great pleasure in the creation or purchase of new canes. At his death, a collection of canes numbering over one hundred passed from Shlomo to Amos. Each one now hung from the rafters of his store, constant reminders of the wealth one could gain from deception.

Although miscellaneous hardware was the foundation of Shlomo's wealth, he felt that his real genius lay in his greatest failure—his kites.

When he was a little boy in Austria, Shlomo had loved to fly a kite his father had constructed for him out of birch wood and dried sheepskin. The kite had been too heavy to fly in light breezes, so Shlomo and his father would venture out only in the windiest conditions. Shlomo's soul had soared with the kites in the buffeting wind on the green fields above Graz.

Faced with the relentless winds of Black Rock Mesa, Shlomo at first remembered his boyhood kite, long ago trampled under by joyless armies. The bittersweet memory vanished almost as soon as it had appeared—swept away, Shlomo thought, by the relentless wind. Like all of the prospectors, Shlomo suffered through untold hardships in the wind. Water was scarce, except for deep wells drilled off the mesa, which were a long walk from the prospecting areas. Normal campfires couldn't be kept; either the flames blew out or the hot ashes scattered unpredictably. Fuel for the fires, usually nothing more than thin juniper or sage, was laboriously carried from off the mesa. Prospectors quickly learned to dig deep fire pits several feet into the ground. The fire pits had to be wide at the bottom to allow the fire sufficient room to breathe, then thinner at the top so that the wind couldn't sneak down and put the fire out. The proper digging of a fire pit took about three days of chipping through hard black slate, an exhausting ordeal for one man.

Prospectors are normally a distrustful lot, loners and fortune seekers unable to tolerate the constraints of normal society and unwilling to try. On the mesa, prospectors found the wind made conversation impossible, and they liked it that way. But weighing against their desires to keep their own company was the harshness and difficulty of life. So, in deference to the wind, the prospectors would build a communal fire pit and speechlessly gather around it each evening for their meals. They stood as they ate, their backs to the wind, communicating by the nodding of heads or by subtle hand gestures, some of which were still in use by modern residents of Black Rock.

One evening, after he had left the communal fire pit, Shlomo had settled into his lean-to, hoping for a night's rest, when the wind tore the canvas of his shelter neatly in half. From the waist down, Shlomo was covered by the canvas, but the remainder released, held only by a rope to the stakes he had set earlier. Lying on his blanket, too tired to spring immediately up to save what remained of his canvas, Shlomo watched the canvas straining in the air, held only by his sturdy rope. Immediately, the memory of his childhood kites flashed through his mind. Then, incongruously, one memory unearthed another, and he remembered when his father had brought home an electric light bulb attached to a generator with a handle—when the handle was turned, the light glowed yellow-orange. Shlomo suddenly sat bolt upright in the wind, staring up at the fluttering canvas. He reasoned carefully: a sturdy kite with its tether passing through a flywheel generator would create enough energy to light ten light bulbs—maybe more.

"I'll be damned," Shlomo muttered to himself, then looked up just in time to see the fluttering shred of canvas tear free and disappear into the darkness. He watched as the canvas danced wildly on its flight to heaven, where it quickly disappeared from mortal sight.

For the next week, Shlomo stayed in the meager shelter of his campsite. Men had tried to create windmills in Black Rock before, it was true. With the windmills, they had hoped to generate energy, just as Shlomo now dreamed. Black Rock Mesa brooked no such technology. Towers, structures, anything over ten feet in height, were destined to be ripped apart by the merciless wind. The bases of these failed windmills still stood on the mesa, their upper structures long ago blown across the state.

Shlomo knew that any normal structure was destined to fail in this place. But kites, Shlomo reasoned, could dance in winds that would cripple and destroy even the humblest of structures. At that time, goats were still available on the mesa, having been considered the hardiest animals by the prospectors and brought as sources of food. The goats were promised nothing more than a short and miserable life on the mesa, followed by an unhappy ending. The unfortunate animals soon were unable to give milk, and the prospectors began slaughtering them for their stringy meat, blaming both the lack of milk and the tasteless meat on the sparse grasses growing on the mesa. After promising a goat owner a share of the profits of his energy-making venture, Shlomo was permitted to slaughter an animal for his idea.

Several weeks later, Shlomo launched his vision. The tether of the goatskin kite did exactly what Shlomo had imagined: it set the flywheel generator spinning as the kite took flight, and this caused the light bulb to glow ... briefly. The modern appliances were brought by Shlomo's brother, Nate, whom Shlomo had wired in New York City, telling of his imminent good fortune:

REQUEST COME TO BLACK ROCK MESA STOP UNTOLD RICHES AWAIT STOP BRING FOLLOWING ITEMS: ELECTRIC FLYWHEEL GENERATOR STURDY ROPE CONDUCTING WIRE SOCKET LIGHT BULBS CHEWING TOBACCO WIFE FOR EACH OF US STOP FORTUNE SMILES STOP SHLOMO.

Nate had collected the necessary items, convincing Rachael, the woman he was courting, that his brother, the prospector, had discovered a thick vein of rich ore. Rachael believed that Nate represented her last chance at marriage, but she was reluctant and fearful to travel so far alone. Rachael's more clever sister, a dark-haired beauty named Ruth, took a good deal of convincing, but finally succumbed to the desperate pleas of her sister. Ruth's desire to protect Rachael from a potentially unhappy union finally moved her to join her sister in the transcontinental trek.

Words were exchanged when the brothers were reunited on the mesa and no fortune was revealed, but Nate was quick to understand the potential represented by the delicate merger of technology and nature and quickly muted his complaint. The women were less forgiving, but were convinced to stay when it was pointed out they had no means to leave and would certainly perish before they even got off the mesa.

After sufficient preparation, Shlomo and his brother had completed the prototype of an energy-producing kite. The morning of the test, they were as excited as schoolboys, fiddling with minor adjustments and quibbling over rope lengths to be used. Amos had attached the heavy rope tether to the kite, but Nate, who was new enough to the mesa to think that the brutal winds were a temporary aberration (a common mistake among newcomers), felt that better flight would be accomplished with a lighter tether.

Shlomo settled the argument with an elder brother's common sense.

"We've only got one weight of rope."

Nate looked at the ground, as if he expected to see a selection of ropes.

"You're right. You're right. Of course."

Shlomo looked up at the fast-moving sky and sniffed. In the old days, on the street in front of his mother's house in Graz, he and Nate had delighted in the afternoon smells of the neighborhood. The boys could identify the dishes by their particular smell as the Austrian women prepared their dinners: the welcoming fried onion smell of *groestl*, the exciting goose liver smell of *buergenlandische gaenseleber* that announced the holidays, and the chocolate smell of his all-time favorite, *Linzertorte*, a specialty of his mother's. But on the mesa, smells had a way of vanishing. The animals were especially vulnerable in the wind. Shlomo had seen men, silent and scentless downwind, capture unwary goats by sneaking up on them and leaping onto their backs, twisting and snapping their necks cleanly as if they were in some rodeo.

The sky on this morning was neither blue nor gray, neither cloudy nor sunny. The sky was movement. Nate had seen a player piano, where the scroll of music turned across the front of the piano. The sky here reminded him of one of those scrolls, moving fast, but leaving a tune in its wake. The tune of the wind was rich and varied, and people who stopped to listen kept listening longer than they intended every time, marveling at the complexity of the sound.

Nate turned and smiled at his brother.

"Brother, it is time to make our fortune!"

Shlomo's face twisted in concentration. With more experience on the mesa, Shlomo heard the undertones to the wind's music. There was a low tone, almost a growl. He scowled.

"It is time," he agreed.

In an effort to boost the endurance of the kite, the brothers had decided to stage their experiment out on the bent grassland just east of the mesa, where the winds were slightly less brutal. The two sisters, neither of whom spoke fluent English, stood close to each other, taking turns serving as a windblock for each other.

They carried the kite sideways to the wind, the same way prospectors tended to carry anything which might otherwise catch the wind. They set the generator down a few yards in front of where Nate would stand and then placed the socket—connected to the generator by a long wire—near a tree trunk for protection. Shlomo then threaded the tether through the flywheel and handed the end of the heavy rope to Nate.

"Hold the loop at the end of the rope, but don't tighten it around your hand," Shlomo yelled above the roaring wind.

Nate nodded his understanding.

"I'm going to carry it out into the field and launch it slowly. Hold tight to the end in case the kite's tether starts to pull out too quickly. If you get into trouble, wrap the rope around the tree."

Nate nodded again and watched his brother take a firm grasp on the kite and walk into the field.

Shlomo would remember later a vague sense of dread as he walked out into the field, still holding the kite sideways to the wind. He glanced back at his brother, who waved encouragement. Further away he saw the sisters, huddled like sheep against the wind, not speaking to each other, but watching intently.

Back by the tree, Nate licked his chapped and painful lips, wishing he had a drink of water. He had only been at the Black Rock Mesa settlement a few weeks, but now he couldn't remember a time when he hadn't been thirsty. The wind seemed to suck the water out of people as fast as they could drink it. He sidled closer to the tree, near the light bulb, where a canteen of water rested.

In the field, Shlomo walked until the slack in the rope had almost been taken up. To walk without allowing the wind to tear the kite took absolute concentration. Several times, as he walked away from his brother, the wind almost ripped the kite from his hands.

"Not yet," he muttered. "Not yet."

At the right time, Shlomo took a firm grasp on the rope about a foot out from the kite itself. His plan, worked out with his brother's assent, was to start flying the kite with only a foot of rope, then to slowly raise the kite, bit by bit, until he had worked his way all the way back to the generator, where he would then switch to helping Nate with the end of the rope.

With both hands clenched around the rope, Shlomo let the wind take the kite. When it was only a foot into the air, he glanced back, delighted, as the flywheel generator immediately began spinning. It spun so fast he could see the sparks flying.

It's going to work! We'll be rich! Shlomo thought. He turned to his brother.

Even at a distance of a hundred yards, and in a vicious wind, a brother can see a brother's successes, as clearly as if they were standing next to each other. Nate smiled and raised the canteen in a toast to their good fortune.

In the field, Shlomo smiled back, then realized his brother had raised a hand to him.

That shouldn't be, he thought. *He should be hanging on with both hands, like me.*

At the tree, Nate finished taking a drink and leaned down to replace the canteen. He had looped the rope around his waist for a moment to briefly free up his hands.

In the field, Shlomo realized his arms were growing tired already, and looked over his shoulder at the distance he would have to cover to get back to his brother. His hands, grasping as tightly as they could, were losing strength. He cursed, thinking of the strength in the arms and hands of the prospectors. If only he hadn't given up, his hands would be strong, too.

He knew he would have to start letting the kite out. He relaxed his hands, allowing only the slightest loosening of his grip. The wind, which had waited patiently for this moment, struck suddenly, ripping the kite upward with an explosive force. Even the strongest prospector would have had to let go of the rope, but Shlomo, strengthened by the fear of losing his dream, and the possible harm to his brother, held on. In a matter of seconds, blood and smoke rising from his tattered hands, he felt the rope slip from his grip. He turned immediately to his brother.

"Let go the rope!" he yelled.

As easily as brothers might sense mutual triumph from a distance, it is equally as true that brothers cannot recognize mutual failures, no matter how close they might be standing to each other. In this wind, at his distance, Nate misinterpreted his brother's failure for further celebration. He smiled and waved, the rope still looped tightly around his waist. Nate looked upward toward the kite and briefly thought how nice it would be to soar in the wind like this kite.

"Like a bird," he muttered. They were the last words he would speak.

Nate looked down from the kite to Shlomo, who was now running like a madman toward him, still yelling. Something, a noise beyond the wind, distracted him—a hissing, then a buzzing, like angry bees. For the first time he saw the rope, speeding away from him fast, impossibly fast, burning the dry grass as it ripped through the flywheel. Before he had a chance to understand, the kite, madly dancing in the upper winds, pulled the rope tight, generator and all, snapping Nate's spine cleanly in two.

Shlomo was still running toward the tree when his brother's body, now ten feet in the air, passed him, flying in the opposite direction. Shlomo looked to the horrified sisters, who, as women, were acutely aware of tragedy at any distance. Shlomo turned and ran after his brother, whom the kite was lifting steadily higher into the air—twenty feet, thirty feet, and higher, until Shlomo could only see the speck of his brother in the sky. Then he was gone. Shlomo collapsed to the ground, covering his eyes with his bloodied hands as if to blot out the whole event. His moans were stolen by the wind.

Emboldened by the horror, Ruth took charge over the next few weeks. She dressed Shlomo's wounds and cooked his meals until his hands had healed. When her sister borrowed twenty dollars and set out for San Francisco, Ruth stayed, telling herself only that this man needed more protection, more soothing. When Shlomo's damaged hands could finally hold the reins of a horse, he set out in search of his brother's body, with the intent of bringing him back to Black Rock for a decent burial. Months of searching turned up nothing, and Shlomo decided that God had plucked his poor brother directly from the earth to whatever home he had in the sky.

Returning to Black Rock, Shlomo was surprised to find Ruth waiting patiently for his return in the fledgling settlement. Ruth would later say she had no idea what made her stay. Shlomo would say it was the mesmerizing wind, but even the hardened prospectors could see the sympathy in Ruth's eyes when she talked of Shlomo's loss. When Shlomo finally returned, they could also see Ruth's sympathy had, despite the inhospitable conditions of the mesa, blossomed into love.

For his part, Shlomo never forgot he had cost his only brother his life. Although he still believed the energy-producing kite was his only inspiration, Shlomo swore off inventions. He resigned himself to formalizing a business of supplying provisions to the dwindling number of prospectors and to the more numerous quarrymen who had given up on gold and had begun mining slate for shipment to the big cities. Before long he had his own shop built, just east of the mesa, to gain some marginal protection from the fiercest winds. And he felt a dissonant mixture of pride and defeat the day the builders put in the plate-glass window that read: Shlomo's General Store.

5.

In most quarters of the United States, a person can always depend on the weather as a ready source of conversation. In Black Rock, there was no weather. There was only wind. The winters were cold, to be sure, and the summers hot. But the weather was secondary to the wind. The wind dominated attention. It allowed no rain, no snow—nothing but the incessant blowing. Citizens of Black Rock referred to the wind as if there could be no other weather. The lone subject of conversation often revolved around the tone of the wind.

The day Tokyo arrived in town Old Man Proudfoot had walked into Amos's store hours earlier than normal. "You hear the change?" he asked Amos.

Amos nodded. "Got lower this morning. Stopped whistling that high note, too."

"Whistle didn't stop," Proudfoot said. "Got higher. High enough that only a dog could hear it."

"So, how can you hear it?" Amos asked. "You a dog now?"

It was an insult peculiar to Black Rock. There were no dogs here, or cats, either—nor birds, nor any domestic animal. People had tried, had brought pets to their homes, but the poor animals went insane after a few months. Most stopped eating and wasted away. The only domesticated animals that survived in the town did so for reprieves of short duration: sheep and goats were quickly slaughtered for food.

"Try to have a conversation," Proudfoot huffed. The old man strode out of the store, damned if he'd interrupt his morning routine again to tell a man something. Amos watched the old man struggle out into the wind, familiar with Proudfoot's unorthodox manner of walking sideways to the wind, crablike.

Well after Proudfoot had disappeared back into his house, Amos watched the street, listening to the wind working for him. He imagined shingles tearing off roofs, fence posts tearing at barbed wire, windows rattling and shattering, tools being swept away in the wind. As sure as the wind would blow, within a month every person in Black Rock would be walking through his door to buy their replacements. He smiled at the thought.

A few months later, the wind brought a different kind of customer: a writer and photographer from *National Geographic* came to visit Black Rock to chronicle the "second-windiest place on earth." All the so-called town experts gathered to meet the magazine crew at Amos's store. This included Amos, of course, with Sis moving silently in the background, Old Man Proudfoot, and Luke, who was respected because of his family's history in Black Rock. Tokyo was there because she was living with Amos and Sis in the room just behind the counter. Tongate, though ridiculed for his gift of gab, showed up in his official capacity as the mayor of Black Rock.

"Second-windiest?" Amos had asked the bearded young man from *National Geographic*.

"That's right," the man answered. He looked down, rubbing his L. L. Bean boots against each other as if he were trying to scrape off some nonexistent mud. "But it is the windiest place in the United States."

"Well," said Amos. "You mind telling us where the windiest place on earth is?"

"In Nepal." The man cleared his throat, then continued uncertainly. "You see, there's this mountain highland in Nepal surrounded by frigid glacial lakes. In the summer, the winds get generated just like off the Great Salt Lake, swooping in on the highlands from all sides …"

Tokyo saw the man's excitement, but her new neighbors were not about to give in.

"In the summer, you say. Wind here blows year-round." Old Man Proudfoot smiled at the small gathering.

"Well, now. That's true. But the Nepal winds are almost twice as strong—"

The man was interrupted by outright laughter from the group. Even the normally reticent Luke, standing next to Tokyo, laughed. She turned to him and smiled. Emboldened, Luke joined the fray.

"Anybody here ever been to Nepal?" he asked.

There were scattered noes from the group and shaking of heads.

"You been to Nepal?" he asked the man.

The man shook his head as well.

"Then ..." Luke paused, at a loss to conclude anything from his questioning.

"Then Nepal probably don't even exist," Amos concluded.

The crowd murmured its assent to the obvious solution, and, only then, when they had disproved the existence of a windier place with unassailable logic, they welcomed the man warmly. His name was Ralph. He was from Chicago. They agreed they had all heard of Chicago, and therefore it must exist.

Tokyo turned to Luke and smiled. "I've been to Chicago," she said.

Tongate cleared his throat and stood. A speech was coming. Proudfoot, who fancied himself a man of the cloth, despite never having been ordained, rolled his eyes as Tongate began.

"As Mayor of Black Rock ..."

"Only because nobody else wants the job," Proudfoot interrupted, leering. Tokyo turned away from him, trying not to see the four gnarly teeth that were left in the old man's mouth. Tongate continued, ignoring Proudfoot's taunting.

"We, the core of the town, welcome this scientific expedition for the value it brings to our people. To the extent our histories can help you discern the problematic climactic conditions, please be unhesitant to avail yourselves of our help. The people you see gathered here today represent the families who chose this challenging clime at the outset and have survived, despite all odds, to the present particular time." Tongate smiled, pleased with his speech, and sat down.

"You're lucky we don't vote in this town, Barney," Proudfoot said, leering again. "Besides, what's science got to do with the winds? Everyone knows it's God's will."

Scientifically, Ralph could explain the cold winds leaving the mountains through a peculiarly formed valley far to the west, and moving eastward over the elevated plains. Winter or summer, the high, flat land was warmed sufficiently by the sun to heat the winds; the heat increased the energy until the winds reached the natural funnel formed by two river valleys. Between the valleys, rising up like a solemn tomb, was Black Rock Mesa. Having nowhere to go but up, the heated, and by now hysterical winds blew up the slopes of the mesa and across, west to east, to scour the mesa until they diffused off the other side.

The wind grew strongest during the hottest days of the summer. On those days the steep western slopes were raked upward by a wind so powerful that quarrymen tested their courage by standing on the edges of the cliff, leaning out, arms spread in a mixture of joy and fear at the weightless feeling of being held only by the wind.

Local legend spoke of a young widow who chose to end her life by hurling herself from the cliffs. A sad and angry note was composed and left on her writing desk, weighted carefully under a large book. Tokyo imagined the widow standing on the cliff, the wind drying the tears in her eyes before they had a chance to reach her cheeks. In her anger, the widow had attempted to hurl herself over the edge, only to find herself lifted by the even angrier wind and thrown backward onto the safety of the mesa.

Again and again, the widow tried to fling herself from the cliffs until, exhausted, she abandoned her attempt and, commanded by a force she did not understand, returned even more angrily to her father's home.

Tokyo had heard the scientific explanation for the wind, but the words turned on themselves without meaning. *A peculiarly formed valley far to the west... elevated plains ... solar radiation.* The man of science had explained it all. But science explained nothing. The widow of the cliffs told Tokyo everything she needed to know.

6.

During the nineteenth century, Black Rock Mesa was universally avoided by most sane Indians. Forced to relocate in the name of *Manifest Destiny*, the Indians, a mixed band of Sioux, Bigfoot, and various other tribes, sought the best and easiest land on which to live. Black Rock Mesa, being neither, was left as a holy land where only brave and eccentric shamans ventured occasionally for vision quests.

When three hardy white men stood side by side in the shrieking wind one summer day in 1947, they were among the first animals of any species to regard the mesa as anything other than a place to be quickly abandoned to memory. Holding firmly onto the reins of their nervous horses, the men discussed the mesa in shouts.

"Flatter than an old tabletop," Noah Christophe yelled. His booming voice carried easily over the wind.

"Look at them rock formations, there," Shlomo Rubenstein said, pointing to an area where the wind had blown away all vegetation and all soil. Only an outcropping of black slate was left, exposed in the wind.

"Some kind of black sheet rock," the third man said. He was known only as Apie, due to his low forehead, dark eyebrows, and diminutive height.

"Just a black rock mesa," Noah agreed, and turned to the smaller man. "Why'd you get off your horse?"

Apie looked into the distance. He suppressed a momentary urge to tell them the truth, that he was tired of riding in the relentless wind, that he was weak and afraid he could no longer keep up the pace, that he simply needed ten minutes out of the saddle. He tried to clear his throat of dust and pointed into the wind.

"I saw something glimmer there."

"What?"

He turned and faced Shlomo and Noah.

"There. I saw something glimmer there."

"Gold?" asked Noah.

The three men were silent for a time, considering.

Shlomo reasoned. "Place like this, would stand to reason the wind would blow everything but the heaviest things away. Leave the heavy stuff lying around. And what's heavier than gold?"

Noah nodded. "A place like this, this terrible, was put here to protect something that God thought needed protecting. Something like gold."

Apie looked back at Chief, his huge red gelding. Having abandoned city life for the West, Apie found his horse to be more than the most reliable means of transportation; he was Apie's best friend. Unflappable, steady Chief, who had seen him through perilous times in ice-cold places and had raced him out of near disasters when it seemed the devil himself was on his heels, was now whimpering pitifully and rolling his huge brown eyes. He patted Chief's neck, silently cursing the fact that he had let the other two men pack all the food. Soon they would eat, mount up, and be out of this horrible place.

Shlomo pursed his lips. "Maybe we should stick around for a spell, you think?"

"The Lord helps those that help themselves," Noah said. "He also said, in the New Testament ..." and here he nodded to Shlomo, who nodded back. "... the Lord said, 'The last shall be first.' Maybe he was blessing people like Apie."

Stunned, Apie realized that his lie had not simply covered his need to get down from Chief out of the strongest wind but had also condemned him to more time in the wind. Could he tell the truth now? He glanced over at Noah and considered. *What the hell am I so damned afraid of with this guy? I'm gonna tell him we should just get out of this damned wind.* Apie ran his tongue over dusty teeth and turned toward Noah, who looked down at him imperiously.

"Doesn't hurt to look around a little," Apie agreed. *Well,* he thought, *they've got the food in their saddlebags, and I'll die of hunger if I go it alone.*

Having achieved a reluctant unanimity based solely on Apie's lie and Noah's silent intimidation, the men set up the first of a series of difficult camps just off the eastern edge of the mesa.

7.

The three men had first met weeks earlier in one of the last Kansas City saloons, where those unwilling to accept the modern world could escape, if only for a few hours, into a bleary past of smoke and whiskey. At the bar, Noah and Shlomo had struck up a spirited conversation concerning the nature of fortune.

"God's will guides us all. We walk his path, we follow his example, and riches will come to us in the end."

Shlomo pursed his lips and sipped at a shot glass of whiskey. He eyed the cup of coffee on the bar in front of Noah suspiciously.

"I'm not sure about that, friend," he said.

"Not sure? The evidence of God's righteousness is everywhere. Why, riding out here, across the great Mississippi, across the great fields and farmlands, you'd have to be a fool not to see it. I left the sin of man in the city where I found it and fled—yes, I admit it, I fled the city. But it was God telling me to go, to go to the place where I knew it would be just me and him, no interference between us. And it came to me as I came here; God is everywhere around us."

Shlomo smiled pleasantly. "I took the train here from New York City. Through Chicago. I didn't see anything that reminded me of God on the way except some men on street corners talking about his will."

Noah shook his head angrily. "No, that's not what I'm talking about. You have as much chance of finding God in the city as you do of finding a wife in this saloon."

Shlomo turned and surveyed the room. A few whores stood at one end of the bar. Taking a momentary break from their futile attempts at tempting the men who had come to the bar solely to drink, the whores busied themselves by talking with each other more loudly than they needed to, all the while watching themselves in the large mirror behind the bar. Shlomo shrugged. This tall religious man was probably right. There were no prospects for marriage here.

"My fortune has always been my family. But times in New York City have been troubled …" Shlomo shook his head and sipped his whiskey.

"God is sending you a message, is what it is."

"What would that be?" Shlomo asked, genuinely curious.

"He's telling you to do like me, to get out and commune with the land to get an appreciation of him." Noah's balled fist struck the bar, punctuating the truth as he saw it. "To find him!"

The bartender eyed him warily. Lots of transients came through his bar, some on their way east, some on their way west. All of them were looking for something, and it wasn't uncommon for them to talk, to yell, to fight, or even to kill. With the depth of his experience, the bartender examined these two men at the bar. Although both were over six feet, the preacher-man was quite big, with jerky movements that were abrupt and tinged with danger. His eyes reminded the bartender of his wife's brother, a young man who had died of scarlet fever. When the bartender had last seen the poor boy, his eyes had the same glistening, feverish look.

The other man sitting next to the preacher-man wasn't big, just tall, and he seemed more careful than dangerous. He spoke slowly, with some sort of a European accent. Polite, he thanked the bartender for the whiskey with a nod and sipped slowly. The bartender hadn't marked these two for trouble, but now the raised voice of the preacher man caused him some anxiety.

Shlomo, seeming to sense the bartender's disquiet, looked up at him and winked.

"I don't think he can give me an appreciation of himself," Shlomo said. The bartender rolled his eyes. This would certainly not help calm the preacher-man down. Without drawing attention to himself, he slowly reached for a wooden club he kept under the bar in case of arguments about politics, religion, or sports. Noah's mouth opened, about to visit the power of his God on this stranger, when Shlomo held up a finger.

"Wait. He can't make me do anything. The Old Testament speaks of free will, doesn't it?"

Noah nodded. The bartender held his breath.

"I left Europe before it took my free will. Joined my brother and his family in New York. My free will took me to the comfort of my family, away from a bad place. A good thing, wouldn't you say?"

Noah nodded. The bartender nodded too.

"Living in New York City, it didn't take me long to see the same thing that made me go from Europe to America was there too: there in the hawkers on the street corners, in every sneering boss asking me to clean up a mess, in every cheap store owner trying to get my money. That's what made me come here, on my way west."

Noah was no longer nodding. He put a single finger to his right cheek and contemplated Shlomo. After a moment's silence, he spoke.

"It was the Lord's will made you move from Europe to America, to New York, and right to that barstool." For emphasis, he struck a large finger against the side of Shlomo's barstool.

"Maybe it was. But you can't know the Lord until you are free. Free of everything. And the day a person realizes that comfort is not something that can be given to him is the day he is truly free. I'm out here, so far from home, looking for my freedom. Then maybe I can get to God."

Noah stood suddenly, his eyes wide, his arms held up above his head. The patrons of the saloon, savvy in the currents of conflict, quieted and watched the two men. The bartender closed his grip on the club, thinking that the point of no return had been reached. His hands began sweating around the club, his breathing became rapid. Shlomo sat placidly contemplating his reflection in the mirrors behind the bar.

"I've traveled this far in wonder of God, and I'll travel as far as he wants me to. And you are traveling too, looking for the wonder of God to bless you as he's blessed me."

From across the room, leaning against the door, wondering whether he would spend his last dollars on whiskey or whores, Apie contemplated the two men. From his vantage point, he imagined Noah to be a preacher, giving some kind of a half-assed benediction to the other man. Apie smiled, thinking of the poor, dumb priest he had fleeced in Ohio, telling the old man he was collecting church funds for the archdiocese.

From across the room, Apie watched as Shlomo extended his right hand to Noah. The preacher stood still, his arms upraised.

"Name's Rubenstein, friend. Shlomo Rubenstein."

Noah blinked at the offered hand but did not take it.

"God has sent us here to this place, together. He has meant us to meet, don't you see?" Noah asked. His arms were still raised, but his voice was plaintive. The bartender realized only now that Noah meant no harm and released his grip on the wooden club. He dried his moist hands on his apron.

In another place, Shlomo would have dismissed a man like Noah as a lunatic, a man so desperate in his need to preach that nothing good could come from following him. But in this place, Noah's words struck him; maybe they were meant to meet; maybe this man, even if he were unable to understand, could lead Shlomo to freedom. Shlomo looked into Noah's intense eyes. Here was danger, to be sure, but the harsh land sometimes required a lunatic to lead. And, by chance—or not—Shlomo had met a lunatic. Strangely heartened, Shlomo smiled, concluding that the path to freedom must travel through, and perhaps with, this man.

"Where does he mean to send us, do you suppose?" Shlomo asked.

Noah smiled back at this strange man of such little belief and shook his hand firmly.

"Noah Christophe is my name. And we'll know when we get there."

"Have a drink with me, friend?" Shlomo asked, pointing one finger at the bartender to draw his attention.

"Normally I wouldn't. The Bible, you know. But his will is strong in this room, and it must be for a reason." Noah paused, as if he were making a monumental decision. Finally, he nodded vigorously. "His will be done. Let's have a drink."

Apie, by this time close to the two men, fingered the money in his pocket. Though he had been in Kansas City only three weeks, the authorities were already beginning to take notice of Apie whenever he entered a public area. Soon, he knew, he faced the inevitable choice between jail and flight. These men at the bar, while tall and strange, were well-clothed and looked as if they had eaten recently. Wherever they were going, they would eat well. He had fleeced worse. With the nerves of a gambler, and the certainty of a man twice his size, Apie threw money on the bar and spoke to the bartender.

"Bring me a bottle of your best for my two new friends," Apie said. The bartender frowned at the dollar on the counter and reached for a bottle of watered-down whiskey.

Noah and Shlomo looked at the small, dark man. Apie looked back at them, hoping that his long-shot bet of parlaying his last dollars into a steady meal ticket would come through. By the end of the evening, the three drunk men, laughing and stumbling, left the bar determined to set out the next day to find their dreams. For Noah, this meant to follow God's will; for Shlomo, freedom; and for Apie, a steady supply of hot meals.

8.

On the first day, Sis led Tokyo to a back room in which Tokyo had difficulty seeing. For the next six months, while she lived in the room, Tokyo experimented with the lighting in a futile attempt to see more clearly. Neither Amos nor Sis seemed to mind Tokyo's incessant rearranging of the stand-up lamps, placing them one day on opposite sides of the room, the next day on the same side of the room. She removed the lampshades. She went into Amos's supply room and pilfered higher and higher-wattage bulbs. One day, Sis entered the room as Tokyo was on a ladder changing one of the overhead light bulbs. As was normal with Sis, Tokyo felt her presence before she heard or saw her. There was simply a change in the quality of the silence, and Tokyo turned and saw Sis smiling her smile in the doorway.

Tokyo stood on the ladder in the center of the room, a blank expression on her face. She had welcomed their offer of room and board in return for the cleanup responsibilities, and after several weeks she had surprised Amos with her capacity for bookkeeping. Despite the welcome, Tokyo felt the distance between herself and the older couple. Sis, though unfailingly friendly, rarely spoke to her. At the dinner table, she would smile and nod at Amos, and Amos would attempt to carry on a conversation with Tokyo, or, if Tokyo was withdrawn, he would carry on a conversation with himself.

Although Tokyo's first impression of Amos was that he wasn't much of a talker, she soon came to find that certain subjects would set him to chattering. But his conversations were unlike any Tokyo had experienced, for they were not so much conversations as they were histories. Sitting at the dinner table, at the counter doing the books, or cleaning the dirt from the floor after the store closed, Tokyo learned about Black Rock and its people. Amos told her about the people who lived there, where they had lived before, what they had done, what they liked and disliked. He told her about the slate: how it was taken out of the quarries and sold on behalf of the Johnson Company, how the quarrymen worked hard, and which of them could be trusted. Normally, Tokyo would have learned by now about Amos's family, and Sis's, but Amos's history mostly seemed to cover other people—everyone except himself.

Sis, on the other hand, seemed content to spend most of her days weaving on a hand loom, producing tapestries and blankets which were sold in the front of Amos's store. Sis worked the loom expertly, sometimes humming a barely audible tune, but more often working in silence. Her blankets were simple, and Tokyo assumed the lack of ornamentation in Sis's work was due to the primitive loom on which she worked. The loom appeared to be made of wood, but bore slate supports on the bottom, which had apparently been added as an afterthought. The shuttle itself was wood, but accented with a smooth inlay which was polished and shiny from use.

Whether she was working her loom or not, Sis hovered in the background, watching and listening. Initially, Tokyo suspected that Sis was incommunicative, but she came to realize that Sis, too, carried on constant conversations. Unlike the conversations carried on by Amos, Sis's conversations were largely unspoken. Sometimes, at the dinner table, Sis's silence spread to Tokyo and Amos, and they sat silent as well. At these times, Amos would often put down his fork and stare into Sis's eyes, and Sis would stare back at him in fondness and placidity. The first time it happened, Tokyo was sure the two were going to excuse themselves from the dinner table and go to their room, but, once again, Tokyo's first impression of these two had been incorrect. Since the rooms behind the shop were small and close together, Tokyo had listened occasionally for moaning and rustling, but she never heard a sound. Only infrequently, in the room next to hers, did Tokyo hear the murmuring of voices in brief conversations. Tokyo imagined the two of them in their bedroom, simply staring at each other. Amos and Sis conversed at those times on some frequency or wavelength that Tokyo could not hear or see.

Once, when the dinner table grew silent except for the sound of Tokyo's utensils against her plate, she looked up, expecting to see the two of them staring at each other. To her surprise, she found them staring at her.

Her first instinct was to excuse herself, but the large kitchen area afforded no privacy. Amos's father had seen no need for privacy in planning the construction of the store. Tokyo's only choice would have been to escape to her own storeroom/bedroom. She dropped her fork to her plate and felt the awkward weight of being observed. She studied the canned peas on her plate, noticing in that instant that the peas were not green, but a strange off-color green tinged with gray, like the pig embryo she had seen preserved in formaldehyde when she was a child. She slowly looked up, to see that Amos's focus had returned to his plate, while Sis was still staring.

Shit, Tokyo thought, looking quickly down again. She shuffled the gray-green peas around her plate with her fork, waiting. When she heard Sis begin eating again, she finished her meal without looking up and quickly stood to help clean the dishes.

The day Sis walked into her room, Tokyo felt similarly trapped. Above Sis, on the ladder, Tokyo could not revert to her normal course of looking down to avoid eye contact, for Sis was below her. Tokyo balanced uncertainly on the ladder as she reached to unscrew the old light bulb.

"I'm Native American," Sis said. "My great-grandparents were Nez Perce."

Tokyo had, of course, heard Sis's voice before, and it had been mesmerizing. Like that first day, when Tokyo had been ready to panic and run from the store back out into the wind, Sis's voice had stopped Tokyo dead, had somehow made her immediately forget the weight of expectation and strangeness bearing down on her from the newness of the people and place.

But Tokyo had never heard Sis string such a long sentence together. Indeed, Tokyo had come to believe Sis was nothing more than a simpleton, kept on by Amos for her malleability and her willingness to cook and clean. Sis's sentences were usually of the two-word variety, pronouns followed by verbs. And although a dreamy singsong quality accompanied her voice, Sis seldom used it.

"You sit," Sis had said on the first day, when she took Tokyo into the back room.

"We eat," was the call to dinner every night.

From Tokyo's awkward vantage point, she looked down on Sis, surprised to hear she could speak more than two words at a time.

Tokyo relied on a blank stare to register surprise, a stare learned over many years of untoward occurrences in her life. In moments of extreme surprise, her stare was punctuated by an exaggerated blink. For the brief moment her eyes were closed, Tokyo sometimes imagined she could reset the scene that had surprised her, to make it into something else. Perched on the ladder, Tokyo blinked.

When Tokyo opened her eyes again Sis was still there, smiling her strange smile. Tokyo shrugged and decided Sis meant her no harm. She took one step downward awkwardly, holding onto the ladder with one hand and reaching over to place the old bulb on a shelf and grab the new bulb from a pack she had placed there. It was a stretch, so Tokyo turned to Sis, gesturing for Sis to hand her a new light bulb from the pack on the shelf. Sis made no move. She didn't seem to understand that Tokyo wanted her to help.

"Can you take this bulb and hand me a new one?" Tokyo asked.

Sis stayed next to the door and looked up at the ceiling, straight up, as if peering through the wood and slate at something perched on the roof of the house. Tokyo rolled her eyes and again turned to the shelf. She reached for the bulbs on the shelf, further and further, until the ladder suddenly tipped. Tokyo threw her arms forward for balance, supporting herself on the shelf and sending the bulbs crashing to the floor. Glass shards scattered in all directions.

The noise seemed to awaken Sis. She looked up at Tokyo, who descended from the ladder, being careful to avoid eye contact with Sis. Feeling shame disproportionate to having broken a few light bulbs, Tokyo felt her face redden. She quickly started scraping pieces of broken light bulbs toward the corner with her shoes, grinding the broken glass into smaller shards.

"You can't see here? It's not just in this room, is it?" Sis asked.

Tokyo stopped scraping the broken glass and looked at Sis. She couldn't recall having told Sis of her problems seeing in the small room; she hadn't mentioned it to Amos either. Tokyo stood upright and shifted on her feet. *I guess I didn't need to*, she thought, *with all this rearranging I've done*. The pieces of glass crunched harmlessly under her shoes as she stood. She felt the glass break, almost distantly, and thought how much like eggshells underfoot it felt. Not dangerous at all, but harmless and weak.

Amos appeared at the door, a dustpan and brush in his hands.

"I heard something break. Figured you could use a hand in here," he said. He stooped and began sweeping the tiny pieces at Tokyo's feet with his hand brush. He paused for a moment and smiled at Tokyo. "When we break something in this town, we like to keep the pieces as big as possible," he said, not unkindly. "The wind, you know," Amos explained, pointing up to the roof with his brush. "It takes dust, pieces of glass, makes them fly all over. In your hair, your eyes, your food." Amos resumed sweeping the shards carefully. "Can't have that," he said, shaking his head. "Gotta clean it up right away."

Tokyo felt heat in her cheeks. "I didn't mean to do something wrong."

Sis smiled at Tokyo.

"If all you do is smile at me like that again, I swear, I'll ..." Tokyo's voice trailed off in frustration.

"She can't see anything in this place because she doesn't understand anything in this place," Sis said, then patted Amos's shoulder as he cleaned. Tokyo noticed Sis's fingers were extended outward to such an angle that they didn't touch his shoulder. Only her palm made contact with Amos. Amos turned and smiled at Sis as she walked out of the room.

Tokyo blinked.

Amos moved across the room with the brush. Although his movements were the gawky, jerky movements of a tall man, he moved with almost absolute silence, and, with the silence, an unlikely grace. Tokyo watched him bend at the knees, sweeping the glass into a neat pile. He pulled out a pocketknife and used it to pry a few remaining glass shards from a crack in the floorboards. The pocketknife was custom made, she could see. The handle was a polished black stone, not dull, but, despite the polishing, not bright either. Tokyo watched him in silence.

As Amos placed the knife on the table, he saw Tokyo staring at it. He smiled as he stood.

"That there's some of the finest slate ever taken from the mine," he said. "My daddy gave me that knife when I was a pup."

"Where is he now?" Tokyo asked.

"Still up in the mine, I guess," he said.

A moment passed as Tokyo watched Amos shift uncomfortably on his feet. There was something he wanted to say, something he wanted to tell her. She wasn't sure she wanted to hear it. She never wanted to listen to men when they got to talking about their fears, their tragedies, their failures. They were not strong; they were weak, and she was tired of their goddamn whining. If she heard it from this huge man, she'd be mean and she'd be homeless in the windiest place she'd ever seen. Before he could speak again, she cut him off.

"What did Sis mean?"

Amos shrugged.

"There's no telling with Sis, not really. You either know what she means right off, or you don't." He paused and looked at the walls of the room. "She could mean anything, really."

Tokyo nodded, not really listening to Amos's words any more than he was paying attention to what he was saying. Tokyo knew she had distracted him, maybe enough for him to leave his sorrows untapped.

"Guess I'll get some new bulbs for you," Amos said, and walked out of the room in his silent way.

After he left the room, Tokyo felt his lingering sadness as if it were a stale smell.

"I can't see it because I don't understand it," she muttered, looking up at the wall over her cot. The blood red tapestry hanging above the cot was the only hint of decoration in a room which appeared to Tokyo to be composed in black and white. Tokyo sat heavily on the cot, staring at the room.

From an objective viewpoint, the room was a simple storeroom. Three walls had shelves built against them. On the shelves were dusty jars, cans, and greasy tools. The smell of oil from the tools was thick in the air. Amos had ordered these items to sell, but his conception of the needs of his clientele was not expert, and this room had become the graveyard of his brilliant ideas.

As she surveyed the shelves, she realized that she had never really looked at the items on the shelves. *Junk*, she had thought, and passed through the room, slept in the room, and tried to live with the room. But now, looking at the shelves as if for the first time, she saw not only junk, but *old* junk. The dust was thick on some of the cans, so thick she couldn't make out the labels. It was the same with the jars. She stood, moved across the room, and picked up a can, reading the label.

"Borscht," she read aloud. "Expires 1-30-87." She shook her head. "Jesus Christ."

One can after another, one jar after another, she saw expired labels. They were uncommon foodstuffs. Some of them were bloated and twisted. She saw sardines packed in lime juice. Marinated parsnips and onions. Tongue in brine. Shredded salmon. Bacon slabs in lard. Salted pork in oil. Goat hoofs. Peeled hardboiled eggs in spring water (an impossibly perky woman smiled from the 1970s vintage label, boasting "Ready to Eat!"). Hearts of palm in vinegar. Several shelves held cans with writing that appeared to be Arabic, the pictures on them the only clue as to what could be within: canned chickpeas, canned lamb (this label had a sheep happily sitting in an open tin can gazing up at two dark-looking children who were clutching spoons), and a set of mysterious cans, all of which carried a picture of a horse standing in a pasture, a huge smile on its face, but no words to describe what might be contained in the cans themselves. Small tin cans were marked "U.S. Army." Larger dented cans had no labels.

On a second shelf, Tokyo looked with wonder at the tools, some of which were only partially covered in their original wrapping paper, a decayed brown cardboard which crumbled at her touch. She could recognize the handheld picks and shovels, but the remainder of the oily, unused tools was a mystery. Most of them looked vaguely dangerous, with sharp, gouging pieces of metal sticking out from wooden handles at odd angles. She picked up one tool and tested its well-balanced weight in her hand. The handle was blond wood; it was no larger than an average hammer. The handle ended at a green metal ring (perhaps aged copper) from which three steel prongs projected. It could have been mistaken for a garden fork, but the prongs were too thick for a garden implement, the ends too sharp. The middle prong projected several inches further than its two mates, and its end, unlike the two others, was V-shaped. Tokyo blew some of the dust from the steel prongs and saw that the tool, like the others, appeared never to have been used.

She brandished the weapon, for that is what she thought it was, as if an attacker were approaching her. Spinning, she warded the phantom attacker off with the device. She paused, face to face with the large red tapestry hanging over her cot. At the tapestry's center, a surprised woman with a long ponytail was holding a pouch outstretched in two hands. Curling, swooping lines were emanating from the pouch. Tokyo shrugged.

I must be going crazy, she thought, letting the weapon fall to her side. She turned back toward the shelves and gently pitched the weapon onto the cardboard from which she had pulled it.

Behind her, Amos walked into the room with a fresh light bulb.

"This oughtta help," he said.

Tokyo turned again, looking up at Amos. She nodded a thank-you, and Amos quickly climbed the ladder and replaced the broken bulb. As he was screwing it in, Tokyo felt again his discomfort, his need to say something to her. She knew again she didn't want to hear it; she had to speak first.

"She might be right. How can I see anything in this room if I don't know what any of it is? Some of this stuff is ancient."

Amos nodded as he worked. When he had finished, he climbed back down and turned to her. A feeling of dread overwhelmed Tokyo when she saw the look of pain on his face.

"Sis says time don't move straight in a place like this. With a wind like this. She says it moves like a kaleidoscope." Tokyo blinked. After a time, Amos looked down and cleared his throat. "She says it's time to eat," he said and left the room.

Tokyo watched Amos walk out, and all the light inside the room seemed to go with him.

9.

If someone had told the three gold prospectors when they first arrived at the windy mesa that time passed differently in such a place, they would have been more than a little puzzled. But, as days gave way to weeks, and the gusts of the wind brutalized them—forcing dust into their eyes, their ears, their mouths, and even between the threads which made up the cloth in their clothes—they slowly came to experience the random nature of time on the mesa.

On one level, the simple act of walking fifty feet became an unpredictable event. In one direction, the wind speeded time, moving a man much quicker than he expected, much faster than his feet were willing to go. In the other direction, the same fifty feet could make a man feel as if he had just climbed a steep slope, and time passed slower by tenfold.

Choices made in the wind had a way of changing suddenly; it wasn't simply a matter of which direction a person headed or even the physical act of walking in the wind. You might start off in a straight line, hunched to face the wind and buffeted by a force that stopped you cold, forcing you to one side or the other—and watch your destination move out of kilter and off to one side while you struggled to get back on track—until you either gave up, your will defeated by the wind, or you let yourself be taken to where the wind wanted you to go and made the best of what it was you found when you arrived.

On an even deeper level, the wind forced a person to look at the world and, therefore the way time passed, at a skewed angle. Facing the wind, head down, shoulders hunched, a person took short, quick breaths with lips tightened over teeth to avoid breathing too much dust, and wondered what had motivated him to get up and try in the first place. Moving *with* the wind (as if a person could cooperate with the wind or be friends with it), an awkward backward lean was required, with arms spread wide for balance but not so wide that the clothes became a sail. And worst of all, slipping at an angle with the wind, where the wind could suddenly throw you down, your posture became an awkward mix of leaning backward and forward at the same time.

The strange passage of time wasn't the only thing different on the mesa. Take for example, the simple matter of a campsite. Noah, Shlomo, and Apie had made rough campsites before in any number of difficult circumstances, and the process was always the same.

First, a suitably flat piece of land was selected. It was best if it were at a higher level than the surrounding ground, but not necessary. Shlomo, who had the foresight to travel with not only the bedroll blanket favored by most travelers, but also with a large piece of canvas and stakes for constructing a lean-to, would carefully spread the canvas on the selected piece of ground and fold it down the middle. By the time he had reached Black Rock Mesa, the process of folding the canvas in half had become a simple matter of finding the well-worn and whitened crease down the middle of the heavy material.

Next, and this step became crucial on the mesa, the canvas was turned so that the fold faced the direction of the wind. In Illinois, in South Dakota, in every state and on every prairie, this step had been a matter of discussion among the travelers. Because the other end of the lean-to would be exposed to the wind, if rain began, or if the wind picked up, the entire structure would be compromised. In other places, the wind was often subtle, even a bit of a trickster, patiently waiting for the unsuspecting to let their guard down, to fall asleep under the stars, content with their shelter until the middle of the night when the wind would awake and sweep in to scatter ashes and dust, and destroy tents and lean-tos. Travelers like Noah, Shlomo, and Apie were experienced in the middle-of-the-night winds and were careful to read the signs and discuss their options before they built their shelters.

On the mesa, there was no discussion. There were no other options. The wind was never asleep on the mesa; it never played the trickster. It blew ceaselessly from the west. Building the shelter was simple. Keeping it built was another matter entirely.

To protect the structure, the men dangled three ropes from the top of the open end of the lean-to. At first, the men had pitched the lean-to at an extreme angle to cut through the wind, but they found the closed space to be too confining. They ultimately decided to pitch the lean-to at a wider angle, giving themselves sufficient room, and to use the ropes to streamline the structure as needed during the long nights. When the wind turned from relentless to savage, the men would pull on the ropes, streamlining the angle of the lean-to, making it cut into the wind at a thinner angle, much like an airplane wing. The men took to holding the ropes in their hands as they slept. Even asleep, they learned to tighten their grip as the sound of the wind changed, pulling the rope as the wind increased, loosening as it decreased. For Noah and Shlomo, deep sleepers under most circumstances, this arrangement was workable, and they could play the ropes in their sleep as if they were fishermen landing a fish. But Apie was unable to find rest with the incessant tugging of rope in his hand.

Noah awoke one morning to find Apie, still prone, angrily tugging on a rope, struggling to keep the wind from taking more of the lean-to than it was entitled to. Apie cursed as he pulled on the rope.

"It is not pleasing to wake to the sound of your language, Apie."

"I'm guessing it would be all right for you to wake to the sound of your tent blowing away, then?"

"The tent's not going anywhere. We've got it."

Noah held up the piece of rope in his hand, showing it to Apie. Shlomo, now awake, did the same.

Apie clenched his teeth.

"Why don't we camp with the horses? Down on the east side of the mesa, just off the table? It ain't near as windy."

Noah and Shlomo exchanged a look.

"You think you're going to find wealth through comfort? You're free to go. You aren't a slave, you know," Noah said.

Apie watched hungrily as Shlomo cut off a piece of salted beef from a slab in his pouch and popped it in his mouth.

"I can't sleep with that damn rope tugging in my hand all night."

Shlomo nodded thoughtfully. "I've got an idea for you, Apie. Try tying that rope around a rock. A big one. Then put the rock under your head. Big wind comes along, it's gonna move the rock. Won't move it as much as when you're just holding it in your hand. It'll only wake you up when it's a big wind."

Noah nodded.

"You want me to use a rock for a pillow?"

Shlomo nodded.

"You're both crazy, you know that? The horses won't even stay up here. But you two do. The horses got more sense than both of you!"

In a quick flurry, Noah let go of the rope and stood. Apie and Shlomo tugged on their ropes to compensate for Noah's release.

"See what I'm doing?" Even though he didn't have to yell to be heard from such a short distance, he was shouting.

Shlomo struggled to grab Noah's rope and held it tight. He looked at Apie, then awkwardly back over his shoulder at Noah who was standing, hands on hips, facing the lean-to and the wind.

"I see you're standing there without your boots looking straight into the most god-awful wind and godforsaken mesa I ever seen," Apie said.

Noah stood in front of the lean-to and shook his head angrily. The suddenness of the harsh wind in his face had caused his eyes to water, and tears cut small clean streams on his dusty face until they disappeared into the forest of his windburned white hair. Noah took a step back, placed his hands defiantly on his hips, and yelled again.

"You don't see what I'm doing, do you?"

Apie looked to Shlomo. Then back at Noah. *The damned fool has lost his mind, and don't it figure?* he thought. *'Cause I'm close to losing my mind in this damn place with nothing to do but hide from the wind.*

Shlomo reached out and chucked Noah on the leg.

"I see what you're doing, friend."

Noah shook his head. Defiant. Proud.

"Only God knows what I do."

Noah stayed rooted in place, squinting into the western horizon. Shlomo sighed and shook his head in response to Apie's questioning glance. He pulled his boots on carefully, handed the remaining tent ropes to Apie, and stood in front of Noah, his back to the wind. *Noah might be touched,* Shlomo thought, not for the first time. *But there's something about this man makes me stay right by his side. Maybe he's one of the fools and madmen I've heard God takes care of.* Shlomo looked in Noah's face and smiled reassuringly. Here was a man making a stand, looking to put down stakes, possibly even to make something of himself. Maybe the sheer force of Noah's stubborn desire to fight for the Lord would spill over to Shlomo, enough for him to find some freedom of his own. *Shoot,* Shlomo thought as he looked into Noah's fierce eyes. *Folks have been following strong men forever, even when a child could tell they're crazy. And some of them do all right for themselves, even if the crazy man doesn't.*

Noah's eyes continued to be fixed on the horizon, his feet still planted firmly on the ground, his hands defiantly on his hips. The wind seemed to sense the affront and gusted brutally in an apparent attempt to knock Noah off his feet, but where Shlomo rocked and shifted to maintain balance, Noah stood as if firmly weighted by tons of rock.

Apie snorted in derision as he looked up at the two men. There they stood, Noah facing the wind as if he were a mountain plopped down from the sky, Shlomo's eyes at the level of Noah's chin, his straight black hair blowing back over his face.

Apie considered. *A couple of fools*, he thought. *I hitched my wagon up to a couple of crazy men, and I'm gonna pay for it. Was it worth it just for the food?* His mother had always said that God looked after fools and … and someone else too, but sure not the Millers. Right, the Millers. That was his mother's father's name. They were never lucky, she was fond of saying. If it weren't for bad luck, they'd have … something. Apie shook his head. He couldn't remember what exactly it was that they'd have had. What was it his mother had said?

10.

He was at the police station. The smell of sweat, piss, and dirt hung over everything. Angry, muffled voices issued from an adjacent holding cell. The damp stone walls held moisture so thick the sleeping men's woolen blankets were covered in dew when they awoke. The men slept on the floor; the holding cell was too small, the number of men too large. The crowded conditions were the result of a fight in the riverfront town of Newport, Kentucky. The mixture of bargemen working the Ohio River, the trappers still plying the woods of Kentucky, and the roughnecks from Cincinnati looking for trouble across the river was like dry tinder to lightning, the sheriff had said. Let them fight now, he had said, turning the lock on the large iron grating. All parties concerned (except for a few hotheads who were subdued by quick logic from the older men and a still fewer young hotheads who were subdued by quick punches to soft areas) knew the cell would be too crowded to fight effectively. Like salmon in a can, a tall blond man had said, leaving Apie to wonder what he meant.

With nothing else to do, they slept back-to-back on the dirt floor. Among the men was Apie. A weak voice next to him was saying, "I'm having someone else's dreams."

Apie looked over at the man lying on the ground next to him. Despite the semidarkness, Apie could see him well enough to be disgusted. What was left of the man's hair was long and gray, splattered with mud. His teeth and eyes were the same musty yellow. The man looked at Apie. Apie stared back, his dark, almost black, eyes invisible to the old man.

"Do you hear me, then? Eh? Do ya? Give me a hand."

Apie was not so young that he hadn't yet learned how to ignore. He pulled his blanket up to his neck and closed his eyes, not yet convinced that he was in any mood to wake up.

"I tell ya. They ain't my dreams. I'd know if they were, wouldn't I? I've been alive near eighty years, and I should know my dreams by now, oughtn't I? And I can tell you these ain't my dreams."

A burly man sleeping on Apie's other side stirred.

"Shut up."

The old man nodded and rolled onto his back. He stared up at the ceiling of the cell. Apie looked at him. He could see the old man's faltering health as if it were dripping off his body. Apie thought he might as well be looking at a pile of rags. He shook his head in disgust. He hated this man.

"Someone else's dreams. I know it." The old man was muttering again.

The burly man leaned up on one elbow. Apie turned to him. *Probably one of the bargemen*, Apie thought. His neck was thick, his arms short and thickly muscled. Here was power to respect.

"There's them in here needs some sleep. Knock it off."

Apie nodded, agreeing with the bargeman.

"Yeah, old man. Keep it down," Apie said, trying to please.

The bargeman looked at Apie.

"Good kid. Keep him quiet."

A sudden flood of contentment filled Apie, and he smiled, eager to do what more he could for the bargeman. He turned back to look at the old man. He must have sensed Apie looking, because the old man slowly turned his head. Apie remembered the haunted eyes, desperate and intense, staring him in the face, inches away. He fidgeted as the old man said nothing.

"What?" Apie hissed, afraid to disturb the bargeman.

The old man coughed, a cough so deep it seemed to come from a stone tunnel within him. He was too weak to lift his arms to cover his mouth; spittle flew from the man's mouth onto Apie. Apie shuddered, remembering the sound of his own father, lying in bed, dying of consumption, coughing until he couldn't breathe anymore, thin like a wisp. When his father finally stopped coughing for good, Apie told his mother at the funeral he was glad his father had died. His mother had slapped him across the face, but it hadn't changed his opinion. There his father had been, young but old in the casket, and never much of a conversationalist to boot. At least now he was quiet and not sick anymore. Why not be glad?

"They're your dreams, aren't they?"

Apie squinted at the man. "Quiet, old man," he said.

The old man reached out and touched Apie's shoulder. Apie looked at the bruised and wrinkled hand, wondering how a man in this condition could be alive.

"Take your dreams back."

Apie knocked the old man's hand away. "They ain't my dreams. I don't have dreams," he said, feeling foolish for engaging in conversation with a madman.

"You don't have them 'cause you gave them away. I've got them. Take them back."

On Apie's other side, the bargeman stirred. Apie was young, but not so young that he didn't already know you only got one chance in life to do things right, and if the bargeman had to talk again, he was going to be talking with those powerful arms, not only to the old man but also to Apie.

The old man began to cough again, this time more violently than before. Apie reached out angrily and put his hand over the old man's nose and mouth. *Goddamn*, was all he thought. Surprised, the old man looked directly into Apie's eyes. Apie looked back, no surprise in his face at all, just a white-hot rage. *It would be so easy*, Apie thought. And the mere thought kept Apie's hand over the old man's face, wondering if indeed it would be as easy as it appeared.

The old man didn't struggle as Apie took his dreams back. A brief shudder, a heaving in his chest, then he was quiet. Apie withdrew his hand and leaned back on one arm, marveling. It had been easy. On the other side of the old man, there was some movement as another scruffy-looking man with greasy hair moved toward the old man, rifling through his pockets. Apie watched without emotion.

"Three quarters," the scruffy-looking man said. "They're yours, I guess, kid."

Apie looked at the money in the man's hand. He was suddenly tired and wanted nothing more than sleep.

"I guess you wouldn't mind if I kept two bits for myself? Let me keep them, and I'll swear the old geezer just kicked off in his sleep."

Apie waved his hand. He was so tired.

The scruffy man nodded and pocketed two bits. He threw the other quarters across the old man's body to Apie. They landed on Apie's chest.

Still on his back, he pawed at the quarters, closed his hand around them, and fell fast asleep.

In the morning, when they released him and the others and took the old man's body away, Apie felt a strange sense of satisfaction, like the kind he got when he finished a long day of work in the hog stockyards and was able to finally scrape the pig shit from his boots.

Then, outside the jail, his mother had met him. She had been angry. "This ain't a big town! What will people say?"

Apie hadn't answered. He thrust his hands deep in his pocket and looked at the ground. He felt the quarters in his right pocket.

"Now you're late for work, too. They'll probably sack you."

Apie withdrew the quarters from his pocket and looked at them. He looked up at his mother, inches taller than him.

A mother seldom is able to notice a change in her child until it is too late to do anything about it. More accurately, a mother ignores all the signs until the bridge collapses and her child leaps away from her to a place beyond her wildest imagination, beyond her reach. The moment of realization is always traumatic, and was no less for Apie's mother in the dusty street of Newport, Kentucky, when she looked in her son's eyes and saw that he was gone. Her head swam, and tears came to her eyes. In later years, she would grasp for an explanation, failing to understand what Apie saw so clearly now, that his path had veered cleanly away from her hopes. There were no explanations, she would ultimately decide; things just were what they were.

Apie saw his mother looking at him as if for the first time. He did not feel changed, not in the least. She might have feared what she suddenly saw in her son, but she had also taken pains to ignore the change. What he had become was what he had been becoming for years. He looked at the quarters in his hand again, then squinted at the nearby barroom. *As good a place to start as any*, he thought, and walked off without saying another word to his mother.

His mother, intuiting that this was the last she would see of her son, watched as he walked into the grimy bar. She would always remember the name of the bar, even though it closed only a few months later. "Riverbend," she muttered to herself, then turned to face the jail. Two ambulance attendants dressed in clean white uniforms were carrying a body on a litter from the jail and loading it into an ambulance. The sheet over the form on the litter covered the person's entire body. Apie's mother quickly crossed herself in the Catholic fashion, remembering what her own mother had said. "Bad luck to see a body," she had said.

"If it weren't for bad luck, we Millers would have no luck at all," she muttered, not for the first time, as she hastened to leave the whole scene behind her.

11.

In the tent, Apie's eyes popped open. That was it! *No luck at all.*

Above him, Noah and Shlomo were still at standoff, just as they'd been when Apie had first seen them in the bar. Noah, a strange mixture of the bargeman's strength and the old man's dementia, was preaching.

"The horses are dumb animals—that's why they cower off the mesa! We are images of God himself!" Noah pointed an accusing finger at Apie, who shrank involuntarily, a chastened dog. "He's wrong! He's wrong! This place is not godforsaken! It's blessed! He gave us free will, and are we to use it to just do what is easy? Is that it? What then? A life of featherbeds and fresh coffee?"

Lying on his back in the shelter, Apie mentally added a Kansas City whore whose name he didn't remember.

"What does it profit a man if he gains all these things and loses his soul?" There was a change in Noah's voice. Noah looked at Shlomo desperately, tears still streaming from his eyes. Shlomo nodded.

"I see what you're doing, Noah. You're a brave man, and I'm with you."

"But he doesn't believe."

"He doesn't have to believe. I don't have to believe. That's the beauty of it. We are who we are, and we're here with you. Maybe that's enough."

Noah exhaled sharply and looked from Shlomo to Apie, who looked up at them both. Apie shrugged.

"Cut me off a piece of that salted beef while you're up, will you?" Apie asked.

Shlomo moved to where he had anchored the pack carefully using heavy pieces of broken slate, and Noah crawled back into the lean-to and pulled on his boots. Apie chewed happily on the salted beef that Shlomo had handed him. It wasn't much, but it warmed him until he could feel nothing but goodwill toward these two men.

"That coffee you were talking about sure sounded good," Apie said. "And the featherbed, too."

Noah looked at Apie, a look which reminded him of his own father's damning judgments. Noah brushed some dust from his boots and looked up at Shlomo.

"Let's find what God's hiding."

And the three men set off to spend another fruitless day scratching the surface of the windy mesa looking for a fortune in gold.

12.

Sometimes after they made love Luke wanted Tokyo to touch the slate bed in which they were lying, just like the first time.

"Look at this bed," he would say, and Tokyo could hear the wonder in his voice. He said *look*, but what he really wanted was for her to reach out and *feel*, to run her hand along the thick stone columns, the smooth and polished slate cool to the touch.

"This slate ..." he would say, shaking his head.

Luke never tired of extolling the virtues of the slate pulled from the remaining working quarry on the mesa. He wasn't sure whether Tokyo was interested or not; she just looked at him in that silent way of hers, with no judgment in her eyes, but no enthusiasm either. She did reach out and touch where he wanted her to touch, enough to keep him thinking she was interested.

"You see, if you supported the weight of the bed by putting the slate on its side, it would flake off and break. But the people who made this bed, they were smart. They lived with the slate. They breathed the slate. They could tell you before they'd dug it up what it would be suited for. This slate was meant to be a bed," Luke said, as if any sane person would agree.

Tokyo only nodded, thinking it must be nice to be so certain of a thing that you could tell, before even pulling it from the ground, that a piece of slate would be useful as a tabletop, or a floor, or as siding for a wardrobe—so certain you could look at a tree and see the chairs, the axe handles, and even the firewood all bundled up inside the bark—so certain you could look at a cow and see the steaks, the saddles, and the shoes all lumped together under the cow's hide.

At first Luke had tried to fill up the space after their lovemaking with words, embarrassed in some ways by the ferocity of their sex. Soon, though, after Tokyo failed to respond to words, Luke fell into brooding silence. The absence of intimacy in lovemaking is seldom a problem on the first few occasions, but becomes increasingly grating as time goes on. Luke knew his effort to share his wonder about the craftsmanship of slate furniture was an attempt to connect with Tokyo and, upon reflection, probably not the best attempt he could have made. But Luke's world revolved around his ability to craft slate and wood into fine pieces, the reality and certainty of which he could feel in his hands.

Luke spent most of his time in the cramped workshop of his house, surrounded by raw materials. He carefully crafted the wood and the slate together to form chairs, tables, wardrobes, and other furniture, then gave them away to other townsfolk, to quarrymen, or to anyone who seemed to have a need. As far as Tokyo could tell, Luke never made any money, nor did he have any apparent income at all. He simply worked in his shop quietly, day after day, alone with his slate and his craft.

Initially, Tokyo hadn't accepted any of Luke's invitations to visit his home, the only home left up on the mesa. It wasn't until she was certain that Amos and Sis were on the verge of kicking her out of her room at the back of the store that she relented. She thought Luke was nervous as he quickly pointed out all of the slate items in his home, telling her in each case not only what they were (that was obvious), but also who had mined the slate in question. It was only later that Tokyo realized it wasn't nerves that caused him to point out the slate, it was history.

"That kitchen countertop. That was my—Amos's dad's addition."

Tokyo looked at the countertop, the one she had since wiped so many times after so many meals. Luke was running his hand along the edge.

"See here, how the edge is rounded? You know why?"

Tokyo blinked.

"If you cut a piece of slate square—ninety degrees, you know?—the edge'll flake easier. But if you file it round, the little layers support each other and they won't flake."

Although it didn't make any sense to Tokyo, she cocked her head to one side in an ambiguous gesture that might have indicated understanding.

"It's okay. Here, feel it."

Why did he think she wanted to touch it? Tokyo reached out and touched the edge of the slate. It was smooth, almost polished. She couldn't tell if the smoothness was the result of wearing over time or an intentional act of workmanship. Her answer came a few weeks later as she watched Luke work in his shop, filing the edge of a slate tabletop.

After each stroke, he blew away what little dust had accumulated and rubbed the edge with a thumb, judging. Then he squinted and took another stroke, repeating the cycle. Luke seemed at ease in a way Tokyo had not seen before. Even his typical grimace had eased; his face now showed contentment, even joy.

As she stood wordlessly at the door of Luke's tiny shop, Tokyo realized he was attempting to take his most intimate relationship and transfer it to her. At that moment she knew the smoothness of the slate was no accident—it was an act of love. Her realization brought anger, sudden anger.

"Why are you telling me this?" she asked. Had she asked softly, had she really wanted to know, Luke wouldn't have felt stung.

"Dunno," he said, dropping his head like an old dog. After a moment, he spoke again. "It's what I do."

Still angry with his bumbling attempts to connect, Tokyo backed away and stood in the kitchen alone, enraged at his misdirected presumption, but unwilling to articulate it. Luke failed to notice Tokyo leaving his shop, but he saw with absolute clarity her subsequent avoidance of not only his shop and his furniture, but also of any discussion on the subject.

"See, now," he had said on her first visit to his home, when he had still harbored hopes she might be receptive to sharing his passion. "I laid this floor and the counters and all, but Amos's dad, he was the slate genius. He found a way to join slate to slate at angles nobody else could, almost like it was wood. And once he got them together, they didn't come apart."

"What about your dad?" Tokyo asked. Luke's mouth opened slightly, a look of shock on his face.

"He's gone," Luke said. Tokyo recognized the face of a man who wished nothing more than to tell her a long story, but at the same time was afraid to tread in a delicate area. For her part, Tokyo had no real desire to know about Luke's father. She looked around the kitchen.

"Why do you live here?" she asked, her hand sweeping toward the window.

"There were more houses up here, in the beginning. They're still here, you just don't see them."

Tokyo waited. Luke looked down at his feet, trying to find words to explain.

"Well, not up here, but down in the quarry."

"The quarry?"

Luke nodded. "That's where they are … where they were built."

"All the houses in the wind are built like boats," Luke said, changing the subject. "See, like this one, they all have a bow pointing straight into the wind, right there."

Luke pointed to the walls, and Tokyo saw how they sloped slightly inward where the ceiling met the wall.

"The pantry is at the front of the boat, so it muffles the loudest of the winds." Luke walked over to the door and opened it, clicking an overhead bulb by pulling a silver beaded chain. "You can hear the wind something fierce, here."

Tokyo walked into the pantry without looking at Luke. It was true; you could hear the wind louder in the pantry. Tokyo walked to the front of the room, the apex of the point, and imagined the house moving fast, as fast as the wind across the mesa. Here was power. She closed her eyes and stretched both hands forward to touch the walls. She could feel the wind sweeping across the bow in small vibrations and sounds which traveled through her hands and into her spine. Tokyo would have stood in the pantry enjoying the power for much longer had Luke not cleared his throat self-consciously.

"Yeah, I used to do that a lot when I was a kid. Don't know what I thought," Luke said.

"You can feel the wind without it having the power over you," she said. "Like you can control it, for once."

Luke laughed, a genuine guffaw. She turned and blinked at him. The harsh light of the single bulb softened his features, making him appear kind, even delicate. *Must be the shadows*, she thought, and snapped the light off.

"Pretty amazing, isn't it?" Luke asked. Tokyo nodded and followed him out of the pantry, toward the inner door at the back of the kitchen.

"Nobody would ever have thought to put a door on this side of the house, or a window even. Windows you can put on the side of a house, but you've got to be careful to only open one at a time."

"Why?"

"The wind will suck everything out of the room. Like a vacuum. *Shooop!*"

Luke laughed again. He pointed at the window.

"Seen it happen. Right here, too." His eyes moved quickly around the room as if he were seeing the contents scattered in the savage wind. Tokyo imagined the kitchen contents sucked out of the window, the walls and cupboards swept clean, the household items traveling toward town like tumbling bullets shot from an errant gun. Now everything movable was heavily weighted or locked behind cabinet doors which were fitted with oversized latches and stubborn clips. Luke followed Tokyo's eyes. "Living up here, you get so that you have to almost learn a new language. You don't think too much about anything other than how to figure out what to do about the wind. Twenty-four hours a day, seven days a week, it's there. To make a house stay put is all you can do."

"Is that all you do?"

"Believe me, it's plenty."

"How do you …"

"I get by. Amos and I've worked some things out. We both get by."

Tokyo nodded.

Luke hesitated. He looked at Tokyo sheepishly.

"You want to see something?"

Tokyo blinked.

"C'mon."

In a moment, she was in his bedroom, standing in front of the bed. Luke smiled broadly.

"I want you to feel something else."

This was more direct than Tokyo had expected. More direct even than her first lover, a fumbling teenager bent on one thing and one thing only—her wanting him and hating him, him forcing himself inside of her in the basement of his parents' house, coming quickly and leaning back, smiling broadly. She had gone home feeling dirty and obvious, greeting her foster parents numbly and bathing for a long time, feeling as small as an ant, then later, oddly, because of her secret, and not in spite of it, suddenly as large, if not larger than, her foster parents. Not because she was a woman, but because she knew, and they didn't.

Luke reached down and swept the blanket from the bed, revealing a dark slate frame. He ran his hand along the mattress support. Tokyo took a step backward, blinking. She was used to a man not saying what he wanted, particularly about sex. She was used to a man sliding up on the subject sideways, like a hyena. Luke looked back at her, sensing her discomfort. He smiled in a way he thought was disarming. Tokyo saw only an uncomfortable grimace.

"This is all slate, with a wood frame. Best night's sleep in the world, Amos's dad used to say. Sleeping on slate."

Tokyo hadn't said much since she had agreed to come to dinner, but Luke felt things were going well.

"Well, not sleeping on slate, really. It's more sleeping on a mattress that's on top of a big slate. Like people with bad backs who sleep on pieces of wood."

Tokyo nodded. She remembered a pool hall somewhere in her life where the bartender bragged endlessly about his slate pool tables covered with felt, so much better than wood. The bartender had been full of shit, she remembered, but he gave her free beers because she always looked sad, and he felt guilty about something he had done in the Philippines during the Second World War. One day she had come in early and found the bartender sleeping on one of the pool tables, snoring noisily, his gut protruding high into the air. She had helped herself to a draft and watched him sleep, comforted by his silent form, until a group of young men had clamored into the barroom, and he awoke with a start, grateful they had been noisy, fearing the jokes they might have played on him otherwise. She smiled at the memory. Perhaps now she was about to sleep on slate, too. She glanced over at a nearby chest of drawers. Luke saw her glance.

"Now, that's mostly wood. The slate's been inlaid into it, like panels in a door." Luke reached out and touched the wardrobe.

"This is like one my dad made, before we lost him."

The silence was unbearable. Not caring about the answer, Tokyo asked, "You lose your father or the dresser?"

Her question caught Luke by surprise. "Both. We lost both." Luke looked as uncomfortable as she had ever seen him. His squint had narrowed his eyes to slits. Not knowing what to do with his hands, he turned to the dresser and rubbed the slate as if he were seeking to smooth the small ripples of stone under his hands. He spoke without turning, his voice strange.

"This is one of the first pieces I made myself. Amos's dad described it, and I made it."

Tokyo nodded again, wondering what he could be talking about.

After they had made love, he turned to her. She dreaded what he was about to say, what she had heard men say before. When they said they had lost something and now it was found, they meant it, but then, sometimes sooner, sometimes later, they realized that they hadn't found it at all and kept looking, leaving Tokyo roughly right where they had found her. Here was another guy, she thought, mistaking an orgasm for something much larger, something almost mystical.

"The slate isn't what keeps me here," he said.

Tokyo looked at Luke. This was a roundabout way of getting to the point, she thought.

"It isn't the slate at all," he said.

Tokyo pulled the blanket up to her neck with both hands and looked up at the ceiling. She knew what was coming.

"It's … it's my family. Like you said, my dad."

Tokyo looked at Luke, puzzled.

"None of them are left but me. I'm the only one of my family. They worked hard; they built this place. It's like I have to stay here, you know? If I left, they'd not only be gone, they'd be dead, too. As long as I'm here, they're not dead. To me, anyway."

Tokyo shook her head. "I've been in so many towns, so many people, and they all want you to be their family or their wife. If I'd tied myself to all of them, they'd have pulled me apart, killed me."

Luke propped himself up on an elbow. "That's the most I've ever heard you say."

Tokyo's face reddened. *Don't get used to it*, she thought.

13.

One morning a few weeks later, they sat at the kitchen table drinking coffee in silence.

"You know what I like about you?" Luke asked.

Tokyo felt the rim of her coffee cup with her little finger. A drop of cream hung to the rim. She ran her finger through it quickly, then brought it to her mouth, wrapping her thick lips around the rich taste.

Luke smiled. "You really don't say much, do you?"

Tokyo smiled and looked into her coffee cup.

Luke stood and walked to the kitchen sink. He looked out at the windswept mesa.

"The first buildings in Black Rock were built with only one door. Can you imagine that?"

Tokyo smiled ambiguously.

"Later people realized that it was best to have sets of two doors— the first one to shield you from the wind. That just got you to the real door of the house. If you only had one door, the wind would get in and rip your place apart every time you opened it. They learned the hard way and put up two doors, with a breezeway like that."

Luke pointed with his chin to the doorway at the kitchen.

"And the door's got to be at the back of the house, protected from the wind. But even so, you still need two doors. And not too many sets of them. One or two was enough, just so you could get in and out when you needed. Too many doors, you got the same problem. Leaks and wind and dust from the mesa."

Tokyo nodded again. This made sense. Too many doors; too much wind.

Luke turned to her and smiled.

"That's what I like about you. Not too many doors."

Tokyo smiled again and sipped her coffee. Just when you thought you knew it all, people would baffle you. Unexpectedly, she felt within herself a slight ray of warmth toward this man.

Later, Tokyo studied Luke as they drove to town in his battered pickup. Others had remarked on the almost comical differences between them: He was tall and blond; she was short, her hair jet-black. He had the high cheekbones, the pronounced chin, and the blue eyes of a prototypical American cowboy; she had the soft, round cheeks, full lips, and dark eyes which betrayed her Japanese roots. She considered his chiseled features and their almost annoying weathered perfection. He didn't seem to mind the sound of the wind roaring past the truck as they drove. He didn't even seem to hear it. Maybe the wind had deafened him, for he didn't seem to hear much. Luke had the bone-weary stare of a Black Rock lifer. Bone-weary, but willful. People would have to be, in light of the tricks nature played on them. They'd have to be simple as well, and not too philosophical—a good breakfast in the morning, eggs and meat, coffee and biscuits, then out to fight the wind.

At forty-five, Luke looked closer to sixty. Women too, tended to age prematurely in the wind. It dried them out young, leaving barren sinews barely covering their sturdy bones. In the back room of Amos's store, Tokyo had seen books with pictures of sailors who'd spent their whole lives at sea. Black Rock was a thousand miles from the nearest ocean, but she saw the townspeople of Black Rock, the same as those sailors, weathered and hard. Their eyes were like Luke's, squinting and blue.

Since then, Tokyo had learned she now lived on a sea, as moving and broiling as the Atlantic she had seen as a little girl. She remembered the gray sky melding seamlessly into the gray ocean, with waves churning and crashing. She had watched, fascinated, for as long as she could, but the combination of the backseat of the green 1952 Buick and the constant motion of the water made her queasy. She squeezed her eyes shut and concentrated on not throwing up, then opened them wide a split second before she erupted in the back seat. Her foster father, an impatient man married to a barren woman, had looked accusingly at her foster mother as they cleaned the back seat.

"Why wouldn't she say anything? We could've stopped the car."

"Sweetie. You okay?" Her foster mother's face was close to her own.

Tokyo said nothing. She looked down at her feet.

Her foster father shook his head. "Why in the dickens wouldn't she say anything?"

Now she looked out the window of the pickup truck, watching the long, thin grass bending under the constant wind. On this sea, as on so many others, Tokyo was a stranger. Her skin was soft, her face rounded unlike the sharp angles of the other townsfolk. Their hair was light, sunbleached; hers was dark, black as ink. They were tall, she was short. Her vaguely oriental features had moved Amos, her first employer in town, to give her the nickname *Tokyo* when he couldn't pry her name from her.

Luke braked harder as soon as the road turned downhill coming into town. Heading this way, Luke had hardly stepped on the accelerator; instead, he allowed the wind to push the truck at its frenetic pace. Heading west, back to Luke's house was, of course, a different matter. Feeling Luke checking the truck's progress, Tokyo looked out of the front windshield. She liked the town slightly better than Luke's house; off the mesa, the winds weren't nearly as bad.

She sighed as Luke drove down the town's main street. As always, she vainly hoped coming to town would provide some excitement, or at least some distraction. She craned her neck, peering ahead. Catching sight of the worn buildings, she slumped sideways in her seat and sighed again. Only three structures were left in town, and, other than Amos and Sis, only Proudfoot and Tongate were regulars. The others came and went from Johnson's quarry as if governed by the wind—men and a few women who came for the good money they could make during the warmer months (or, if they were farmers, for the good money they could make during the colder months), then disappeared when their pockets were full, or at least full enough to happily leave the wind in their past. They'd be back when their pockets emptied again. During the months they stayed in Black Rock, Old Man Proudfoot charged them ten dollars a day to stay in his "hotel"—a glorified bunkhouse built by one of the prospectors who had founded the town many years ago.

Tokyo's disappointment in the reality of Black Rock mirrored that of the early prospectors who had established the town forty years earlier. From as far away as Denver and Salt Lake City the men had flocked to the mesa, making a hard journey through Bear Creek Canyon or through Diamondville and Kemmerer. Spurred by the rumors of gold, the men had arrived with hopes of a new gold rush, determined to ignore the wind and make their fortunes.

"We're here." Luke jangled the keys from the ignition and flipped them into the breast pocket of his denim jacket.

Luke had carefully parked so that his door was what the locals called "with the wind." Tokyo slid to his side of truck; it had only taken a few weeks to understand that only one door of a car could be used in this place. Instead of exiting immediately, Luke paused for a moment, squinting out at the store, seemingly searching for words. She waited for a moment, eyes forward and unreceptive. Luke would have welcomed even the brush of their course clothing, but he could see that a door that had briefly been open within Tokyo was now slammed shut. He sighed and opened the car door, hunching his shoulders to walk into the wind, leaving Tokyo to watch his steady progress. Tokyo felt a sudden, unexpected revulsion toward Luke, almost shuddering from the force of her feeling. The sameness of this place, the sameness of Luke's need, his apparent confidence in her utter predictability, all combined to convince her with complete certainty that she must leave him, and this place.

14.

A few months after they first arrived on Black Rock Mesa, Noah, Shlomo, and Apie were ready to give up and leave as well.

Noah had concluded that God was even more clever than he had thought, putting this awful place here on earth to show mortals he was hiding something worth fighting for, then deftly placing whatever he was hiding somewhere else.

Despite Noah's charisma, Shlomo was just short of concluding that living in a place like this, with two other men and no prospect of fortune, was never going to give him freedom.

And Apie, who had conclusively judged this place as a barren hell the first time he saw it, eagerly looked forward to the first town they could find, for strong drinking, for women, and maybe even for a fight with someone he was sure he could best.

Apie was tired of the mesa. While the other two prospected, Apie, who had plenty of interest in gold, but none in fighting the hard wind to scratch at the rocky soil, was usually left to scrounge for food. He hunted either on the mesa, which offered little save for a stray and scrawny form of goat which was stringy to eat and nearly impossible to catch and kill, or down off the mesa, where at least game birds could live in the scrub vegetation. The unspoken agreement among the men was equal shares in whatever they could find, either food or gold.

His constant complaining aside, Apie kept his end of the bargain well enough, but since open discussions about an abandonment of camp had begun, he thought to hasten the decision by killing and eating what he could off the mesa and telling his fellow travelers he could find nothing. Hunger had motivated Apie's will over the years, and he expected it could influence even large men like Noah and Shlomo. Maybe even *especially* large men like Noah and Shlomo, though neither man had ever claimed a right to a greater share of food than Apie merely because of size. But to Apie's acute disappointment, hunger seemed to do little but stiffen Noah's resolve.

"Another week or so," Noah was saying.

Shlomo nodded.

"Just to make sure," he said.

Apie shrugged and looked to the nearby horses. Several weeks after they had first arrived, Noah had finally relented to Apie's and then Shlomo's suggestion that God probably wouldn't mind if they slept in the relative shelter of the eastern slope of the mesa as long as during the day they were willing to fight the wind looking for gold.

Noah and Shlomo started up the hill to face the wind. Noah turned back to Apie.

"See if you can't shoot one of those goats, Apie. They'd even taste good right about now."

Apie nodded and looked at the fire pit as the others walked away. While they were up on the mesa, Apie had constructed the fire pit by digging into the ground about four feet. At first he had slanted the walls outward as they reached the top of the pit, as anyone might, so that the walls would support themselves. Later, after watching ashes and fire being swept out into the wind, Apie dug a new pit more vertically, cursing as he carved his way through layer after layer of slate.

Noah and Shlomo disappeared over the edge of the hill, and Apie sat listening to the noises the wind made you think you were hearing. He admitted to himself (but not to the others) that it was not only the sheer volume of the wind that kept him awake but also the haunting sounds he heard within the wind. During the last few months, he had spent entire nights wide awake and listening. He had listened to the two men sleeping: Noah so quiet you thought he might be dead, and Shlomo snoring so loudly he was clearly audible over the roaring wind. He had to rinse the dust out of his mouth and off his teeth every morning. Apie lay awake, listening to them, wondering how in sleep the two men seemed to exchange personalities, the noisy one becoming quiet and the quiet one becoming noisy. Maybe, he thought, that's why these two stick together, because they need to steal each other's dreams every night. Only Apie remained unchanged; just like during daytime, he lay nervously between the two at night, watchful, tired, and awake.

Apie looked out on the landscape and tried to find the source of the noise. The wind, of course, but the wind itself didn't sound like anything, not unless it moved against something. And the wind had long since scoured this place clean of everything except some sparse grass, probably clean of all the gold, too. But there was the relentless sound, the whistling, the *whooshing*. It never stopped. *Well*, he thought. The wind had run him ragged, and these other two as well. These two were about to give up, and he'd follow them as far as the next town, then abandon them. Abandon wasn't even the right word. They wouldn't even miss a beat if he left. For now, Apie decided, he could take it for a few more days if he had to, at least until he could figure out how to steal as much as he could from his companions before leaving.

Sitting, listening to the howling wind, Apie squinted. He shook his head. He covered his ears with his hands. He waited.

The noise of the wind showed no signs of understanding he was only a few days away from leaving, that he didn't have to take much more of this. It howled in his ears, seeming to vibrate down into his marrow. He shuddered. A few more days of this would be impossible. He pivoted, turning his back to the wind and bowing his head, thinking that he was lucky to be here and not up on the mesa where the wind was worse.

A few more moments passed, and Apie raised his head. The horses, huddled close against each other, seemed to be sharing his pain. They had learned to keep their eyes closed unless feeding and had taken to facing sort of sideways into the wind. The men had discussed this posture (thinking naturally that the dumb beasts would face away from the wind), and decided that the horses were not so dumb after all. If you watched them for a time, it became clear that the horses had formed an unspoken agreement: one horse would block the wind for as long as it could stand it, protecting the other two, then move to the calm side and let the next horse take its turn. Apie had watched this slow dance for many days, just as he was watching it now, but he did not comprehend the animals' cooperation until Shlomo had pointed it out. To him it had been obvious why the animals refused to stand with their backs to the wind—the damned wind would blow their tails out of the way and come right up their asses.

Now he watched the horses change positions, with Chief taking the wind-blocking position, his blood red saddlecloth flapping in the wind. *The saddlecloth must be annoying*, Apie thought, moved slightly by altruism but mostly by boredom. *Maybe I'll just go and tie it down.*

Apie stood. Walking with the wind, he moved much more quickly than he had expected. It seemed to him that as soon as he thought about walking to Chief, he was at his horse's side. The wind could give one a sense of power, whereby a person had only to start out toward a goal to find himself there, as if simply thinking it made it happen. Of course, the wind could also give a sense of helplessness if one were to walk against it, but Apie on this day felt almost omnipotent, one moment thinking he should be at Chief's side, the next moment being there, with no vivid recollection of the steps he took in between. It was almost as if he had been pushed along by a mighty hand. The wind screaming in his ears, Apie luxuriated in his power, forgetting for the moment he would soon feel powerless as he battled his way upwind back toward the fire pit.

Apie struggled with a piece of leather he used to tie down Chief's saddlecloth. It had come loose from the other side, and, try as he might, he couldn't quite reach it from the windy side. He lunged for the strap, but it danced playfully out of his reach. The wind was once again playing tricks on him, taking back its power as quickly as it had granted it.

"Goddamn wind," Apie snarled.

He lunged again, but once again came up empty. Chief, unaccustomed to having a man scrapping about under his belly, moved his forelegs nervously.

Apie stood up and patted Chief's neck to quiet the horse.

"Easy, Chiefie. Easy."

Chief opened one eye and reluctantly turned his head to look back at Apie. Chief had never particularly liked his master, but under the circumstances, he had begun to look at Apie as the most benevolent of men. Chief seemed to sense Apie's agitation at being on the mesa, and was therefore willing to be patient while he worked things out. Ultimately, Chief knew his master would move toward comfort rather than away from it. The other men's horses were more nervous, certain of their masters' intentions to stay right where they were.

Apie patted Chief's neck reassuringly, seeming to read the horse's thoughts.

"We'll be off this place soon," Apie said. He stroked the horse's neck, wondering why more people couldn't be as silent and good-spirited as this animal.

His thoughts were interrupted by a sound, unlike the wind, from Chief's other side. He moved back and looked over his saddle, but saw nothing except the other horses. He shrugged, thinking about the number of times the wind had played this particular trick on him.

Under his hand, he noticed a ripped and tattered corner of the wool saddlecloth. Again, the experience of the mesa came into play for him. If you left something ripped, even slightly, before you knew it, the entire thing would be in tatters. Apie squinted, considering the saddlecloth and the torn corner. The saddlecloth had been with him nearly as long as Chief, it had been a gift … well, not really a gift, since the man who he had taken it from was drunk at the time, dead drunk and lying on the muddy boardwalk in Louisville, but Apie had lifted it from the uncomprehending man's horse as the man watched, so that had to be better than stealing. If the drunk had wanted to keep it, he'd have found a way to get up, Apie had told himself at the time, practicing an excuse he might be forced to give to the authorities. The saddlecloth had meaning, since it was one of Apie's few possessions he could even argue had not been stolen, and Apie was damned if he would let the mesa take this away from him too.

The wind seemed to pick up its pace, the sound level increasing to a continuous scream. Apie turned to face it.

"You ain't taking me!" he screamed into the wind. "Or my horse!" He looked at the tattered saddlecloth, and ripped a piece off the end, holding it up to the wind.

"Or my goddamn saddlecloth!"

Apie knew screaming into the wind was useless, but he had never been one to restrict his behavior to the useful. As he bellowed, he realized the sound of the wind was less punishing.

Maybe that's why Noah talks so much. So he don't hear the wind, Apie thought. He dropped his hand to his side, feeling the saddlecloth flapping against his side. If only he could keep talking all the time, never hearing the wind. Chief snorted at his side, and Apie remembered why he had gotten up in the first place. He still hadn't tightened down the other end of the saddlecloth, and Chief was annoyed, shuffling nervously. Suddenly, Apie was struck by an idea.

Apie raised the strip of material and looked at it. It might just be enough, he thought. He lifted the jagged strip to his head, tying it tightly around his ears. As he expected, everything, especially the wind, was muffled. Apie smiled broadly and spoke to the wind.

"If I can't hear you, you ain't there," he yelled.

For the first time on the mesa, Apie felt somewhat in control. He smiled and ducked down to reach for the leather strap. Somehow he knew that the strap would no longer be out of his reach. His face pressed to Chief's warm belly, Apie reached under and thought he felt the strap. He grabbed, but came up empty. He dropped to one knee in order to see under Chief and came face to face with a man, holding the strap in his hand, reaching across to hand it to Apie.

Apie scrambled backward on the ground, on all fours, incongruously thinking that this was the easiest time he'd ever had moving into the wind, making a mental note to try to duplicate the maneuver even as he was panicking.

Apie stopped a few yards from Chief, crouching on the ground and looking back at the man visible on Chief's other side. The man peering under his horse was an Indian, his hair long and black, tied tightly in a long ponytail held in place by dozens of thin silver bands decorated with turquoise. His skin was wrinkled and red. Apie could never judge the age of people in general, and Indians were tougher since after they were kids they all tended to look alike until they got the gray hair.

This Indian, dressed in leather riding gear like Apie, stared placidly at Apie, who was still holding the leather strap out to him, a kind of peace offering. The wind lifted the man's ponytail, the silver bands clinking against each other.

Apie considered. The only thing that could bring a person up to a place like this was mischief. Apie had come to live off two more gullible men, so the explanation for his presence was obvious. But Indians could be shiftier, lulling you with their silence until they killed you and took your horses. That's what this one was going to do. Saddle up the horses and take them away. Probably leave Apie dead or dying as he whooped his way back to trade the horses for a bottle of whiskey. But Indians didn't behave like that anymore, did they? *The hell they didn't*, Apie thought. He decided to shoot the Indian on the spot. That'd show Noah what he was made of once and for all.

It was not until Apie had passed sentence on the Indian that Apie noticed his rifle was out of reach, strapped to Chief's saddlebag.

The Indian gestured, holding the strap out to Apie. He was saying something, but Apie couldn't hear it over the wind and under his new saddlecloth earmuffs.

I'll kill him after I tie down Chief's saddlecloth, Apie thought.

Apie moved to Chief's side and took the strap from the Indian's hand. He nodded a forced thanks, tied down the cloth, and stood next to his horse, eyeing the rifle. As luck would have it, the Indian stood on the other side of Chief, stroking the animal, his hand inches from Apie's rifle. The Indian suddenly smiled and pointed to his own ears. He said something.

Apie raised the strip of saddlecloth covering his ears. The Indian nodded and spoke again.

"You didn't hear me either, but I sure as hell exist. Name's Panchese. Want some food?"

Apie immediately put his plans for murder on hold and gestured hungrily to the fire pit. The two men walked toward the fire without speaking, trudging with difficulty into the howling wind.

15.

When Noah and Shlomo had returned from the mesa, they were surprised to find Apie had company at the fire pit. But their surprise quickly gave way to laughter when they spied Apie's new headgear.

Apie saw Noah laughing, a rare enough sight, but between the wind and the saddlecloth wrap, he couldn't hear what Noah said.

"What?" Apie asked.

Noah looked at Shlomo, and the two men began to laugh harder.

"Don't think your hat's gonna fit over your headband," Shlomo said.

"My what?"

The two men sat down at the fire pit, shaking their heads in laughter. Angry, Apie took off the saddlecloth wrap and threw it to the ground, or intended to, but the wind snatched it first. It would have blown it out of sight in seconds if Panchese had not reached out and deftly caught it.

"What are you laughing at? What?"

Noah looked up at Apie, appraising. He was still smiling.

"You think a piece of wool is gonna keep out God's word? Is that what you think?"

Shlomo looked to Noah suddenly. "Maybe he's hurt. Maybe the Indian hurt him."

Panchese shook his head. "He just don't want to hear no more, that's all. He ain't hurt. At least his body ain't hurt. His mind, I can't say ..." Panchese winked and held the band out to Apie, who snatched it from the Indian.

Apie struggled with his headband, pressing it painfully down over his ears until it hung loosely around his neck.

Noah walked slowly over to Panchese and looked at the Indian. Panchese, sitting cross-legged on the ground, squinted up at Noah, appraising.

"My people have legends. About the tall ones, the ones who dress in black." Panchese nodded at Noah and held out a chunk of salt beef. Although he was hungry, Noah made no move for the food. He looked to Apie, who, with no such hesitation, greedily took the offered piece and used his teeth to tear off a piece. *Might as well eat while Noah kills this godless Indian for me*, he thought. *Preachers hate Indians. Always have.*

Noah looked down at Panchese and, as Apie had suspected, all the preacher saw was an Indian.

"My people worship in houses of prayer and men dressed in black lead the worship."

Panchese nodded soberly and waved his arm around him. "My people worship here."

"I can't think," Apie complained as he chewed his salt beef. "I can't think with this damn wind. We've got to get out of here, can't you see it?" Noah and Shlomo exchanged looks. Apie looked desperate, maybe even dangerous.

"Your God doesn't want you to hear anything but him. This place is sacred that way." Panchese was smiling as he spoke. Noah turned angrily to him.

"Don't you be telling me about my God, you savage! Don't tell me what my God is telling me, or wants to tell me, or even what he wants to hide from me."

Panchese's smile grew larger. "Gold, eh? You can't find no gold, can you?"

"It doesn't mean it ain't here, friend, it just means we ain't found it yet." Shlomo was the voice of reason.

"It ain't here." Panchese shrugged as he spoke. He gestured for the men to join him on the ground next to the fire pit; he was tired of yelling over the wind.

"The legend of this place, and the wind, is sacred to my people. The legend I cannot tell you."

Apie shook his head. "Some legend. It's windy. What else is there?"

Panchese ignored Apie. "But I can tell you of the black flake stone that lies beneath your feet. The stone that my people take from this place for use in our villages. Black gold."

Noah looked suspicious. "Black gold?"

Despite the wind and the makeshift earmuffs, Apie could hear clearly any mention of gold. "An Injun trick," he snorted.

In answer, Panchese scraped at the soil around the fire pit with his heel. In a moment, he had uncovered a piece of black slate, which he lifted and handed to Noah.

"This? It's nothing but slate! We've seen plenty of it!" Noah tossed the piece away.

Panchese shrugged again and stood. "The white men killed my people, killed the buffalo, took my land. And still I give you a gift for nothing more than friendship."

"Some gift," Apie spat. He turned to Noah with a malevolent look. "Let's kill him and take his horse."

Noah stood angrily and walked away from the fire pit. He stood five feet away, facing the wind. Panchese rose and moved slowly, almost imperceptibly, toward his horse as he watched Noah carefully, sensing that this somber man might quickly grow hostile. Apie, desperate to rid the confusion in his mind with the clarity of a killing, stood and inched toward the gun in Chief's saddlebag.

Panchese, by this time a few feet from his horse's side, broke into a run and leapt nimbly onto his horse's back. Apie, thinking he was about to lose his opportunity, ran toward Chief. Noah, still facing the wind, was oblivious to the minor drama playing out behind him. As Panchese trotted away on his horse, Apie pulled his gun from his saddlebag and aimed. As he pulled the trigger, his eyes narrowed. *Got you*, he thought.

But Shlomo, who had seen many men and animals die in his lifetime, had decided that today was not a day that he wanted to see more, and, with exquisite timing, cracked his whip down on Apie's hand at the moment that Apie squeezed the trigger. The bullet struck the ground three feet in front of Apie, who howled with pain and dropped the gun. Incredulous, he turned to Shlomo, who was shaking his head.

"I won't let you kill that man," Shlomo said.

Noah, who had turned toward the sound of the gunfire, strode up to Apie and struck him across the face with the back of his hand. Apie fell to the dusty ground, shaking his head in an effort to regain his senses. He thought back to the bar in Kansas City, trying to figure whether his dollar bet was now going to pay off in the worst way. Bad luck, his mother would've called it. And yet, there, in the dust in front of him, not three feet from his grimy face, was his gun. Maybe this would be good luck after all, he thought. The Indian had gotten away, but these two might make up for it.

Shlomo sensed where Apie's thoughts were headed and snatched Apie's gun from the ground just before Apie's hand got to it. He then handed it to Noah, knowing Apie wouldn't stand a chance against the bigger man. Methodically, Noah opened the chamber and slowly emptied the bullets onto the ground.

Shlomo, realizing the threat from Apie was over, turned to Noah. "You know something? Back east, there's nothing but slate quarries. People use the slate for all kinds of things. Foundations for buildings, floors, counters, what have you."

Noah nodded.

"But when was the last time you heard about a slate quarry west of the Mississippi?"

Noah nodded again, thinking. Suddenly, his face broke into a wide grin.

"If this is the only slate for five hundred miles around, it's as good as gold, ain't it?"

"That Indian gave us a gift after all, didn't he?"

Although it was true that Apie was not bright, or even of average intelligence, his mind was nimble enough to follow any logic, no matter how twisted, as long as that logic led to a payout of some kind. He crawled to his knees and picked up the chunk of slate that Panchese had offered them.

"Damn! We could get rich off this rock?"

Noah bent down and put his face only inches away from Apie's. "Lord help me, Apie, if you take more than five minutes to get out of our sight, I'm going to shoot you with your own gun."

Apie's mouth opened to argue, but no words came out as he watched Noah stand and grimly remove his pocket watch from his trousers. Finally, Apie found words. "But we could finally hit it big! We'll be rich!" Apie turned to Shlomo, who remained silent, contemplating how his gut-level bond with Noah seemed about to pay off. "You can't chase me off! Not now! You can't cut me out of my share!" Apie's tone had changed from pleading to anger.

In answer, Noah opened the cover of the watch and wiped the dust off the glass facing. Weeks earlier, he had broken the watch while scraping at an unusually difficult piece of ground which he had felt almost certainly hid gold. Now, looking the watch, he wondered vaguely whether he would ever again have need of knowing exactly what time it was. Here, now, he knew that he didn't have need of the actual measuring of five minutes. If the Lord told him that five minutes had passed, and this miserable weasel-like man was still here, then the Lord was giving him permission to kill him.

"It was just an Indian," Apie argued, as he rose to his feet. Noah stared impassively at his watch. Apie turned to Shlomo. "It was just an Indian!"

Shlomo nodded. "He was, Apie. And he was a man who did us no harm."

Noah looked up from his watch and into the wind. The Lord had brought him here for a reason, and that was to make him rich so that he could spread the Word even more widely. Noah looked back at Apie.

"Don't do this, Noah!" Apie looked as if he might cry.

Noah snapped the cover of his watch shut, gripped the gun as one would a poisonous snake, tight around the barrel, and began looking for bullets on the ground. Before he had found the first one, Apie jumped up on his horse and spurred Chief east, with the wind, as fast as the suffering animal could gallop.

PART TWO

THE PICNIC

1.

In time, three solitary buildings were erected on the downwind side of the mesa, which soon came to be considered the "town" of Black Rock. The first building had been Shlomo's store and home. The second was Noah Christophe's home, and the third was what today's architects would call a "multipurpose facility," serving as an impromptu bunkhouse, whorehouse (to which Noah turned a blind eye for business's sake), and saloon for quarrymen with enough money to afford the meager rent. Rent, of course, was paid to Noah, while provisions were supplied by Shlomo (including hard liquor, which at first drew protests from Noah, but soon he was convinced by Shlomo that his source of willing quarrymen would certainly dry up quickly if drinking were not allowed. Noah spent an evening consulting his well-worn Bible before he agreed that somewhere between "As ye sow, so shall ye reap" and "Give unto Caesar," there was certainly room for a strong drink), and everyone, whether sober or drunk, was happy with the arrangement.

Noah took a wife named Daisy (a stage name from her previous employment at the aforementioned whorehouse), though Noah simply referred to her as Wife. Theirs was a marriage of impulse rather than courtship, due to a realization Daisy had one evening. She had been counting the money given to her by a tired, but pleased, quarryman, when she happened to glance in the dingy mirror in the quarryman's room. What she saw was not the bouncy blond-haired singer she had wanted to become; rather, she saw a woman no longer young, and one who might not always have a ready source of income from giving pleasure to others. Outside the window, the wind howled. Daisy shivered despite the odorous warmth of the quarryman's room. She had been raised in Virginia, near cool, green mountains with running creeks. She remembered the mist which covered the farms surrounding her home in the mornings, how the summer sun would bake the mist away slowly, patiently, the way she would wish a man to make love with her. The wind in this place blew like the quarrymen made love: fast and powerful, leaving emptiness and longing in its wake.

As a child, she had wanted nothing more than to grow old on her parents' farm, but the Depression had rid her family of any property, then of any security, and then, before she was old enough to understand, she was on her own with nothing to support her but a loud singing voice (which was not good) and her looks (which were). She had traveled through cities and towns, villages and encampments, spiraling slowly downward, never finding anything resembling Virginia. She had ended up in Black Rock because, although the winds were bad, the competition was limited, so she made more than anywhere else she'd been before. But, that morning, seeing the lines which had formed below her cheeks, the sagging flesh which frightened her like nothing else, she resolved to leave the town, leave the wind, and start a new life somewhere else, probably California.

On her way out of the bunkhouse she stopped in Shlomo's general store. There, she told Shlomo's wife, Ruth, her one friend in town, that she was leaving.

Ruth, a dark-haired beauty who had cut her hair short because of the wind, nodded her sad understanding.

"I'm not surprised, Daisy. It's a hard place."

They both stood at the counter, watching Ruth's son, Nate, play on the floor near his father.

"You know where you'll go?"

"Somewhere you can walk around outside. Somewhere you can sit by a creek and eat fried chicken and drink lemonade with some friends on a nice summer day. Somewhere you can let your hair down and laugh. Somewhere with no wind."

The door opened with a bang, and Noah entered. His eyes gleamed with fervor.

"I have come here with an idea, Shlomo," Noah said, ignoring the need to greet his longtime companion. "Have you ever considered why the men like staying down in the quarry? Even when they aren't working?"

Shlomo nodded, knowing better than to ask Noah where his thoughts were headed. Noah, in the manner of men who have spent long hours together, continued. He knew that Shlomo would have agreed with this obvious truth.

"We're going to move the town."

Also in the manner of men who have spent long hours together, Noah turned to gauge Shlomo's reaction to a pronouncement that he knew would be a shock. As he had expected, Shlomo's face, which was normally in motion, froze. During moments like these, and there had been many of them, Shlomo doubted Noah's very sanity. Was it madness or determination that lit Noah's face? Partly, Shlomo knew, he stayed with Noah because of his friend's single-minded conviction, which had allowed them both to prosper relative to their former poverty. At times, Shlomo saw himself as just another quarryman, putting up with Noah's often unreasonable demands and imperious nature for the sake of a few dollars. But, unlike the other quarrymen, Shlomo could also admit it was his friend's shining vision which drew him to Noah; indeed, the more Noah treated Shlomo as a friend, the more Shlomo craved his friendship. He enjoyed Noah's power by mere proximity, without being burdened by Noah's beliefs.

Noah turned briefly and tipped his hat politely to Ruth and Daisy. Daisy, curious by nature and in no hurry to rush off into the wind to find a quarryman who was willing to give her a ride off the mesa, decided to stay to see what Noah was talking about.

"I have taken the trouble to ask the men. The men told me. They like staying down in the mine because of the lack of wind."

"That's why I stay in here, Noah. No wind in here." Shlomo pointed to the four walls of his store. Noah looked around, squinting at Shlomo's meager protection from the wind, from God's will. *It can last only as long as our Lord wants it to last*, he thought.

"We've done well here, haven't we?" Noah asked. "We have walked through the valley of the shadow of death and emerged unscathed."

"Not much on valleys," Shlomo said. "Or walking. But you're right— we're doing right by ourselves. Our families." Ruth smiled. Shlomo was a good man and cared for her well, even in this place.

"You make your living off the men who need equipment, and I sell the slate. We both have wealth."

"Not wealth," Shlomo quickly corrected, anxious to avoid tempting fate with boasts. "But a living."

Noah laughed. "True—only the Lord can give wealth. We have given ourselves a living. But suppose we could attract more townspeople. There'd be more people to buy equipment from you."

Ruth nodded. Shlomo shrugged indifferently. As a concept it made sense, but convincing someone to move to this place meant a firm commitment. Ruth had returned here after she had seen her sister off, but only after Shlomo had promised to marry and care for her in the manner she would like. Although she was better read than most, her material desires were few enough to be fully satisfied by Shlomo. He was solid in a way she hadn't thought possible in a man, and his permanence attracted her and kept her rooted to his side. Quarrymen were by nature transient and couldn't promise the kind of care one promised a wife. The concept made sense, but making it happen was quite another thing. Shlomo glanced over at his wife's friend, Daisy. She was an example of the type of temporary citizen who came to Black Rock, stayed long enough to realize there was nothing here for her but wind, and then left.

"And for me, hiring the trucks to take the slate to Denver nearly eats up all the money that devil Trilling pays me for it. And what he charges his customers in markup is a downright sin."

Shlomo, having heard Noah's complaints about the paltry return on his slate as an incessant drumbeat, nodded for the thousandth time.

"You could sell it yourself. Make the markup yourself."

"I'm not a devil like Trilling! I ask what's fair!"

"I know, I know. But what are you talking about, Noah? Move the town?"

Here, Noah took off his hat and smiled again. Shlomo could not recall a time when he had seen Noah smile, laugh, and take off his hat all within the span of fifteen minutes.

"In the mine, we're down to about forty feet. The wind doesn't blow down there. Not like above." Noah gestured with his hands. "We'll build our houses in the pit. We'll live like Christians, no offense intended. Our children will play outside. We'll build a church, a school. We'll have roots."

Shlomo considered. "This ain't a place where roots come easy. The wind is hard, and so is the ground."

Noah responded slowly, thoughtfully. "We've worked hard, dug deep. We never thought we'd go so deep. The walls are too steep to go much deeper. So steep we can't get the wagons all the way to the bottom. Makes getting the slate out tougher."

Shlomo nodded. He well knew the quarrymen's incessant complaints at having to haul great slabs of slate up the precarious, steep trails. It was backbreaking work. "If you built a new quarry," Shlomo reasoned to Noah, "you could start over, build wagon ramps right in. But you'd need a good reason to get this lot to start a brand-new quarry, working in the wind. Living in the bottom of the quarry would be a good enough reason, I guess."

Noah paused, angered by the suggestion that his inspiration was motivated by personal profit. Before he could speak, Shlomo continued. "If you built the ramps right to start, you could get more slate out. More money."

Noah frowned, unwilling to chastise his friend too harshly, for he knew he would need Shlomo's cooperation. "That would be a byproduct of our creation of a new home. If God wills it so, then his will be done."

Business talk bored Daisy; men became indecipherable to her when they spoke this way. She turned to Ruth. "Well, good-bye."

Noah turned quickly and fixed Daisy with a glare. "Where are you going?"

Daisy, a hard woman, but not one accustomed to the imposing figure of Noah Christophe, stuttered a bit as she answered. "I … I'm leaving."

Noah reached out and held her arm firmly. He turned and faced Shlomo. "You see this woman? What she is doing? She's leaving. Do you know why?"

Daisy struggled slightly to release her arm. Noah's grip tightened. He looked at her again.

"You're hurting my arm."

"Why are you leaving?"

Daisy turned to Ruth, who nodded.

"Because of the wind."

Noah nodded. "You see, Shlomo?" To Daisy, he asked, "And if you had a home with no wind? And a family? And a church? Would you still leave then?"

Daisy ripped her arm free from Noah's grasp.

"Listen, mister. I've heard more promises out of men than any of you."

Surprised by the woman's tone, Noah turned and looked at her. "The Lord teaches us to promise only what we can deliver."

Daisy stepped back, rubbing her sore arm, looking wildly from Ruth to Noah. When a person is leaving a place for the last time, it is not unusual for even the most familiar people, places, and things to look entirely different. Perhaps it is the knowledge of seeing a thing for the last time which leads a person to see the dust in the cracks of a wood floor, to see the tarnished streaks on a window, or to see the age in a friend's face. At such times, the heightened acuity, whether physical or emotional, can lead to an overwhelming feeling of limitless possibilities. The soul seems to say, "These things I've taken for granted all this time—these things that seemed so real—they can all go away with the snap of my fingers." At such times, large gambles often look small, since the consequences could be quickly left behind in one's past, particularly if things didn't work out right.

Daisy looked up at Noah. He was not handsome, but his boldness attracted her. True, she had seen bravado in men before, but few of them had lived up to their boasts; normally, their attempts to make good amounted to a few dollars thrown on an unmade bed. Noah was already a man around whom an entire town and business revolved. In the end, Daisy's recall of her aging image in the mirror that very morning emboldened her as much as the feeling of omnipotence which accompanied leaving this windy place for the last time.

"What are you promising?" The night before, flirting with the quarryman, she might have said the same thing, but her tone was hard now, demanding.

Noah looked down at Daisy, then over at Shlomo's son. He was acutely aware of his own lack of progeny, particularly a son who could bear his name. This woman was flawed, as were all women, but Noah harbored no illusions on the subject of love. If she could bear children, the discussion was at an end. "It would be easy to leave, woman. The Lord is testing us with his might. With the wind, the harshness of this place. But you don't have to leave. You can tell the Lord you respect his power, and show him you're willing to take all he's got. Then, he'll love you even more."

"My name's Daisy."

Noah nodded. "Of course it is. I know you, and I know what you are. Do you know what you want?"

Daisy swallowed hard and looked at Ruth, who shrugged. Years later, Daisy wondered what her life would have been like had she done what any reasonable woman would've done—simply walk out. But Daisy had been caught in that strange ether between what was old and worn and what was new and fresh, that moment when a slight notion or wisp of a thought could be taken by the wind and suddenly become real, and at that moment, caught in a maelstrom of change, she looked up at Noah and thought to herself, *This man could provide security, anyway*, and she nodded to Noah. He smiled a kind smile, the sort of smile a proud father might smile at his toddler, and then nodded briskly. It was the last smile Daisy was to see Noah direct toward her until the birth of their second child, and only boy, Luke.

2.

Another aphorism peculiar to Black Rock, which could possibly have been coined by Daisy at that moment in Shlomo's store, was: "Never decide anything in the wind." As much as one might want to take the saying and internalize it, townsfolk meant it literally; they knew that the mind did not think clearly under the imposing wind. Decisions to mend fences, to purchase new equipment, to pull a load of slate from a precarious ledge in the quarry—all these were decisions that townsfolk knew better than to consider out in the wind.

But Daisy was not the only person guilty of being buffeted by Noah's wind in Shlomo's store that morning. Shlomo, a man who no longer relished either change or new ideas of any kind, considered his options, and he was struck with the realization of his dependence on Noah and all of his whims. *If Noah were to move the town to another location, what good would it do for me to remain here? To whom would I sell my wares? Would I be forced to move to another town and start again?* With a resigned sigh, Shlomo agreed to cooperate with Noah's scheme.

Once they agreed on the idea, the two men started planning in earnest, though they kept their plans to themselves to prevent any organized opposition from the quarrymen. The planning process took several months. First, the location and digging of a new quarry was a matter of some discussion. Noah ultimately decided the location should be as close to the mesa's eastern edge as possible to easily access the one road that served as the main thoroughfare on the mesa, beginning off the eastern edge in the town and ending abruptly at the first quarry at the western cliffs.

Finally, in early spring, after spreading rumors of gold strikes at the eastern edge of the mesa, Noah had little trouble convincing the quarrymen to abandon their precarious work in the first quarry and begin working anew nearer to Black Rock. Their enthusiasm waned when Noah disclosed his plans to rebuild Black Rock in the depths of the first quarry. Having spent long hours, day after day in that bleak quarry, the quarrymen found even the harsh winds were a welcome change at day's end. They were cheered when it became clear that not enough homes could possibly be built in the quarry to house them, at least for the current season. Although Shlomo had expressed willingness to abandon the fiction of gold mining, Noah would not hear of it.

"Men are frail," he snapped at Shlomo. "They won't understand what we're trying to do here."

"You pay them a fair day's wage for a fair day of quarry work, Noah."

"Mine work, but that's not the point. These men believe in nothing. I need to make them believe in the Lord. First, I make them believe in gold. Then, I switch the gold for the true gold, the Lord."

"How?"

"The men see the rewards of hard work in a cruel place. They see no reward in this lifetime."

"Because there's no gold."

"Exactly. Then they start looking for an explanation. For some way of figuring out why all the hard work makes sense."

"And you'll give it to them."

"That I will," Noah agreed. After a moment, he added, "Through the Lord's will."

By the time his wife had given birth to their first child—a girl named Prudence—Noah, with the help of the barely cooperative quarrymen, had begun reconstruction of the same three buildings which were found in Black Rock. These he would replicate at the bottom of the quarry. Shlomo helped as best as he could, providing tools and advice, but little in the way of manual labor.

After several months' hard work, these first three buildings were completed. On moving day, as Daisy (already pregnant with their second child) packed the last items of her now-six-month-old daughter's clothes, she turned to Noah and suggested that they have a picnic once they were moved in, to celebrate their new town.

"After all," she reasoned, having lived long enough with Noah to know how to get what she wanted, "it was the Lord's command to rest on the Sabbath."

Noah nodded noncommittally, idly wondering how long it might take to bring his wife into the right way of thinking.

3.

The reticence to speak, once learned in the open wind, extended to the inside as well. Most Black Rockers (except a few like Tongate, who construed the inability to open his mouth outside as an absolute invitation to open his mouth indoors at any time and for any purpose) kept their mouths closed, unless there was an unquestionable need for speech. Even Amos, though given to the occasional burst of chatter, eventually would revert to a wall of silence. To outsiders, even outsiders like Tokyo who had raised her own lifelong practice of silence to an art, the silence of the town was off-putting. Tokyo was unused to a silence in others which might last longer than her own. She preferred instead the high level of noise one could normally expect from others. Here in Black Rock, she couldn't help but feel that she, the observer, was now the observed.

Amos looked up from the stillness of his counter as Tokyo and Luke walked in the door. Luke's face, twisted in what he thought was his usual good-natured half smile, looked to Amos as if he were in pain. Tokyo stood blinking at Amos. Amos smiled at both of them, not saying a word.

Inside his store, Amos was safe as long as he kept the roof and siding in good repair. Next to the door, near the large, expensive plate-glass window, were two overstuffed easy chairs Amos had bought years ago with the intention of creating a comfortable talking area. But after the window had shown a propensity to crack and shatter on repeated occasions from the force of the wind, the regular patrons of the store—Proudfoot, Tongate, and Luke—chose instead to congregate at the counter for their conversations, safely out of proximity to the large window.

The long counter had been constructed of several slabs of slate within a sturdy wooden frame. Each slab had been chosen with care by Amos's father and placed carefully to form one seemingly unbroken plane. Shlomo had made sure to use thick slate, guarding against the possibility of random cracks.

Like most Black Rockers, Luke was not much on conversation, and even less so around Amos, about whom he had mixed feelings. Had Luke the ability to do so, he sometimes thought, he would have avoided Amos completely. At least, he believed he would. But as Tokyo watched over the years, she realized that Luke was drawn to Amos in some way, drawn like a gambler to Las Vegas.

"What do they do over there at night?" he had asked Tokyo when she had first moved in with him.

Tokyo shrugged. "They're like you or me. They eat, they work."

"Do they talk to each other?"

After a long pause, Tokyo shook her head and laughed. "I never heard them fuck, if that's what you really want to know, Luke."

Luke looked down at the floor, then up at Tokyo again. "I want to know what they talk about."

Tokyo thought for a long time. Finally, she shrugged again. Luke's repeated questions were tiresome, and she hoped her repeated nonanswers gave him less and less of an incentive to continue his queries. She could usually outlast almost anyone else in a game of this kind.

"They don't talk very much. Sis kind of sings. And Amos nods a lot."

For her part, Tokyo liked the fact that Luke was nervous around Amos. In his house, or surrounded by slate and wood in his shop, Luke was at ease, in his awkward way. But here, in Amos's store, Luke was as jumpy as a lizard making its way across a sunbaked rock. Tokyo smiled as Luke walked toward Amos, who waited patiently for Luke to speak.

"Amos."

"Luke."

Tokyo resisted the urge to roll her eyes. Maybe because she had observed people for so long, or maybe because she lived with Luke, she knew without a doubt that Luke wanted something from Amos. Another woman would have asked Luke what it was he was looking for out of Amos, but Tokyo had never bothered. She assumed Luke would be baffled by such questions. Besides, having lived in both households, she knew what she cared to know.

She watched Luke study a display of steel wool wrapped in plastic. He pursed his lips thoughtfully as he examined the packages. Steel wool could be useful around the house; it could buff slate and clean dishes. It could clean paint from tools, and it could ready wood for joining. But it didn't last like a file. The more you used steel wool, the more of it you needed. It just didn't last. Luke shook his head disapprovingly. Amos watched him without comment.

"A man is coming."

Luke, Amos, and Tokyo turned toward Sis, who had come into the room silently from behind the counter. Her sweet singsong voice floated in the room, up among the canes hanging from the rafters. Tokyo looked over at Sis, who was smiling her odd smile at Tokyo. Half expecting to see a man standing in the doorway, Luke and Amos turned toward the door and looked. Seeing no new arrivals, they turned back to what they had been doing. Luke replaced the rolled steel wool to the stand.

Sis, having delivered the message she felt was appropriate, smiled at Luke and walked back into the kitchen. Luke looked at Tokyo, then at Amos, then back at Tokyo.

"What does she mean? You have any idea?" Luke asked.

If Amos made Luke nervous, Sis sent him up the river. As he realized that neither Amos nor Tokyo had an answer for him, Luke's nervousness threatened to shake him to the ground. He tried to focus on the steel wool again, but he was about to burst. What he usually did at such times was make things, clean things, or carry things. Here, in Amos's store, he was in a fix. The only thing he could realistically do was to carry things, but, first, he would have to do one of his least favorite things, which was to spend money to buy the thing he was going to carry.

Tokyo smiled at Luke and walked over to the housewares. She picked up a package of sponges and held it out to Luke. Luke's mouth opened and shut, then opened again. *He looks like a guppy*, Tokyo thought, and she smiled.

Mistaking her smile for reassurance, Luke returned her smile gratefully. Tokyo again resisted the urge to roll her eyes. To fill the empty space left by Sis's indecipherable prediction, Luke decided to splurge. He stepped forward and took the sponges from Tokyo's hand and in one motion placed them on the counter in front of Amos. Tokyo smiled again, secretly proud of her triumph. Manipulating Luke was easy, she reflected, then turned to the shelves to search for items she might want in the future, when Luke was similarly malleable.

"Sponges, eh?" Amos looked from Tokyo to Luke.

"Guess we need them, Amos," Luke said. "Tokyo's in charge of the woman's work in our house."

"And Luke's in charge of the less important things," Tokyo said without looking up from the shelf of canned peaches she was eyeing hungrily. She imagined the sweet syrup cooling her scratchy throat.

Luke made a noise with his lips. Tokyo knew by the sound he wanted her to look at him so he could make clear he had only said it to fill space, that he meant no harm. Inclined to use his pain to her advantage, Tokyo kept her eyes fixed on the peaches.

Luke realized he might be watching Tokyo a long time if he hoped she'd turn and smile at him again. He turned away. "What'd Sis mean, Amos?"

"No telling with Sis, really," Amos replied. "Seemed she was talking to Tokyo. You expecting someone?"

Tokyo shook her head without turning. She rolled her eyes, a gesture only the canned peaches would see. Amos might as well have asked if she was expecting to win a million dollars.

"She's not expecting anyone," Amos said.

Luke nodded and looked at the sponges on the counter. "I wasn't expecting to buy sponges."

Tokyo turned to Luke and sighed. She watched him count some change out onto the counter. She was stunned by a realization.

"You don't save things because you're cheap! You save them because you don't like coming here! You don't like seeing Amos and Sis!"

Luke had the look of a man who has seen a family member shot. Amos hesitated for a moment, then walked silently away, politely appearing to search for something he had left under the counter.

"What the hell are you talking about?" Luke hissed.

"They make you so nervous, you'd rather use old stuff than come down here."

"She's crazy, Amos," Luke said. "Don't pay no attention; she's just trying to stir things up like she does."

"Nothing," Amos said. "Means nothing. We all have our little peccadilloes."

"I like coming here. I do." Luke's voice was plaintive.

Amos stood up and looked directly into Luke's eyes. "She doesn't know a thing about our families, Luke. She has no idea why you might want to be here. And not want to be here."

Puzzled, but with practiced indifference, Tokyo turned to look out the window. Two men were hurrying across the street, the wind billowing their long coats as if they were being inflated.

"Tongate's coming," she said, and it was a warning, similar to a foghorn on a lighthouse. The people of Black Rock knew when to beat a hasty retreat, and Barney Tongate's approach was one of those times.

"Ring me up," Luke asked Amos.

"You could stay a while," Amos said with a grin.

Luke grinned back. "Don't think so."

4.

Daisy was genuinely surprised to find the wind was significantly calmer at the bottom of the forty-foot quarry—New Town, as they now called it. Had she spent time thinking carefully about the wind-block provided by the huge black walls, her surprise would have been lessened, but Daisy was not a person who spent time thinking carefully. On the first day, she simply stood on the black slate of the quarry bottom and marveled at the lack of wind. No windier, she thought, than a blustery spring day in Virginia. As a girl, she had loved those days when the wind seemed to blow both cold and warm in each gust, when she could feel the battle of winter and summer against her cheek, changing wildly from one moment to the next. And here, standing on the bottom of the quarry, the few gusts reaching her cheek were both cold from the furtive winds of the mesa and hot from the radiant heat of the sun against the slate. But even a person who chooses to live on memories invariably realizes every place has its drawbacks.

Before she had walked into Shlomo's store, before she had met Noah, and before Prudence was born, Daisy would have literally jumped at the chance to live in a place with no wind. But now, sitting on the front porch of her home, Daisy nursed her daughter and looked with distaste at her new world, a world filled with darkness.

Slate was, after all, black. And in this place, New Town, as Noah called it, not only was the slate underfoot, but it towered up on all sides, forming a permanently black horizon. At its widest, the quarry's diameter was only about three hundred feet. In fact, if you could carve a giant wooden salad bowl with four rough-hewn corners and paint it black, then could somehow place a few tiny homes at the bottom of the bowl, you would have some idea of what New Town looked like. The floor of the quarry was rough and inclined slightly. The incline was lowest toward one wall of the quarry, the wall where the quarrymen had cut steep trails into the sheer slate wall. The incline of the quarry floor then proceeded upward toward the highest ground, forming a mild peak about two thirds of the way toward the opposite wall, then declined again until it met the other quarry wall. Noah chose the highest ground as the site for his home, not considering the view from his relative height would be only slightly more interesting than any other place on the quarry bottom. It seemed natural for him that he should command the high ground, so that he could be closest to God. In this place, close proximity to God brought with it the benefit of close proximity to the sun, and this was important in New Town, for the sun, even when it was overhead, seemed to be absorbed by the ground and the walls of the quarry. And the sun was rarely overhead. At the bottom of a man-made, four-cornered sinkhole like New Town, the sun was observable only for a matter of a few hours, even in the summertime. In the winter, the angle of the sun was so extreme that the bright rays only reached about ten feet down the northern wall of the quarry. Fortunately, the blackness of the slate absorbed what little sun did shine and helped to keep New Town far warmer than it would have otherwise been.

To reach the bottom of New Town, one could either trust to luck, descending the rough and sinuous trails, each of which was carved precariously from loose shale and slate, or use the faster system of rope ladders with wooden rungs that had been lashed to the side of the quarry. The simple act of getting in and out of New Town, especially with young children, was so slow and difficult that Daisy and Ruth rarely ventured up and out of the quarry.

"Maybe when the children are a little older," Ruth would sigh, and Daisy, who spent most of her time with Ruth, would nod silent agreement.

Another drawback, one that became a short-lived personal obsession to Noah, was the lack of foliage in New Town. Noah spent countless hours replanting small saplings, flowers, and other greenery, only to find that anything he tried to plant refused to grow. He even transported sandy soil to fill the small holes he had dug in the slate, but the plants refused to live.

"Can't be lack of water," Noah said. "Water table's right below the surface."

Daisy nodded and said, "Maybe the roots can't get through."

"Wife, I've seen bushes and such growing out of the side of granite mountains. I've seen flowers blooming in the hottest hell of a desert. The

Bible talks of the garden, where all things grow. The Lord tells us that anything can grow anywhere. Are you arguing with the good book?"

In the face of an angry Old Testament, Daisy usually kept her peace. She knew there was no sense arguing with Noah, but this time she couldn't help herself: "You're the one arguing. You're arguing with plants that need more light than they can get down here. Find some mushrooms or something, you'll do okay down here."

Noah's mouth hung open. Daisy waited silently for Noah's stern admonishment. He had never struck her before, never even raised his hand, but somehow she dreaded his stern words more than the harshest beatings from any of the violent men she had known. Head down, facing away from Noah, she hunched her shoulders and waited. When the expected words failed to materialize, she turned cautiously. To her shock, Noah stood in the same spot, his mouth hanging open.

"I'm sorry, Noah. I ..."

"Good God in heaven, you are right!"

Daisy stopped, incredulous. "Me?"

Noah nodded. "The problem is vanity! I'm trying to grow fancy plants, flowers, and trees. The Lord didn't start with apple trees."

No, Daisy thought, *but he sure as hell finished with an apple tree.*

"I have to plant the simple grasses of the mesa here. Sage, and juniper too, maybe. From such a simple start, the Lord our God made the garden plentiful."

Suitably inspired, Noah began a long trial of uprooting and transplanting various types of simple plants from their homes off the east side of the mesa and moving them to New Town. Quarrymen were again cajoled and then offered payment; most of them were happy to dig something other than slate. They dug around juniper and sage where Noah instructed, carefully lifting the greenery with large clods of loose stones and earth still clinging to the roots. These they lifted into the slate wagon. With the carelessness of men who are being paid to do a simple but strenuous job, they failed to lash the plants to the wagon, assuming the weight of the roots would keep the plants intact. Noah, intent only on pointing out the ideal plants to be uprooted for transport to New Town, assumed the men would have the sense to secure the plants carefully. As the first wagon pulled away, up the slight incline toward the mesa, he smiled.

"This is the beginning of our garden," he muttered to himself.

A few minutes later, after the first wagon had disappeared over the horizon, Noah was startled to see uprooted sage and juniper plants tumbling past him in the wind, amazingly fast, some even rising and jumping up to thirty feet in the air. Within minutes the wagon reappeared over the horizon, the faces of the quarrymen beet red with windburn and chagrin. Noah saw no need for admonishment. The quarrymen immediately set to work lashing shrubs into the wagon firmly, grumbling only to each other about the additional work they had caused themselves.

Had he been inclined to read omens truthfully, Noah would have immediately given up his effort to green his garden. Indeed, a man other than Noah would have given up his effort after the first few flowers and trees had failed to find purchase in the gloom of New Town. Of course, a man other than Noah would by now have been safe in Kansas City or Salt Lake City, lifting his face occasionally to be warmed in the sunshine, remembering with ill humor his days on the difficult mesa.

When, after painstaking weeks of futile attempts, Noah discovered that even the simplest, most godforsaken grasses refused to take root in the black, flaky ground, he began to harbor secret doubts about the soundness of New Town. But as he looked up from yet another clump of withered grass, up beyond the black sides of the quarry to the quickly moving sky, he knew beyond doubt that he was being tested yet again, and his resolve to meet the test grew stronger. What was needed, he decided, was not greenery, but rather like-minded hardy people like himself. The people would be the green carpet to cover his garden.

5.

After his failure to transplant greenery to New Town, Noah boldly predicted that some quarrymen would choose to move there and establish a true community. But while several quarrymen stayed in the bunkhouse in New Town, only one thought to try to build a house next to Noah's and Shlomo's, and his reasons were far from spiritual.

Jim Sweetwater had wintered in Black Rock for five years, drawn like so many by the steady money offered for working under such hard conditions. A farmer by vocation, Sweetwater supplemented the meager earnings from his farm just north of the Bear Creek Canyon with equally meager, but reliable, earnings paid to him by Noah for scraping slate out of the quarry at Black Rock. Every November, after his harvest had been collected and sold to a man Sweetwater regarded with the same esteem as Noah did his slate merchant, Sweetwater gave most of the proceeds to his wife Norma to spend over the winter. He then rode south and east to Black Rock.

After Sweetwater's first day of work, Noah judged, with the degree of certainty only the deeply religious enjoy, that Sweetwater was a good worker and a good, God-fearing man. Within a week, Sweetwater was supervising the work of the other quarrymen—men who, in some cases, had been working the quarry for several years. But, unlike Sweetwater, they had neither the desire nor the ability to direct others on how to work more efficiently. Sweetwater's abilities flowed naturally from the long hours he had spent toiling alone on his farm. Without help, he had learned efficiency as a matter of survival and in the quarry used his self-provided education to Noah's benefit. More importantly, none of the others stood in God's graces in quite the same way as Sweetwater. Noah, standing as usual in a protected spot in the quarry, nodded with satisfaction as he watched Sweetwater work.

A good Christian, Noah thought.

Although Noah tried frequently over the years to convince Sweetwater to become a full-time resident of Black Rock, Sweetwater would only shake his head and gesture vaguely in a direction he thought to be north.

"Can't leave my farm, Noah. Can't leave my roots." Although he had spent many years alone working his barely productive farm, Sweetwater was a keen reader of men, as evidenced by his ability to supervise the normally lazy, and often belligerent, quarrymen. Noah, being less deceptive than the average quarryman, was easy enough for Sweetwater to read. Noah would not argue further if Sweetwater insisted that his roots were elsewhere.

"Can't argue with that, Jim. No, by God in heaven I surely can't." Sweetwater nodded.

In November, after his harvest, Sweetwater returned to the town of Black Rock and was surprised to find the store empty. The construction of New Town had begun shortly after Sweetwater had left back in the early spring, and Noah's silence about the venture had included all his quarrymen—so Sweetwater had no knowledge of the move.

Saddened to find the old town of Black Rock abandoned to the wind, Sweetwater stood inside Shlomo's empty store and listened to the pitch of the wind. As typically happened in one's first days back on the mesa, the wind seemed louder than he remembered, louder than he could stand. Past experience had taught him that his sensitivity would diminish over the next week or so, to the point where it would become at least tolerable. After listening for a brief time, Sweetwater came to the conclusion that the quarry, like his farm, must have turned barren, and the normal bounty of slate Noah and the others had pulled from the quarry was no more. His only option, it seemed, was to return to his farm and his wife. This was penance, he thought, for the vague thoughts of abandonment he had harbored during the difficult trip. Just prior to his return to Black Rock, Sweetwater had left Norma with less money than usual, and she had noticed.

"What's this?" Norma had demanded, looking at the crisp bills on the kitchen table.

"That there's your money. For the winter, like always."

Norma didn't need to count the money to know that something was drastically wrong. She shook her head, an exaggerated motion which caused the flesh hanging from her neck to move from side to side. Jim, who remembered having married a younger, enthusiastic woman, had to look out the window to avoid the wave of revulsion at the sight.

"How the hell am I supposed to live on this?"

The conversation degraded through noise and unpleasantness to the point at which Jim packed his small bag and left for the quarry, not particularly caring whether he ever saw Norma again.

Penance notwithstanding, Sweetwater was in no particular hurry to return to Utah and Norma. Before leaving, he decided to visit the mesa one last time. Sweetwater didn't know why he wanted to see the mesa, but he was sure that he couldn't leave Black Rock unless he did so.

Up on the mesa, as he walked the trail to what he thought was the quarry, he was surprised to find wagons of slate piled to capacity in what appeared to be a newly begun quarry. Noah, who had been expecting him for several weeks, detached himself from the quarrymen and walked over to Sweetwater, smiling.

"Jim," Noah smiled. "The Lord has brought changes."

"I see that, Noah. I'm surprised."

"And this is not all."

Without another word, Noah led Sweetwater to New Town. As he stood at the bottom of New Town next to Shlomo, Noah, and their small families, Sweetwater shook his head. In his simple way of looking at things, it seemed to him that Noah had made it more difficult to make money from mining slate.

"You took your farm, your best soil, and you covered it up with houses," Jim said. When Noah hesitated, unsure of Sweetwater's thoughts, he continued. "The slate, it's your farm. It'd be like me building a big house on my cornfields, plowing the crops under. Wouldn't make sense." Sweetwater shook his head, troubled.

Noah nodded thoughtfully. He felt the eyes of the others on him. Even Shlomo watched carefully, for he still questioned whether the creation of New Town was a perilously bad idea. Noah, perhaps sensing his longtime friend's unspoken discomfort and perhaps harboring doubts of his own, was careful to moderate his public views. "That may be, Jim," he said carefully. "We have condemned ourselves to more hard work and more hard living than we otherwise might, but the Lord will provide."

Realizing it wasn't his problem, Sweetwater went back to work. *As long as Noah provides,* Sweetwater thought, *the Lord can do what he wants.* As for Shlomo, because he felt unable to make money without Noah's burgeoning business, he swallowed his concern and stayed at Noah's side.

Noah had ample chances over the winter to work next to Sweetwater. During those times, Noah took full advantage, pointing out at every opportunity the benefits of starting a community in New Town. The winter work was more difficult than any previous experience Sweetwater had had on the mesa, since the quarrymen were starting over, working largely without any protection from the wind. Noah, who was in the process of digging his second "mine," was happy to see the effect of the wind on the quarrymen.

"They're working quicker, Jim," he said to Sweetwater one day. "The Lord is making them work quicker."

Standing next to Noah, Sweetwater turned his back to the wind. If anyone was foolhardy enough to stand still long enough in the wind to watch the two men talking, they would have reflected on the oddity of their postures. To speak on the mesa, and, more importantly, to be heard, both men had to turn with their backs to the wind and face the same direction. Eye contact was rare during conversation, and the quarrymen were prone to looking at the horizon as they spoke. While they were working in the quarry, though, eye contact occurred frequently, since it was too difficult to yell over the wind. One quarryman might make eye contact with another in order to communicate a need for help lifting a particularly large piece of slate. Once eye contact was made, hand signals were used. An elaborate system of these had developed, most of which were related to moving, breaking, or picking up some heavy object. Various other hand signals were designed to get another man to look in a particular direction, to back away, pay attention, or to just plain stop.

Not unexpectedly, the hand signals that developed on the windswept second quarry became difficult to abandon, even when the second quarry became deep enough to protect the men from the wind. Although the hand signals were certainly not necessary in the safe confines of New Town, they were used incessantly by Noah with Daisy, his daughter, and with Shlomo's family, even when making common requests for a glass of milk or another cup of coffee.

Although Daisy had quickly grown accustomed to the hand signals used by the quarrymen to communicate, each time Noah pointed to his coffee cup and raised his eyebrows or gestured for Daisy to sweep the kitchen clean, she felt as though she would shriek. Her only defense to the silent instructions was to not understand them and to respond to his gestures with a furrowed brow.

"I want you to sweep the floor," Noah would say. "Do you not understand the English language, Wife?"

"I understand the English language fine, Noah."

After several years of silent warfare, it began to dawn on Daisy that Noah thought he was speaking out loud when he gestured to her. He no longer saw any difference. The realization stunned her. The wind was strong, she knew, but a wind strong enough to alter a person's conception of speech itself was incomprehensible. Although this could have been a reason for her to become less irritated, she failed to take the opportunity.

She looked out of her window onto the black street of New Town and shook her head as she watched Sweetwater and Noah exchange hand signals in the semidarkness. Her ability to read the hand signals the two men exchanged gave her an ability to eavesdrop she would otherwise not have enjoyed, but the conversation she was watching did not please her in the least, for Noah was once again trying to get Sweetwater to agree to move to New Town. Not for the first time, Daisy tried to remember whether Sweetwater had been one of the quarrymen she had entertained in the days before she had married Noah. Other quarrymen, even the ones who openly leered at her behind Noah's back, caused her no embarrassment or discomfort. Sweetwater's calm demeanor betrayed no signs of untoward recognition; this agitated and even shamed Daisy.

"You and your wife can move in to a new house we'll build, right next to mine and Shlomo's," Noah told Sweetwater, as Daisy watched. "Right there, we could build it. Ready by spring, it could be."

Although it was still winter, Sweetwater felt the oncoming spring in his soul—a minor tugging which would, he knew, grow into an outright obsession to begin tilling a fertile field under the warming rays of the sun. The high walls of slate that defined the boundaries of New Town were no barrier to Sweetwater's ingrained farming instinct, learned over years and years of hard work in the fields.

And yet, a poorly formed and hazy thought resurfaced, competing with Sweetwater's desire to return to Utah and till the soil. Here was a new start, the thought seemed to be saying. Here was a new beginning. There was no penance necessary, no fear attached. Here, at the bottom of this dark pit with this strange man, was freedom.

Sweetwater looked to where Noah was pointing and thought of Norma, of her twisted, angry mouth as she sneered at him for being such a poor provider. In Black Rock, Sweetwater knew he sat at the right hand of Noah, which made him probably the second-most important man in the town. He also knew, with the same degree of certainty, that he was the second-most important person in his farmhouse back in Utah.

"My wife, she might not move in with me, Noah."

Noah considered, his face puzzled. Daisy, who was watching the two men standing on the rapidly darkening path which served as New Town's main street, saw the two men finally shake hands gravely. As Noah walked back up to the door of his house, he was smiling, a smile which made Daisy shiver. Once inside, he took off his heavy coat and handed it to Daisy. His face, she noticed, was glowing the way it did when he talked about God.

"The Lord has provided us a new townsman, Wife. A first seed to make our garden complete."

Daisy nodded and peered out at the darkened figure of Sweetwater, who was looking at a barren piece of slate where he imagined his house would be built.

"What about his wife?"

"He says he's not going back to his wife."

Daisy turned. The radiance Noah had exuded when he walked into the house had vanished. Daisy knew better than to ask questions, and instead moved to light the kerosene lamps on either side of the large kitchen table. Noah thoughtfully watched her.

"He's not right with the Scriptures, Wife."

"Not if he's leaving his wife, he's not."

"But we need him in our garden to serve the Lord." Noah sighed heavily and sat down at the kitchen table, gesturing for a cup of coffee, which Daisy supplied without argument. "The Lord will provide an answer," he said.

6.

The Lord did provide an answer, delivering Norma on the first day of spring, just as Daisy and Ruth were setting out slate bowls of fruit and baked biscuits on long wooden tables. The culmination of Daisy's desires, the picnic was an event which she had pursued for months. It was to be a celebration of a happy coincidence: the completion of Sweetwater's house and the coming of spring.

For some time, using a variety of excuses, Noah had managed to delay Daisy from any real consideration of a picnic, but eventually he realized that Daisy wasn't going to let go of her frivolous scheme. The Bible gave no real instruction on the subject of picnics, but it was more than mildly illuminating on the subject of women who want something badly. Indeed, Noah looked no further than the story of Eve to determine that Daisy was not likely to forget about what she wanted. Noah thought long and hard about the picnic, particularly wondering where the snake could be found in New Town, and how on earth he could turn Daisy against the idea.

One evening, sitting in the shadows of the kerosene-lit kitchen, Daisy, having just put Prudence down to sleep, sat down across the table from Noah. Noah, who was reading his Bible at the time, felt Daisy's eyes on him and looked up from the Scriptures.

"I want to have that picnic."

Noah exhaled and looked out into the pitch-black night. In the window, he saw the flickering reflection of the kerosene lamp, his tall figure dressed in black, somewhat slumped forward in his chair, and the figure of his wife sitting ramrod-straight. One of them, Noah realized, was ready for a fight. He looked back at Daisy, whose eyes were shining. *This must have been what Adam was up against*, he thought.

He opened his mouth to speak, but Daisy beat him to it. "It isn't wrong to celebrate what the Lord has given us, Noah."

Noah nodded. "But your celebration isn't for the Lord, is it?"

"It's for all of us, Noah. God is in all of us. In the quarry—"

"The mine."

"The mine. In you, in me, in Shlomo, and Ruth."

"Who is the snake that has been whispering to you, Wife?"

Now it was Daisy's turn to stare out into the blackness outside the kitchen window. Like Noah, she could only see her own hazy reflection in the wavy glass.

"There's no snake, Noah."

Noah shook his head sadly.

"There is always a snake, Wife. And you may be mine."

Daisy stood angrily, her chair tipping backward and clattering to the floor. In the next room, Prudence stirred and whimpered in her crib.

"We're *all* snakes, Noah! Just like God's in all of us, we're *all* snakes!"

"I lead my life by the Good Book. I avoid the serpent of temptation. I walk through the fire unharmed, like Shadrach and Meshach. I work for him alone. I do what he tells me."

"And he told you to live in the bottom of a well? He told you to treat your wife like she doesn't exist except to make dinners and make babies? I want something else!"

Noah, who had thus far taken pains in their marriage to avoid complaining about the lack of a male child, paused, trying to determine whether this was an opportune time to raise the issue. He looked up at Daisy, standing on the other side of the table, leaning forward, her hands pressed against the table, her breath coming quickly, her belly round with child, her breasts heaving slightly under her housedress. Daisy's eyes were fixed hungrily on Noah. Her cheeks and arms were flushed with anger. Noah shifted uncomfortably in his seat, looking down for a moment.

Noah pursed his lips in thought. Finally, he reasoned, "We could pray at this picnic. To give glory to him."

Daisy knew better than to disturb Noah when he was trying to rationalize.

"Outside, in New Town. We could see his blessing in the lack of wind."

Daisy turned to pick up the chair and nodded as she sat down.

"We'll wait for spring, though. And praise him for getting us through another winter. A hard winter, at that."

106

Daisy had no idea why the concept of the picnic was so important to her and was glad nobody asked. Although New Town protected its few inhabitants from the roughness of life on the mesa, the wind was still the overwhelming truth in New Town. They might not be able to feel it as much, but they could see it above them, see it in the fast-moving clouds and occasional slate projectiles launched by the wind down into their sanctuary. Indeed, Daisy began to think of the wind up on the mesa as a tight lid on the darkness of New Town. The combination of sweeping wind and omnipresent darkness created a riptide of confusion where they met, and the same riptide tore at Daisy's soul in ways she did not understand. The picnic, she felt, was a focus that could help, and she dedicated herself to its preparation.

When spring approached, Daisy and Ruth spent hours each day planning. They knew the group would be small, but nevertheless they discussed every detail carefully. Daisy, being only a month away from her due date, worked at a pace that sometimes frightened Ruth, supervising the carving of long stretches of slate which would serve as wooden table supports, spending inordinate amounts of time studying catalogues and ordering canned goods from Shlomo, and trying to determine how many quarrymen would actually show up. Fire pits of the kind normally seen on the mesa were dug, which were to serve as barbecue pits. Several pigs were delivered, shaken by their journey across the mesa and squealing miserably as they were lashed one at a time to the back of a large quarryman who carefully descended the series of ladders to the bottom of New Town.

Noah watched the preparations with a combination of fear and amusement. He feared any activity not designed specifically to honor his God, and was amused by the depth of Daisy's immersion in the details. If she were a man, he reflected, she could have taken Sweetwater's place. As the weeks went by and Daisy's activities continued unabated, a dim realization crept into Noah's mind.

The night before the picnic, Noah entered the kitchen to find Daisy once again working furiously. The kitchen was hot, the oven having been loaded with coals and worked for over forty-eight consecutive hours. Noah looked at the huge pile of biscuits and the canned fruit on the table and nodded.

"You're having your picnic, Wife."

Surprised at the kindness of his tone, Daisy turned and looked at her husband. Her hair was disheveled, her apron dusted liberally with flour, but she was smiling broadly.

"Thank you, Noah."

Noah nodded an acknowledgment and poked one of the biscuits with a long finger. The surface of the biscuit flaked just the way Noah liked. She watched, delighted, as he tasted the crumb which stuck to his finger and nodded his approval.

"When this picnic is over, Wife, then you'll see what it is to be idle."

Daisy brushed the hair from her eyes and cocked her head. Her smile thinned. "What do you mean?"

"I mean this: I've watched you doing all this, planning all this. It keeps you moving. But when it's over, you will be alone with me and your family. You cannot see it now. You cannot see it *because* you are moving. Like the wind." He paused for a moment, considering. "But," he concluded, "you will be alone."

7.

In the truck heading back to Luke's house, Tokyo held the package of new sponges in her hands. They were brightly colored and proudly proclaimed their synthetic superiority over natural sponge. She would use the green one first, she decided. Then the pink one. Save the yellow one for last. She shook her head and smiled. *The things a person can think about.*

"Nice sponges," Luke said.

Was he kidding? No, of course he wasn't. "You drove all the way down there to buy sponges? That was it?" Tokyo asked.

Luke was silent, looking out at the windswept mesa as he drove. He raised his eyebrows and breathed in through his nose, exhaling slowly.

"I guess."

Tokyo looked out the window in disbelief. "I thought you wanted to go down there."

"I did. Didn't want to buy anything, necessarily. Don't even know why I bought those."

Tokyo paused, considering whether she should ask, then gave in to the temptation. "What was Amos talking about? What don't I know?"

For one of the few times since she had known him, Luke laughed— really laughed, from his belly and his heart. But it was over quickly, a staccato burst of laughter that Luke cut off as if with a razor blade.

"You don't know half of what you think, Tokyo."

Tokyo's face flushed immediately. She felt the heat in her face and the throbbing in her temples. Her hands clenched around the sponges. She imagined the sponges to be Luke's soft neck, with her squeezing and squeezing until her fingernails were white. His neck would feel this way, soft at the edges and hard at the core. It would be easy, she thought, but not really, not really so easy.

They drove in silence the rest of the way to Luke's home. When Luke parked the truck in front of the house and got out, Tokyo paused for a moment, until she was sure that Luke was looking back at her. Without a glance in his direction, she stepped out of the truck and threw the sponges up into the air. As would any light object on the mesa, the sponges arced wildly, first upward, then to the east. The wind seized them and carried them fifty feet before they hit the ground. Tokyo stood watching them for the few seconds during which they were still visible, then turned and walked past Luke, whose mouth was open in shock despite his years of training on the mesa.

As she walked past Luke, Tokyo smiled. "You don't know half of what you think you know," she said.

If anger were readable on some sort of a scale; if you could plug in a meter and point it at someone to figure out whether they were angry or not, and *how* angry they were, you might think you really had something. But the meter really wouldn't tell you a thing. To know whether someone is angry can be useful, since you could use the information to change lanes on the highway, or stop arguing with the policeman who is giving you a ticket, or even to let your kids play the stereo as loudly as they want. But what the meter wouldn't tell you was the vitally important piece of information: *Why* is that person in the next car angry? Why is the policeman angry? Why are your kids so damned angry? *Why?*

Then again, for some people, the meter would be helpful only if they pointed it at themselves.

If Tokyo had been asked, she would have said that she rarely spoke a word in anger. But if you trained one of those anger meters on her, the needle would rock as violently as the wind sweeping across the mesa. And now, as she walked by Luke into the house, her anger was off the scale, and Luke, following her in, was not too far from her level.

Slamming a door shut in Black Rock was not unusual, for the wind made such an event necessary and commonplace. Black Rockers had long since stopped taking the gesture of slamming a door as a sign of anger, since the act was so common as to be meaningless. Just as the wind had robbed the town of speech, it had also contrived, in subtle ways, to deprive the town of ways to display emotion—not from feeling it, though.

Though he knew it was pointless, Luke did his best to slam both the outer and inner doors shut as he followed Tokyo into the kitchen

Tokyo turned and blinked at Luke. He stood in the kitchen, trembling with rage.

"Why'd you do that?" he demanded.

Tokyo looked out the window and shrugged. After a long pause she turned back to Luke. The pause had drained him of his anger, as she hoped it might. He seemed deflated, slumped in a chair.

"You never explain, do you, Tokyo?"

Tokyo blinked.

"You don't understand about this place." Luke shook his head and looked down at the table. Reflexively, he rubbed the edge of the slate table with his fingers, feeling the smooth layers of filed slate. *If only everything could be as smooth as this slate*, he thought.

Tokyo, still standing, decided she was tired of people telling her what she understood and what she didn't.

"I understand all I need to understand, Luke," she said.

Luke looked up at Tokyo. Was he about to cry?

"No, you don't. And you want to know what else? You don't want to understand." Luke's voice was rising, working back into the anger that had caused him to slam the doors. "Because you think you know everything already, you don't really want to understand. You want to stay in your bitter little world. It's like you're happy to be mad."

Another of the truisms created by the relentless wind of Black Rock held that to fight the wind was useless. Physically, this dictum was self-evident, as walking straight into the wind was normally an impossibility. This was particularly true when the wind took on its most dangerous form at ground level, when the tone of the wind was a high-pitched scream, barely audible to the human ear but so resonant as to be unmistakable, layered on top of a deep bass humming that townsfolk immediately recognized. If you were caught in a normal wind in Black Rock, you were wise to sidestep it, and attack it from angles. If you were unfortunate enough to be caught in the more dangerous sporadic gusts, it necessitated covering up and waiting until the wind normalized.

In some ways Tokyo was ideally suited to live in Black Rock, because an inextricable part of her character was an ability to wait out a wind. She knew from long experience that to argue with an angry person was useless. She listened and watched, hoping that Luke's anger would soon diminish into the sad depression that followed most tantrums. But now she was unsettled, because Luke was standing, hands and arms trembling, staring at her with an intensity she had not seen before. Going against her instincts, she filled the silence with words.

"It was an accident," she said.

Luke looked disbelievingly at Tokyo. One of her eyes was practically shut as she squinted back at him. She didn't even care if he knew she was lying.

"Don't lie to me anymore, Tokyo."

"What have I lied about?" Tokyo shot back.

"What haven't you lied about?"

"I'm here, isn't that enough?"

"It might be okay for you, Tokyo, but we all have pasts. I have them, Amos has them ..." and here Luke paused and seemed to choke on his words. "Our families have them. It's what this place is all about. It's thick all over us here, Tokyo."

Tokyo looked into Luke's angry, pleading eyes. Although she had always assumed that she would leave Luke at some point in the future, she hadn't thought that moment would come so soon. Luke seemed to be shaking apart in front of her, and most men would turn it right around on her, she knew. Maybe not right away, but for sure by the next morning, when they woke up as if from a hangover. Thinking of the next morning, of Luke's likely rage at having opened up this way, she made a decision. She stalked into the bedroom and began gathering some of her clothes into her duffle, which she had always kept handy for just such occasions.

"What are you doing?" Luke was standing at the door. Tokyo refused to look back at him.

"What the hell does it look like? I'm leaving."

Luke didn't move. He didn't say a word. Tokyo kept packing. Then, in a low volume, almost too low to be heard over the howling wind, Luke spoke.

"I haven't asked anything of you."

Tokyo zipped her bag and looked up at the ceiling. Here was the accusation and the simpering plea stopping just short of a question, all rolled up into one. She had expected it.

When Tokyo hoisted the nylon bag's strap over her shoulder and turned to face Luke, he saw both her determination and her lack of sympathy.

"And that's all you want out of me, isn't it? To ask you the questions, the questions to let your poor soul come clean?"

Luke's eyes became cloudy. He looked beyond Tokyo. Sensing she had struck a soft point, Tokyo approached the doorway and stood in front of Luke.

"I can't make everything all better for you, Luke. You need your mama to do that. I've got nothing to tell you. I sure as hell can't answer your questions. And you've got nothing to say to me because you can't answer mine."

Luke stood aside and let Tokyo walk past. She didn't look back as she walked out the door and into the wind. Luke asked her a question as she stormed past him into the breezeway, but he spoke in low tones, barely audible. She didn't register his question until she was out the door and walking down Luke's long driveway to the road, fighting the dangerous crosswind the entire way. When the question registered, she grew even angrier and ground her teeth in determination.

Back in the kitchen, Luke watched Tokyo walking, and repeated his question in the relative silence of the empty room.

"Why don't you have a past, Tokyo?"

8.

When Noah had decided to kill Apie, he hadn't hesitated, nor did he think to question his decision. He knew with a degree of certainty most people would find chilling that Apie should be killed. Noah knew nothing of Apie's past misdeeds; he knew nothing of Apie's inclination for random violence, knew nothing of Apie's own tendency for snap decisions which brought with them significant changes in someone's life—usually someone other than Apie. Noah only knew Apie had crossed a line, a vague line separating the righteous from the unholy, a transgression which required the terrible swift judgment of the Lord—acting through Noah, of course.

Later that evening, Shlomo thought to question Noah about his threat to kill Apie.

"Threat?" Noah asked, genuinely puzzled.

Shlomo considered, staring a long time into the fire pit. Glowing ashes floated slowly up the few feet of the fire pit until they emerged into the air, where they were swept savagely away. All Shlomo could see was an orange blur of movement, a series of miniature shooting stars five feet in front of his face. The men wisely sat with their backs to the wind, keeping the ashes in front of them at all times.

"Don't get much heat this way," Shlomo said, wondering how they could build a downwind device to trap the heat but avoid the ashes. Squinting, he envisioned baffles made of heavy slate, screens of wire mesh, and warm wind-blocks made of canvas.

"Threat?" Noah asked again.

Shlomo paused a moment to return from thoughts of his invention. "Apie. You said you'd kill him."

Noah's face reflected the strange flickering glow of the fire as tongues of flame were buffeted in the swirling wind.

"That Indian said this place is sacred," Noah said.

Shlomo nodded. "He did."

Noah threw a small piece of slate into the fire. "He was wrong."

114

Although Shlomo had not known Noah long, he knew enough to realize a sermon was coming.

"This place is not sacred. This place is evil. More evil than any place I've ever seen on this earth. The wind is the Lord's voice, and you know what he's telling you? Telling me?"

Shlomo shook his head.

"He's telling us, and any other God-fearing soul, to get off this mesa quick as they can go."

"And that's why Apie left?"

Noah laughed. "Apie is weak."

And Shlomo returned the laugh. "And we are what?"

Noah put his hands on his knees and leaned forward. "We," he said, "are staying."

Shlomo considered. The man could be mad. But even madmen could prosper—Shlomo had seen it happen. "Are we going to be rich?"

"Rich in spirit, friend."

Shlomo considered again. He squinted off into the distance, in the same direction that Apie had disappeared. Finally, Shlomo looked back at Noah.

"I'm turning in, Noah."

Shlomo laid down under the semicover of the lean-to, being careful to wrap the tent cord around his wrist loosely before he settled in. In the haze between wakefulness and sleep, he thought of lions, roaring incessantly, loudly enough to frighten him. He tried to see their eyes, but they refused to face him, try as he might. Finally, the head of one of the lions moved toward him, and he saw the eyes, a yellow gold color he had never seen before, shining and clear, staring straight into his eyes so directly that Shlomo felt a pain in his heart. The lion stared for a brief time, then licked its lips and yawned. Suddenly, Shlomo was riding a horse on a calm, sunny day next to a creek of fresh water, but he was fearful. As the horse bent his neck to drink from the creek, Shlomo had the sudden sense that the lion would leap out from under the water. He tried to pull his horse away, but thirsty, it stayed standing in the creek, drinking its fill. A sudden roar behind Shlomo startled him and he awoke, sweating, to the roar of the wind. Shlomo looked over to find Noah sitting wide awake, nodding his head occasionally as if agreeing with some voice only he could hear.

9.

On the first day of spring, Daisy and Ruth instructed laughing and hungry quarrymen to place the bowls of carefully prepared picnic fare on the tables—at the same time sternly admonishing them to not pilfer biscuits and bits of fruit before it was time. Daisy's warnings were met with even more laughter by the quarrymen, since it was well known that Daisy had for a long time lived with this day in mind and no amount of stolen biscuits would dampen her enthusiasm. Nor did she feel hampered by her pregnancy, now eight months along. Daisy felt as lithe and buoyant as a swimmer. Despite the many admonitions in the Bible against it, Noah felt pride in the organizational capabilities displayed by his wife.

"Looks like you might have some competition there, Jim," Noah said to Sweetwater.

Sweetwater laughed and watched as Daisy directed the group of twenty quarrymen and her daughter Prudence, and Ruth's son Nate, who, in turn, was tending to his baby brother Amos. Shlomo limped behind the quarrymen, helping as well as his ankle—an invented malady that some time ago had turned painfully real—would allow.

Nate, who had been instructed to carry buckets of water from the shallow well at the end of New Town's Main Street, was just walking back to the tables with the first bucket when he happened to look up at the ladders fixed to the side of New Town's walls. He stood for a moment, shocked, his mouth open, then ran as quickly as he could to Daisy's kitchen, where he knew he would find his mother. He burst in, breathless, sloshing water from the bouncing bucket. Ruth turned immediately and smiled.

"Nate, you are going to have to clean up all that water from Mrs. Christophe's floor, and I mean now."

"There's someone coming. A big lady!"

Daisy and Ruth exchanged puzzled looks and walked out of the house, followed closely by Nate. Outside, the group of revelers had already noticed the woman. They stared, transfixed, as a rather portly woman worked her way carefully down the series of ladders.

Sweetwater stepped apart from the others and looked up. It was early afternoon, and the sun was just dipping below the false horizon of New Town, just behind the woman on the ladders. But even with the glare of the sun, Sweetwater recognized the woman immediately.

"Good God," he said, to no one in particular.

Norma Sweetwater had come to New Town not to claim her husband, but to punish him. Sometime during the cold Utah winter, on a day when the furnace, temperamental at the best of times, had chosen to give Norma a reason to spend even more money that she did not have, she had first felt that Jim might not come back. On such a day, at such a time, most people, and especially a mean-spirited woman of low intelligence, would choose to ignore such nagging feelings as unfounded fear. But as the short winter days grew longer, Norma's suspicion grew into an absolute certainty. Her husband had abandoned her. And when the middle of February passed into March and Sweetwater failed to appear, Norma decided to take action.

A quick inventory of her assets told her that she could not survive long without him. She knew that her age and her appearance, while once described as "pleasant," had deteriorated to the point where the only bond she was likely to form with a man was represented by the ring around her finger. Her father, a minor bureaucrat in the Recorder of Deeds office in the county seat, gave her the final piece of information she needed. She could not sell the farm and take the cash left after the couple's many loans, because she needed Sweetwater to sign the deed. Her only decision, as she saw it, was to find Sweetwater and make him pay, one way or another.

"You think you should go up there and help her?" Noah asked Sweetwater, for he and the others had seen the unmistakable recognition in Sweetwater's posture.

Sweetwater looked up at his wife, who at that moment was struggling, with a dangling foot, to find the top rung of the next ladder. She reached blindly with her foot, finally finding a purchase and letting her hands slip from the higher ladder. She landed with a plunk on the lower ladder. Some of the men standing next to the tables winced involuntarily. Others exchanged knowing looks, quick judgments on the prospects of a safe landing.

"She's a strong woman, Noah. She'll make it all right."

Noah nodded thoughtfully and looked toward Daisy. She shrugged.

"Well, let's wait for her before we eat, at least," Daisy said.

Sweetwater nodded his agreement, and Daisy and Ruth went back into the kitchen and mixed great buckets of lemonade for the quarrymen to drink as they watched Norma work her way down to the bottom of the quarry. Had Noah not maintained the high level of vigilance which prevented the quarrymen from adding alcohol to the lemonade buckets, the quarrymen would have been inclined to place bets as to whether and when the fat woman would fall from the ladders. The quarrymen also were delighted to see Sweetwater, their normally controlled foreman, shifting uncomfortably as he watched his wife. One quarryman turned to another and gestured toward Sweetwater.

"Think Jim would get a payoff if she fell?"

Noah, inclined to ignore the merriment around him, and wary of what might happen when the woman reached the ground, preferred to ignore her approach. Sweetwater, however, was trying to convince himself that somehow his wife's approach could be beneficial.

When Norma's foot finally hit the rough slate at the bottom of New Town, a great cheer went up from the quarrymen. Noah and Sweetwater walked toward Norma, who leaned heavily against the lower wall, trying to catch her breath. The quarrymen, delighted with the unscheduled entertainment and the forthcoming feast, chattered happily among themselves, watching Noah and Sweetwater approaching Norma.

"You bastard," Norma panted, as she squinted up at her husband.

Noah, normally in command of most situations, patted Sweetwater on the shoulder.

"This is a good man, woman."

"This is my husband, preacher. And he left me with no money and no way out back home."

"I'm not a preacher," Noah said.

Norma looked up at Noah, uncomprehending as to why any sane person would dress up like a preacher if they weren't one. In an instant she lost interest, and her attention returned to her husband. Sweetwater was staring at the slate under his feet, nervously flaking bits off with the toe of one of his boots. Noah patted Sweetwater again on the shoulder.

"I'm sure, woman, that—"

"Name's Norma."

"I'm sure, Norma—" Noah began again, but was interrupted.

"Are they eating down there? I'm hungry."

Noah and Sweetwater turned toward the revelers, seemingly surprised to find tables laden with food and drink waiting for them.

"Are those biscuits?" Norma asked, squinting. "I'll deal with you later," Norma said to Sweetwater and waddled toward the food.

Sweetwater looked down the street at the group of quarrymen, many of whom, he knew, were snickering at his plight. He sighed and wished the picnic had never started.

10.

Tokyo staggered down the long driveway. Because the rough pathway was built into a crosswind, she could move forward only with difficulty, forever correcting her direction due to the pressure from the west. As bad as the driveway was, she knew once she turned onto the main road leading off the mesa she would be pushed by the wind from behind, toward the town. Incongruously, walking with the wind had always presented more of a problem for Tokyo because of her small frame. As she leaned back awkwardly, the wind tended to force her steps as she walked, threatening to knock her to the ground. A simple tumble without protection on the open mesa could quickly become an uncontrollable slide across the ground, faster and faster until she was torn apart by the rough surface. Alternately, she could turn west and walk into the wind; that would be exhausting, yes, but she knew from experience she could better maintain her balance leaning forward in a more natural posture. The only problem with this choice was that it led nowhere but to an abandoned quarry she knew little about and then to the cliffs beyond. She was certain she would be unable to fight the wind much beyond the old quarry.

She glanced at Luke's house, only a quarter mile back, a small ship embedded in an immovable black sea. She had known this moment would come just as it had come with other men; yet, as always, she was surprised at how quickly the thought had become reality. She was walking away from another house, another man. The only difference she noticed was the physical difficulty of this escape.

As she resumed her trudge, she unexpectedly thought of her mother. Tokyo's earliest memory was of watching her mother—her birth mother—walking away from her. She remembered a different path, a leafy one, the green, slow-moving creek, the heat of the day. She remembered crying, great chest-heaving sobs, and feeling the cool moss of the pathway against the backs of her legs. Her mother didn't turn; she kept walking slowly away, her print dress clinging to her back where she was sweating. Her mother's hair was jet black, like Tokyo's. She couldn't see her mother's face, but she knew her mother was crying too.

When she remembered her mother, this was the only image she could conjure: the print dress, the sweat, the black hair, and the tears. Shortly after the time by the creek, her mother had gone away. She had never heard from her again until she received news of her death in an insane asylum in upstate New York. By then, Tokyo didn't think about her mother, didn't even conjure up the memory by the creek, unless it happened on its own, like today.

Luke had asked about her, had asked until she was tired of telling him that she didn't remember. And yet Luke kept asking, as if knowing something about her mother would somehow have told him something important about Tokyo.

"I only remember my foster parents. And I don't want to talk about them."

"But, you didn't know your parents at all?"

Tokyo shook her head and looked down.

"Why do you care?" The anger in her tone was unmistakable. It had been Luke's turn to look down.

Now, at the end of Luke's driveway, Tokyo decided to head west, away from town and escape. Into the wind. She would fight the wind sent straight from hell.

It struck her face, forcing tears from her eyes. Despite the importance of maintaining a delicate balance, Tokyo angrily wiped the tears away. She hadn't cried and meant it for as many years as she could remember. Crying was a weakness or a tool, depending on whether it was her doing the crying and why. She had no time for women who lost control and cried, and even less respect for men who did.

Inside Luke's house, of course, he would be watching, waiting for her to turn around and come inside. Despite his experience with her stubbornness during their time together, he would expect her to turn around, not solely because she was a woman in a bad place, but because any person, animal, or insect, given a choice, would have returned to the relative safety of Luke's house after only a few moments. He wouldn't understand Tokyo's stubborn insistence.

Sitting by the window, watching her progress intently, Luke shook his head in disbelief as Tokyo turned left onto the main road. She was walking away from the town, into the teeth of the wind, toward the west. It made no sense.

"My God, she's stubborn," Luke muttered. He stood up and put on his jacket, then sighed and reached for the keys to his truck, just as Tokyo had known he would.

11.

The nonbelievers never see it, but even the most ardent believers harbor self-doubt. The nonbelievers see in the believer only strict adherence to dogma. The believers stride purposefully through life, determined to serve their beliefs. The nonbelievers watch, partly in awe, partly in jealousy, seeing only gray where the believers see black and white.

But, Noah, the believer, harbored self-doubts. He harbored doubts of the existence of a divine plan, doubted whether he played a part in the plan, and doubted whether the plan would lead him ultimately to paradise. In his rare silent moments, Noah considered the world and his place in it. He looked at the swirling chaos all around him, then at the relative peace he had scratched out in New Town. Surely he could keep the doubts at bay by creating his own paradise here on earth, removed from the savage winds of the unprotected mesa to the dark calm of New Town. Surely the Lord would look with favor on those who followed Noah into his own garden.

But the doubt remained: What if he didn't? What if the Lord saw Noah's creation of paradise as nothing but vanity, doomed to failure in a thousand ways Noah could not yet see? Noah's response to his nagging doubt was to face the wind and shoulder a heavier burden. Ultimately, Noah decided, the Lord would make his judgment, and, whatever that judgment was, Noah would obey.

Noah's fears of the Lord's adverse judgment were confirmed at Daisy's picnic. Beginning the day of the event, he regretted having thought to prove his perseverance to God. After the picnic, Noah realized with absolute certainty that the Lord was displeased and that he would be punished severely. He did not, however, regret having surrendered to Daisy's desire; to the contrary, he was thankful, for it was only through the picnic that he had realized his error.

At first, Norma's ominous appearance unsettled Noah, but the bustle of the picnic carried his vague misgivings away as neatly as the wind. Soon he began mingling happily with the other quarrymen, seeing this as nothing short of a God-given opportunity for him to convince others to join the small hardy band of New Town. Daisy, as always mindful of her husband's location and humor, was delighted to see him lost in earnest discussion with various quarrymen. She saw his earnest entreaties from a distance, and, despite her often distant relationship with him, felt a surge of warmth.

Norma, on the other hand, seemed to care little for appearances. She had helped herself to large portions of fresh biscuits and potato salad and impatiently waited for a healthy slab of the pig which was roasting over a shallow fire pit. Now, with her mouth full of half-chewed food, she was berating her husband loudly, without apparent humility.

"Did you think I'd let you just leave me? Is that what you thought?"

For perhaps the hundredth time in the short period since she had arrived, Sweetwater, who towered over his wife, bent his head submissively and failed to respond.

"You made a deal, Jim," she said, holding up her hand to show her simple wedding ring. Sweetwater nodded.

"And now you're thinking of breaking it?"

Ruth and Daisy, standing nearby pouring lemonade, exchanged glances. Sweetwater had always treated the two women well, and it appeared he could use a hand. Ruth cleared her throat and smiled sweetly.

"Norma? Like some more lemonade?"

Norma turned to Ruth. Her eyes narrowed.

"You two knew he was married, didn't you? All of you knew, but you didn't think about me, did you?"

"If we had known you, we might have thought about you," Ruth consoled.

"Life out here is different, Norma. We don't ask questions ..." Daisy's explanation trailed off. How could she explain life on the mesa?

"Well, that day's over now that I'm here. I ask questions," Norma said proudly, holding her glass out and shaking it from side to side for Ruth to fill. As Ruth poured the lemonade, Norma looked up at the fast-moving clouds, then at the sides of the black quarry. The sun, which wouldn't set above on the mesa for another several hours, was just now sinking behind the great western wall of the quarry. On the main street of New Town, twilight had come.

"What the hell are you doing living in the dark?" Norma asked. "This is some kind of hell!"

Those sitting close enough to Norma to have heard her actual words stopped talking and stared. Those not close enough were quarrymen who were well trained in reading the subtleties of variable and changing winds and therefore knew enough to read when a silence should catch and be extended.

It seemed to Norma that the quarrymen parted like the Red Sea, and there at the end of the dry canal stood Noah, who seemed to have grown several feet in height. He strode to her, covering the ground in three steps. He towered over her as he spoke.

"This is no hell, woman. This is home! This is paradise!" His voice was loud, as if he were standing in the pulpit of a large house of worship. Those few quarrymen and children who were still talking quieted and stared. Even if he was pigheaded and wrong, Noah was a man to whom Black Rockers listened. After all, were it not for Noah, no one in the town would be capable of earning a living.

When she had been a child, in the one-room schoolhouse she had attended, Norma's Mormon schoolmaster had beat her continuously for her unwillingness to conform. She remembered his black frock coat, so much like Noah's. More than his coat, it was his eyes she remembered, bright and insistent, like Noah's, but even as a child she had been perceptive enough to see the tinge of madness. Despite the beatings, Norma had not learned to keep her mouth shut. Her parents had been asked by the church elders to remove her from the premises when she had the equivalent of a fourth-grade education and to bring her back only when she had learned discipline. Norma's education level had therefore been permanently fixed at the fourth-grade level. Her father had rationalized her failure in education as of no significance in any event, what with her being a girl about to turn into a woman and have babies. Norma had treated his opinion with the same respect as she had the schoolmaster's and thereafter attempted to make life as difficult as possible for her father, just as she had for the schoolmaster.

Looking up at Noah, Norma saw not the man, but an unbroken chain of sanctimonious preachers who thought they knew best. This man, she thought, had probably had a good deal to do with convincing her only source of income to abandon her on a barren farm. Well, she thought,

Jim wasn't the only person who was going to have to pay the price. She glanced around at the silent faces, sensing at once their awe and fear of this man. She hated the obedient faces around her, faces that seemed to merge into one tepid flock of sheep. Even her husband seemed to merge into the crowd, what little backbone he had once had lost forever in the presence of this preacher. Even if no one else in this dark place was willing to stand up to him, she would be damned if she'd shut up now.

As she opened her mouth to speak, Norma became aware of a sudden great tiredness in her limbs. Noah's face began to swim slightly. She thought it best that she sit down for a moment before she told Noah exactly what she thought of him and his "paradise." She leaned heavily against the table. Her breath was raspy, and she became aware of a heavy chill.

"Do you hear me, woman?" Noah was insistent. Daisy and Ruth once again exchanged looks.

"Noah," Daisy said, "I don't think she's well."

Noah looked at the sagging woman in front of him. Her skin was pale, her eyes fluttering.

"This woman is possessed by a demon!" Noah said.

Ruth, who had, along with Daisy, taken one of Norma's arms, faced Noah, shaking her head. "She's not possessed, Noah. She's sick."

Noah ignored Ruth and Daisy and put both his hands on Norma's face. She was sweating, a cold, clammy sweat that Noah had seen before in dying men and hogs about to be slaughtered. He shook his head, taken for the moment with the idea of the evil demon lurking within this stranger.

Somewhere within her delirium, Norma looked up at this preacher with his cool hands. His face was contorting, moving back and forth erratically, and she gamely tried to follow it, but the waves of nausea became worse. Finally she closed her eyes for a moment, then looked up. Yes, that did it. Noah's face kept still for long enough for Norma to see into his bright blue eyes. He looked so much like her schoolteacher, she had to tell him. Norma tried to open her dry mouth to speak. She thought she was speaking, but could hear no words other than Noah's.

"In the name of the Lord, our Father, I expel the demon from this woman!"

Norma licked her lips, concentrating on a face that was once again bouncing back and forth in her vision. She opened her mouth to speak to this preacher, but instead vomited all over him, a torrent of half-digested potato salad, hog, lemonade, and biscuits.

Noah backed away, his eyes wide with surprise and disgust. He felt the vomit dripping from his black clothing and heard the silence of the quarrymen and their families around him. He tried to speak, but instead watched his wife and Ruth help Norma to the ground.

"She's possessed," Noah whispered, mostly to himself.

"She's sick, Noah. She's just sick." Daisy was mopping Norma's forehead with a dishtowel. Norma's fat cheeks were sagging, her eyes glassy and rolling. Sweetwater stepped forward and kneeled down to look at her. As he did, she turned her head to the side and vomited again, a hard green slime disappearing on the black slate at Noah's feet.

"Daddy?" Noah turned as young Nate tugged on Shlomo's sleeve. "Daddy, I don't feel well."

Shlomo nodded and looked to Ruth, who came to Nate's side.

"Honey? Are you okay?"

In answer, Nate bent over and vomited heavily on the ground. Shlomo turned toward Noah.

"He ain't possessed too, Noah," Shlomo said. "Ain't possible. He's got a different God than her."

Noah nodded. He turned to the quarrymen. One of them, back near the fire pit, was suspiciously sniffing something on his plate. Noah's eyes narrowed. The quarryman threw the plate on the ground and looked up.

"This hog's bad," he said. "Them that's eaten it, gonna get sick."

There was murmuring among the quarrymen. Noah heard someone say, "We're all going to get it now." Noah glanced over at Daisy, who was looking a bit pale.

"See, Noah? It's just a bad hog, is all." Daisy smiled weakly. "Not everything is a message from heaven."

Noah and Shlomo had been the only people in New Town not to eat any of the poisoned hog: Noah because he had not found the time yet to eat, and Shlomo out of habit. Noah shook his head as he watched his wife sag perceptibly and sit heavily on the stairs of their home. She was wrong, he knew. Of the two of them, Noah was certain he knew how to read a sign from God. And his Word could be seen not only in the heavens and on the earth, but also in a bad hog.

12.

If a person found it necessary to do so, walking into the wind could be accomplished, not through strength, but rather through guile and patience. Theoretically, one could tack, zigzagging back and forth across the wind, much as a sailboat would head into a stiff breeze—but only the strongest men could really hope to pull off such a tactic. And not since the old days on the mesa had anyone even tried.

Mostly, when forced to walk into the wind, Black Rockers chose to take small steps, always leaning heavily into the wind, each step being no more than three or four inches. If a person were savvy enough, he would wait for the occasional lulls in the wind, each one mere seconds in duration, and use them to lunge forward a few extra steps. The wind, sensing it had been outsmarted, normally followed such lulls with savage gusts. If the subsequent gust caught the walker unaware, or awkwardly in midstep, the wind could throw him backward, far beyond the minor gains he had been able to steal from the wind. Most walkers avoided attempts to cheat the wind and instead chose to take short, balanced steps. In this way, progress could be made much in the same manner as climbing a steep hill.

Tokyo didn't hear Luke's truck pull up next to her. She knew he was there only by the shadow which fell across her feet. She didn't look up immediately, but rather continued her trudge into the wind. The truck crawled forward at her pace. Luke rolled down the window and yelled to be heard.

"Tokyo!"

She turned her head, tears forming in her eyes from the wind. Angry that he might think she was crying, she turned her head back toward the ground.

"Tokyo, get in the truck!" There was a pause, a change in his tone—it became more pleading. "C'mon!"

In the truck, looking out at Tokyo, Luke bit his lip. Head down, her small frame was struggling in the wind. Luke had seen men, large men, use more energy than they had ever dreamed possible and collapse in the wind, exhausted. If Tokyo collapsed, she might be blown completely off the mesa. Worse, he noticed her nylon bag slung carelessly over her shoulder. She knew enough to keep the bag hidden under her coat, but her anger had dulled her caution and fully half of the bag was exposed to the wind. If the wind were to catch the bag, it would act like a parachute, launching her backward to be dragged mercilessly across the mesa. There would be no way to save her.

"You have to get in, Tokyo!"

Involuntarily, Luke had used language which Tokyo refused to let go by.

"I don't *have* to do anything. Nothing!" She was panting, her breath coming hard.

"You can't make it much further."

"See what I can do," Tokyo spat.

"Where the hell are you going? The town's the other way."

Tokyo smiled to herself as she walked. Of course it was. Had there been any doubt whether Luke would actually come out to pick her up, she had removed it effectively by heading away from town. He wouldn't understand where she was going. It would be totally unexplainable to him, she knew. She trudged slowly forward, satisfied in his apparent consternation.

Luke stopped the truck and considered. It was probably good she was walking into the wind. If she had walked in the other direction, going with the wind, she'd probably be dead now, having been pushed uncontrollably by the wind until she fell and rolled on the ground—each roll would be as if she'd been struck a heavy blow. Too many rolls and she would have been unconscious and battered, lying in a shallow on the side of the road.

Luke, although determined, was also mindful of Tokyo's stubbornness. He saw she was already struggling, but also saw she would sooner be infested with lice than get in his truck. Soon she would tire even more; then the wind would push her backward, as if she had started downwind in the first place.

Putting the truck back into gear, he pulled up in front of her and stopped the truck.

Tokyo, momentarily grateful for the wind-block provided by the truck, halted to catch her breath. Luke opened the door and stepped out. She looked up at him: his craggy face, his grimace of a smile.

"Kind of windy out for a walk, Tokyo."

"I'm going. Get your fucking truck out of my way."

Luke leaned heavily against the truck. He looked sad.

"You're not mean to me because it's your nature, Tokyo. You're mean to me because you have to be. It keeps you closed up."

In answer, Tokyo strode around the truck and resumed her march. When she was facing the wind again, walking slowly away from the truck, she knew she would be in trouble if she allowed Luke to become angry enough to leave her here, but she was determined to walk until she collapsed. Collapse was preferable to surrender. Luke brought the truck up next to her again and rolled down the window.

"You've got to win, don't you, Tokyo?"

She acted as if she were unable to hear.

Luke revved the engine and popped the clutch, which he had been working in and out to stay aside of her. The truck leapt ahead a few yards, then slowed down again to Tokyo's pace. An observer would have thought it a comical parade, the pickup truck followed by the slight Japanese woman. Walking behind the truck, Tokyo realized her stride had become easier. Watching in the rearview mirror, Luke kept pace with her stride, blocking the wind for her as best he could. If she wouldn't get in, he could at least protect her.

Behind the truck, Tokyo considered. In the face of the wind, she would fail, and be forced to accept Luke's offer quickly. Back here, breathing the exhaust fumes from his pickup, she could choose how far and how hard she wanted to fight. When she felt it was time to give up, she'd give up.

PART THREE

NEW TOWN

1.

Outside on the windswept mesa, and even in the slightly calmer town, quarrymen quickly learned not to open their mouths. Besides wasting their voices in having to yell over the howling wind, opening their mouths for even a brief moment allowed slate dust to enter and coat their teeth and mouth with a layer of fine dust. No amount of water, whether used as a drink or as a rinse, could relieve the gritty taste. The only solution was to not speak in the first place, or better yet, not even to open their mouths. Given the choice between grime-covered tongue and teeth and not speaking at all, most Black Rock citizens kept their mouths shut.

Even with the ingrained reluctance to open his mouth, during his lifetime the average Black Rock citizen could expect to ingest over forty pounds of slate dust. Some slate dust, of course, was inhaled and contributed to coughing spasms and black lung, making walking into the wind for those so afflicted much more difficult. But the ingested slate, interestingly, worked as a charcoal filter of sorts in the digestive systems of the Black Rockers, and it was rare indeed when someone complained of a stomach ailment due to something he or she had eaten.

In fact, it was unusual for a germ to infect the town. The local townsfolk correctly assumed they were seldom felled by the flu or even the common cold for the obvious reason: If a virus was transferred from person to person by a cough or a sneeze, it would have to be a very strong virus to make its way through the wind to a second person's mucus glands. Viruses, it was said, if they made it onto the mesa at all, were quickly swept through town and, it was assumed, didn't land until they got to Kansas or possibly even Nebraska. A scientist would have called it biological isolation—essentially, they were an island. But the townsfolk knew it was much more. In fact, the closest Black Rock ever came to anything resembling an epidemic was that infamous day that came to be known simply as "The Picnic."

In the aftermath of the picnic, Shlomo took it on himself to scrub the vomit from the black slate of New Town. Normally Shlomo would have deferred to Noah's work ethic, but Noah had been strangely silent, spending the day sitting on the front porch of his house as the town's collective gastrointestinal upheaval ran its course. In the face of his friend's silence, Shlomo did what he thought would raise Noah from the demiworld in which he seemed mired. Shlomo himself cared little for the smell, but the thought of passing time waiting for either Noah to speak or for the New Town sufferers to stop retching was not acceptable.

Shlomo carried bucket after bucket to the shallow pool at the low point of the town. Originally, the hole had been dug as a well, but the water had bubbled up to form a small pond of frigid water. Shlomo was grateful for the ease with which he could dip the buckets into the water and carry them back to the still-standing picnic tables. He poured the water over the reeking slate as Noah watched.

"More I pour the water, the more I smell it," Shlomo said at one point, taking a break from his labor and leaning against a vomit-stained table.

Noah turned his head upward, watching the clouds racing across the limited horizon. It was an uncharacteristic gesture of contemplation on Noah's part. Shlomo followed his gaze.

"Sun's setting. How's Daisy feeling?"

A look of confusion came over Noah's face. He opened his mouth as if to respond, but no words came out. To Shlomo, standing in the fading light of New Town, Noah looked as if he were befuddled, one of those crazy people Shlomo remembered from the city. They looked normal, as did Noah, except they didn't hear or understand a word that was said to them. You only found out by asking them a question.

"Never mind, Noah. I'm sure she'll be feeling better." Shlomo looked down at one of the buckets he was carrying, still half filled with water. "I think giving everyone sips of this water helps. It's got some slate dust in it, and that works like a filter in their systems to clean them out. Kind of like charcoal, you know?" Shlomo paused and chuckled. "Of course, they've been plenty cleaned out by now, eh Noah?"

Seeing no response was forthcoming from Noah, Shlomo nodded silently and walked toward his own home.

On his porch, Noah sighed deeply, acutely aware of the stench of vomit on the street in front of him. He could have gone inside or even climbed up on the mesa to avoid the smell, but he preferred instead to be faced with his own folly. Here, listening to his wife and daughter retching and sobbing inside, he looked out on his paradise in bafflement. The street was littered with the prone and suffering forms of quarrymen too ill to climb the ladders or even reach the safety of their bunkhouse. The Lord was sending a message of disapproval, and it was Noah's duty to sit here amid the Lord's work until he could see the message more clearly.

As darkness fell, Daisy's cries grew louder in the house, sometimes waking young Prudence in her crib. There was a certain ebb and flow to Daisy's discomfort, which at first was bothersome and distracting to Noah, but soon became almost comforting in its regularity.

In his own house, in bed asleep, Shlomo dreamt of escaping hell.

As the sun crept across the high wall of New Town the next morning, Shlomo awoke, disturbed by the cries of the damned he had heard in his dreams. Ruth, who had regained a more healthy color during the night, stirred and smiled at Shlomo.

"You're feeling better?" Shlomo asked.

Ruth nodded a reply and quickly rose from bed to check on the children. Of course, her greatest concern was for the baby, Amos. During her illness, she had stoically cared for her sick children, jettisoning every thought or action which would be extraneous to their health. Now, she thought of Daisy for the first time, pregnant and facing the same task of caring for Prudence. After she saw to the children, she would visit Daisy to offer help if it were needed.

Downstairs, Shlomo looked out of his front window and shook his head at the figure of Noah, still transfixed on his porch. He listened to the sounds of his wife moving upstairs. With the familiarity of a husband, he contentedly noticed that the sound of her footsteps was firmer and stronger. As he listened, Ruth walked to the stairs. By her footsteps, he could hear she was carrying Nate—weak, but healthier. As she reached the bottom of the stairs, she came into sight, and Shlomo felt a rush of gratitude for her return to health—in no small part due to the easing of his own burden in caring for the needs of his family which he otherwise would have left to her.

Ruth joined her husband at the window and squeezed his shoulder. She smiled reassuringly, knowing he would relax when he saw her health had returned. Shlomo smiled back at her, then nodded out the window.

"He's still out there." Ruth looked out at Noah, still staring at the street in front of him.

"How long?" Ruth asked.

"All night, I think. I'll go see what I can do."

"Make sure Daisy and Prudence are okay."

Shlomo nodded, pulled on his suspenders, and limped to the door. He smiled ruefully at the pain in his ankle. His feigned limp had become real somewhere down the line; Noah opined it was God's punishment for Shlomo's lies—just punishment in Noah's eyes. At present, Shlomo blamed his pain on the day's hard work of toting buckets of water from the pool at the end of the quarry to the stinking street in front of Noah's home.

"Guess I'm entitled to a little pain," Shlomo said to himself as he limped onto his own porch.

As Shlomo paused in the sunlight, attempting to get a bearing on the day, he noticed that some of the quarrymen had awakened from their stupor and were heading to the ladders to begin the climb up to the mesa. Surprisingly, Noah was not leading them to the mesa, but rather remained sitting on his porch. In most circumstances, Noah's desire to supervise would have emerged, leading him to criticize or cajole the workers down to the last detail, even if it were a criticism of the method with which they were ascending the ladders. Today, Noah simply watched the quarrymen climb. Puzzled by his friend's lassitude, Shlomo limped over to Noah's porch.

"Looks like the men are going off to the quarry."

From the porch, Noah looked down at Shlomo, as if surprised to see him standing there. Inside, Prudence began to cry in her crib.

"Aren't you going to go help them?"

Noah looked down the street to the series of ladders. Sweetwater and his wife were just struggling up the ladders, leaving New Town and the mesa, probably forever. Noah pursed his lips, considering the distinct possibility that he would never see either one of them again.

"Let them go," Noah said in a voice which Shlomo had never heard. It was the voice of a smaller man, a weaker man, a defeated man.

Shlomo pointed to the house behind Noah. He heard Prudence's cries, the cries of a child desperate for something which, in the unmistakable way of a child, she seemed utterly certain she could not live without.

While the crying struck at Shlomo's soul, Noah seemed not to hear his daughter. "By them, I mean Prudence and Daisy. They feeling better?"

Noah waved vaguely over his shoulder and resumed his study of the street. The quarrymen were either heading toward the mesa or had disappeared into the bunkhouse. Those in the bunkhouse were simply biding their time until they felt sufficiently recovered to ascend the ladders; thereafter they would, Noah was sure, never live in the bunkhouse of New Town again. He felt their unspoken mass decision as if it were written in burning letters in the air in front of him. The street was empty.

Shlomo glanced in the window of Noah's house and saw Prudence standing in her crib, crying with all her might. It wasn't Prudence's crying that caught his interest; there was something else.

"Noah, what's going on in there?"

Noah waved again, as if he were brushing flies away from his face and shoulders.

Shlomo turned toward his own house and waved urgently to Ruth, who quickly put Nate on the ground and Amos in his crib. She ran to the porch. Ruth knew Shlomo was a man not given to urgent gestures; rather, he was a calm man, prone to reasoning his way smoothly through urgent times, often to the acute irritation of his family and friends. But today he waved with a jerky awkwardness, and Ruth immediately sensed his need.

On Noah's porch, Ruth recoiled slightly at the stench emanating from Noah's black frock coat, still stained from Norma's vomit. She turned to Shlomo quizzically. He shrugged and pointed inside to Prudence.

"If Daisy's too sick, I'll take care of Prudence," Ruth said, moving toward the door.

Noah didn't move. Ruth and Shlomo exchanged looks as Ruth pushed open the door. As soon as she took one step inside, she heard a sound, an unmistakable sound and turned urgently to Shlomo.

"Get water and bring it back here now!"

As she ran inside the house, she pulled a blanket off the large chair in the kitchen and ran by Prudence. A quick glance told her of Prudence's improved health. Her dirty diaper and desperate cries for food would have to wait. Not understanding, Prudence, who had quieted herself to heaving sobs when Ruth had entered, began shrieking again as Ruth ran through the room.

Ruth paused outside of the door of Daisy's bedroom. Prudence's cries in the front room heightened Ruth's sense of danger. She peered into the darkness of Daisy's room, trying to block out the fear.

"Daisy?"

Ruth pushed the door open a crack and looked in. Amid the bloody sheets of her bed, Daisy smiled weakly up at Ruth as she nursed her new baby. Tears formed in her eyes as Ruth came to the side of the bed.

"It's a boy, Ruth. His name's Luke, after Noah's father." She paused a moment. "Noah's gonna be so happy."

2.

When the visitor burst into Amos's store, as strangers always did, neither Amos nor Sis seemed surprised. Proudfoot and Tongate on the other hand, would have expressed surprise at practically anything, and the entrance of a stranger in a place where few strangers ever came was enough to send them around the bend. The two men habitually used the process of shelling and eating peanuts at the counter as a distraction to help them through long days; each day was so like the next it seemed one glasslike plane. The advent of a newcomer to Black Rock was more than enough to stop their desultory trudge across the unbroken plane of another day.

As the door flew open and the man entered the store, Amos reflected ruefully: "Bad luck for him he came in when these two characters are here." Amos glanced over at Proudfoot and Tongate, both of whom had stopped munching on peanuts. As the two men turned to stare at the stranger, Amos deftly closed the open end of the burlap sack of peanuts. *Good luck for me, though,* Amos thought.

Tongate wasted no time in walking over to the man, who was shaking the dust out of his jacket onto the floor. The man seemed stunned by the amount of dust his own clothes had collected during his short exposure out-of-doors. He shook his head and slapped the sleeves of his coat, watching the dust drift upward in the air. He shook his head again, until he noticed the men staring at him; one of them was walking toward him. He realized at once he had probably created quite a mess.

"Welcome to Black Rock," Tongate said, extending his hand.

The visitor took down his hood. He was old, and his face was tan; his cheeks were so smooth and shiny that it seemed as if he had never shaved nor would he ever have to do so. His eyes were dark and bright, his hair black and short. He took Tongate's hand.

"Black Rock?" the man asked.

"The name of our humble town," Tongate began. "The name comes from—"

"The mesa?"

Having been interrupted, Tongate squinted at the man. "Well, yes."

"Didn't think it was just a black rock quarry," the man said, winking at Tongate.

He walked past a somewhat befuddled Tongate and toward the counter.

Amos smiled a welcome. "Most strangers stop here looking for gas."

"This a gas station?"

Amos shook his head. "No, no gas here."

Tongate noisily resumed his seat. "What Amos here means—"

"I think I know what he means. You don't get many strangers in here, am I right?" The man paused for a moment, then looked back toward the door. "Sorry about the mess. It's really windy out. All the dust. If you give me a broom …"

Amos smiled again and shook his head. Sweeping dust in a place like Black Rock made no sense until a person was absolutely certain a door would be closed for a good long time. The man seemed to understand Amos and nodded; it was a combined gesture of thanks and agreement.

In the silence, Tongate smiled thinly, pulled a few hidden peanuts from his pocket, and cracked them in his hand. Hearing the noise, Amos flinched.

Tongate cleared his throat and began what he imagined would be a short speech of explanation. "Due to the constant harsh winds, Black Rock is not conducive to visits from strangers. Most seem to think it's a hard place to stop. Even for a few hours." Tongate stopped speaking when he noticed the man was paying absolutely no attention to him. The stranger had noticed Sis. Though she normally hid in the background, now she stood next to Amos and smiled sweetly.

The man directed his attention to Sis. "I spoke to you on the phone, didn't I? I'm Penn."

Sis nodded.

"Do you know where I can find her?"

Sis nodded again as Tongate and Proudfoot exchanged glances. Amos made as if he were inspecting his latest shipment. He noticed a case of mothballs had somehow been included, a useless item in Black Rock, as there were no moths on the mesa or in the town. There were no flying insects or birds of any kind, for that matter. In the silence, Amos smiled.

A stranger shows up, that'd itself be enough to stop those two characters from stealing my peanuts. But now he's looking for Tokyo? That'll really set them off. Maybe they'll finally leave the peanuts alone. As if in confirmation of Amos's thoughts, he listened as Proudfoot cleared his throat, a long, exaggerated rumbling which led to an uncontrollable coughing fit.

Undisturbed by the eddies of interest in the store, Penn followed Sis with his eyes as she moved to the hook on which hung a jumble of keys. She took the keys for Amos's truck and patted him on the shoulder. She gestured at Penn to follow, and he did so without a second glance at Proudfoot, Tongate, or Amos. As they left Amos's store, Tongate, by this time exasperated, stood in front of the counter firmly.

"As mayor of this town, I think it would be prudent for you to tell me who this man is and what the hell he is doing here."

Proudfoot stirred. "Don't use language, Barney."

"I'm sorry, but don't you think Amos and Sis ought to be more—"

Amos sighed and looked up at Tongate. "I don't know who he is. He called here a couple of weeks ago. Talked to Sis. He wanted to see Tokyo. Don't know why. Have to ask him."

Tongate nodded and resumed his seat. His brow was furrowed in thought. Suddenly, he looked up, his eyes wide.

"He looked like a lawyer," Tongate began, nodding his head as his idea gained momentum, "and a smart one at that. Maybe Tokyo has come into an inheritance, and he's come to tell her about it."

Proudfoot rolled his eyes and shook his head. "And what's she going to do with it, Barney?"

Tongate nodded with certainty. "She's going to invest it. In the town. In us."

Amos, slow to anger and slow to reveal his feelings directly, stopped eyeing the mothballs and looked at Tongate, incredulous. "Barney, that woman blew in here one day with the wind, and she's gonna blow out the same way."

Tongate smiled triumphantly. "That's only what she wants you to think, Amos."

3.

In his truck, Luke inched westward along the road—a direction in which he had rarely ventured, since his home was the last living landmark on the western portion of the mesa. He occasionally glanced in the rearview window to ensure that he was driving slowly enough to continue blocking the wind for Tokyo. Had Luke heard the words Tongate had just spoken, he would have agreed wholeheartedly. Tokyo reveled in her stubbornness and seemed addicted to her unpredictability. As angry as he was at her behavior, Luke knew he wouldn't leave her on her own. There were thousands of reasons not to abandon a person on the mesa without protection. Severe physical harm and death topped the list. In his truck, Luke seethed silently as he realized the reason he had his truck between Tokyo and the worst of the wind was not so much protection as it was love. He couldn't explain his love for this angry woman, yet there it was within him, a love he had yet to express in words. Besides, what were words to Tokyo? She would ignore them or turn them on him angrily in some mean-spirited way, and he would regret having uttered them. He could just as soon scream into the wind for all the good it would do. Better to leave the words unspoken, to hint at them with care and steadiness, at least until the hints became too broad and too desperate. Not telling her would be easy; it avoided the hurt she would bring. She almost seemed to sense she could hold him at bay with her silent anger; she could keep him bottled up inside himself as long as she wanted. *Sure,* he thought, *I save myself the scene she would make. But I'm playing right into her hands.* He shook his head angrily and turned his head to spit a bit of slate dust out of his mouth. Normally he would have spat out the window, but with Tokyo behind the truck, he chose to spit onto his pants. He idly rubbed the bit of saliva on his jeans with an open hand and glanced once again at Tokyo's image in the rearview mirror.

Tokyo was tired. She had walked farther than she had thought possible and now struggled to make every small step. The duffle bag didn't help matters. Despite the cold day, she was perspiring heavily, the sweat on her face drying into salt streaks almost immediately. Her thoughts were simple: Luke would know she wouldn't go back to his place, so he'd suggest Amos's. She would reluctantly agree. She'd get to Amos's place, stay there until the bus came through, and ride on, maybe to a place in the desert where the winds only blew at night and the daytimes were hot, still, and acrid.

To her right, Tokyo noticed the ground sloping upward, forming what she suspected was the rim of the old quarry. She'd never been out this way before, and had heard very little about this quarry. Unlike the rest of the scrubbed and flat mesa, Tokyo saw, there were various outcroppings of slate—remainders of the scraping and clawing of quarrymen from countless years ago. Tokyo turned slightly to survey the broad mesa. As the only characteristic feature of the mesa visible from horizon to horizon, the old quarry appealed to Tokyo as good protection from the vicious wind, far more appealing than Luke's truck. She was too tired to walk much further, even with the wind-block provided by Luke's truck. Gathering herself for the effort, she stopped walking forward and turned crosswind toward the old quarry.

A few moments later Luke glanced in the rearview mirror and saw nothing but road. Panicked, he slammed on the parking brake and heaved his weight against the door, opening it with difficulty. Normally he would have moved the truck sideways to the wind so that opening the door would not have been such a burden, but he was afraid in so doing he might expose Tokyo to the wind. He was certain she had stumbled and was likely prone on the roadway. Worse, she might have already been swept completely off the road.

Outside the truck, he quickly confirmed his worse fears: she had been swept away by the wind and had vanished completely. He checked both sides of the truck, then underneath, but there was no trace. Exasperated, Luke put one hand to his head and scratched mightily. Up and down the road, he saw nothing but the same windswept view. *She's small, but not so small the wind got her up in the air that quickly*, he thought. Other than the road, there was no place for her to go, unless … turning, he slowly realized she must have headed for the quarry.

As Luke stood outside the truck, his eyes slowly drifted to the rim of the old quarry. A sense of dread crept up his spine and then flooded his brain.

Luke hesitated a moment, then began walking slowly crosswind. He moved slowly, stepping carefully toward the eastern rim of the old quarry. Tokyo, well hidden in a shelter of slate on the western rim, watched his approach.

As Luke walked toward her hiding place, she steeled herself for the confrontation. Just as she was about to stand, she noticed Luke was not behaving in the manner of a person who is searching for someone; instead, he seemed almost transfixed by the black water that filled the quarry. As Tokyo watched, befuddled, Luke stood on an outcropping of slate and looked down into the quarry, not idly, the way someone might watch the ocean at a beach, but intensely, in the manner of someone who has lost something.

Good Christ, Tokyo thought. *He thinks I jumped in.*

As a Black Rock lifer, Luke knew, almost instinctually, how to behave out on the mesa, particularly how to move with the least resistance to the wind, which, of course, included never sitting with your face to the wind. But now, Luke sat down on a piece of slate with no protection from the wind—worse yet, facing the wind—and stared down into the quarry. After a moment, he lowered his head into his hands and shook his head slowly back and forth. Tokyo watched him from across the quarry for a long time, watched the sobs shaking his body. She was angry and determined, but she couldn't stay here and let him grieve for her this way. Slowly, she stood up, dropped her duffle, and, carefully, so as not to be blown into the quarry, walked around the rim on the well-worn path. When she reached him, she stood behind him, feeling an unexpected longing to reach out and comfort him, to stroke his hair, to ease the tension in his neck, but she resisted. It was over between them—this was no time for compassion. Still, something had to be said.

"Luke!" She had to yell to be heard over the wind.

Luke raised his head from his hands and looked back to her. His eyes were red from crying. Tears in a man. A weakness which normally repulsed her. She took a few steps closer. *So I don't have to yell,* she told herself.

"I didn't jump in, Luke," she said. She smiled thinly.

Luke sighed deeply and turned back to the quarry as if he were reading a book. After what seemed to be a long time, he shook his head slowly and feebly gestured to the quarry with his head. He said something, but his words were carried away with the wind.

"What?"

Luke looked up at Tokyo, then yelled up at the sky, a deep, throaty man's scream. "I hate this place." He was half angry, half crying, seemingly talking to Tokyo, but also to someone else who, quite clearly, was not sitting with him on the rim.

Tokyo blinked. The previous tension between them was gone, but it had been replaced by something inexplicably darker. Luke nodded down into the quarry and resumed staring at the silent black water. Surprisingly, the wind seemed to pass right over the quarry; the water's surface was broken only by minor ripples reflecting the grayness of the windswept sky. Soon, Luke's head dipped into his hands, and he was sobbing again. Tokyo shifted uncomfortably and glanced over to Luke's pickup truck. Mercifully, she saw a means of distraction.

"Luke. Someone's coming."

Luke looked toward the road. Amos's truck was parked next to Luke's. Sis was walking toward them. With her, trailing a few steps behind and struggling to keep up, was a man—not Amos, but a stranger. Although he could not yet see the man's face, Luke could tell the man was a stranger. His stumbling gait betrayed his lack of experience walking in the wind. Sis, on the other hand, seemed to glide over the jagged slate toward them, low to the ground and graceful. Indeed, Sis's movements in the wind were unlike any Tokyo had seen, almost as if Sis followed secret steps of a dance known only to her and to the wind. Even the natural movements of Amos and Luke, longtime Black Rockers, looked clumsy next to Sis's skill. Entranced, Tokyo stared at Sis's progress toward them, oblivious to Luke or the stranger, conscious only of the dancelike quality of Sis's steps: balanced, poised, and comfortable in a way that Tokyo couldn't have imagined, whether in a quiet room or in this vicious wind.

Sis arrived at Tokyo's side and smiled, the smile of a doctor coming to a patient's sickbed during a fever.

"How do you manage to move like that in this wind?" Tokyo yelled over the wind.

Sis smiled and squeezed Tokyo's shoulder. Tokyo felt Sis's physical strength, and, inexplicably, Tokyo also was overwhelmed by a sense of the dryness of Sis's hand through her jacket, even through her shirt. Seeing

Sis was not going to answer, Tokyo finally looked back at Luke and was exasperated to see he had once again turned to stare into the quarry.

A few steps behind Sis, the stranger had stopped and was staring at Tokyo. His gaze was neutral, without judgment, but not without interest. Tokyo stared back for a moment with her normal disdain, then blinked and turned to watch as Sis walked to Luke's side.

Sis put one arm around Luke's shoulder and spoke into his ear for a few moments. Luke began nodding his head slowly in the manner of a man resigning himself to a bad fate. Finally, Luke stood and nodded ambiguously at Sis, then at Tokyo. Tokyo gestured to the slate outcropping in which she had hidden; Sis and Luke nodded their agreement. Tokyo followed them into the wind, and the stranger fell in behind them. When they were all safe in the shelter, Sis spoke.

"We catch our breath, then we go home."

Tokyo ignored the man when he resumed staring at her; she watched Luke instead, fascinated. He was barely with them, just on the edge of resuming his catatonic staring at the quarry. It was as if a mermaid were swimming in the black water of the quarry, singing a bewitching song to him. He seemed to be alternately aware and unaware that he was accompanied by other people. Glancing at Sis, Tokyo saw she was staring at her as well. *Great. Luke's gone overboard, and these two are staring at me*, she thought.

"He thought I fell in," Tokyo explained.

Sis smiled again, this time a quizzical smile. "No, he didn't," she said.

Characteristically, Tokyo was unwilling to let anyone tell her she was wrong about anything. "You weren't here, Sis," she said in a venomous tone.

Sis looked up at Luke, who was once again staring down into the water.

"No, I wasn't. But he was," Sis said to Tokyo.

They all fell silent. After a moment, the man spoke for the first time. "Shouldn't we get out of this wind?" To him, the shelter was just short of a living hell, with the wind ripping savagely around them.

Sis nodded and took Luke's arm. He was willing to be led, and so she led him back out into the crosswind and toward the road. From the safety of the shelter, Tokyo watched them walking, then looked back at the man.

"What are you staring at?"

"Sorry," the man said and looked down.

Tokyo grabbed her duffle and followed Luke and Sis to the road, then downwind carefully toward the trucks. Sis climbed into Luke's truck to speak with him. Tokyo, taking advantage of what seemed to her to be an excellent opportunity, climbed into the passenger side of Amos's truck. To her dismay, the stranger climbed in beside her. They watched in silence as Sis talked earnestly with Luke. Her words seemed to bring him back to life; he began nodding and even spoke a few words. Finally, Sis left the cab of Luke's truck and stood in the road watching as he put the pickup in gear and turned east toward home.

Tokyo, bothered by the silence, spoke as soon as Sis had sat in the driver's seat and allowed the wind to slam the door shut.

"What the hell was that all about?"

Sis didn't look at Tokyo, who was sitting between her and the stranger. Instead, she looked back toward the old quarry rim and then gestured with her head toward the man. She spoke gently, in her singsong way, but loudly enough to be heard over the whistling of the wind.

"This man has come to see you. He is Penn."

Tokyo turned and looked at Penn, who smiled cautiously. This could mean anything, Tokyo knew. Given her expertise in leaving no tracks in even the lightest of snowfalls, this man would have to be some kind of a genius to have found her, or worse, have a damn good reason. Usually, the only people who had damn good reasons were cops. Tokyo blinked and considered. She had stolen nothing, at least since she had left Sioux Falls five years ago. And she had left Sioux Falls in the same way she was planning on leaving Black Rock: anonymously, on a bus, without telling anyone where she might be going. *Anyway*, she thought, furtively assessing the man to her right, *this guy is no cop*. And if he wasn't a cop, it really didn't matter what he wanted. She turned back to Sis and was further angered to see Sis smiling, seemingly enjoying Tokyo's obvious discomfort.

"What happened back there?" Tokyo demanded.

Sis turned the ignition and paused before she put the truck in gear, searching for the right words.

"Luke wants something he lost," she finally said.

"Who doesn't?" Tokyo asked. She was unsure which was more exasperating, the nonsensical answer or Sis's tone of certainty. Tokyo thought of Sis as a simpleton, but Sis was speaking more today than Tokyo had heard her speak during all the months she had spent in the store. Like the wind outside the truck, the swirling eddies in the tight cab of the pickup were threatening to blow Tokyo off some indistinct edge, an edge inside herself, less tangible than the quarry rim which had so fixated Luke, but no less perilous.

Sis turned the truck around. "Who doesn't?" she repeated. She let out the clutch, and the truck began moving east along the road toward Black Rock.

4.

While Ruth cared for Daisy, Shlomo took the infant in his arms and carried him to the porch to meet his father. Still wrapped in bedsheets, the baby squirmed uncomfortably in Shlomo's arms. The sun had risen high enough to reach the porch, and Shlomo welcomed the warmth on his face. He walked slowly out toward Noah, who still sat motionless in the chair.

"Noah," Shlomo said.

Noah stared straight ahead.

"Noah," Shlomo said again, stepping into Noah's line of sight, "Daisy's given you a boy."

Aware first of the shadow cast across his clothing, Noah glanced down at it in puzzlement. After a moment, he looked up at Shlomo, then at the bundle dwarfed in his friend's long arms. He appeared puzzled, the way a person might when listening to a foreign language for the first time.

"Your son, Noah. She's named him Luke," Shlomo said, offering the child for Noah's inspection.

Noah's hands shook as he placed one on each of the great arms of the chair. He shifted his weight to the edge of the seat and slowly rose to his full height. Shlomo held the squirming baby out to Noah. As Noah reached for his son, he stopped suddenly and squinted toward the open door of his home.

"She's fine," Shlomo reassured. "The bad hog must've started her labor. She's tired out, but Ruth's taking care of her."

Noah took the bundled baby from Shlomo's arms and held his child close to his chest. To be sure, he had held Prudence in his arms when she was an infant, but this child, his son, felt distinctly warmer. As infants, Prudence and Luke would have been indistinguishable, bundled tightly so only their faces were visible, but as he held his son, Noah's heart opened to possibilities he had previously willfully ignored, possibilities which included male progeny bearing his name, the Christophe name.

150

Noah's legs weakened as he imagined his sons, his grandsons, and their sons and grandsons, all bearing the Christophe name and spreading the Word. He sat back down in the chair and stared out at the wet slate, then at the vomit stains on his coat, and finally back up at the fast-moving sky.

"This is my penance," Noah said, without moving his gaze from the sky.

"This is a gift, Noah. A gift from God."

Noah turned sternly, eyes flashing. His voice, until now uncharacteristically muted, boomed: "Knowing when and what your penance is, that's the gift from God." Despite Noah's harsh tone, Shlomo was relieved to hear his normal volume.

Shocked by the sudden loud voice, the baby began to cry weakly. Noah looked down at the child sternly.

"He's crying. He knows what he's been born into."

"He's hungry, Noah." Shlomo stepped forward and took Luke from Noah's arms. No matter how Noah might misconstrue his son's hunger, it didn't mean Shlomo had to watch the child cry desperately. He walked into the house with the bawling infant and handed him to Daisy, who accepted him and wordlessly moved him to her breast. When Shlomo returned to the porch no more than two minutes later, he was shocked to find Noah on his knees, head tilted upward, tears streaming down his face.

"I'm a creature of vanity, Lord. You have shown me. I will stay in this place, with this stench, and be reminded of your will every day. And my children will see your glory through my folly and your sound punishment." Noah closed his eyes tightly and shook his head from side to side in an exaggerated motion which rocked his whole body. He was moaning quietly as he rocked, his lips forming gibberish of some kind, unformed words he could feel but not say. Shlomo stood silently behind him, watching his friend pray.

Shlomo had lived with Noah a long time and had long since grown accustomed to his passions. Indeed, it was Noah's passions, both good and bad, which kept Shlomo by his side: Shlomo wanted to be near the flame which burned so brightly, hoping the light would help him illuminate corners within himself which would otherwise be dark, corners which might contain possibilities of wealth or freedom which otherwise would never be realized. Once Noah made a decision, there was little anyone could do to dissuade him. Even more, there was little anyone could do to even understand the decision. One could only wait for the loud and lengthy explanation which was sure to come. Noah followed his own path and explained to others only when he felt they should follow, which was most of the time.

In the weeks following the birth of his son, Noah resumed his management of the new quarry, but he no longer tried to persuade quarrymen to move into the New Town. Indeed, Noah seemed not to notice even Sweetwater's abandonment. Norma had shamed Jim all the way back to their struggling farm in Utah. Noah had resumed his duties as the head of the quarry, working even harder to scratch out a living, secretly doubting whether he could ever prosper from land so barren and so clearly put on earth by God solely to punish Noah.

Soon, as Noah had foreseen, the quarrymen began abandoning the sparse bunkhouse in New Town and resuming residence in the former town of Black Rock. Before long, the only regular residents of New Town were the two original families.

One day, Shlomo considered his situation. He had stuck with Noah for a good long time, staying close for his own reasons. But now Shlomo realized that the closeness of the two families was what had made him stay—and it was that clear Ruth and Daisy could not live without each other. At the same time, Shlomo knew that he and Ruth and their sons couldn't stay, not with all his customers back in Black Rock.

From Shlomo's perspective, the friendship between the two women was odd; while Daisy was worldly, Ruth was bookish. Ruth saw Daisy's disinclination toward education, but Ruth respected Daisy's depth of experience in the ways of the world, experience that Ruth would never have or dare to have. Ruth listened with wonder to Daisy's matter-of-fact reminiscences of her life. Daisy's stories were not embellished for effect, nor were they minimized to protect pride; she was without guile. Day after day as Daisy recounted her life to her friend, Ruth grew closer to her, especially sympathetic to Daisy's choice of husband, a choice Daisy never seemed to regret, at least not out loud. Ruth had no desire to be Daisy, either past or present, but she felt as fascinated and empathetic toward Daisy as she did to characters in her favorite books. The vicarious thrill of Daisy's past was addictive, and her burdened present commanded sympathy. Ruth grew close to Daisy for both reasons.

Even now, Ruth's and Daisy's infant sons, Amos and Luke, shared an oversized wooden cradle that Shlomo had made for them. Shlomo had chosen to use wood rather than slate only due to a spare load of fine black walnut which had been delivered to him by mistake months earlier. Rather than waste it by sending it back, Shlomo used the wood for various projects. Shlomo now sat on Noah's porch with Ruth and Daisy as he ruminated. Ruth sang to the two infants as she rocked the cradle. Shlomo and Daisy both watched the familiar figure of Noah descending the ladders carefully. He moved more slowly than most, perhaps due to his methodical nature, perhaps because his black coat caught on the edge of the ladders occasionally. As he descended the ladders, the long shadows of the afternoon sun cut odd angles across the ground and moved slowly toward the porch.

Daisy, who realized that the exodus of quarrymen back to the old town had created an unpleasant dilemma for Shlomo, sighed as Noah finally reached the bottom of the quarry. Just as Noah started his way around the ever-larger pool of water at the base of the quarry wall, the sun set completely on New Town. Total darkness would follow soon. Daisy shuddered at the thought and turned to Shlomo.

"What will you tell him?" Daisy asked.

Shlomo considered. In his practical way, he finally shrugged and turned to Daisy.

"I'll tell him the truth, Daisy. Can't do less than that for Noah. You know that."

"I'll miss Ruth."

Ruth stopped singing to the babies and looked up at Shlomo. He was not surprised to see tears in his wife's eyes. Her sadness at the prospect of leaving her only female companion was palpable. Shlomo sighed heavily again, wondering whether she could ever be happy again if he took her away.

"He thinks creating this place was wrong," Shlomo said. "Most people, they'd have left here once they figured that out—but not Noah. He thinks God wants him to live here, like some kind of penance. He doesn't care so much what the quarrymen do. Probably, he won't care so much what I do. It's only him that's got to stay here. That's what he thinks, anyway. Was like that from when we first saw this place. This godforsaken place. Wants to stay right here. And I stayed with him, didn't I?" Shlomo caught Daisy's eye and saw sadness welling up in her eyes. *They could be sisters, these two*, he thought. But he nodded kindly to Daisy and said, "Same as you, I guess, Daisy. You and me, we ain't that different."

Daisy nodded sadly and watched her husband stride toward the porch. He stopped some distance from the houses near the edge of the pond that had grown from the first well dug in New Town. He reached down into the water and fished out a distinctive piece of whitish gray slate and moved it to the edge of the water. He shook his head as he carefully placed the slate on dry land and looked up as Nate and Prudence ran toward him. They stopped, standing almost at attention as Noah surveyed them carefully.

"Did one of you children move this stone?" He pointed down at the whitish gray slate. Prudence and Nate shook their heads vigorously.

"You told us never to touch it, sir," Prudence reminded him. As a child of Noah's, it did not occur to Prudence that a person could do a thing contrary to what her father ordered. Nate was equally well schooled in the boundaries of behavior.

Seeing the children's fear of disapproval, Noah was pleased. "That's right," he said and walked toward the other adults on Shlomo's porch. *They should fear me as they fear God.*

On the porch, Noah greeted Shlomo, Ruth, and Daisy with a silent nod. It was not unusual for the families to be gathered outside when Noah returned from the quarry. But today, Noah immediately sensed something different, an air of expectation, of nervousness. Standing on the slate in front of Shlomo's house, Noah took off his hat and glanced over at the empty quarrymen's barracks. After such a promising start, Noah reflected, he was now standing with the only people hardy enough to face the Lord with him. *They might not share my belief, but they stand with me. And so they stand with him. He will reward them.*

"Ruth's made a fine dinner for us," Daisy volunteered.

Noah nodded. The two families, more now than ever before, had taken to eating meals together, especially dinners. During the day, the children played together as Daisy and Ruth took turns caring for the babies. Shlomo busied himself carving or making furniture. Well aware of the harsh conditions that had drawn the two families together, all welcomed a regular dinner. Noah seemed at his most relaxed during the dinners, whether in his own home or in Shlomo's. The more people who sat at his table, the greater his power of influence grew. And even deeper, although he would have denied the feeling as sinful pride, the mere fact that his "family" had grown affirmed his confidence in his ability to influence. He had created a thriving, if modest, business which had drawn hundreds of men as workers; he had created two towns, and, as an ultimate act, had blurred the distinction between families of different faiths until they all relied on him and him alone. Here, he had become powerful.

But now he looked at Shlomo, and his self-confidence eroded in a deep sense of foreboding. He looked to his wife, who kneeled next to Ruth at the cradle. Daisy seemed to be comforting Ruth, who wiped tears away from her face with outstretched fingers and then rubbed her fingers against her housedress.

"What has happened here?" Noah directed his question to Shlomo, as if only he could answer the question. Shlomo bit his lip and sat down on the cold slate stairs of Noah's porch.

"Can't make a living down here, Noah. Not now."

Noah froze.

"The quarrymen, they're up in Black Rock. If I let it go, someone else is gonna take my store, my business. It's why I stayed here with you, Noah. For my business. But here …" Shlomo's voice trailed off.

Noah was aware of Ruth and Daisy staring, waiting for his response. One of the babies awoke, crying loudly for milk. Neither Ruth nor Daisy looked away from Noah, but Ruth, recognizing Amos's cry, leaned forward and brought the baby to her breast. As was his custom, Noah averted his eyes.

"Then you'll be moving back," Noah said.

Shlomo nodded. Daisy sighed loudly.

"I'll move up there tomorrow or the next day, Noah. Ruth will stay here for a spell, I expect until she and Daisy get everything straight with the babies. There's all kinds of shapes a family can take, and I figure these two ladies got one right here under our noses."

Ruth and Daisy stared at Shlomo in disbelief. Shlomo smiled down at Ruth, her tears now tears of joy, then over to Daisy, who put her arm around Ruth.

"Now, not for too long, you two. Maybe just until winter's over," Shlomo said, feigning sternness.

Shlomo waited as Noah climbed the stairs and sat heavily in one of the large chairs. In the cradle, Noah's son was awake and crying. He gestured to Daisy, who lifted the baby up and into his father's arms. Noah looked down into his son's helpless face. The baby's face was contorted in an exaggerated cry that made his mouth appear to take up his entire head. His eyes were shut tightly as he cried, but tears flowed nonetheless. Noah's face was expressionless; he might have been looking impassively at a wagon in a purveyor's shop or reading the Bible. As the baby continued to wail, Daisy moved forward and tried to take him from Noah's arms, but Noah shook his head without looking up at her.

"No, Wife. He's going to have to learn. There are things that just can't be cured by crying. Things that can't be cured, except for living through them."

Daisy took a clumsy step back from Noah and watched as her helpless child cried for food in her husband's arms.

5.

Shlomo felt old.

Breathing heavily from having climbed up the series of ladders, he waved down to Ruth, who had worried at his slow progress up the quarry wall. When he had given her ample reassurance, he turned, leaned heavily on his cane, and contemplated the arduous trek he faced across the mesa to the town. Even though he would be traveling on horseback, the trip could take all day.

"Gotta get going, Noah. Long trip."

Noah reached out and held Shlomo firmly by the shoulder.

"I've got a wagon for you. Two horses." He pointed.

Shlomo turned and saw a quarryman sitting unhappily in the driver's seat of a box wagon. Two horses, nervous and half crazed by the wind on the mesa, pawed the ground under the quarryman's uncertain rein. Shlomo knew Noah would have been reluctant to take the horses out of the rotation in the quarry, reluctant to lose the wagonload of slate the horses would have carried. Sitting up on a horse, progress would have been achingly slow as Shlomo fought the wind's attempts to knock him down. But in the semiprotection of the back of the wagon, the trip would be more tolerable. In gratitude, Shlomo nodded as he studied the wagon. He was about to speak, when Noah cut him off.

"Don't thank me. This man picks me up here every day, takes me to the mine. It's just a bit further to the town."

Shlomo, who knew quite well the distances involved, did not respond as they climbed into the wagon. The driver, who faced the arduous trip with no protection, found little comfort in the extra few dollars Noah had promised him for ferrying Shlomo to Black Rock. Noah, his hat tied firmly under his chin, sat bolt upright next to the unhappy driver, as he turned the horses toward the new quarry and old town. Sitting in the protected well of the wagon, his back to the wind, Shlomo was able to glance back only once at the rim of the New Town quarry as it receded from view. He wondered how long it would be before he saw his sweet wife.

The distance to the new quarry passed surprisingly quickly, and Shlomo was impressed with the strength of the horses. Whether the horses moved rapidly with the wind due to good training or the vain hope they could minimize their suffering by hurrying, he couldn't say. Some said animals were dumb, that they couldn't understand the concept of hurrying to get the bad part done quickly, but, having lived on the mesa as long as he had, Shlomo knew better. He knew a horse could learn, and learn quickly, the danger of idling in the strong wind, no matter which direction they headed. He also knew Noah to be a fine judge of animals: even in the early days Noah could pick a strong-hearted horse out from a corral in the blink of an eye.

When the wagon reached the new quarry, which, to Shlomo's surprise, was crawling with workers and already fairly deeply dug, the wagon stopped on the path to Black Rock. Surprisingly nimble for his size and age, Noah jumped to the ground by vaulting over the sideboard of the wagon. He looked into the new quarry for a long moment, cataloguing the quarrymen's many transgressions for criticism. Then, satisfied with the clear necessity for his further supervision, he walked back to Shlomo, who was still hunched against the wind in the back of the wagon.

"Good-bye, Shlomo." His tone was grim, final.

Shlomo looked puzzled.

"Noah, I'm only going to town. We'll see you soon."

Noah smiled and shook his head.

"Your God hasn't spoken to you. Mine has."

Shlomo considered. If his God had spoken to Shlomo, what would he have said? Would he approve of Shlomo's decision to abandon his friend and even his wife (albeit temporarily) in order to protect his business? Would his God even care about something which, in the grand scheme of things, appeared to be so small and inconsequential? Was it bad for a man to leave his family for a time to give him a chance at more protection for them in the long run? Would his God have punished him for attaching himself to Noah's ascendancy like some kind of a parasite, for desperately hanging on to his friend's black coat for the meager living he could scratch out of the land? Or would his God see Shlomo's attachment to Noah as a vain attempt to fulfill some greater need?

Shlomo sighed deeply. His God, Shlomo decided, was in a different place, speaking to different concerns than Noah's God.

"You can give glory to your God in the old town, Noah. Just like always. You don't have to live in darkness." Shlomo's prior attempts to convince Noah to move to town had tested the strength of the two families staying together. Now, in a last attempt, Shlomo appealed directly to Noah's pillar of belief.

Noah smiled thinly. "It's true. I can give glory to my God anywhere. But I can receive my punishment in only one place. In darkness."

With that, Noah nodded to the driver, who obediently flicked the reins. The horses, grateful to be doing something other than standing in the howling wind, resumed their slow trot to Black Rock.

6.

Amos, standing in his usual position behind the counter, looked up idly at the collection of his father's canes hanging from the rafters. As he had so many times in the past, he resolved to do something about the cobwebs and dust. Amos kept a mental list of tasks to be performed around the store—small household chores which he knew would make their lives in this place slightly more tolerable. He lovingly added to and subtracted from his list, never setting aside time to actually perform the chores. Rather, as he did now, he delighted in planning how he would take a ladder, remove each of the canes from the rafters one by one, hand them to Sis, who would clean them off with a rag, probably a rag soaked in hot water, possibly with a touch of white vinegar (any other type of cleaner might inadvertently stain the wooden canes and streak the carved ones). Then he would take a modified mop, one he would spend some time making, the head of which would form a ninety-degree angle, allowing him to reach the top and bottom of the rafters. The mop would have to be rigid enough to clean without bending out of shape so would probably be made out of some sort of reinforced metal, since neither wood nor slate would work. Finally, Sis would hand the canes up and Amos would replace them. They would look fine and shiny with the sunlight dancing in among them from the front window; perhaps, when the front door was opened, and the wind set them clattering, their sound would be brighter. Amos glanced at the filthy front window. Of course, if he wanted the light to shine on the canes he would have to keep the windows clean. And with the dust in the town, keeping the windows clean could be an everyday chore. In the end, he reflected, all chores came back to the wind, and perhaps it was the relentless wind which restricted Amos's ability to actually perform his chores. Or maybe, he thought to himself with a slight smile, he conveniently used the wind as his excuse: it was just his nature to enjoy planning more than the actual work. As he heard the door in the back of the store open, he shook his head in self-amusement, knowing that he would, in all likelihood, end up doing nothing about the cobwebs, but would happily plan to clean them up countless more times.

His scheming was interrupted by the slamming of the back door.

"Sis?" Amos called. "Did you drop that man off at Luke's?"

In answer, Sis glided out of the back room. Amos saw Tokyo and Penn walking behind her. Tokyo looked embarrassed; she clutched her worn nylon bag.

"Well," Amos said when Tokyo and Penn walked into the front of the store, "seems like we've added one." He glanced down at Tokyo's small duffel bag and pursed his lips. Sis smiled and touched Tokyo lightly on the forearm. Her hand, dry and cool, sent an involuntary shiver up Tokyo's arm, making her want to leap into the air.

"She wants to stay in the back room a while," Sis said. She took her hand away from Tokyo's arm quickly, like a leaf would blow away in a strong breeze.

Had there been even an infinitesimal chance she could find another place to stay until the bus came through, Tokyo would have snapped rudely at Sis's presumption to know what Tokyo wanted before she had even asked. But, having spent a good deal of time with Sis, she knew better than to argue, especially when Sis was dead-on right. Tokyo chose instead to adopt a supplicant's appearance. Head down, she looked up at Amos through her dark eyelashes, then quickly down at the ground.

"That's a problem, isn't it?" Amos asked.

Tokyo held as still as possible. She saw Amos's boots in front of her, his weight shifting uncomfortably from one foot to the other in his worn leather boots. She noticed that the heavy cord he used for bootlaces was thin and worn where it stretched around the eyelets. Soon, he'd need new laces. When she had lived with them before, Amos and Sis had relied on her to notice such things and to order them without direction. But now? She glanced over at Sis's feet, the simple laceless shoes she favored, her weight equally distributed, her feet not shifting an inch, impassive.

"What I mean is, if one of them stays in the back room, where's the other one going to stay?" Amos continued.

Sis nodded. Tokyo looked up at Penn, realizing instinctively he was no longer a stranger. Now, he was competition. Penn smiled back at Tokyo in a way he hoped would be disarming. Tokyo was mildly shocked to see that his teeth seemed to come to points. Not just his eye teeth, but all of them. *Great*, she thought. *I'm competing with Count-fucking-Dracula for a bed.*

Penn was still smiling. All Tokyo could see of him was his teeth. "No need for that," Penn said. "I can stay in a hotel."

Amos laughed. "You could, I guess. But there isn't a hotel within a hundred miles of here. Maybe more."

"No hotel? But—"

"Nope. No hotel. Proudfoot's house is a bunkhouse, but it's just for quarrymen. Nobody in their right mind would stay there, and the quarrymen wouldn't allow it. Dirty place. Rough crowd."

"Doesn't sound too good," Penn said, looking downcast.

Amos nodded. "No bus service either. Barely have phone service out this way."

Tokyo started. "No bus service?"

Amos shook his head. "Bus stopped months ago, Tokyo. Didn't pay. Didn't you know?"

Tokyo pointed at Penn. "How'd he get here?"

Penn looked at Tokyo. "Is that your name? Tokyo?"

"He called a couple of weeks ago, spoke to Sis. Described you. Got a ride with the hardware truck when he came in yesterday," Amos explained. "Got me some new sets of hard ground rakes, you know the kind? Heavy steel tongs on 'em. Good for scraping—"

"When's the hardware truck come through again?" Tokyo interrupted, a hint of panic in her voice.

Amos considered. "Well," he said, "when I call in an order, I think. Maybe another month or two."

"But, surely one of the other service guys are due?" Tokyo looked desperately around the front room of the store, finally pointing at the peanuts. "The food service guy? The appliance guy?"

"You in a hurry to go somewhere, Tokyo?" Amos looked at Sis, who merely shrugged and gestured to the front door with her eyes.

Immediately, Tokyo realized she had been too direct. Her face reddened. In the following silence, Penn sat down at one of the benches in front of the counter.

"I guess I owe you an explanation," he began, directing his attention solely to Tokyo. Involuntarily, her teeth clenched tightly, so tightly that her jaw ached. Before Penn could continue, the door at the front of the store opened and the wind swept into the room, silencing the room, and precluding the possibility of any words being spoken, at least temporarily. In the entrance, Luke stood mutely for a brief moment until he remembered himself and shut the door, too late to keep some of Amos's lighter items from hurtling from their shelves to the floor in the wind. Luke seemed oblivious to his breach of normal Black Rock behavior. His face bore a stunned look, as if the length of time he had spent on the mesa earlier that day had addled his wits.

Luke faced the others, his eyes intense. Even Penn knew enough to be silent as Luke approached Tokyo. Something in the air was charged between the two of them, so much so that Penn imagined Luke was unaware of anyone else's presence in the room. Tokyo looked up at Luke. He no longer seemed on the verge of tears, but neither was he tightly composed. He was unsettled, as if the wind had found an unprotected crack and blown inside of him and was unable to get out, rustling through his body, his mind, and even his voice. He started to speak, then stopped. He cleared his throat, twisted his lips in a vaguely reassuring manner, then started again.

"I wanted to make sure you got here okay."

Tokyo nodded and blinked. Slowly. Her face, as usual, betrayed no emotion. The silence continued, silence loud enough to convince the others in the room to mind their own business. They complied as best they could: Sis moved into the back room to resume weaving, and Amos busied himself behind the counter, whistling tunelessly. Penn studied the canes hanging from the ceiling in genuine wonder. Finally, Tokyo spoke, so softly that Luke had trouble hearing her over the whistle of the wind.

"Phone broken?" she asked.

Luke grimaced, his attempt at a smile.

"You could have called. Would have saved you the trip." Tokyo's eyes darted back and forth as she spoke, noticing bits of peanut shells left on the counter, obviously from Old Man Proudfoot or Tongate, noticing a dead insect of some kind, dried and slightly shredded lying at Luke's feet where the counter met the floor. Her eyes shifted quickly to Luke's eyes, then away again when she sensed his yearning.

"I'm just going to stay here with Amos for a few days. That's all. To get my head straight," she said, answering the question Luke had traveled here to ask.

Luke squinted at Tokyo. A moment passed, during which he seemed to come back to his senses. He nodded to Tokyo and glanced over at Amos and nodded a greeting, which was returned by Amos. Luke pointed to Penn in the Black Rocker way, a subtle uplifting of his chin in Penn's direction.

"Who's he?" Luke asked Tokyo.

Tokyo looked down again. "I don't know. He says he came to find me."

Luke nodded slowly again. "Well," he said, "if you're gonna stay here, where's he going to stay?"

Tokyo smiled. "Maybe with Proudfoot?"

"He looks too young to die," Luke said. Luke and Amos chuckled.

Tokyo smiled up into Luke's suddenly laughing eyes. Her own eyes, Luke saw, had softened, and although he did not consider himself overly experienced or even perceptive in the mysteries of relationships, he would have sworn she was feeling something of what he was feeling: the simple joy of having built a bridge—a bridge powerful enough to withstand even the wind on the mesa, yet fragile enough that a word or two from either of them could break it. And so, rather than acting on his burning desire to sweep Tokyo up in his arms and drive her back home, he instead turned toward Amos and arranged to give Penn a ride back to his place and provide him with a room to stay for a while, until something worked out with Tokyo, with Penn, or otherwise.

7.

"Aren't you curious who he is? What he wants?"

Tokyo blinked slowly, considering Amos's questions as Sis moved around the table, clearing the remnants of breakfast.

Tokyo shook her head. "You ever have a stranger track you down to tell you something good, Amos?"

Amos smiled and shook his head. "I have, and I haven't." Amos stood and set to work, and Tokyo resumed the familiar rhythm of life in the store. The night before, she had found that her back room was unchanged. There was still the familiar storage area, the red tapestry with its faded image of the Indian woman opening a pouch, the vaguely stale smell of the air, and the aura of the past thick in the place.

The next day, as the late afternoon shadows crept slowly into the front of the store, Tokyo sat rustling through invoices that Amos had asked her to organize. The clacking sounds of Sis's loom in the back room were regular and soothing, serving as an odd sort of background percussion to the high notes audible in the wind. Sis sat at her loom working day after day, with a transcendent grace, producing tapestries and coarse rugs with simple designs. Although some were sold in the front of the store, Amos collected each of Sis's final creations, storing them on shelves in the back room. For her part, Sis wove at her loom for neither profit nor pride, but seemingly for the calmness it induced.

When she had first noticed the loom, Tokyo had mistaken it for a stand-up piano, for it was not an old-style loom, but rather a Shaker-style loom. It had been made in Quebec and ordered specially by Amos for Sis. Tokyo had realized her mistake the first day when Sis sat down at the loom and began expertly pressing the foot pedals and moving the shuttle. If it were possible for a motion to be smooth and savage simultaneously, Sis's hands, moving lightning-fast as she passed the shuttle back and forth at the loom, combined the contrary qualities. If her weavings were simple, her movements at the loom were mesmerizing to anyone who watched her, and, since the first day, Tokyo and Amos had spent many days either watching Sis at her loom or listening to the sound of her work from the front room.

On this day, as Tokyo listened to the reassuring sounds of Sis's loom, she reflected that Sis had resumed her usual state of silence. Tokyo imagined Sis to have used up some sort of yearly allotment of words with her recent conversations. Amos, who Tokyo knew was only pretending to be busy behind the counter, finally cleared his throat and resumed his line of questioning.

"What do you suppose he wants?" Amos asked. Tokyo looked up, distracted. She wrinkled one eye and considered. Finally, after a few moments, she shrugged and returned to counting invoices.

"He seems like a nice fella, anyways," Amos concluded. Sis's loom clacked in the back room as a few more minutes passed in silence.

"How do you think he's getting along with Luke?" Tokyo spoke without looking up from her paperwork.

"What's to get along with?" Amos said, genuinely puzzled. "Easy to live with Luke. I mean, it seems easy, anyway."

Tokyo looked up at an embarrassed Amos. To his relief, she was smiling, almost laughing. "Easy. That's right, Amos. Like living with Sis," she said. "No fuss, no muss." After another pause, Tokyo placed both her palms on top of the invoices on the counter, a signal that she wanted to talk. Amos, welcoming the chance to speak with someone other than the loitering regulars of Black Rock, waited as Tokyo formulated what she wanted to say.

"He was sitting at the quarry," Tokyo said. "He came unglued." Amos nodded, and Tokyo continued, "I don't know what Sis said to him. Do you?"

"Sis didn't say," Amos replied.

"What was he doing there? She said he was looking for something he lost."

A dark flash of pain clouded Amos's face. Tokyo could feel the atmosphere in the room change, as if the setting sun was taking any hint of light out of the room with it. Aware she might have transgressed some unknown boundary, she began shuffling through the invoices again, content to let the matter drop. Amos came around the counter and stood at the end, one booted foot propped up on the dingy brass rail. He stared out through the dust-covered window at the setting sun. The only sounds he was aware of were the rustling of Tokyo's invoices and the whistling of the wind. In the back room, Sis's loom had stopped. She was probably starting dinner, he thought, feeling reassured by the predictability of his household. As the sun set, he craned his neck, watching it begin to disappear behind Proudfoot's house across the street. From the corner of her eye, Tokyo watched the bright light illuminate Amos's face. He blinked once or twice, then turned away.

"Sometimes, when the sun is right, you can see the houses. Some say you can, but I never have. Nobody ever has." Amos said, then paused. "I don't need to go there." He shook his head, a final gesture.

Tokyo had no idea what Amos meant. She watched as he walked back around the counter to resume his normal place. She turned to look out the window at the remnants of daylight. The brightness of the setting sun surprised her. She closed her eyes and turned away, but the bright white spot stayed with her under her eyelids. Her eyes still closed, she remembered rubbing her eyes as a child, watching odd yellow shapes come and go, then blackness, then other colors, purples and greens, and she would keep rubbing and watching her own private world until she had passed through layers upon layers of lights and colors, until she felt open and exposed and ready to surrender to anything or anyone.

When she turned and opened her eyes, Amos had left the room, and she was alone in the semidarkness.

8.

Back in town, Shlomo had set about restocking his store. He worked through the days, relishing the additional hours of sunlight which the surface of the earth afforded. To his surprise, a thriving group of quarrymen had already returned to Black Rock, forming a community which, shockingly, seemed to work well even in Noah's absence—perhaps, even, because of it. Upon Shlomo's return, one of the quarrymen skirmished with Shlomo briefly. The man had squatted in Shlomo's store for several months and believed himself entitled to stay and even share in the resumption of Shlomo's business. The dispute between the two men grew heated, but Shlomo turned the tide when he pointed out that the man was simply living in the store and had failed to resume any business. The man, dirt-poor at birth and only marginally less destitute now, was larger and tougher than any other quarryman and so had stubbornly lived off Shlomo's abandoned goods, shortsightedly refusing to sell the goods, preferring instead to hoard them for his own future use. The argument unequivocally ended when Shlomo threatened to ask Noah to intervene as the arbiter. The squatter, reluctant to face the judgment of a man who had helped keep his family fed over the long winters, submitted meekly and returned to the quarrymen's barracks, leaving Shlomo to clean the mess.

Shlomo enjoyed the rhythm of his days cleaning, stocking, and bartering, and most of all he enjoyed the general freedom from any constraints upon his time. Suddenly, Shlomo no longer was restricted by the children's schedules and, if he chose to, he worked long into the night pounding nails or moving shelves. When he grew too exhausted to do more, he delighted in sitting at the table in his back room making lists of the improvements he would undertake the next day.

As the weeks went by and his business became steady again (surprisingly quickly, Shlomo thought), Shlomo considered the joy he felt and the general good-natured camaraderie which the quarrymen displayed. He couldn't quite put his finger on it, but something about Old Town had changed.

One day while smoothing a pine board with a homemade scrub plane, Shlomo heard the door to his store open, and the wind blew wood chips and shavings into every corner and under every low-hung shelf. Shlomo didn't look up immediately. Rather, with his back to the door, still bent over the wooden sawhorses, he carefully noted each of the places into which the shavings from his scrub plane had been blown. The boisterous quarrymen who had been sitting at his counter sharing preposterous tales of sexual conquest had immediately quieted and were staring grimly at the door. A familiar shadow fell across Shlomo's pine board. He turned, delighted.

"Noah! You're a sight, you are!"

Noah only nodded as Shlomo took both of his arms in his hands, up around the biceps, in greeting. Noah's eyes were fixed on a point behind Shlomo.

"You boys not working today?" Noah spoke to the quarrymen at the counter.

The quarrymen looked guiltily at each other.

"No, sir," one of them volunteered. "We made enough for ourselves this week."

Shlomo shut his eyes, knowing what his friend's reaction would be. Noah jerked away from Shlomo's friendly grasp and walked slowly over to the bar to face the three men. Judging from Noah's angry countenance and the three men's grim demeanors, a man just walking into the store would swear a fight was about to break out.

"You made enough for yourselves this week," Noah repeated.

Two of the quarrymen nudged each other and began to shuffle to the door. The third, a braver man named Lyle, stood his ground and stared back at Noah.

Noah took a step closer to Lyle.

"You think you've done enough for the Lord, son?"

Lyle smiled. "I've done enough for me. The Lord looks after them that helps themselves."

Shlomo shut his eyes again, abandoning any thought of walking behind the counter to retrieve his floor broom just now. Instead, he contented himself by scraping wood shavings together with the inside edges of his boot. "It's a start, anyways," he mumbled to himself. Noah rose to his full height, readying himself for the diatribe that was to follow. Shlomo, figuring he had some time before Noah turned back to him, limped to the shelves and began removing canned goods. Once the shelf was cleaned, he would remove the shelf itself to clean underneath.

"Well, then. I suppose it's okay," Noah said without venom or apparent judgment of any kind.

Shlomo, who had been mentally designing a small hand broom which could make it unnecessary for him to laboriously move canned goods from the lowest shelf in order to clean underneath, was so shocked to hear Noah's meek response that he looked up suddenly. He banged his head hard against the top shelf, upsetting cans and boxes of laundry detergent. Rubbing his painful head, he turned to see Lyle walking triumphantly to his friends at the door, who appeared to be as shocked as Shlomo. The three men opened the door, blowing the rough pile of wood shavings Shlomo had scraped together back into their hiding places. Shlomo rubbed his painful head as he watched the mess recreate itself. *Guess I ain't used to life up above yet*, he thought.

Noah sat heavily at the counter and took off his hat.

"The Lord is testing me, Shlomo. Testing me severely."

Shlomo gestured to the door. "Don't pay no attention to Lyle, Noah. He's young and full of himself. Fancies himself a fighter. You know the kind. I had one in here, eating my stock—"

Shlomo quieted as Noah shook his head and reached into his jacket pocket with an exaggerated solemnity. He withdrew an envelope, already torn open. Carefully, as if the letter inside were hot to the touch, Noah extracted a one-page letter with the thumb and finger of one hand. He held the letter out to Shlomo the same way, as a person would hold a dead rat by the tail.

"A man came to me, handed me this letter. He said I'd been 'served.' He came all the way up onto the mesa to say that."

Shlomo winced involuntarily at the legal word. *Served*. He'd heard it before, seen it before. As he reached out to take the letter, Shlomo noticed Noah's hand was shaking.

"I'm not what you'd call experienced with legal matters, Shlomo. Your people know more about this sort of thing."

Shlomo nodded and read; he was too familiar with Noah's prejudices to take offense. When he finished, Shlomo read the letter again, then placed it on the counter and whistled softly. Noah, sitting at the counter on one of the high stools, had taken his coat off and was running his hand through his white hair. He looked up to the ceiling and spoke softly.

"It's a big, wide country, Shlomo. A lot of land in it. You and me, we've covered a bit of it ourselves."

Shlomo nodded and smiled. "Those were times, Noah."

"They were indeed," Noah said, his tone contemplative, even dreamy. After a pause, he continued, suddenly angry. "Never did I think, in all the travels we made over the land, that the Lord wouldn't command me to stop somewhere to set down roots. And this," Noah banged his fist on the counter, "is the place. The wind, it was a signal, a sign. The Lord wants me to triumph over the bitter conditions. He wants New Town to be a home."

Noah's anger receded abruptly. He shook his head sadly and once again resumed the tone of uncertainty. "Or he wants it to be my prison. The living reminder of my weakness. A warning to all of us. His punishment is indeed severe, but I accept it. I must accept it."

Shlomo had never heard Noah's voice so meek. He seemed plaintive, even close to tears. Shlomo put a kindly hand on Noah's shoulder. Noah sniffed and nodded. He continued, more quietly.

"The Lord has even blessed me with his highest compliment. He has given me doubt. He has let my mind wonder whether this is the place for me to set down roots. Whether I should have moved on. But here I am, too old to pull up roots now, too old to do much of anything but pull slate from the mine and sell it to keep my family fed. And now this. More trials from the Lord." He gestured to the paper on the counter.

"That's not from the Lord, Noah. That's from a man. And he isn't testing you, he's suing you."

9.

To say the wind was particularly harsh on any given day would be meaningless to a person who had only just arrived on the mesa. From the quarrymen who had spent their days toiling on the mesa, such a statement would have elicited snickers. But Shlomo, sitting in the back of the wagon with his shoulders hunched for protection, could feel that the wind was noticeably worse today. At first, he explained it away by assuming his relaxing respite in the store had weakened his ability to deal with the harsh wind, but as the wagon lurched over the mesa toward New Town, he noticed a distinct worsening in the wind. Instead of the relentless, steady wind, the conditions today were the most fearful that men faced on the mesa: the wind blew in harsh staccato bursts, seemingly every five to ten seconds, separated between by the normal relentless howling.

A wind like this was as dangerous as standing in the surf of a storm-swept ocean. Any one wave could knock a person down, but in and of itself was not dangerous unless a person didn't have time to prepare for the next wave. Today's wind, Shlomo reflected, was a wind that could knock you down and never let you get to your feet. Before you knew what had hit you, the next burst would be on you, and you'd be down and tumbling.

Sitting erect beside his grumbling driver, Noah lurched back and forth in the wind and with the motion of the wagon, holding tightly to the specially installed handrails. Under the best of circumstances, he would have been unable to reach into his pocket and reexamine the letter he had received, no matter how compelled he felt to do so. The wind would have ripped it to shreds, leaving nothing but a scrap of paper between his fingers and the unpleasant memory of what he had already read repeatedly. The wind today, he knew, made it doubly difficult and therefore out of the question. In any event, he had no desire to read the letter again.

This man who had sent the letter, this Burton Johnson, seemed to say he owned the whole mesa. Noah shook his head at the thought. He had read the letter enough times before he showed it to Shlomo to quote the words. "All rights and appurtenances thereon," the letter said. "Including riparian rights." The words made no sense to Noah. The words spoke of the law. He knew only one Law, and this letter's rude interruption into his world only served to increase the nagging doubts he harbored.

As the wagon approached New Town, the road turned slightly so that the wind was no longer directly impeding the wagon. The horses gratefully trudged crosswind toward the rim of New Town. In the back of the wagon, Shlomo contemplated whether he would be happier to see his wife and children or to have the protection from the wind in New Town. He smiled ruefully at the thought. The wind, on some days, could turn even a strong-willed family man into a coward. Regardless, Noah needed support, and Shlomo had decided to accompany him to provide what little Noah might accept. To see his family again was a welcome bonus.

The wagon stopped near the rim of New Town, and Shlomo jumped down on the lee side, hanging onto the wagon before he turned to look down into the quarry. When he did, he was stunned.

From above, it appeared as if the water from the pond had crept up to the very steps of the houses. Shocked, Shlomo turned to Noah.

"Noah. The water!"

Noah nodded and looked down. He was unable to see his stone marker from here, but he assumed he would find it under a foot or more of water, as he had for the past several days. Shlomo peered down, motionless.

"The bunkhouse looks like it's flooded."

Noah nodded again and gestured to the series of ladders. The two men worked their way down the wet and slippery rungs. Water seemed to be bleeding out of the walls in a thousand places, a continuous trickle which dampened everything in the quarry. Shlomo silently wondered how much unseen water was leaching into the quarry from below. When the two men reached the surface of the water, Shlomo noted with alarm that it appeared to be nearly ten feet above where it used to be.

"Papa!" Nate was sitting in a dinghy, waiting to ferry his father and Noah to the edge of the pond. His face was radiant, excited. Shlomo stepped carefully into the dinghy, and Noah followed. Shlomo leaned forward and kissed his son, then faced him as Noah took the oar and rowed toward the houses.

"Where'd you find the boat, Noah?" Shlomo asked.

Forgetting he could communicate with words rather than gestures, Noah jerked a thumb upward. When it was clear no further information was forthcoming, Nate smiled up at his father. "One of the men in the quarry is a boat maker. He made the boat. I get to row it, sometimes. But not today." Nate's eyes were smiling, a secret joke between father and son. Shlomo smiled.

Nate's hair and eyes were his mother's, Shlomo mused. And if it were possible to love someone more than he loved Ruth, then he loved his young son Nate with all the strength in his body. He leaned forward again and gave Nate another kiss, embarrassing Nate in a happy way. Stumbling over his words in excitement, Nate turned and pointed out the changes of the past several weeks to his father.

"See there? Remember the steps you carved between the bunkhouse and our house? That's where we tie up the boat now. Mr. Christophe says that soon we might have to move into his house, if the water keeps coming."

"The water has tapered off. It will not rise past the foundation of your house." Noah's certitude ended the topic, despite Shlomo's questioning look. Noah concentrated on the deep black water as he rowed.

"At least I don't have to walk for the water no more," Nate said.

"'Any more,'" Noah corrected. Nate grinned at his father, again, a secret joke.

"Any more," he repeated.

That night, after dinner in Noah's house, when the women were putting the babies to sleep in their shared bassinet and Prudence and Nate were playing together, Noah took the letter out again and placed it on the table. Daisy nervously looked from one man to the other, studying them closely as if she would be able to tell the future by their faces. Shlomo picked the letter up and reread it, moving his lips silently. Many of the words were new to him and, he was certain, new to Noah. But the message was clear.

"Do you know this man?" he finally asked, placing the letter flat against the table and smoothing the creases with his callused hand. "Burton Johnson?"

Noah shook his head. For the past several days, he had asked himself the same question, over and over, but, as now, was unable to place the name.

"I'm no lawyer," Shlomo said. "I've seen a few, in Chicago years ago, other places." Daisy and Ruth exchanged glances over the cradle.

"Is what he says true? He can kick us off the land?" Daisy asked. Noah turned and fixed his wife with a glare. Daisy, however, stared back at him. "We've fought hard for this place, worked hard. And if someone's gonna take it all away like that—" Daisy snapped her fingers. Finally, under Noah's steady glare, her gaze fell to the floor. "We've got a right to know too," she mumbled.

Noah turned back to Shlomo. Confusion threatened to erode Noah's unshakable faith. Shlomo tapped the letter with a finger.

"The long and short of it is this. This Johnson fella seems to say he owns the land. If he does, he can kick you off of it, I guess. Kick you off the mesa, out of the quarry, out of this house—"

Noah stood angrily. "That's man's law. God's law isn't the same, Shlomo." He whirled and pointed at Daisy. "Even that poor woman understands his word. If a person makes a place his own with his hands, his work, then how can someone else take it from him?"

"We're gonna find out next week. Letter says this Johnson fella's gonna be here. With a magistrate. Says they're gonna set it all right."

"A magistrate," Noah repeated. "An official. A man of honor, maybe. We'll show him what we've made here. The new mine. And most of all, New Town. A home, a place of our own. He'll understand."

Ruth cleared her throat. Shlomo glanced over at her, then spoke. "Ummm, Ruth and I were talking, Noah. She's a little concerned about the water."

"What?"

"The water. She says it's been coming up."

Noah stood up and looked out into the evening. As usual, the darkness of New Town limited his view to no more than a few feet in front of his porch. Despite the darkness, he could see where the rough-hewn slate of the street ended and the smooth black water began. The moon, directly overhead, reflected brightly in the black water.

"I told you the water has slowed down." Noah spoke without turning. "It's just got to seek its own level, like anything. And it's almost there."

In the silence that followed, Ruth urged her husband on with a glance. Shlomo hesitated, then asked, "How do you know it's slowing down?"

Noah turned. "I mark it every day. It used to come up nearly three feet a day. Now, it's only a foot."

Shlomo shrugged. Ruth stood up and leaned against the slate of the kitchen counter, peering out at the water.

"At that rate, it's gonna drown us in a couple of months," she said, an edge in her voice.

"The Lord will not let a thing happen to you or to this place," Noah responded, but the words sounded weary, as if he were tired of repeating himself.

Daisy, knowing better than to display anger in front of Noah, sat down at the kitchen table and placed her hands carefully on the cool slate tabletop, palms down. She looked up at her husband and saw doubt in his face. This was a time to be careful with him, she knew.

"Husband, the Lord will provide. But maybe he's providing something that isn't what you think. You see a mesa like this, with this wind, you see a town where everyone got sick, you see this letter threatening to take it away, you see the water. You see all this as the Lord telling you to fight. What if he's telling you something different?"

Noah stood by the window. When a steady man, a man of self-assurance, questions himself, he relies on his unchanging appearance to hide his feelings. He doesn't notice the slight twitches, the subtle grimaces and movements which reveal his true concerns to those who know him best. The others watched Noah standing at the window for what seemed like a long time. He turned and looked at each of them. They doubted him, he knew. Worse, they doubted the Lord. He began speaking, quietly at first.

"The Lord doesn't always send a straight signal, that's true, Wife. And I've considered what he's saying here. Over and over. At first, like you said, I thought to myself he wanted us out of here, after he sent us that bad hog. I prayed on that for days, weeks. But then, when the water started coming, I started getting a feeling. And now, with this letter, it makes the feeling stronger. The Lord wants me to face my own Armageddon. He's bringing everything to a head, and he's doing it at once. I'm going to stand right here and meet his wrath head-on, and he's going to see I'm worth something to him, that I'm his servant forever!"

"Hush, Noah. You're waking the babies." Ruth scurried to the cradle to comfort the children. Shlomo and Daisy didn't move. Noah's face was shining, and his eyes were bright as he looked at them.

"Don't you see how he's testing us? Now he's sending this man. When this man looks down into New Town and sees us living here, what we've built, he'll feel the Lord in what we've done, and he'll do right by us."

"After he leaves, Noah?"

Noah's face darkened. "If the Lord keeps the water coming, then after he leaves …"

Ruth looked up from the cradle. Noah inhaled sharply.

"After he leaves, we'll move back to town. We can serve the Lord just as well there as we can here."

Daisy began laughing, a giggling laugh of relief, and Ruth silently thanked God for Noah's compromise, even if Noah had convinced himself he hadn't compromised.

Daisy gestured to the letter.

"How long until he comes?"

"Next week," Shlomo said smiling. "Guess we can hold out that long, eh?"

10.

Luke stood at the kitchen window watching the sun set. On the mesa, the wind seemed to distort the sun, particularly as it set. The closer the sun approached the horizon, the more it seemed to vibrate and dance. Just now, the sun seemed to have jumped to the south several inches, then back again. When Luke was a child, he had been told it was the wind pushing the sun in a particularly strong gust, and he had believed it until he knew better, but even now, looking out the window at the dancing sun, he thought it might be true.

Penn, sitting at the table behind Luke, had slept poorly since he had come to Luke's. Indeed, for the past several months, he hadn't slept well as he traced Ayako's tracks from Pittsburgh, to St. Louis, to Sioux Falls, to Black Rock. He had explained to Luke the details of where he had been, but never disclosed that he had been following her. Luke had listened politely to Penn's travelogue, but without apparent interest. Penn expected Luke to ask why he was tracking her, but Luke feigned no curiosity. Instead, he seemed more interested in showing Penn the slate in his home and explaining about the wind and the mesa. Sprinkled among Luke's talk of slate and wind, an occasional tidbit of the past was revealed, always in a roundabout way with no seeming relevance to a prior conversation. When Luke turned from the window, Penn, though he had only spent only a few days with Luke, knew Luke had something to say.

"They say there have been times the wind has stopped. Completely stopped." Luke raised his eyebrows, considering the absurdity of the proposition.

"Of course," he continued, "none of us has ever seen it. None of the regulars—Black Rockers, we call them …"

Penn nodded.

"… None of the quarrymen, none of the old Indians, none of them has ever seen it themselves."

Not able to help himself, Penn asked, "Then how do you know it happened?"

"That's what they say," Luke said and turned to stare back out the window.

Penn looked at Luke's back. Like most of the others Penn had seen in the town, Luke's shoulders were stooped and rounded, perhaps, he thought, from the effort of walking into the wind.

The wind. Penn shook his head. Maybe what Luke said was true. A wind like this couldn't continue forever; it had to stop sometime—if for no other reason than to recoup its strength for the next blow. Even God had to rest.

"You married to her?"

Luke's question caught Penn off guard. Luke hadn't betrayed the slightest interest in Penn or his reasons for seeking Tokyo out, but here it was, out of nowhere.

"She's never met me. I've never met her."

Luke nodded and smiled grimly. "Me neither," he said without turning.

Penn nodded. "She doesn't stay in one place too long. Stands to reason nobody would get to know her."

At this, Luke turned. "Who is she?" he asked. He had been careful to avoid any talk of Tokyo with Penn, even to avoid the appearance of interest, partly out of an ingrained reticence to engage in conversation, but mostly out of a desire to not appear as desperate as he felt. But now, living with this man who seemed to know the answers to Luke's questions, it seemed silly not to ask. He had to know, and his desire finally overcame his fear. Penn owed him nothing. He could refuse to answer the questions, even after Luke's hospitality. *Hell*, Luke thought. *She's refused to answer anything and how long's she lived here? Why should this Penn be any different?* Luke had feigned disinterest, but now he could do so no longer. He had to know and finally asked, despite his anxiety over Penn's possible answers.

Penn nodded again and took a sip of coffee. Not for the first time, he tried to explain what he knew of Ayako.

"Last place she lived was Sioux Falls. Lived with a guy who worked in a meat factory. Name was Hingham. Still is, I suppose." Penn grinned self-consciously at the joke. Luke, too focused to have noticed, seated himself at the table across from Penn. Penn sipped his coffee and considered the cup. It was made out of some deep blue ceramic material. The dish in which it rested was clearly the product of the quarry. Rounded cups apparently were beyond Luke's skill with slate. Some coffee had spilled into the dish, and Penn carefully lifted his cup and poured the contents of the dish into the cup.

"Hingham was a quality control inspector at the slaughterhouse," he continued. "They called it a 'meat processing plant.'" He was what they call a 'QC' inspector. They've got names for everything now. Anyway, they killed the hogs and hung them up; they split them right down the belly and spilled their insides out onto the floor. The 'kill floor.'"

Penn sipped his coffee. Luke, as he had expected, winced at the image.

"Hingham stood to one side with a flashlight; he looked up into the empty cavity of each hog hanging from hooks as the conveyor moved them by. Slow work. Every room in the slaughterhouse was thirty-five degrees, three hundred sixty-five days a year. Cold work. If he saw a carcass that had fecal matter still in it, or a piece of stomach or intestine or something, he marked it with a large red slash. The next station on the conveyor line lifted the marked carcass and sent it back for someone to clean out with a high-pressure spray. What a way to live. Cold and wet all day."

"God," Luke said.

"Yeah," Penn agreed. "But Hingham always figured he was lucky, since the next guy on the line had a tougher job, lifting two hundred pounds of hog off the line. And at least he wasn't the one killing the hogs with the electric charge. He spent his days doing his job in the plant and his nights at home, quiet. Watching the television maybe—he loved football on the weekends, he told me—or on some nights even going out drinking with the fellas. But he was always quiet, kind of withdrawn. She liked that kind."

Luke cleared his throat, suddenly self-conscious.

Penn sipped his coffee and cocked his head, listening to a note in the wind he hadn't heard before. It sounded as if a large animal was suffering, moaning deeply.

Luke nodded. "It does that sometimes."

"Damnedest thing, that wind. Well, Hingham stood there in the cold meat plant, watching three hundred hogs an hour go by, peering into them for traces of shit. Born and raised in Sioux Falls, fished in the Big Sioux River, dropped out of school when he was fourteen to join the union and make some money. Never thought much exciting would ever happen to him.

"Then one day, he meets this Japanese woman. Young, kind of different for Sioux Falls, looks-wise, and quiet. She doesn't say much, kind of like Hingham. She doesn't even seem to have a name. She spends a lot of time with Hingham though. He just calls her Blackie, for her hair. He doesn't even care when the folks at the plant, his family, and folks at church start talking about him, commingling with a Jap. Talking about Pearl Harbor and all, real dummies."

Luke's face had lost some color. His coffee, sitting in front of him, was cold.

"I don't have to tell you if you don't want to hear."

Luke shook his head. Penn took a deep breath.

"When she moved in with him, he was happy, maybe for the first time in his life. He didn't ask much out of Blackie; she didn't ask much out of him. They got used to each other, the two of them. He liked having her around, she seemed to like being around, staying inside most of the time, not doing much of anything as far as anyone could tell. People would go by the house and see her, staring out the window, not doing a thing. Just thinking, they figured. But she kept the house clean and cooked him dinners. Hingham was happy."

"Then one day, three years after she moved in, almost to the day, she was gone. Didn't say a word to Hingham—just left. I asked him whether they had argued, whether she had said anything, but he couldn't think of a thing."

"'She just got restless the last couple months,' was all he said."

Luke shook his head.

"At first, Hingham worried she had stolen from him, but she didn't take anything, left with just what she had brought. When I saw him, it was five years later. He was still living in the same house, a nice one—those meat jobs do pay pretty well. It had been five years, and he started to cry when he told me about her."

"What … what does she want?"

Penn leaned back in his chair and tilted his head up toward the ceiling.

"I've got no more of a chance to answer that than poor Hingham does. She lives off the land, so to speak. Like the old explorers did."

Luke scratched at the side of his face. He could see Hingham coming home from work, his bloodstained clothes wrapped up in a bundle in the back of his pickup truck. He saw Hingham open the door to his simple, clean house—kept clean in large part by Tokyo's efforts. He saw the look of expectancy on Hingham's face: not exuberant, but quietly pleased at the knowledge that he would find a quiet woman, one who wouldn't demand anything out of him, anything at all. And he felt Hingham's shock when he realized she was gone. He almost felt the nausea rising in Hingham's throat, the bitter, helpless feeling.

He saw himself in Hingham's house, looking desperately for Tokyo and not finding her, not even finding a note. Across the table, Penn watched Luke. Luke's breath came quickly, as if he had been walking against the wind for an hour.

"She's going to do the same to me, isn't she?"

Penn finished his coffee and placed the cup carefully in the saucer. "I don't know," he said. "But it's a good guess."

Luke seemed to wilt. As a tall man, he usually dominated a room, and people sharing space with him were always aware of his position. But now, Penn imagined Luke had melted, his rounded shoulders becoming even more stooped, his face blank and staring at a spot seen only to him on the kitchen table. Penn now knew of or had met every one of her men. All of them, without exception, had retreated into themselves in quiet pain when she had left. This time, however, he had the unpleasant task of watching the man crumple before she had even left. *Odd*, Penn thought. *She was a closed book, but these quiet men grieved for her as if for their own mothers.*

"I figured I knew her," Luke said, a hard edge in his voice. "Figured she was just quiet. But it wasn't that. She just didn't want me to know her. Maybe I just didn't want to know what she really was either."

"What is she?" Penn asked. He had seen this anger before in men.

Luke looked up, his eyes cold. Penn watched Luke slowly resume his normal size.

"Damn it," Luke said, banging an open hand on the table palm-first.

Like Hingham, Luke was angry, hurt and alone, in a kitchen like Hingham's, maybe with more wind outside, but it had just as much wind inside. He looked up and sucked air sharply through pursed lips.

"What's she to you?"

Penn didn't hesitate. "Nothing at all. I need to tell her something. A couple of things, actually."

"How come you didn't just tell her at the store?"

"I spent a lot of time just getting to her through where she's been. No hurry to tell her right off."

Luke stood up and seized his coat. "I know I'm not going to get what I want out of her. God knows. But damn it, I want to tell her something too. Just like you." He was silent for a moment, aware that he was talking to a stranger, talking more to this stranger than he did to most people. He knew there was no need to explain what he was feeling to Penn; Luke was barely able to explain what he was feeling to himself.

"I lost a lot of things out here on the mesa. Never had a chance to ask them why."

Penn nodded.

"But Tokyo, if I lose her … well, before she leaves, at least I can ask her. I can find out why she's leaving."

Penn shrugged noncommittally. Although he had never met Ayako, he felt instinctually she would be hard-pressed to answer Luke's questions, which is why Penn planned not to ask her any. He knew what he needed to know. Ayako could hardly even be told things, and she certainly couldn't be asked.

Luke, having watched Penn carefully for a moment, suddenly broke off and walked to the kitchen window, apparently deep in thought. Penn hesitated as Luke buttoned his coat and lifted his heavy band of keys off some scattered papers. Luke looked intently around the kitchen, finally fixing on Penn's coffee cup and saucer. He strode quickly over, picked up the cup and placed it on top of the papers on the slate kitchen counter. He nodded with satisfaction, then turned to Penn.

"What are you waiting for? Let's go see …" Luke hesitated. "What did you say her name was?"

"Ayako," Penn replied. "Her given name was Ayako, but she's had a lot of names."

Luke opened the door to the breezeway, and Penn stood up to follow. Even with the outside door closed, the two men could feel the cold wind. Behind them, the papers rustled under Penn's cup and saucer. Just before he opened the outer door, as Penn was following Luke out, Penn heard him repeating her name to himself.

"Ayako," Luke whispered. "Tokyo."

11.

Noah traveled back off the mesa with Shlomo to prepare for their families' return. Just as Shlomo had enjoyed the past few weeks of freedom alone in his store, Ruth and Daisy looked forward to the prospect of a few days without Noah's presence. Their anxiety concerning the creeping black water was more than offset by the delightful prospect of packing their belongings without Noah's suffocating supervision. The water had slowed its advance perceptibly over the past few days, and the prospect of a week of freedom was enough for them to shoo Noah off without a second thought. Indeed, the women conspired eagerly to be left alone.

"It just makes sense," Daisy volunteered to her husband before he departed. "You and Shlomo will be able to spend some time figuring out what you're gonna do with this Johnson fellow."

Once they returned to the town, Noah and Shlomo busied themselves readying their houses for their families. Neither Noah nor Shlomo spent any time planning or even talking about what they would do when Johnson appeared, although his impending arrival was never far from either man's mind.

"The Lord will provide," was all Noah would say, verbalizing a platitude he had repeated to himself thousands of times since the letter had arrived.

Noah assumed Johnson and the magistrate would be coming from the east, since the letter had been sent from Philadelphia. And, since the road to the west of New Town terminated at the western edge of the mesa, Johnson would have to come through Black Rock. He would stop at Shlomo's store; everyone felt compelled to do so after the long journey to Black Rock. It was clear from the letter that Johnson was claiming the land on the mesa, but neither Shlomo nor Noah gave voice to the fear that he might also be claiming the land surrounding the mesa, including the town.

As the last remaining residents of New Town, Ruth, Daisy, and the children were ecstatic to be leaving. They spent their days packing boxes and their evenings together in Daisy's home. Though it had slowed, the water had reached the first floor of Ruth's home, forcing them to move everything to higher ground. To save the trouble of moving the boxes into Daisy's house and then into the boat to take to the ladders, the women, and Nate and Prudence when they could help, moved the boxes and furniture to the slightly higher ground on the quarry floor beyond Noah's home.

Months earlier, before Shlomo had left New Town, the two families had sat quietly inside to protect themselves from the first cold day of winter. Nate and Prudence had sat quietly as Ruth read them a children's book. Neither Ruth nor Daisy ever acknowledged that Ruth was a better reader than Daisy, but an implicit understanding led Daisy to abdicate responsibility for the children's education to Ruth. Predictably, Noah had opposed the idea of reading anything other than the Bible.

"My child is going to grow up a God-fearing Christian child," he said one evening, not caring that Ruth and Shlomo were in the same room. Shlomo was imperturbable under most circumstances with most men, and particularly with those on whom he relied most. He rightly assumed that a tolerant demeanor could improve business, while a spirited, defensive demeanor could ruin it. And, he understood that Noah's convictions ran deep and that he was not likely to consider whether someone's feelings would be hurt. Although Shlomo was not an observant Jew, he sometimes expressed surprise to Ruth that Noah made no attempts to convert him. Ruth had only smiled and reflected on the extent to which Shlomo was blind to Noah's reliance on him; were Noah to stretch his passion for Christian beliefs to Shlomo, even Noah knew the bond between the men might break. But Noah was unafraid to extol the virtues of Christianity in raising children; he felt his concern was justified and inoffensive.

"They'll be reading, Noah," Ruth assured him.

"The only reading I ever did was the Bible. It was all I ever needed," Noah said.

Shlomo leaned back in his chair. "When I was growing up, Noah, there was a school near where I lived in Graz. Nobody but good Christians could be students. In fact, they didn't let anyone but Christians even go into the school. Not even to deliver a cake. Not to visit, not to deliver mail, not even to clean the toilets. I went to another school, mostly people of my kind. But my friends and I, we wondered about that school, the mystery of it. What were they doing in there? What secret books did the teachers have that they took off their highest shelves, blew the dust off of, and taught the little Christian girls and boys? We wondered and wondered."

"One day, my brother Nate, he had an idea. We'd sneak into the school at night and steal the secrets they had in there. Then, we'd be just as smart as the little Christian boys and girls. Now, Nate," he said to his son, "stealing isn't right, but my brother was young, and we were curious. And the time, well … the times were different."

Nate looked up at his father and nodded. His eyes were wide. Shlomo glanced over at Ruth, who was smiling.

"So late one night, we snuck out of our parents' house. This could've gotten us in hot water. Something fierce. But we did it anyway. Nate had convinced me to go along, to see the great mysteries."

Noah, listening as intently as Nate, observed, "Adam and Eve."

Shlomo laughed. "Nate and Shlomo. And we learned the same lesson. We snuck into the school, through a window. Then up into the classrooms. We went to the bookshelves, took down some books. You know what we found?"

The room was quiet. After a moment of enjoying the expectation, Shlomo spoke.

"They were reading the exact same books as us."

Even Noah smiled as Shlomo repeated himself.

"The exact same books as us."

"'As *we*,' Shlomo," Ruth corrected. "Too bad you didn't stay in Austria and improve your reading."

"If I'd have stayed there, I wouldn't never have met you. I did the right thing."

And so Noah relented to allow a Jew to teach his daughter, even while, at every opportunity, Noah preached the gospel to Prudence. And, without mentioning it to either of them, Noah resolved to teach his son everything he needed to know. Ruth could do what she wanted with Prudence, since she was a girl. His son, Luke, would be Noah's sole province.

Months later, as the two women sat in the same room, their husbands miles away across a nearly impassable mesa and the dissonance of Prudence and Nate's early-evening argument having just subsided, Ruth and Daisy were left to contemplate the coming changes in their lives. Daisy was knitting, humming a song softly to the two infants in the large cradle.

"Do you worry about the wind?" Ruth asked suddenly.

Daisy put down her knitting and smiled.

"I used to," she said.

"But not now?"

Daisy shook her head.

"The children haven't really been up there. Prudence was too young to remember. They don't know …" Ruth's voice trailed off.

"They've heard the stories. What Shlomo has told them. What Noah has told them."

Ruth laughed and considered. Noah spoke of the wind as a force of God, sent to earth to make them all hardy, god-fearing people. Her husband, on the other hand, accepted the wind as an immutable fact of life, like back pain or a runny nose. Were it not for the wind, Shlomo often said, there would be something else. Indeed, Ruth thought to herself, he was right. The water, the ever-creeping, cold, black water, was proof.

"It's nothing like *living* up there, though," Ruth said.

Daisy put down her knitting and leaned back in her chair. She looked up at the ceiling of her house which for so long had been all she ever wanted out of life. The walls were sparsely decorated out of necessity, since bringing any of her niceties down the ladders was unthinkable. Indeed, when Daisy thought of the strain of hauling all her worldly possessions up to the rim, she shuddered.

"Getting up there is just a first step, Ruth," Daisy said, still looking up at the bare wall.

"What do you mean?"

"I think Noah's beginning to see the light. And if this fellow that's coming doesn't kick us out—which I half hope he does—I think Noah's gonna let us move. Out of here. Somewhere that isn't harshlike. We can go to California, Ruth. We can live like normal folks, in a house with red shingles, with flowers that grow, with markets filled with things to eat." She paused again, then looked at Ruth, determined. "He's changing, Ruth, really he is. He'll have his battle with the wind, with the water, and with this Johnson—then we'll leave. You'll leave too, with us, because we can't be apart."

Ruth shook her head, dubious. "I can't see that, not with Noah. Things have got to be tough for him. It's his way of proving something to himself, somehow."

Daisy nodded distractedly and said, "But maybe he's changing. Maybe the Lord is changing him, Ruth—maybe it's us; maybe it's life." She paused. "Maybe it's that damned wind up there. Maybe this Johnson fellow will just get the law to boot us the—boot us off the mesa, and then he'll have to move. He'll just have to."

The two women were silent for a time. In her mind, Daisy saw the unshakable image of herself and her children on a spring day in a garden, too beautiful for words, and Ruth, sitting next to her, could not see the vision but could feel the intensity of her friend's desire. She knew enough of Daisy's whimsical nature to allow the image to fade on its own. Finally, Daisy picked up her knitting, trying to remember where she was in her count.

"Shlomo can't leave. We can't leave. His business is here," Ruth said.

"He'd follow Noah," Daisy responded, her tone desperate.

"Mmmmm," was all Ruth said. She stared out at the water.

Daisy, still counting her stitches, murmured, half to herself, "Maybe none of us can leave. Maybe that's just it."

12.

Most self-made men enjoy nothing more than to spend every possible moment reminding anyone willing to listen about their poverty-stricken past. Burton Johnson was such a man. He had driven from Salt Lake City in a shiny new car, bought from a grateful owner of a Buick dealership, who had taken a full-cash payment without discount. Johnson had wanted the biggest, brightest, newest car the dealership had to offer, and the owner happily obliged. As Johnson drove off the lot, the owner marveled to himself.

"Man didn't even care to hear what kind of car it was," the dealer said to one of his perennially underachieving salesmen. "He still might not know. He just asked for the biggest, most expensive car we had and bought it without even looking at it. Didn't even mind when I charged him for the floor mats." In the following silence, the salesman shifted uncomfortably from one foot to the other. The owner finally glanced over at him accusingly. "Why can't you bring in customers like that?"

The magistrate from Salt Lake City who accompanied Johnson on the long drive to Black Rock was less happy than the owner of the dealership. In fact, Magistrate Tiller, a good Mormon, took a visceral dislike to Johnson from the moment he laid eyes on him. Johnson, who was accustomed to people reacting negatively to either his wealth or his vaguely unkempt appearance, was not intimidated and attempted to win Tiller over with conversation.

During the drive, Tiller avoided looking at Johnson, who, despite his fine clothes and jaunty demeanor, reminded Tiller of nothing more than a common felon. His language was course, and his attempts at ingratiating himself into the magistrate's good graces were crude, even bordering on unlawful.

Johnson drove the car quickly away from the dealership and, once he picked up the magistrate, drove even faster—too fast for Tiller's taste. He sped up even more on the long, flat road which led to Black Rock. The two men were quiet for a time, Tiller out of an unpleasant mixture of fear and distaste, and Johnson out of amused deference to the other man's clear discomfort. Finally, after hours of silence, Johnson grew bored and shifted uncomfortably in his seat.

"Like to drive this baby?" Johnson asked.

"No, sir," Tiller responded.

Another handful of miles went by.

"Doesn't matter to me about insurance, you know," Johnson said. "You crash it, I'll just get me a new one. Or just take the money and blow it on some broad."

"No, thank you." Tiller's tone was cold, as if he were talking to a petulant child.

"I wasn't always rich, you know," Johnson said.

"Pardon me?"

"You heard me. I said I wasn't always rich. Was pretty damned poor, really."

Tiller paused. "You must be gratified, then."

Johnson hesitated. As a rich man, he had little time for irony. His first money had come from an oil well which struck mere days after it had come into his possession by questionable means, means which had faded into history in no small part due to Johnson's successful attempts at obfuscation. At the beginning, there were rumors of threats, gambling, and even violence, but people no longer paid attention to the mysterious rise of the man; instead, they dealt primarily with the power Johnson wielded. And Johnson wielded the power confidently, with even a hint of arrogance. There was nothing, he often said, that he feared.

But he was lying. In fact, Johnson's confidence could be easily shaken by confrontation with a person of steady convictions, whether from strong belief, sound education, or good manners. Unfortunately for Johnson, Tiller appeared to be a man who combined healthy amounts of all three qualities. In Johnson's experience, the only way to overcome these qualities was to fight them head on.

"How much do you make?"

Tiller, who had been reflecting on the unparalleled level of discomfort he felt riding with this man, coughed in surprise.

"Excuse me?"

"Money, magistrate. How much do you make in a year?"

Johnson smiled and glanced into the rearview mirror, then quickly over at Tiller, who, to Johnson's delight, appeared tongue-tied. Johnson waited a moment before rescuing his uncomfortable passenger.

"I mean no offense. Don't mean to be a snoop. I'm just trying to make a point here. Whatever you're making now, it's got to be more than the first time I ever set foot in Utah. Got to be." A pause. "I hope, anyways."

Magistrate Tiller cleared his throat. "I understand your point. Perhaps we can agree you were poor. Now, you are not."

"We can agree on that. We sure can," Johnson replied.

Another handful of miles passed. Tiller leaned against the passenger-side door and allowed himself to be lulled by the regular rhythm of the tires passing over the cracks in the road. After a time, he pulled a pair of reading glasses from one jacket pocket and a small, inspirational novel from another. He put the glasses on and began to search for his page.

"Do you want to be rich?" Johnson asked.

Tiller looked up from his book and directly out at the road in front of the car. He could answer honestly, he supposed, and tell Johnson of his large family's difficulties, particularly since the state had recently decreased the pay for magistrates, pay which had been meager to begin with but now was too little to even consider sending his sons to law school, pay which Tiller knew he must supplement in order to care for his family. Tiller demurred to tell Johnson the truth, though—he had the distinct impression that truthfulness could only lead to further conversation, which, Tiller knew, would be unpleasant.

"I never thought about it," Tiller lied.

Johnson laughed. "Everyone thinks about it, magistrate. Even the richest people in the world, they think about being richer. I think about it, all the time. How can I get richer? And you mean to tell me you don't?"

Tiller was silent. The lack of courteousness in his driving companion was staggering. Even worse was Johnson's apparent lack of good business sense. Johnson knew Tiller would be the arbiter of his claim about this land called Black Rock Mesa, but here he was, basically calling Tiller a liar.

"I don't think about it," Tiller repeated, his tone somewhat peevish.

The hell you don't, Johnson thought. Then he said, "It wouldn't take much for you to be rich. Richer than you are, I mean."

Tiller closed his book on his lap, took off his glasses, and considered the elegant simplicity with which he had just been offered a bribe. Johnson's lack of explicit language allowed him the ability to deny, but Tiller knew he was free to accept. He thought briefly of his family—his poor wife, his struggling sons—then he answered in a voice filled with a conviction he instinctually knew would end the subject entirely.

"I suppose I could. I am here not by choice, but out of deference to my job as county magistrate. I am paid by the government per diem, plus expenses. I make do with my arrangement."

Johnson drove in silence. Finally, he spoke again. "You know, most of the things I do are for only one reason, and that's to make more money. That's all I care about. But if you think that's what we're doing up here, you're wrong, dead wrong. There are other things in life, you know."

Tiller looked out the window at the beautiful desert landscape, dotted here and there with sage and juniper, an occasional bluebird flashing in the sunlight. He considered the possibility he had misjudged Johnson, that there was more to the man than his wealth and arrogance. In a muted attempt to mend a divide between the two men, Tiller nodded and gestured, a sweeping gesture of his hand.

"There surely is, Mr. Johnson. This is a beautiful land, and I can see why you'd want a part of it to call your own."

Johnson looked over at Tiller, an expression of shocked surprise on his face, then he laughed—laughed hard. As he laughed, he pushed the accelerator harder, and the car flew faster down the road. Tiller, even more uncomfortable now in the seat next to Johnson, was quiet for a moment.

"Perhaps, Mr. Johnson, it would be better if we kept our conversation to a minimum. So as not to create the appearance of impropriety concerning the matter I am being asked to judge."

Johnson leered over at Tiller, his eyes gleaming. "Good point, magistrate. Let's do that." And the car was silent for many miles more, until Johnson pulled it to a stop in front of Shlomo Rubenstein's store.

13.

On the morning Johnson arrived in Black Rock, Noah stood in Shlomo's front room among the shelves, attempting to select dry goods for Daisy's pantry. Noah was unsure of which items to choose and needed to rely on Shlomo's advice as to which would be useful.

"The flour and sugar, of course," Shlomo said. "Some chocolate—if it isn't a sin, that is."

Noah turned to Shlomo and allowed himself a smile. "Chocolate isn't a sin, Shlomo. It's liquor that's a sin."

"I figured if it tastes good …" Shlomo said.

"Don't blaspheme, Shlomo," Noah said. Noah's spirits seemed good, even buoyant, as he lectured partly in jest. "God doesn't care about your religion, but he does care if you blaspheme."

Shlomo leaned against a shelf and smiled. "I grew up in a time when chewing gum was a sin. We'd see my father, or worse, my grandfather coming, and we'd swallow whatever we had in our mouths, for fear that we'd get whipped. Even a piece of grass from a field. Sins."

Noah examined a can of mixed vegetables. "These look old," he said, holding the can for Shlomo's perusal.

Shlomo pursed his lips as he looked at the slightly dented can. He reached out and took another can off a shelf. "Nah," he finally said. "These stay good forever."

"'Eternity is mine and mine alone,' sayeth the Lord," Noah said, still studying the dented and hopelessly out-of-date can in his hand. "Or he should have," Noah added.

Shlomo chortled. "Now I sell gum. Lots of it, too. The wind dries out the saliva in everyone's mouths, so they want gum."

"Times have changed," Noah said, still distracted.

Shlomo wiped the dust off the top of a can with one finger, then replaced it on the shelf. He rubbed the finger against his thick wool pants. "Maybe times haven't changed, Noah. Maybe everything's just the same; we're just older and looking past things. Things that used to be

194

so damned important to us, like whether we got whipped for chewing gum."

"Like whether to stand up for the Lord and fight?" Noah challenged.

"I don't mean New Town, Noah. You fight harder than any three people I know. I mean something else. But I can't put my finger on what it is."

Noah stopped collecting items from the shelves and stood up straight, thinking. In this area of the store, the light bounced through the cans and boxes at crazy angles and just now it seemed to be emanating from a place directly behind Noah, so brightly that Shlomo was aware only of the outline of the huge man dressed in black, his black hat high on his head, still tied under his chin despite being indoors. The dust from the shelves swirled through the air, bouncing and flowing on unseen currents of wind which had somehow found cracks in Shlomo's walls. Shlomo watched as the dust eddied and suddenly leapt around Noah, and Shlomo remembered the dark black-and-white etchings he had seen as a child, the dark man in dark clothing, face unseen—the devil.

Finally, Noah nodded his head and resumed his selections. "You were trained well is all you mean, Shlomo. You were trained well."

Shlomo smiled and exited from between the dark shelves. When he glanced out the window, he noticed a fancy car parked in front of the store. A tall man had gotten out of the car and was clearly struggling in the wind. A smaller man was helping to guide him up the stairs to the doorway, but his progress was impeded by the taller man's long black coat, which kept billowing out and wrapping itself around the shorter man's head.

"They're here, Noah," Shlomo said.

Noah came out from between the shelves and stood next to Shlomo. "The day of reckoning, I suppose," Noah muttered. Then, after a pause, "His will be done."

Shlomo gestured to the distinctive magistrate's black robe. "The man in the coat, the tall one. He must be the magistrate, I reckon. The short one, that must be the Johnson fella, the one says he owns the land."

Noah nodded. Shlomo threw the door open, and the two men entered. There was a brief silence as Johnson extricated himself from

Tiller's coat; he had hoped for a grander entrance. Finally, Johnson emerged and leered triumphantly at Noah and Shlomo.

Even though many years had gone by and Noah and Shlomo had forgotten more than they could remember, there were some things, some indelible experiences and people, which neither Noah nor Shlomo could forget. For a moment, the sight of the short man standing in front of them struck both Shlomo and Noah dumb.

Shlomo was the first to find his voice. He extended his hand to Johnson. "Hello, Apie," he said. "Long time."

PART FOUR

TOKYO'S SONG

1.

Walter Deilly sold flags. In the early days, he would ruefully recall, the main variable he had dealt with was the length of the flagpole involved. But later, as tastes became more sophisticated, the factory he represented began to send catalogues filled with various types of flags, flags that caused Walter to shake his head in dismay.

"Look at this," he would say to no one in particular, as he sat in a diner somewhere in Greeley, or Cimarron, or Bear Creek. The waitress, usually a woman—who had seen her share of men talking to themselves when what they really wanted was to talk to her—would nod as Walter thumbed through the pages, revealing hundreds of flags. There were flags with horses on them, with flowers, with Easter Bunnies, with jack-o-lanterns, with state mottoes, with foreign symbols, with long-forgotten designs, and with abstract designs which the flag maker was hoping would catch on.

The waitress would know after a few seconds that she wasn't interested in this man or his catalogue. She would know, if she had been around a sufficient number of years, how to quickly and efficiently end the budding conversation with this corpulent white-haired salesman.

"More coffee?"

Walter would nod or shake his head, depending mostly on the length of the coming drive and his assessment of his bladder's capacity. The waitress would walk away, and he would continue shuffling through the pages until he arrived at the flags he knew, the only flags he could sell with any enthusiasm. These were the American flags.

"Now, that's a flag," he would mutter to himself. He would pay his bill, leaving a modest-verging-on-insulting tip, then set off to a new territory to sell flags.

"The trick," he often instructed young field representatives, "is to sell the country. Don't sell a flag; nobody wants one. Hell, truth to tell, nobody even needs one. Sell them on the United States of America. Sell them on that, and you'll sell more flags than you'd ever think possible. You'll sell as many flags as I have."

One sweltering summer day, Walter's car, an unruly Chevrolet with one hundred fifty thousand miles on it, balked at climbing a mountain pass in Utah, and Walter was forced to take it to a service station. The mechanic, uninterested in flags, but curious about traveling, eschewed Walter's sales efforts, pointing out that his garage didn't have a place to put a flag, other than on top of the gas sign, and that the oil company that rented him the place wouldn't allow it.

"We got this lease, you know? Part of the franchise deal. Nothing higher than the oil company's sign. They're tough on that. You travel a lot?"

Walter looked up from his catalogue. The mechanic was leaning under the hood of his car, unbolting something with a socket wrench. Walter liked the pleasant clicking sound of the socket wrench. The ratchet sounded like industry. Like money. He remembered the years he had sold tools to local hardware stores. *Easy money*, he thought to himself, smiling.

"Hundred fifty thousand on that car," Walter said.

The mechanic nodded and frowned, thinking that if the car made it another hundred and fifty miles he would count it as a miracle. Salesmen like Walter, accustomed to picking up small signals, could see this man's lack of faith in his Chevy.

"It got me this far," Walter said, a slight note of defensiveness in his voice.

The mechanic, a man who had grown up working on practically every internal combustion engine ever invented, was embarrassed. In his experience, to insult a man's car was to insult the man. He quickly tried to change the subject.

"Where's the strangest place you've ever been?"

Without hesitation Walter snapped his catalogue shut and answered. "Black Rock."

The mechanic looked puzzled.

"Head south from here a hundred fifty miles, then east another hundred. South of Bear Creek."

The mechanic shook his head again.

"The damned windiest place on earth."

The mechanic smiled. "Good place to sell a flag, I guess."

Walter shook his head and leaned back. He noted a small refrigerator humming quietly underneath a workbench in the garage. Sitting here in the shade he was cool enough, but he wondered idly whether there was pop or beer to be had.

"No, sir. The worst place on earth to sell a flag. I was there, must be five years ago. Car was new then—well, almost new. Don't know what made me go there. Guess I figured, like you did, that people would need the flags all the time; they'd fly pretty enough, straight out in the wind. Pretty as a picture, they'd be. And I figured I'd be able to sell one of the specially reinforced flags. Worth more money, all that heavy material and extra stitching. More money for the factory, more money for me. Commissions."

"Well, I show up in the town, you can't even open the door on the car, it's so damn windy. I fight it for a while, then have the brilliant idea to turn the car around. Door opens right up that way. See, the car's blocking the wind." Walter gestured with his hands, and the mechanic grunted. "But damn if I could shut it. I had to turn the car around; left me in the same predicament. Damn wind," Walter said, remembering.

The mechanic nodded. He was leaning against the side of the car, Walter noticed, without having set a rag or newspaper against the paint. His greasy clothes would leave a mark, and Walter would have to clean it off himself.

"I get out and go into this store. There's a big guy in there with a little Japanese gal. The big guy owns the store, so I start talking to him, generally like, not mentioning anything about flags yet. Figured I'd try to tell him they're good to have on hand. To sell, you know. You should think about it too. Anyway, I talk to the guy a little bit, but I find out he's a Jew. No sale there, so I ask about anyone else in town. The guy, the tall one, finally asks me what I'm selling. I tell him it's flags. Well, the Japanese gal—she hadn't said a word—starts laughing until I think she's gonna bust a gut. Laughs and laughs, and I'm asking her what's so damn funny, but she doesn't answer; she just stops laughing finally and looks at me. So there I am, with two impossible sales. Some Jap, probably here illegal, and a Jew. I'm gonna sell either one of them a flag from the US of A? Never happen. Don't get me wrong; some of my best friends are Jews; it's just that you can't make any money if someone's gonna bargain with you all day, then pass. What's in that fridge—you have a beer in there for an old man?"

The mechanic, sufficiently drawn into the story, considered for a moment, then nodded. He walked over to the refrigerator and withdrew two Budweisers. Cans, Walter noticed, disappointed. He lifted the pop-top and took a long, refreshing drink, suddenly aware of how happy the simple things made him these days.

"So, finally, the tall guy tells me about another guy in the town, might be interested. Lives across the street, but I'm standing there thinking that if I try to carry my catalogues and samples across that damned windy street, they might end up in St. Louis, with that wind. So I tell him I'll wait for the guy to come into his store."

"The wind was that bad," the mechanic asked, "that you couldn't walk across the street?"

Walter put his beer down on the floor next to him and leaned forward. The mechanic was interested enough, he thought to himself. He might make a sale after all. Maybe even trade a flag for the work the guy was doing on his car.

"The wind there was unlike anything I've ever seen. What's the fastest you ever drove, friend?"

The mechanic considered, then smiled in the way of a man who has been asked to reveal the thing he is proudest of in his life. Feigning reluctance, the mechanic said, "Well ..."

Walter smiled encouragingly.

"I did one-ten one time, in my brother's car. An Olds. Four-four-two. Fast car."

Walter whistled a low, soft whistle. The mechanic beamed.

"Think about what it would feel like if you'd rolled down the window and stuck your head out. That's what the wind was like."

Now it was the mechanic's turn to whistle softly.

"Yes, sir. That's what the wind was like. So you can see why I didn't want to walk across the street. Didn't want to risk it. I figured the best I could do was to get back to my car and get the hell out of there, but I had driven a long ways and wanted at least to try to make a sale. But this gal, this little Japanese thing, she turns all mean on me. All of a sudden, she's shaking her head, looking at the tall guy. Don't remember his name."

"'Don't let him stay here,' she says to him. You don't need anything he's got,' she says."

"Well, the tall guy looks at me and I look at him. He doesn't want to kick me out, I can see that right off. But this mean little thing, I swear, she goes on."

"'Please, she says to the big guy. Please, make him leave.' Then she takes him where I can't hear and talks to him for a while."

"Now, normally I can take a hint and would've gotten the hell out of there, but I had driven a hundred miles to get to this place and I was damned if some little Japanese gal was gonna kick me out of town. So I go up to the tall guy and I say, 'Look, if it's that important to your wife, I'll leave, but you know it isn't right.' Now the tall guy knows I'm right, and he looks at the Japanese gal. I thought she was angry before, now she's out of her mind. She puts on her jacket, all the time calling me every name in the book, and calling him every name in the book. She buttons the jacket, opens the door and that wind whips in. It was dead winter, and that little gal runs out into the street. I half expected her to end up in St. Louis. She sort of runs zigzag across the street, and I see her knock on the door across the street and someone lets her in."

"I look at the big guy. 'Sorry about your wife,' I say. He smiles and says, 'She's not my wife. She's a boarder.' Now, I'm thinking she's more than a boarder, if she's talking to the store owner that way, but I don't stick my nose in anyone's business, I surely don't. So, if he wants her to be a boarder, that's fine with me."

"'How come she wants me out of here?' I ask."

"'She wants you out of town,' he says. Then he laughs. 'She gets strange ideas sometimes,' he says."

"I don't say anything, I know when to shut up. After a while, I see her coming across the street with another guy. *His* name I remember. It was Tongate."

The mechanic, who had resumed working on the car, snorted.

"Yeah, great name, huh? Anyway, just before they open the door, the guy looks at me, his head tilted sideways sort of, and says, 'You remind her of her father.'"

The sound of the socket wrench stopped. The mechanic's head slowly rose from under the hood of Walter's car, his eyebrows arched. Walter nodded in return.

"Must've been a good-looking guy, eh?" Walter smiled. "Anyway, what do you say to that? So she walks in with this Tongate guy, walks right up to me, and I think she's gonna spit in my face. I'm about to say something like, I'm not your father, I'm not even Japanese, and she spits out something like, 'Either sell your goddamn flag to Tongate or get the fuck out of town.' Excuse my language, if you're a Mormon, but that's what she said." The mechanic waved a hand from under the hood. Walter nodded to himself, happy to have a nonreligious man working on his car. A religious man would be less willing to deal on the price.

"Everyone's kind of quiet, then I introduce myself to Tongate, and he tells me he's the unofficial mayor of this place, and how he'd be happy to talk to me, real formal-like. Doesn't take five minutes of talk at the counter when I realize he's no buyer either, he's just a goddamn windbag. I go through my spiel anyways, just in case, and all the time I can almost hear the Japanese gal's foot tapping behind me, waiting for me to be done, and if I'm not done soon, she's gonna put her foot right up my ass. This Tongate guy, though, wants to talk, you know? He's one of those talkers, likes to hear the sound of his own voice."

From under the hood, the mechanic grunted.

"So I'm listening about what a patriot he is, about how this town is the windiest place on earth, but they persevere and all, and I look over at this Japanese gal, and she looks ready to blow. I'm thinking to myself, 'If I'm such a problem, why doesn't she go in another room?' But I see in her eyes what it is: she's one of those women who just hold their ground, you know what I mean? Some women—not just women, men too, sometimes, and now that I think of it, mostly men—they take a stand and they won't back down; who knows why? You can't make a sale to one of these, and, truth to tell, it's tough to make a sale when one of them's even in the room. They've got principles, at least they think they do, but what they got mostly is that they're angrier than hell and they want to take it out on someone. And that day, it was me. I guess because I looked like her father."

The mechanic emerged from under the hood again and looked up at the Coca-Cola clock on the garage wall. He made a minor effort to wipe the grease from his hands, then opened the driver's side door. Walter frowned at the smudge on the door handle and clucked his tongue when the mechanic held the steering wheel in one greasy paw while he fiddled with the ignition. Walter could already feel the grime he would find under his hands when he touched the wheel later. He knew from prior experience it would be days until the steering wheel felt normal again.

"Almost there, are you?" Walter asked.

In answer, the mechanic turned the ignition, and the engine coughed and ran. He revved the engine a few times and nodded in satisfaction. The rattling, knocking noise had gone away, Walter noticed with satisfaction. The mechanic turned off the engine, got out of the car, and walked over to his standup work desk, beginning to figure the bill.

"Well, anyway, I glance over at her for a second, just a second, mind you, and she comes stomping up to me."

"'Let me see one of those flags,' she says. So I pull out one of the big ones, one of the super-strong ones we sell to folks who put them on top of skyscrapers and such—it's pretty windy up top on those places, you know. I've got a new angle now, I figure. If I'm so bad, I'll stay until she buys one. But she's a step ahead of me already, turns out."

"She takes the flag and tucks it under her coat, grabs me by the arm and we go outside. The big guy and Tongate come to the window to watch, but they don't come out. They're smart, I guess. So we go right out into the middle of the street. She starts digging her heel at the street."

"'Tell me how you're going to dig a hole for a fucking flagpole, she says.' She says it, just like that, screaming so I can hear her over the wind. And I look down at where she's digging her heel, and I see she's not even making a dent. The road—now get this—I thought the road was macadam, but it was black slate. Shale, like. I reached down and saw that it would flake off a bit in layers if you worked at it, but that damn wind had scrubbed all the soil off the earth and sent it who knows where, leaving all this shale."

"Well, if you know a thing about soil, you'll know you can't dig a hole for a flagpole proper in slate. No, sir. And normally we use cement or rock to anchor our poles once we've dug a hole. Cement wouldn't take to the sides of a slate hole, the slate would just flake away, and the whole thing would come down before too long, especially with that wind. And rock fill in that town? Forget it. Gone in a couple of days."

The mechanic poked his small calculator with the eraser of a greasy pencil, nodding his head occasionally as Walter spoke. Walter licked his lips and craned his neck in a vain attempt to see the numbers on the calculator.

"So I look down at this little Japanese gal; she's looking up at me like she's won. A great victory, you know the type. Stood up to a man, I guess. So I say, 'You could always hang a pole on a house.' She laughs and points at the houses. Kind of sweeps her hand down the street pointing."

"'You're a fucking idiot,' she says. 'Look at the roofs. They're made of the same stuff as the street.' So I look where she's pointing, and I'll be damned if the roofs of all these places aren't slate. Not the kind of slate shingles you see in some places, but slabs of the stuff, laid on the roofs of houses. Unbelievable, never seen it before or since."

"But something about this little gal's attitude, you know? Made me want to be right. I mean, I fought for my country, you know? So, there I am in the middle of this street, barely able to stand up, and I see that this girl wants to be right just as bad as me. So I say, 'You could always put one on the side of a house.'"

"She doesn't say anything for a while, you know? Just stares at me. Then she starts yelling, screaming. 'I don't want you here, the town doesn't want you here! Can't you see from the wind? Get the hell out!' Well, I don't need to be asked twice, but I'm not going to be ripped off by some foreigner either, so I hold out my hand. Don't say a word, just hold out my hand like this."

Walter held his hand out and narrowed his eyes. The mechanic didn't look up from his desk.

"She knows I want the flag back. She laughs and takes it out of her jacket, the wind is whipping it, let me tell you. Then you know what she does?"

The mechanic grunted and shrugged.

"She lets it go! Into the wind!" I grab it with one hand, manage to get a corner of it before it gets blown away. One of these flags, I tell you, they go for two hundred dollars. But, you know, you could get one—lesser quality, of course—for less. Anyway, I grab onto the end, and I won't let go. But that damn wind takes me, the flag is working like a sail on a boat, and I'm the damned boat. In a second, I'm getting dragged down the street, on my butt, going faster and faster. I figure I'd better let go, but I'll be damned if the copper ring didn't catch on one of the buttons on my coat. Kept dragging me even after I let go. Shows you how well made the damn things are, really. But what a way to find out, huh? Didn't even have time to pray or nothing, I figured I was a goner."

"I woke up back in that store, blood all over me from scrapes and such. An Indian woman was cleaning me up. The tall guy was there, some other folks, and that Japanese gal in the corner, quiet now, but watching me with those mean little eyes of hers. They told me the flag dragged me for almost a mile until my coat button let loose, taking a big swath of material with it. I liked that coat too, you know? Still got a scar on my arm where I scraped it on the ground. Here."

The mechanic nodded without inspecting the proffered arm. He wrote numbers on the bill and underlined one of the numbers at the bottom of the page twice.

"It wasn't fifteen minutes before I was up and out of there. All kinds of people staring at me. Normally, I'd have asked her for the two hundred bucks, but I figured I could tell the factory I had used it as a sample, and it had got ruined. What would they care? And it beat staying there."

"Here's your bill." The mechanic pointed out numbers on the bill as he spoke. "I figure eighty-five bucks for the parts. I'll charge you twenty-five for the labor. And a dollar for the beer."

Walter sighed and unrolled bills from his pocket. The mechanic watched, counting to himself as Walter unfurled the bills.

"Pretty strange place, it sounds. That Sheet Rock," he said.

"Black Rock," Walter corrected, handing the money to the mechanic. "But the strangest part was when I left, going through all those people toward the door, I wanted to give that Japanese gal a look, you know? Just a hard look, show her I wasn't beat. So I walked, real slow like, not looking at her until I was right next to her. And then I turned, quick. And when I looked at her, I'll be damned if there weren't tears coming down her face."

2.

Luke and Penn had just entered Amos's store as Walter paused in front of Tokyo on his way out. Though Luke had arrived too late to see the salesman dragged through town by the wind, he had heard the news. Luke was not surprised that a man who couldn't have been in town any more than three hours could already be sideways with the wind and with Tokyo. He was, however, surprised when Tokyo looked up at the salesman as he was leaving and tears were streaming down her face. The salesman, now with a slightly confused expression on his face, limped past her to the door.

Sis, who had helped Walter to the door, took Tokyo's arm as she returned and led her, sobbing, past the counter and into the back room.

Penn, Luke, Proudfoot, Amos, and Tongate, each of whom knew better than to ask questions, watched as Walter got into his car with difficulty. Proudfoot shook his head.

"That," he announced, "is a lucky man."

Amos leaned against a shelf of tent anchors. "Reminds me of what happened to my uncle. Damned if it doesn't," he said. The other Black Rockers nodded in agreement, and Penn, not for the first time since arriving, realized this town was filled with people for whom the past seemed part of the present.

In the back room, Tokyo was conscious of Sis leading her to her bed and patting her on the arm. Sis took a step back from Tokyo and stood in the center of the room facing the bed. As Tokyo held her head in her hands, staring at Sis's feet in front of her, she was genuinely embarrassed at the sobbing which she could not control. As the tears gave way to awareness of Sis's presence, she glared angrily at Sis's feet.

"Leave me alone, can't you?"

The feet didn't move. Tokyo stopped crying almost immediately. This time, more angrily, she said, "Get out!"

Again, Sis's feet didn't move. Tokyo raised her head and was surprised to see Sis smiling dreamily, looking past Tokyo at the tapestry hanging on the wall. Wondering at Sis's lack of attention, Tokyo looked back at the tapestry. She had, when she first took the room many years ago, inspected it, mostly to gauge whether it might have any value and to catalogue it for later should she need it. But the worn threads and nondescript black and red design of a woman—apparently an Indian woman—opening a pouch was uninteresting to her, and probably valueless.

But now, in light of Sis's almost reverential study of the tapestry, Tokyo took time to look at it again. In the tapestry, the woman's eyes were wide, an expression of surprise, even, perhaps, terror on her face. Black lines of thread began at a source within the pouch and swirled up and around the woman, forming dizzying circles in the sky. Smaller pieces of black thread seemed to represent birds struggling amid the black swirling threads, and, in one corner, another group of people stood in a clear pose of grief. Once again, Tokyo determined the worth of the tapestry to be close to zero. She turned from the tapestry to Sis, who seemed enraptured.

"What?" she asked angrily.

Sis finally emerged from her reverie and seemed surprised to see Tokyo. She smiled and asked, "I sit?"

Until she was ready to resume control of the situation, Tokyo knew she needed to be alone. Sis, normally attuned to another's discomfort and willing to quietly glide out of a room, today seemed strangely oblivious.

"I need to be alone," Tokyo said firmly.

With a glance up at the tapestry, Sis sat down on the bed next to Tokyo, who considered whether she should use bodily force to eject Sis. Before she could decide, Sis turned toward her.

"No problem. I'll talk, then I'll leave. Okay?"

Knowing well Sis's inability to string more than a few sentences together, Tokyo decided to accept Sis's bargain. She would listen in return for the solitude Sis promised. She nodded assent.

Sis reached out and touched Tokyo's shoulder. Tokyo flinched, as if Sis's touch were painful.

"You only feel trapped," Sis said.

"I don't need you to tell me that," Tokyo said, her tone biting. "I can get up and leave this place anytime I want."

Sis nodded and smiled. She put both her hands in her lap and glanced back up at the tapestry.

"Let me tell you how this place got to be how it is," she began. "Many years ago, before cars, before the quarries, before even the first white people had come here—"

"I don't need a story, Sis. Don't tell me fucking fairy tales."

Sis was quiet for a moment. For the first time, and with some pleasure, Tokyo thought she saw a flash of anger in Sis's face, in her eyes. "You don't have to listen. I am not keeping you here. You are here."

Tokyo lowered her head and muttered, mostly to herself, "Whatever the hell that means." When she raised her head, she expected Sis to be gone. Most people, once given a taste of Tokyo's venom, retreated either out of fear or out of the disinclination to be in close proximity to such mean-spiritedness. But Sis remained on the bed. She began talking again, and Tokyo, despite her impatient desire to be alone, resigned herself to listen.

"The people who lived here, they loved the mesa; it was a holy place. But back then, there was no wind. This was a place of green grasses, of trees, of creeks, and good earth. The Indians were given this place by Moneto and loved and respected it.

"Back then, when an Indian maiden came of age, she was sent off, away from the tribe, to the mesa to find her song. Her song was the song of her heart, and she could only find it by herself. And when she did, she became a woman. Ages went by, and maidens who had wandered off to find their songs came back to the tribe as women who could sing, and the tribe grew great and strong with their songs.

"Then it came time for one maiden to find her song. This maiden was a restless child, always fighting, always angry, and always looking for something better for herself. When the time came for her to go apart from the tribe and find her song, she left determined that she would find the best, most powerful song ever found by a maiden. This, she thought, would take away the coldness she felt when the others in the tribe shunned her. This, she thought, would take away the laughter of the other children. This, she thought, would make them love her.

"So she went off looking for a song, went away longer than any maiden had ever spent away from the tribe looking for a song. It wasn't that she couldn't find a song, no …" Here, Sis smiled and made a sweeping gesture with her hand.

"She found one song after another, but none of them was as powerful as she needed. So she kept searching. One day, in a deep wood, she came suddenly into a clearing, a flat grassy place that she immediately recognized as holy. And there, in front of her, was the pouch in which Moneto kept all the songs for all the Indian maidens, for all the Indian fathers and grandfathers, and all the Indian mothers and grandmothers.

"'With this, I will be the most loved Indian in the tribe,' she thought, and ran for the pouch. She opened the pouch to hear the wonders of the songs.

"And the songs came out, all of them at one time, like you see in the tapestry. So many songs. And the songs were like a wind, a wind stronger than any Moneto had ever let blow on earth. Moneto wanted nothing more than to protect the people and the holy place. But the maiden's opening of the pouch was to be punished. The people cried, but Moneto wouldn't listen, so angry Moneto was. Moneto said the songs and the wind would stay on the mesa.

"And the songs stayed on the mesa, and they scoured the trees, the creeks, even the soil, leaving only the black slate and the people, and soon the people of the tribe left or died and only the maiden was left with the wind and her songs."

Sis stood suddenly and walked to the door. Tokyo blinked slowly.

"Pandora's box," Tokyo said.

Sis smiled and shook her head. "No," she said. Then she was gone.

3.

Apie stood in the front room of Shlomo's store and extended his hand to Noah, who stood silently in quiet incomprehension. Noah turned to see the letter on the counter, then back at Apie, trying to link the two in his mind. He gave his head a shake, to see whether the movement might help, but still he saw Apie, leering and extending a hand in greeting.

"It's polite to shake hands. At least, that's what the cultured folks tell me, Noah," Apie said.

Numbly, Noah extended his hand, and Apie pumped it vigorously, all the time grinning broadly.

"Bet you two old prospectors never thought you'd see old Apie walking into your place, did you?"

Shlomo shook his head. "I surely didn't, Apie. You're about the last person I expected to walk in through that door. Come on over to the counter, I'll get you a cold lemonade."

The men walked over to the counter and sat on the stools. Noah stood apart from the others and attempted to understand what Apie was doing back in Black Rock. The last time Noah had even thought about Apie was when he had watched Apie's form riding with the wind for all he was worth toward the eastern edge of the mesa.

Shlomo good-naturedly set out lemonade for the men, and Apie drank his in great gulps. Tiller sipped his drink carefully, wiping his lips with the thumb and forefinger of his free hand. Apie smiled as Shlomo refilled his glass. "Nothing stronger than that for an old friend, Shlomo?"

Shlomo glanced at Noah, who showed every sign of never speaking again.

"Maybe over in the quarrymen's barracks. Noah doesn't allow it in here."

"No, I don't guess he would." Apie turned around and looked at Noah. From years of experience, he knew better than to stand in front of a taller man. The taller man always felt superior in such a position. Rather, he had found that sitting comfortably in the presence of a physically larger man was sufficient to cause discomfort and even irritation. Apie clasped his hands around one of his knees and smiled politely up at Noah, enjoying his position of power.

Noah inched forward, finally finding words: "You … you're Johnson?"

Apie smiled. "And I was back then, too. Ain't that a kicker? I'm a real bastard. Some folks knew me by my mother's name of Miller, but my daddy's name was Johnson. I started going by his name after I got rich. If you'd have killed me, you'd have killed Burton Johnson, not just Apie Miller."

Noah looked at the glass of lemonade on the counter in front of him. Although he was thirsty and the open door had blown a good bit of dust into his mouth, he didn't reach for it. Indeed, the room seemed to be swirling slightly around him, images of Apie's leering smile, Shlomo's normal good-natured civility, and Tiller's quiet elegance competing for his attention. It seemed as if the wind had blown into the room and into Noah's soul. His eyes rested on Tiller for a moment, who, though certainly not as uncomfortable as Noah, was having trouble determining just exactly what was happening.

Apie followed Noah's gaze. "That there's the magistrate, Noah," he said. "Magistrate Tiller. He's going to set everything right."

Noah looked back at Apie. "Set it right?" The words were strained, almost croaked.

"The good Magistrate Tiller here, he's the law. Isn't that right, magistrate?"

"I have been sent as a representative of the court. The Federal Claims Court. To adjudicate Mr. Johnson's claim."

"Fancy talker, isn't he?" Apie asked, not really expecting an answer. "You see, Noah. I got rich. Not rich from gold, like we wanted, but rich from oil. It's like gold, only better. 'Cause it keeps on coming up out of the earth. Gold you take out once, and it's gone. And when I got rich, I enjoyed being rich a while; then I started thinking about all the stuff that had gone wrong on the way to getting rich. All the people that had gotten in the way. There aren't many I haven't already paid back, I mean one way or another. Just a few I need to settle up accounts with. And your name came to mind. So I figured I could wait for God to take care of you, or I could maybe push God along a little, with the help of the law, like Mr. Tiller here."

Noah swallowed with difficulty. "There's your law, and then there's God's law," he said.

Apie nodded. "Yup. And in God's laws you don't need no deed. But here in Magistrate Tiller's laws, you do. And I got one. To the whole mesa."

Tiller opened a small leather satchel and removed some papers. He spread them out on the table and pointed to various provisions. "You see, here. And here. Mr. Johnson purchased two tracts of land from the Federal Land Management Company. This is the entire extent of Mr. Johnson's ownership."

Shlomo whistled softly. "The whole mesa. And halfway down to the town."

Apie cleared his throat and smiled. "In the old days, I might've taken matters into my own hands. Don't need to anymore."

Noah squinted and looked at Tiller. "The law. Your law. I came a long way to live in a place where the only law I needed to think about was the Lord's law. The Good Book. My family was born here, raised here. We've made this place our own. You can't kick us off the land."

"Oh, Noah. I'm not chasing you off the land. That'd be rude." Apie shook the empty lemonade glass at Shlomo, who refilled it thoughtfully. If Apie had gone to the trouble of buying the land, of bringing the magistrate all the way out here, he must want something. And if it wasn't to kick them off the land …"

"What's the Bible say, Noah?" Apie asked. "Eye for an eye?"

Noah nodded numbly.

Apie turned on his stool, and the edge of harshness which had been perceptible in his tone turned suddenly into unadulterated meanness. He smiled wickedly at Noah and pointed a finger. "I'm not going to threaten you, like you did me, Noah. I'm not going to look for bullets to put in a gun to shoot you. I'm gonna let you do it yourself. Tell him, magistrate."

Magistrate Tiller shifted uncomfortably in his seat. When he had first heard of the case, he had expected Christophe and Rubenstein to be the same caliber of scoundrel as Johnson. He had adjudicated cases between such men before, in dung-encrusted cattle towns, in fertile farming valleys, and in dusty fringe towns struggling to survive on the edge of the desert. Inevitably, his decisions did nothing but heighten tensions between the combatants, sometimes with fatal consequences.

To his surprise, however, in the little time he had already spent with Noah and Shlomo, he realized these men were different than Johnson. When he looked at Johnson, it was almost as if he was looking deep into a cave, squinting through the darkness to see this cretinous being smiling maniacally back up at him through a cloud of dimness and filth. Neither Noah nor Shlomo seemed to have this cloud of evil surrounding them; instead, they seemed to Tiller to be simple folk, the kind he was predisposed to favor. And Noah had a preacher's bearing, even if his seemed to be an odd house of worship.

Tiller sighed unhappily. No matter how much he favored the two simple men, the law was the law. "Well, you see, gentlemen, Mr. Johnson has brought an action, not of trespass and eviction, but rather conversion, detainer, and retinue."

Shlomo, Apie, and Noah were silent.

"That clears that up nice, doesn't it?" Shlomo said to ease the tension.

"In other words," Tiller continued, "Mr. Johnson doesn't want to remove you from the property. He wants damages for what you have taken from his property since the date he bought it until now. And in the future, should you decide to stay, he wants you to pay rent." Tiller picked up his glass and sipped the lemonade noiselessly.

Noah, genuinely confused, addressed Tiller. At least he could look at the magistrate without revulsion. "What damages? We haven't damaged anything. What damages?"

Apie sprang from his seat and moved to Tiller's side. He rifled through some papers and pulled one out of the sheaf, holding it out for Noah's inspection.

"See here, Noah. Slate, we figure, averaged twelve dollars a long ton. I've owned the land four years now, so, depending on what you've taken, you owe me twelve dollars a ton for four years. That's damages. Big damages."

Stunned, Noah put his head in his hands. As a businessman, even one of God's businessmen, Noah was gifted with a mathematician's quickness. He had already calculated a rough amount in his head, more money than he could ever consider. He shook his head and looked up at Shlomo. *Armageddon,* he thought. *Armageddon, pure and simple.*

"It gets even better, Noah." Apie continued. "You owe me rent, too. Magistrate Tiller figures about thirteen hundred dollars a year for the whole mesa."

Noah took a deep breath and looked up at Tiller. "I haven't got the money. I can't even raise two hundred dollars together."

Apie, having prepared for this moment since the drunken night in Chicago during which he had hatched his plan, leered at Noah. "That's okay, Noah. I'll let you work it off." And in case Noah had not understood, Apie added, "You work for me now."

4.

Ruth heard the huge splashing sound outside the house and ran to the porch, searching desperately first for Nate, then for Prudence. When she heard it from inside, the sound had panicked her, and she envisioned one of the children, despite the warnings of Daisy and Ruth, falling off the porch and into the frigid water which now lapped up to Daisy's house. Even as she ran to the porch, she knew the splash was far too deeply resonant to have been a small child, but the echo of the sound in the quarry could only mean danger.

The men had been gone nearly a week, and the water, which had slowed when the men were last in the quarry, had resumed its advance a few days after their departure. It had now swamped Ruth's first floor and had Daisy's porch surrounded as if it were a pier jutting out into a lake. To allow Daisy and Ruth to reach the little remaining higher ground where all their earthly possessions sat in various states of readiness for moving, Daisy had cleverly removed a piece of the railing from the dry end of the porch.

The children enjoyed jumping down and collecting pieces of loose slate from the high ground and taking them to the porch to throw and skip them into the black water. The sound of the stones hitting the water was not unusual, but the size of this splash could only have been something much heavier.

To her relief, Ruth saw both Prudence and Nate standing on the porch when she ran outside. She turned and reassured Daisy, who had been nursing Luke inside.

"What was that?" Ruth asked the children.

Nate pointed out to the water, in which unusual concentric ripples were spreading from a point near the series of ladders.

"A big piece of slate fell. There."

Ruth squinted up to where Nate was pointing. The black-on-black ledges of slate were hard to distinguish, but she could clearly see a gash of slate missing about halfway up the wall of the quarry. It was missing from the wall on the deeper end of the quarry and appeared to have taken most of the ladders with it when it fell. Now when they left, they would have to climb. They wouldn't be able to do it alone. Now it was likely the larger pieces of furniture, which would have been difficult to fit into the boat and to wrestle up the ladders under the most favorable of conditions, would have to be left behind. Ruth looked up grimly. Where the slate had been, she could see a trickle of water.

Ruth turned to the frightened children. To distract them, she asked, "You children aren't throwing rocks against the side of the quarry, are you?"

"No, ma'am," Nate said.

Ruth looked back at the wall. Whatever it meant, she decided, it wouldn't matter for long, since they were going to be leaving New Town as soon as the men returned. And the sooner, she thought, the better. She smiled reassuringly at the children and turned to reenter the house.

"Look!" Nate cried.

Ruth wheeled around and peered back up at the wall just in time to see a chunk of slate, bigger than a wagon, dropping from the wall and hitting the water. Large waves rippled out from the wall toward their porch. When the waves reached the porch, they lapped up onto the dry wood, causing the children to retreat. Ruth watched them, remembering the seashore and her own sister in another time, another place. Suddenly, Prudence pointed up at the wall where the slate had just detached.

"A waterfall!"

And there, where Prudence pointed, was a flow of water from the side of the quarry wall, only now it was stronger, like a flow of water from a sputtering mechanical pump. The stronger bursts of water leapt away from the wall and fell in a rough stream through the air to the surface of the pool. Ruth reached out and took each child by the hand and led them inside, all of them taking one last look at the arc of water falling gracefully from the wall of New Town.

5.

Tokyo was staring up at the tapestry in the back room when Penn walked into the room. She looked at him, then, as was her habit, looked quickly away. What she had already seen of him, she didn't like. He was a small man, well-groomed. In her experience, Tokyo's association with such men had not been happy. Men such as these were full of themselves and often confident to the point of arrogance.

"They call you Tokyo." It was a statement, but sounded for all the world to Tokyo like a question. When she didn't respond, Penn continued. "But it's not your real name, is it?"

Tokyo sighed impatiently. "You came a long way to tell me something I already know." She looked at his feet from the side of her eye, careful to avoid any real eye contact.

Penn surveyed the storage shelves in the back room in silence, then gestured toward a stool Amos used to reach the highest shelf.

"Mind if I sit?"

Tokyo blinked. Wrongly assuming her silence to be assent, Penn sat on the low stool.

"Your name, it's Ayako. Your mother named you after her grandmother."

Tokyo stood angrily and looked at Penn for the first time. He was at ease, comfortable. Too comfortable for her tastes. "Are you a cop or something? Did I steal from somebody? Did I take some silverware from somebody, some special family stuff that I don't remember? If I had it, you could have it back. But I don't have anything, not even much of a place to stay, you can see for yourself. So if that's what you're looking for, you might as well just turn around and go back and tell them I haven't got a thing." Tokyo paused, breathing rapidly. "And if they know me, whoever they are, they already know that about me. So do you."

Penn was smiling. He shook his head. "I'm not a cop."

"Then get the hell out of here."

Penn made no move to stand. Tokyo, frustrated, stamped a foot hard against the floor. In the next room, she heard the dishes in the cupboards rattle from the force. "Get the hell out of here! Sis doesn't listen to me, you don't listen to me, who the hell is going to listen to me? Get the hell out!"

Penn stood, his face serious. "Okay. I'll leave."

"That's what Sis said."

Penn walked to the door, then stopped. He didn't turn around, but put one hand up against the cool glass of the door when he spoke.

"Your mother, she was Japanese. You remember her, maybe. But maybe not. You were young when she left. Only three. She went into an institution, and you went into a foster home. The Coles. In Massachusetts. They treated you well, clothed you, fed you, but they were strict. And Mr. Cole was the worst, wasn't he?"

"Get the fuck out of here."

"Your mother died; you got word of that, I'm sure. You never knew what she went through."

"You did?" Tokyo asked, her anger and spitefulness overcoming her desire to end the conversation quickly.

Penn turned and looked at Tokyo over his shoulder. He closed his eyes, then opened them after a moment, a gesture of vague confirmation. Tokyo thought he might start to cry. His voice cracked when he spoke again.

"You didn't know your father. He went away before you were born. Left you with your mother, Mari … Ayako, I'm your father."

Tokyo was only aware of the sound of the wind as she stood in the room with her father. The wind moaned, reaching small crescendos every five seconds, then returned to a softer note, and started over again. Tokyo was suddenly tired. Her eyelids were burning, her limbs heavy, as she sat down on the bed. In the next room, Sis began working her loom. The usually reassuring sound only added to Tokyo's exhaustion.

Penn leaned up against the door heavily, as if he, too, were tired. Tokyo narrowed her eyes.

"What's your name?" she asked. Her tone was muted. The sound of the wind was deafening, pressing in on her brain and threatening her core. Most days, she stood up to the wind, fought it, and even ridiculed it, but today, she felt defeated. She shivered slightly, then reached for the scratchy wool blanket which served as a bedspread. She wrapped the blanket around her shoulders and waited.

"Penn Taylor."

"What do you want, Penn Taylor?" Her voice was a monotone.

"I … I wanted to find you. To see you."

"Are you dying, Penn Taylor? Do you have some rare disease? Have you come to make your peace with your daughter? Do you want me to tell you about how I laid awake at night wondering who my father was and where he was? Was he dead? Was he in heaven with my mother? Or was he Cole, that mean-spirited son-of-a-bitch and the joke's on me? Do you want me to run to your arms and cry? Do you want to fuck me like you did my mother? What do you want with me, Penn Taylor?"

Tokyo's voice hadn't changed from a monotone, but the moaning wind provided ample punctuation. The wind was angry and remorseless. It was a force of nature incapable of thought, incapable of sorrow. It moaned and roared steadily, occasionally raising itself to a scream.

Penn started to say something, but Tokyo stopped him by raising one hand. "If you don't get out of here, now …" Her voice trailed off.

Penn nodded and disappeared from the doorway.

Exhausted, Tokyo fell backward onto the bed, staring up at the cobwebs in the rafters. Her head hurt behind both temples and at the base of her skull, a throbbing pain which threatened to blind her. She closed her eyes and wondered vaguely when the next vehicle of any kind would be leaving Black Rock. Perhaps, she thought, she could put up with Tongate's blather for a few hours. He could be easily manipulated to run her to the nearest town where she could catch a bus for Salt Lake City. She would tell him secrets, some lies, some truth. He would take her anywhere for gossip's sake. She'd take the cash from Amos's lockbox when he wasn't there, having prepared him for this day by being scrupulously honest when it came to even the pennies left on the counter.

But what if Tongate discovered the tie between Penn and Tokyo? He would want to stick around to watch the fun, she thought grimly. So little ever happened in Black Rock, a long-lost father-daughter reunion would be just the ticket for the nosey bastard, Tokyo thought. On the other hand, she considered whether she could use Penn's revelation to her advantage. He was not Japanese. There was little resemblance she could see between her own features and Penn's. She could deny what he said as the ravings of someone she had hurt in the past.

"What'd you say to him?"

It was Luke. His tone was gently accusing. He would assume she had offended Penn, much in the way she regularly offended Luke. She opened her eyes and looked at the ceiling, marveling at the stillness of the cobwebs in the rafters. Despite the wind, she was consistently surprised, both in Amos's store and in Luke's house, how few cracks the wind found to blow into. Luke always said it was because the old-timers knew how to build on the mesa. As far as she could tell, everyone else in town complained of poor workmanship in their houses. They complained of the wind finding cracks in their homes and disrupting their kitchens, their bedrooms, their bathrooms. The cracks enabled the wind to take hold, to widen the cracks, and blow even harder into their lives. Only constant vigilance against cracks could protect them. Tongate alone could have kept Amos in business for a month every year with the amount of spackle he purchased to seal cracks in his walls.

"I mean, his face was white," Luke said.

Tokyo didn't bother to look at Luke. She remained focused on the ceiling. "Did he say anything to you?"

Luke shrugged. "He told me about you, about where you've been. He told me about Sioux Falls."

Tokyo closed her eyes again. Things couldn't possibly be worse. She suddenly propped herself up by on her elbows. "Did he tell you why he's been following me?"

Luke shook his head. Tokyo fell back on the bed. "Can you ask Amos for some aspirin?"

Luke nodded and turned away. The wind diminished to a low moan, and Tokyo heard Luke's careful steps walking to the front of the store, heard the loom stop, the murmuring of voices and finally Luke's footsteps back toward her room. She propped herself up on her side when Luke sat on the bed. She threw the aspirin into her mouth and paused for a few seconds, letting the acidic taste burn the back of her tongue slightly, then swallowed from the glass Luke had brought her. She put the glass down on the floor awkwardly. Luke hadn't moved. He was looking at the floor.

"I don't want you to leave, Tokyo. I know you want to leave, but I don't want you to leave. Not like this."

You don't know how badly I want to leave, she thought. She blinked once, slowly. She could lie to Luke, she'd lied to him before. She'd lied to more men and women than she could think of. Lying came naturally to her. None of the people around her, neither the women who had called her friend nor the men who had called her lover, had ever understood this about her—they simply didn't exist except as a means for her survival.

"I know you won't come back to my place right now," Luke said, but his voice was laced with hope. She heard it. She had heard it before in Luke, in others.

"All I'm asking you is that you don't leave yet. When you want to leave, I'll drive you. All the way to Salt Lake City, if you want. I won't make a stink."

Tokyo was unaware of Luke having actually driven any farther away from his home than the town during the five years she had lived in Black Rock. She looked at him carefully. Most often, she had taken up with weak men, men who she knew looked to her for support, since they were easy to manipulate. But at the same time, these men had a tendency to crawl under her skin in a way she found appalling.

Luke had been one of these men since the day she had met him. But, as now, he could surprise her. He was asking for himself, of course, but he didn't have the weak, pleading, almost infantile look of yearning she had seen in so many men. Instead, behind his eyes, she saw something beyond the quiet, craggy exterior. What she saw, she marveled, appeared to be strength. He wasn't lying. He'd take her wherever she wanted to go and, once they arrived, would watch her walk away without so much as a word.

"You go back, Luke," she said. Her tone was soft, even kind. She looked up into Luke's eyes for a moment, silent. "I promise I won't leave without telling you," she said, and she surprised herself by meaning it.

6.

As a man of religion, Noah had managed to keep desperation at bay by simply banishing doubt, and, when failure threatened and even came to pass, Noah would say, with true feeling, "It was God's will."

But even the firm footsteps of the most religious man—a man who can accept earthquakes, sudden deaths, and crops destroyed by disease—can falter when confronted by the evil acts of another person which are directed precisely and intentionally toward him. A man like Noah, who had willed the hope of gold and wealth into a thriving business of a slate quarry, who had maintained at all times the glory of God's plan, now found himself dumbfounded. Confronted by Apie, who had apparently harbored a grudge for more years than either Shlomo or Noah could remember, Noah knew desperation for the first time.

He tried to plead with Tiller; he tried to reason with Apie, but it was no use. Tiller remarked only that the judgment he was to make was made simple in this case since neither Noah nor Shlomo, nor, it appeared, anyone in Black Rock or on the mesa, could produce any competing deed or interest of any kind in the land owned by Mr. Burton Johnson. Tiller pronounced this judgment almost ruefully, but Apie cheered considerably when Tiller showed Noah the settlement papers he had drawn up, papers which Shlomo and Tiller explained quietly to Noah as Apie looked approvingly at the items for sale in Shlomo's shop. From their explanation, it seemed to Noah that Apie would take most of the sparse profits from the quarries for the next thirty-five years. During that time, Apie would hold off rent, but then rent would start in thirty-five years, in the same amount as the reparations that were due.

"What about you?" Noah asked quietly.

Shlomo shuffled through the papers. "It don't say nothing about me, Noah."

Noah nodded and watched as Apie groomed his hair in the reflection of the front window.

"What if I don't pay? You put me in jail?"

Tiller cleared his throat. "No, sir. You can't be put in jail for not paying a debt. It just doesn't work that way in this country."

Noah shook his head. On another day, in another time, he would have loudly opined on the evils of debtors who failed to pay their creditors. Prison was certainly the best fate for such scofflaws. But today, he considered the Bible's words on forgiveness, particularly of the wealthy toward the poor.

"What if I leave?" Noah asked.

The wind whipped down the street in a long steady gust. Apie remembered the difficulties of living in the wind as if it were yesterday. He turned from the window. "You stayed here a long time, Noah. Put up with a lot of things other men wouldn't have. So I figure, you'll put up with me. You might figure God sent me back to you."

"If you saw what we had made here, Apie. If you saw New Town, the new mine, you wouldn't be doing this," Noah's tone of near pleading made Apie smile. Shlomo, back behind the counter, shook his head sadly.

"Maybe so, Noah. But, really, I might not do this to a friend," Apie said. "This is really working out just like I figured. I'm really enjoying myself here."

Noah looked back at the papers on the counter. Apie watched Noah's eyes with pleasure; he looked like a nervous racehorse frightened in his barn by a loud noise.

"Before I sign, come out and see what we've made. See what this place means to me, to my family, to Shlomo and his family."

As a wealthy man, Apie had no engagements so pressing they couldn't be put off, particularly if he had the prospect of humiliating an enemy instead. The brief image of Noah, standing in the same wind in which he had humiliated Apie was too much to resist. He smiled at Tiller, doubly pleased that he had not even had to bribe the magistrate for such a good result.

"Magistrate Tiller? You have the time?" Apie asked. Not bothering to wait for a response, Apie turned his back on the magistrate. "Well, let's go out and look at what you've done to my land, Noah."

7.

As a little girl, Ruth had heard stories of frontiersmen who, surrounded by hostile Indians, had run into the family cabin and shut the doors and windows. Later, rescue parties would come across the burned remains of the family and their settlement and sometimes exclaim at full powder horns and unused rifles. Ruth had always wondered why no one had thought to fight back, why the families huddled together in the house with closed doors and windows until doom overtook them. Now, with the two families closed up in Daisy's house, Ruth realized how debilitating fear could be.

Ruth and Daisy were similarly paralyzed with fear. The natural response to run back inside and bolt the doors made sense—they couldn't see the gushing black water, and there was some solace in their willing blindness. But even inside, they could hear the sound of the water, punctuated by additional splashes of what sounded like more slate breaking loose from the sidewall.

Daisy leaned over the cradle and rocked it gently, returning to instinctive motions in part to try to calm herself. Ruth turned to the children and tried to distract them by suggesting they read to each other.

"Now?" Nate asked. "I want to see the water." But his mother's look was sufficient to quiet his complaint, and he and Prudence went inside to find their books.

"Daisy," Ruth whispered when the children had left the room. "We have to do something."

Daisy's eyes were blank, her expression confused. "But the sun's going down. Tomorrow we'll see how much the water's come up ..." She was interrupted by a huge cracking sound, a sound like thunder, followed by a deep splashing, this one very close to the house. The children silenced at once, looking toward the adults. Ruth looked up at the ceiling, then down at the doorway as a puddle of water forced its way under the front door and into the house. Ruth tried to catch Daisy's eye, but her friend was concentrating on the babies.

In the face of Daisy's obvious self-denial, Ruth steeled herself and walked to the front porch. She gasped at what she saw. The water already covered the porch and was only an inch below the level of the doorway. She could make out two large streams pouring from the side of the quarry. To her, they looked huge, almost as if two mighty rivers had been displaced and left to drain into their quarry. Between the huge streams, intermittent spurts erupted from other places, punctuating the steadier streams. She noted with dismay that most of the series of ladders fixed to the side of the quarry had now totally vanished.

Worse, Ruth saw that the boat had been struck by falling slate and now lay swamped in the water, its bow still tied to a rope attached to the porch railing. She tugged at the rope and drew the boat toward the porch, but stopped when she saw the piece of jagged slate protruding from the splintered bottom of the dinghy. She turned and walked to the doorway.

"We can't wait until tomorrow, Daisy. Look."

Daisy ignored Ruth and continued rocking the babies, both of whom were incongruously sleeping soundly. Her voice was shaking but determined. "The men'll be back tomorrow. It'll be a week then. They'll know what to do." She shook her head, refusing to move.

Ruth rushed back into the room and took Daisy brusquely by the arm. She marched out to the front porch with Daisy in reluctant tow. Daisy's eyes widened as she stumbled into the ankle-deep water.

"Get the children," Ruth hissed. "We've got to get out."

The cold water seemed to awaken Daisy. She nodded quickly and ran inside. Ruth walked to the deep end of the porch, where the boat was moored. She took the rope in one hand and pulled the swamped boat to the shallow side of the porch. When Daisy appeared at the door with Nate and Prudence, she turned.

"Get the cradle."

Ruth stood on the porch, considering the level of the water and the amount of dry slate left in New Town. The house, she thought, would certainly be swamped by morning. But the dry land looked as if it would last until then, if not completely dry, with only a foot or so of water. Most of the furniture and household goods already looked as if they were on an island. If it came to it, they could perch themselves on their possessions. Their clothing wouldn't be in the water too long, provided the men returned when Ruth and Daisy thought they might.

"What do we do with it?" Daisy asked from the doorway. She held one end of the cradle and Prudence and Nate held the other. Ruth gestured to the boat and dragged it through the shallow water at the door. As she bent to pick up one end of the bassinet, she felt anger—anger such as she had never experienced, anger making her stronger than she knew. She jumped into the water next to the boat and wrenched the slate from the bottom. The hole was large, but perhaps if they covered it with canvas and weighted it down with the cradle it would hold. If it came down to it, the cradle would probably float; unlike most of the other furniture, it contained no slate in its construction. *Thank God*, Ruth thought.

As Daisy and the children watched from the porch, Ruth pulled the boat to dry land and tipped it, spilling the black water out. She turned and looked for suitable material for patching, mentally running through her possessions until she thought of the old lean-to material that Shlomo had brought with him, even to New Town. She ran to a box and opened it, pulling out the material and placing it in the bottom of the boat.

Once she returned to the porch, Ruth lifted one end of the cradle and Daisy and the children the other end, and they carried the cradle to the boat, placing it clumsily on top of the canvas. The babies, awake and alert, both began whimpering.

"There, there," Daisy said.

Ruth pushed the boat into the water, holding the rope in one hand. As she watched, water trickled beneath the canvas and pooled in the bottom of the boat, but seemed to slow and even stop.

"Mama, there's not room for all of us in the boat," Nate said.

Ruth's heart was crushed by a weight she had never known before. She swallowed hard and blinked back tears, then turned to the children. "We're going to just wait here," Ruth said. "Noah and Papa will come back and help us out."

Ruth sat heavily on one of the chests of drawers and considered her feet. They were cold, almost numb. The water had wicked up the long skirt she was wearing until it had almost reached her waist. She reached into a drawer and withdrew a pair of her husband's wool pants, then searched a nearby box for dry shoes and socks. She immediately began to remove her dress and shoes.

"The water's cold," she said to the others. "We've got to make sure we keep dry."

Nate looked suspiciously at the rising water. The boat, overloaded with the cradle and low in the water, rocked ominously. "The water's gonna be up here by morning," he said.

Daisy looked up at the sun, just about to disappear beyond New Town's false horizon. Nate was right, she knew, but Ruth seemed so certain. Like Noah. Maybe that's what had attracted her to Ruth in the first place, she thought, and smiled.

"You're a good friend, Ruth."

Ruth glanced up from hurriedly tying the heavy boots she had found. Daisy's face, once smooth and pampered, still retained the loveliness that had attracted so many men, but it was hidden behind a coarser exterior, almost as if Daisy's younger self had worn away, leaving in its place the same eyes, the same lips and mouth, but a thinner and tougher skin. It was hard to tell whether the lines running from the corner of Daisy's eyes and spreading into her cheeks were from the laughter of her early days or from the crying of more recent times. She reached out and stroked Daisy's cheek gently.

"We'll be all right, Daisy," she said. Daisy nodded, fighting back tears. Daisy looked down at her dress, still soggy from having fought through the water. "You'd better change clothes, Daisy. Get a pair of pants on. It'll suit better."

Daisy busied herself looking through the trunks, while Ruth made sure the children were dry. She had put Nate and Prudence in charge of watching the boat, and they were taking turns holding onto the rope which was tied to the bow.

While Prudence held the line tightly, Nate reached down and marked the edge of the water with a jagged piece of slate. After his turn to hold the rope came and went, in all about ten minutes, he reached down to find the piece of slate, but to his surprise found that he could no longer reach it without going into the water up to his knees. He looked back up the slight incline to where his mother was arranging their belongings, then back at the piece of submerged slate.

Children are well-known to exaggerate, and for that reason are themselves given to great care when opining on a matter of importance to adults. Nate assured himself that Prudence had a firm grip on the rope and shuffled the few steps up to Ruth. Ruth saw Nate's fear and tried to reassure him by smiling as she stacked the last of several wooden storage boxes on top of the furniture.

"Come here, Natie," she said.

Nate allowed himself to be enveloped in his mother's arms, and he closed his eyes for a moment. Close to her, he felt the scratchy wool of her trousers and smelled her distinctive smell even over the cold dampness of the quarry. He opened his eyes and saw Daisy, sitting nearby, seemingly ignoring everything but the stream of water pouring into the quarry. She was still wearing her soaked dress, having numbly forgotten what it was she had been looking for among her belongings. Her head was uplifted, her eyes disbelieving as she watched the water fall into New Town. Nate could see that Daisy was frightened, and he had no desire to frighten her further. He looked up at his mother, his eyes open in a way that he knew would lead to a question.

"What is it?" Ruth asked.

Nate swallowed and looked down at Prudence, who was edging back from the water, waiting impatiently for Nate to take his turn with the rope.

"The water's coming too fast," Nate whispered, making sure Daisy couldn't hear. "It'll be up to here in no time."

Ruth looked down to the edge of the water, now only ten feet away. The porch of Daisy's house was now completely underwater, and, judging from the front door, it appeared as if a foot of water was already in the house. *It can't be coming that fast*, Ruth thought. *It can't be.* Then to Nate she said, "It'll be okay, Natie."

Both Nate and Ruth turned as Daisy gasped; they followed her shocked gaze up at the wall. A new geyser of water had sprung from the side of the quarry, a geyser so large and powerful that it spread out over almost the entire quarry, falling like a powerful rain on the water and the little remaining dry land. The new geyser seemed to engulf the two large streams of water, merging into an impossibly large waterfall. In a matter of moments, they were all soaked.

Prudence, frightened by the roaring sound of the water, ran to her mother. Ruth leapt to the boat and wrapped the line around her hand three times, then turned back to Nate, who had followed her down to the water. The noise of the rain was like the noise of the wind on the mesa, she thought, shaking her head in a vain attempt to clear it. Ruth looked up and saw the blue sky through the mist of water falling into the quarry, the clouds moving quickly in the wind. As much as she hated the wind, she wished with every fiber that she could be there now, in the sunshine, above this horrible pit.

She looked up to Daisy, who had wrapped Prudence in her arms and was walking toward the water.

"Daisy! Stay up here! It's more …"

Ruth stopped and looked down at the water, now up to her ankles. Nate was shaking, clutching his mother's leg in abject terror. He had never learned to swim. None of them had. Where would they have done so? And with the temperature of the water, would it have mattered? Ruth looked to the babies, Amos and Luke, blinking and crying in the rain. Ruth turned desperately to the families' combined possessions. She noticed a picture-size mirror which Daisy had kept, a mirror that had allowed Daisy to admire her image from the front and from the side at once.

"Nate! Get me that mirror! Nate!" Nate looked to where Ruth was pointing and numbly obeyed. He dragged the mirror to her with some difficulty, hip-deep in water, then helped her place it carefully over the cradle, the hinge serving as a sort of peaked roof over the cradle and the boat. Ruth nodded with satisfaction as she watched the water hitting the mirror and dripping over the side of the boat. "That'll keep the water off them," she said to Nate. He nodded up at her, and she couldn't tell whether it was the rain or tears on his cheeks, but she held him tight as she let go of the rope to the boat. Nate buried his head in her wet clothes.

Wiping the rain away from her eyes, Ruth looked at Daisy, who was standing knee-deep in the water, frozen with fear. Prudence had climbed out of her mother's embrace and sought refuge on top of one of the wardrobes which were now slightly submerged. She was holding one of Shlomo's jackets over her head to protect her from the water. Still holding Nate, Ruth walked over to Prudence and sat down with her, hugging her with her free arm. Grateful for Ruth's touch, Prudence burrowed into Ruth as far as she could. Quickly, without even an awareness of having made a decision, Ruth stood.

"I want you two to get into the boat," she said to the two children. Nate's grip tightened on his mother's leg. Prudence looked desperately to Daisy, who looked wildly confused. "Come on, Nate," she urged.

Nate loosened his grip from her leg, and she waded to the boat, first lifting Prudence and then Nate into the dangerously overloaded boat.

"Mama," Nate's voice was shaking. He was terrified.

"Shhh," Ruth said, brushing the water away from her face. "I'm going to hold onto the rope. You two try to hide under the mirror so you don't get wet. It'll be like a tent." Shivering, Prudence nodded uncertainly and pushed the mirror slightly.

"But it's wet down there too," Prudence said.

Ruth pulled the boat closer and looked into the bottom. Prudence was right, a foot of water had collected in the bottom, and the level was rising further. The weight of Prudence and Nate wouldn't be enough to sink the boat entirely, she judged. If they sat quietly and kept bailing, they might keep afloat. *But if Daisy and I tried to get in …* Ruth let her thought go unfinished; instead, she bit her lip and rushed back to their housewares. She seized a coffee can filled with glass beads and emptied the contents into the knee-deep water, then handed the empty can to Nate.

"Keep the water out with this, Nate." Nate took the coffee can and held it numbly, as if he were unable to understand her words. "The water, like this." Ruth seized the can angrily and bailed a few scoops of water, then handed the can back to Nate. Surprised by his mother's anger, Nate started to cry. She glanced over at Prudence, who was blinking repeatedly as the water fell from the sky into their boat.

"Mama!" Nate cried, holding his arms out to Ruth.

Ruth considered. Even with the children bailing, the boat would certainly swamp. But it was a better chance for the children than staying on the furniture, which she knew would sink. Even filled with water, the boat might float if the children didn't panic. They had to stay on the boat. She looked back at the wardrobe which was perched on the highest point of land; it was nearly submerged. Her shock at the quickness of the water's advance had given way to anger and action, but now she was left to wait. She and Daisy could hang onto a piece of furniture, but the water was cold. They wouldn't last twenty minutes, even partially submerged. Ruth glanced at Daisy, who had dashed toward the boat and seized Prudence in a crazed panic, hugging the child so tightly that Prudence was bent over backward, her back as flexible as a rag doll. Daisy was blubbering, near hysteria.

Ruth looked up into the sky. The sun was about to set, and any ability to find a hold on the walls and climb to safety had vanished as the chunks of slate continued to fall from the quarry walls. Ruth shuddered as she considered what might happen if the boat strayed too close to the sides of the quarry.

"Nate," she said, pulling the boat close to her. "Take the oar and stay out in the middle of the water. You hear me? The middle of the water! Do it now." Nate picked up the oar.

"But what about you and Aunt Daisy?" he asked.

"We're fine. You stay with the boat; it's safer because you're smaller. We're taller; we can stand above the water. We'll be okay," she said.

Nate looked doubtfully at his mother and shook his head. Ruth felt a sense of love, intense love, toward the two children who were clutching to the sides of the boat, both of them shaking with fear and the cold. Ruth had spent little time contemplating her own death, and on the few occasions she had done so, she always imagined darkness and pain; children and love had never been part of the equation. The pain, she knew, would come soon, and she hoped, with an intensity she had never known, that the children would be spared. She squeezed Prudence and Nate tightly, silently thanking God for having them near.

"I love you," she said. The children clung to her until she pushed the boat away, motioning to Nate to paddle into the middle of the water. Ruth turned to find Daisy and take what steps they could to safeguard themselves.

Daisy, up to her waist in water, appeared to have entered a trance, still transfixed by the geyser of water falling from the side of the quarry. Ruth followed Daisy's gaze and looked up at the water as well. The last rays of the sun reflected off the top of the streaming water and had formed a rainbow which arced from one side of the quarry to the other. Despite herself, Ruth smiled, blinking up into the black rain.

"Maybe it's a good omen," Ruth said, and she closed her eyes.

8.

At those quiet luncheons after funerals, grieving families talk in low tones about how soon things will get back to normal. They eat the sandwiches put out for them, the bread as cold as the meat from having spent the morning in the refrigerator, they sip their lemonade or soda pop, and they hope to not always feel dazed and stupid. Most of all, they look forward to waking up the next morning when all of this will be over.

Then the next morning comes, and they wake up into what they hoped would be a "normal" world and find instead they are still stunned and shocked and grieving. Despite the emotional truth of what they are feeling, more than a few of these people look in their mirrors and nod their heads bravely, determined to act "normal," repressing something important and unpleasant deep within themselves, hoping it won't emerge at an inopportune time. But it always does.

The townsfolk of Black Rock allowed life in Black Rock to slowly return to "normal" in the days following Tokyo's confrontation with the flag salesman. Penn returned to Luke's house and even started to work with him crafting slate furniture in Luke's cramped workshop. Tokyo returned to her back room and helped Amos with the small chores as well as working on the books and endless inventory reconciliations. Neither Sis nor Penn nor Luke talked further about what they had said to Tokyo, nor did any of them speculate about what the future held; they simply concentrated on what they perceived to be their tasks in any given day and endeavored to complete them. They ate dinner, talked about the wind, and retired to a fitful sleep, telling themselves the wind sounded normal, as if such a thing could be true.

On one such morning, before the sun had even come up, Tokyo awoke. Usually slow to come to consciousness, Tokyo opened her eyes quickly, surprised to find herself lying in bed. Her dreams had been filled with confused images of her mother, and the wind, intermingled with vain attempts to find a safe place to make love with Luke. Realizing slowly it had been a dream, Tokyo relaxed and stared up at the tapestry to her right.

Since Sis had told her the story of the Indian maiden, Tokyo had a new appreciation for the tapestry. Before, she might have glanced at it without even noticing the pattern, but now, after Sis's story, she was drawn to the maiden's eyes, the fearful, surprised look on her face and the swirling winds emanating from the pouch in her hands. Tokyo blinked slowly and rubbed her face, feeling with her fingertips the salty remains of dried tears at the corners of her eyes.

The wind sounded odd this morning. Typically, a whistling sound of this sort meant some part of the store's exterior had broken loose and would be a project for Amos all morning, a project he would actually have to undertake, patching and hammering until the wind's damage had been repaired. Only then would the familiar sound of the wind blowing over the store return, and Amos would nod happily and move on to his normal planning of chores.

Tokyo knew beyond doubt that she had changed. If she hadn't, she would have already left this strange place. Indeed, her plans of stealing money from Amos and taking the next truck out had been set years before Luke had asked her to stay. But yesterday the supply truck had come and gone, and Tokyo had watched it go, helplessly, wondering why she had failed to go. She had trudged through the remainder of the day confused and angry, seemingly unable to do anything beyond what was normal for her Black Rock self. And last night, as she lay down in bed listening to the wind, she had vowed to take some action the next day, action that would move her out of pretending to be normal to actually being normal. She had made such vows before, but this time she was determined to follow through. Her brave decisiveness of the previous evening evaporated in the haze of morning semiconsciousness. At such times, waking and moving were struggle enough for Tokyo.

But on this morning, as in past mornings during the last several weeks, she vowed again to talk to Luke. She knew her release from this place had something to do with him, something well beyond her promise to him. Her anger at this fact was all-consuming and caused her to nearly leap out of bed.

As Tokyo grabbed her clothes out of the drawers of the bureau in her room, she noticed, not for the first time, how the drawers were so finely fit within their openings, so snugly she felt the slight breath of wind each drawer released as she closed it. Luke had made this bureau. She knew this workmanship was the result of Luke's endless hours in his shop. He would say of this perfectly fitted drawer that it was *snick*.

Something about Luke's tedious attention to detail left Tokyo with no choice but to talk to him today. She reached for a bulky sweater to pull on over her white tee shirt, then pulled on a pair of sweatpants with a faded University logo, an old pair of Amos's which had shrunk beyond use. Before she walked down the hall to the bathroom, she took an extra hooded sweatshirt, for the mornings in the front of the store and at the breakfast table could be cold.

As she walked down the hall to the kitchen, she heard Amos and Sis stirring in their room. She could hear no words. She smiled wryly. Maybe she stayed in Black Rock for the silence of the people. Maybe the reluctance of Luke, of Amos and Sis, of anyone other than Tongate to do much talking at all—maybe it was the silence that kept her here. The silence was more than worth the price of living with the noise of the wind.

In the kitchen, she thought about Penn. Her father. Not for the first time, she considered whether he could be lying, but was answered once again by the questions: Why? Why would he lie about this? Why would he be here?

"Looking for you, maybe."

Tokyo turned to see Sis enter the kitchen. Tokyo hadn't known she had been talking out loud, and felt embarrassed and angry once again for sharing her thoughts unknowingly with Sis.

"Why, after all these years? For what?"

Sis shrugged as she bent to watch the pilot flame in the stove ignite one of the burners. She took a stained coffeepot from the rack and filled it with water. Tokyo watched Sis work absently, as she did most mornings. Her simple movements reminded Tokyo once again of some slow dance, the music for which only Sis could hear. Her graceful movements in the kitchen were a welcome transition into the day for Tokyo, a distraction which helped her to forget the difficulty she faced in waking.

"Being my father—it doesn't mean anything to me," Tokyo said to Sis's back. Sis didn't turn, but her movements stopped for a moment. Then she resumed filling the coffeepot. Tokyo, even more angry and embarrassed for having engaged, cleared her throat. Finally, Sis turned and placed three coffee mugs on the table, smiling at Tokyo.

"Everyone has a father," Sis said. "Why should you be any different?"

9.

It was late morning by the time Apie, Tiller, Shlomo, and Noah had gotten into Apie's car. Apie watched Noah carefully, waiting for some sign of respect for the brand-new car. But Noah, who had spent little time in the mechanized world, and less noticing the shiny cars produced by large companies for men like Apie, sat impassively in the front seat as Apie drove.

As was his custom, Apie drove fast, though not as fast as he would have liked, due to the headwind. He glanced now and again at Noah, who seemed to be squirming in his seat. Noah shifted back and forth, then put one hand up on the dashboard to support his massive frame. He leaned backward, pressing so far into his seat that Tiller, sitting immediately behind him, felt the pressure of Noah's back on his knees, which were pressed up against the back of his seat from behind.

Apie peered out the window as the car sped over the rise and onto the mesa. "Just like the old days, eh? Only a lot easier in this car."

"You know the way?" Shlomo asked.

Apie laughed. "Ain't but one road, Shlomo. Just tell me when to stop." He glanced at Noah again and grinned. "Too fast for you?"

"Eh? Fast? I didn't notice. But this vehicle is so cramped I can't understand why you drive it. Of course, I suppose it's a special one, made for smaller men like you."

Apie's smile disintegrated, and he pressed harder on the accelerator. He glanced again at Noah and knew in an instant that Noah meant no harm. Noah assumed the facts as he saw them, but still the words rankled. As if to escape them, Apie drove faster, and the car cut through the headwind with a distinct whistle. In the back seat, Tiller looked over at Shlomo nervously.

"I didn't buy this place because of you, Noah." Apie pointed out of the windshield. "I didn't know you were still here. Never would have figured it. But when I found out you were here, it made it so much better. Yes, indeedy." Apie drew out the last syllable. "Indeed-eeeee."

Noah nodded as the car approached the new quarry. He pointed. "This is the new quarry. Let's stop and I'll show you—"

Apie shook his head. "I want to see the old quarry first. Then we'll come back."

Noah twisted in his seat. "Well, then. Let me tell you about New Town. My family lives there. And Shlomo's. We built something out of nothing there. We triumphed over this living hell on earth and planted roots."

"I don't have a family, you know," Apie interrupted. "I did once, sure. My folks, I mean. I never married. Family died off. Just me and my money. Lots of women, for sure. But no family. Why have one? Never needed one, really." He spoke quickly, in staccato bursts.

Noah bit his lip. In the back seat, Shlomo shrugged, Apie watched him in the rearview mirror.

"I dreamed of this place, you know," Apie said. "Couldn't get it out of my goddamn dreams. Sorry, magistrate. Just couldn't stop hearing the wind, seeing the damn wind, even feeling it in my goddamn dreams. Couldn't shake it."

Shlomo leaned forward. "It gets that way on you, Apie. You ain't the only one."

"What about you, Noah? You dream of this place?"

Noah ignored the question, instead pointing to the mounds of unsalable slate which rose near the rim of New Town. Apie slowed the car near the outcroppings of slate. Shlomo and Noah, their spirits lifted at the prospect of seeing their families again, got out and began moving expertly toward the quarry. Tiller was stunned by the force of the wind that burst into the car. He leaned backward, blinking his eyes rapidly to keep them moist. Apie grinned back at Tiller and yelled to be heard over the wind.

"You ever seen anything like this, magistrate? Worse than the town, huh?"

Tiller seemed frightened. Apie, facing backward in his seat, took a moment to enjoy the magistrate's discomfort. Shlomo and Noah were disappearing from view behind a slate ledge.

"Let's go see what I bought from under old Noah's nose, magistrate."

Tiller leaned to his left and shut Shlomo's door. "Let me gather myself for a moment, please," he said. Apie shrugged. The man sounded like a girl.

"Suit yourself, magistrate. But I want to see this."

Apie got out of the car and walked slowly into the wind. The path from the road to the rim of the quarry rose slightly for twenty yards, then, he supposed, began downward into the quarry. As he left the road, the path turned crosswind, and Apie cursed under his breath, remembering all the times he had been blown hundreds of feet out of his way when walking crosswind. With great difficulty, he stayed on the path, sometimes grasping the slate outcroppings which upon closer inspection were actually piles of slate, remnants deemed useless by the quarrymen.

"Doesn't matter now, does it?" he said to the wind. "I own you now. You can blow me from here to kingdom come, and I'll still be on my own damn property. How do you like that?" As if in answer, the wind began a series of rapid gusts, each one buffeting Apie to his right. He moved closer to the slate outcroppings and stopped walking, waiting for the particularly hard gusts to stop. When he was satisfied with the wind's relative moderation, he began up the last five yards to the top of the path.

As he crested the path, he became aware of a sound just audible over the wind. It was a strange sound, like the sound of a coyote howling in pain. *Probably the damned wind trying something else,* Apie thought. He stopped for a moment to get his bearings, then continued walking, straight up the path toward the sound.

At the top of the path, Apie nearly ran into Shlomo, who was standing upright, and Noah, who was kneeling, clutching onto Shlomo's jacket with both hands. Noah's hat had blown off and was nowhere to be seen. His head was back, his mouth open. He was howling, howling loudly like the coyote Apie had imagined, his eyes wide and unseeing. His words were only occasionally comprehensible, interspersed with wails and moans. Noah turned toward Apie, not even recognizing him, then turned back toward the quarry.

"Dear God ..." Noah said, and his voice choked off into another wailing howl.

Apie looked down into the black water which had filled the quarry overnight. On one side of the quarry he saw a bubbling under the surface of the water which he supposed to be the water source. Shlomo, who seemed to be only slightly more lucid than Noah, turned to Apie, his face white and filled with horror.

"Where's the quarry you took my slate out of? Where's your families?" Apie asked.

Noah pushed himself desperately away from Shlomo and fell heavily on the ground next to the slate rim. His actions reminded Apie of a wild animal caught inside a trap. He put his hands to his face, almost clawing at his eyes. Shlomo, in a state of shock, pointed down to the black water.

"There," he said quietly, just audible over the wind. "Down there."

Apie took a few steps forward past Noah and Shlomo to where he could get a full view of the water-filled quarry. He turned back to Shlomo and Noah. "So when did they move out of there? Where are they now?"

Shlomo shook his head. "The quarry ... it was safe a week ago."

Apie, never the smartest man in any group, suddenly understood. "You mean they drowned? They're really down there?"

Noah suddenly stopped moving and stared at Apie. His lips moved as if he were trying to speak, but no sounds came out. His eyebrows were knit together in consternation. Apie, who had come to Black Rock in part for just this moment, was confused. He turned away and looked at the water, shaking his head. Suddenly, he stopped moving and pointed.

"There's something floating!"

Noah remained on the ground. Shlomo numbly limped forward a few steps to Apie's side. As he peered down to where Apie was pointing, he suddenly stood bolt upright and turned to Noah. "Noah! It's the cradle!"

Only dimly aware of the meaning of Shlomo's words, but hearing the note of hope in Shlomo's voice, Noah stood and joined the other two men on the lip of the quarry. Where they were standing, they were well-protected from the wind and could easily hear each other. Noah looked down to where the other two men pointed. Below them, floating as Ruth had hoped it might, the cradle pressed up against the side of the quarry.

"Damn," Apie said. "What's in that?"

10.

Luke awoke suddenly, gasping for breath, his arms flailing. As his eyes became accustomed to the familiar darkness of his bedroom, his rapid breathing slowed. It had been a dream. He was safe. He looked down at the foot of his bed to where he had pushed his blankets. Beneath him, the sheet was soaked with sweat. His forehead and hair were also damp. He wiped the moisture away with a trembling hand.

It had been a dream, a dream he hadn't had for years, a dream he dreaded. The dream was always dark, wet, and chaotic. In it, Luke is in a cradle with Amos next to him, and water seems to be raining down on them from a darkening sky. There are splashing noises and women and children's voices pleading, arguing, crying. Suddenly, the cradle is lifted into a small boat by a woman who looks like she is in agony. Soon it grows very dark, and the rain stops. Something has been placed over the cradle. The woman commands a little girl and a boy to climb into the boat on each side of the cradle. Luke sees the terrified faces of a boy and a girl as they clutch the sides of the boat. Luke keeps hearing screams, "Mama! Mama!"

He sees the boy and girl desperately trying to grab their mothers. He sees two women, one trying to soothe them, the other clutching her hair and face in paralyzed terror, then grabbing the girl to hug her. Then the boat is pushed off. The screams grow louder now, echoed by the sobbing of the mothers. The boat is rocking horribly. Then one of the mothers throws herself into the water after the boat, screaming, "Prudy! Luke!"

She tries to swim but is soon flailing and choking. The other mother screams out, "Daisy, you'll drown!" Then she jumps in after Daisy but soon starts struggling herself. Daisy pauses for a moment in the dark water, turns and looks Luke in the eyes and, without a word, sinks under the surface. As she sinks, Luke feels his own lungs crushed with the incredible weight of a breath he cannot take.

Next to him, in the boat, the girl shrieks. The other woman is faring no better in the cold water as her head bobs below the surface, then reappears gasping for breath, then goes under again. As the water overwhelms her, she mouths some words that seem to be a desperate prayer for the children's safety. Then she's gone and the boy is crying, "Mama! Come up! Mama!"

The end of the dream is always murky. There is a huge crash and suddenly the screaming boy and girl vanish and bits of wood and a coil of rope land in the cradle. And then there is just the sound of water hitting water, and babies crying and crying.

Luke woke up crying and choking from the dream. Too exhausted to do anything but remain motionless, he calmed himself by listening to the harsh screeching wind. After a moment or two, against his better judgment, he glanced over to Tokyo's side of the bed and felt again the pain of her absence.

11.

Shlomo turned to Noah. "The babies, Noah. They saved the babies."

Noah nodded and began taking off his heavy black jacket. Shlomo watched his friend carefully fold his jacket and place it on the slate near his feet.

"But the ladders, they aren't there, Noah. There's no way to get down there."

Noah looked down below his feet to where the series of ladders should have been. Instead, he saw broken slate and streams of ice-cold water trickling from innumerable cracks in the side of the wall. It would be impossible to climb down, impossible to climb back up. The surface of the water, he figured, was twenty feet below him. His house, his wife, and his daughter were some sixty feet below the surface. The cradle carrying his son and Shlomo's seemed to have a rope entangled in it. It was close enough to him that he could swim to it and maybe, if he was lucky, attach the rope and toss it up to Shlomo. Shlomo could pull the cradle to safety.

Noah looked at the steep, wet walls of the quarry. There would be no climbing out of the quarry; he would be sacrificing his life for the children. He wouldn't be there to guide them, to teach them. They'd be on their own.

Noah began unbuttoning his billowing white shirt. His skin beneath his shirt was pale and ghostly. Shlomo watched as Noah bent down to remove his black boots. "The water's too cold, Noah. It'll chill you and you'll sink like a stone," Shlomo said.

Apie nodded anxiously, his fantasies of vengeance evaporating as he began to comprehend the horror of this tragedy. "You don't even know if they're alive!" he said.

Noah ignored them and continued undressing. When he was down to his trousers, he stood upright and put his hand on Shlomo's shoulder.

"If they're alive, you raise him right. You raise him to love this place. He's got to love it, because this place killed all of us. I didn't know it, but it killed me a long time ago—I've just been too goddamned stubborn."

"Noah, we can drive back and get help. We can get ladders …"

Apie nodded, suddenly moved by a desire to be helpful. "We can, too. Noah, look. I'll drive back to the other quarry. The men—"

"By the time you get back, I'll be dead. That's what you wanted, isn't it? You're the devil, come to chase me to hell."

Apie shook his head. "I'm no devil, Noah. I ain't the one dressed in black."

Noah looked down at his black trousers, a stark contrast to his pallid body. He looked back up at the sky.

"But we are all as an unclean thing, and all our righteous acts are as filthy rags; and we all do fade as a leaf; and our inquiries, like the wind, have taken us away."

And with a solemn nod to his old friend, Noah jumped from the lip of the quarry and hit the surface of the unforgiving cold water.

12.

In his workroom, Luke used a fine steel file to smooth the corner of a large slab of slate. In time, the slate would serve as the inset on a table, a replacement for the one which had dominated Luke's kitchen for years. The current one appeared fine, even beautiful, to Penn, but Luke seemed absorbed in the project, and, to pass the time, Penn decided to help. The two men worked wordlessly, sometimes for hours, with Luke grimacing slightly now and again when he was particularly pleased with some aspect of his new table.

Shortly after noon each day the two men climbed into Luke's truck and drove in silence to Amos's store, where they sat down to lunch with Sis, Amos, and Tokyo. None of them spoke, except about the normal topics: the wind, the weather, the town. Proudfoot and Tongate would saunter into the store after lunch, and the group would listen to Tongate's blather until Luke stood, nodded a silent thanks to Sis and Amos, and walked out with Penn.

As the lunches passed, Penn began to realize he was participating in some kind of long waiting game. Amos and Sis were waiting, it seemed, because they knew of no other way to survive. There was no event they were expecting; rather, they stood like passengers awaiting a bus which had been due hours ago, passengers who had long ago forsaken impatience for a wordless stupor.

On the other hand, Luke was clearly waiting for a sign from Tokyo. He glanced at her when he knew she would notice, certain she knew he was looking for a sign. He did it with subtlety, yet not enough subtlety to hide his motives. Tokyo couldn't be sure of what he wanted, but, whatever it was, she felt unequipped to supply it.

Like Sis and Amos, Tokyo was waiting for no particular event; indeed, she had gone to great lengths to avoid "events."

Penn was amused as he thought of his situation. *As much as she has tried to avoid it, here I am, sitting at the table, observing her and all these people. Waiting.* How he would approach her, tell her there was nothing he wanted from her, tell her in a way she wouldn't buck and run, he couldn't tell.

"What are you doing living out here, Luke?"

File in hand, Luke looked up at Penn. Fine slate dust covered Luke's blue jeans and old leather work shoes. Luke leaned forward and blew the dust onto the floor and felt the corner of the slate with his thumb. "Look at that," he said, holding the slate up for Penn's inspection. "Feel it."

Penn reached out and touched the slate corner with two fingers. It was smooth and still warm from the friction of the file.

"I mean, here on the mesa. With your skill, you could make a lot of money in the city." Penn gestured vaguely at the various pieces of furniture surrounding them, some completed, some still pieces of wood and slate bound together with nothing more than an idea.

"I live here," Luke shrugged.

"But, I mean …"

Luke stroked the corner of the slate with his file. He winced, then stopped. "The guy who raised me, he knew my father. Told me my father was big on roots, you know?" Luke shrugged again, as if there were nothing left to say.

"How do you survive out here? It's not a place to live."

Luke sighed and placed the file on the worktable carefully, as if he were afraid to make a sound. He needn't have bothered, Penn thought. Today's howling wind would obliterate any sound below a loud voice. Penn watched Luke's lined face, the distinctive grimace which could mean anything from physical pain to happiness. Finally, Luke looked up at Penn, his blue eyes shockingly bright. He hunched his shoulders, then dropped them again. "It's just like any other place, I guess."

Penn smiled, thinking of the places the Army had taken him. He had a brief flash of himself years earlier in Bangkok, his crisp khaki uniform losing a slow war of attrition to the dense tropical humidity; he was waiting impatiently for his Japanese girlfriend on her aunt's screened porch. Thailand, Japan, New York City, upstate New York, Chicago: these were a few of the places. No, this place was most definitely unlike any other place. He shook his head as he listened to the wind's outright roar outside the house. The wind seemed malevolent to Penn. He could picture its unseen hands prying at the house, looking desperately for cracks to start, to widen, then to tear. He had seen the massive erosion caused not by water, but wind on the scratched surface slate of the mesa, and he wondered how men and women of flesh and bone could survive here. Or even want to.

"How do you make a living, though? You don't sell any of your furniture."

"Don't need much. Amos sees to what I need. That's it." Luke twisted in his seat. "Looks like it's time for lunch. You coming?"

"Why not?" Penn replied. What alternative did he have? The two men brushed the wood and slate dust off their clothes. Penn watched the sunlight catch the waves of dust in the air, watched the dust drift lazily in a shaft of sunlight until it was caught from some unseen intrusion of wind which had found a crack somewhere in Luke's solid house, a crack too small to detect, watched the wind obliterate the lazy dust in an explosion of movement. Penn pursed his lips and blew, watching the dust circle around his breath, a weak imitation of the wind outside the house.

In his truck, driving toward town, Luke reflected on Penn's inquisitive nature. He had imagined Penn's questions would decrease in number and frequency as the days wore on, but he had thus far been disappointed. Penn had a knack for asking questions, Luke thought, a knack so irritating that Luke considered letting his impatience and anger show. It might be good, Luke thought. Teach him when to stop. But even the thought of displaying anger tired Luke beyond all measure. Silence was better, more forgiving.

Penn had already sensed the other man's ongoing discomfort. At worst, Penn knew, he would be kicked out of the house and driven to town. There he would do his best to find a ride to the next town, since he was certain beyond doubt of Ayako's unwillingness to share a house with him for even one night. He wondered if Luke kicked him out whether he would have the chance to talk to her before he left town. Penn glanced over at Luke, who concentrated on the windswept road in front of the truck. Although they were riding with the wind, the truck rocked wildly as rogue gusts pushed the truck from behind at irregular intervals.

Watching Luke's strong hands working the steering wheel, Penn suddenly realized his fears were unfounded. Luke wouldn't kick him out of the house. As long as Penn was present, Luke's waiting game with Ayako would remain unchanged. Even more, Penn realized, Luke might believe Penn's presence would push Ayako toward Luke—the known versus the unknown—a man she had lived with for years versus a man who had appeared mysteriously and announced his relationship unexpectedly. Penn smiled broadly at Luke.

Feeling Penn's eyes on him, Luke turned his head briefly. He raised his eyebrows, an unspoken, "What?" Emboldened by his realization, Penn eagerly asked, "Do you love her?"

Luke's grip tightened on the steering wheel. His jaw clenched. He had never even explained to Tokyo how he felt about her, in large part because he had no clear conception in his own mind. From the outside, one would have said he depended on her housekeeping skills. But his feelings went beyond the simple creature comforts and occasional physical contact with Tokyo. He needed to be near her for some reason he couldn't articulate, even if they didn't talk to each other for hours, even if her anger had built up and made any communication impossible. That Tokyo had never asked Luke such a question was a relief; he would have been hard-pressed to explain. The past weeks without her had been unbearable. The wind seemed louder, Penn's questions more irritating, and even Sis's normally reliable cooking seemed tasteless. Luke knew he depended on Tokyo in some inexplicable way; her quiet presence was reassuring to him, more reassuring than a person who talked a lot. Or asked a lot of questions. If he couldn't explain his feelings to Tokyo, how on earth would he explain them to Penn?

"I'm her father, you know."

In consternation, Luke looked over at Penn. Did he read thoughts?

Penn looked back out the front windshield. "Not that it matters, really. I just wondered."

Neither man spoke again until the truck had reached the street outside Amos's store. Luke turned off the engine, and, instead of getting out, he reached over and held Penn's arm, just below the older man's elbow. His grip was firm, but friendly.

"I don't know, Penn. If I knew, I guess I'd tell you." He paused. "I guess I would." Luke nodded, his own exclamation point.

Penn nodded, but Luke retained his grip. "Do you love her?" Luke asked. Penn looked down quickly and examined the worn rubber floormat at his feet. Luke let go of his arm and shook his head. "It's easy to ask questions, isn't it?" Luke opened the door and jumped to the street, then slammed the truck shut and walked toward the store in a straight line, as if there were no wind at all.

13.

"I never meant for him to die," Apie said, somewhat plaintively.

He sat at Shlomo's counter supporting his head, staring forward. Behind the counter, Shlomo had opened a can of condensed milk and had mixed it with water. He carefully placed the mixture in a pot and heated it. Apie watched as Shlomo, his hands trembling, tested the temperature of the milk with his middle finger, then wiped his hand on the back of his pants. From a cabinet he took the smallest teaspoon he could find and walked over to the cradle, reaching in to move the heavy blankets he had heaped on the two cold babies.

Carefully, he spooned a small amount of the mixture and placed it outside of Amos's lips. The baby stuck his tongue out, refusing to feed. Shlomo dipped his smallest finger in the milk and placed some on Amos's lips, with the same result. He then moved the spoon to Luke, who eagerly accepted the spoon and turned his head to hungrily watch it withdraw from his cradle. Amos was moving his tongue, having cleaned the sweet milk off his lips, and Shlomo sighed gratefully as his son accepted a small spoonful more.

"I never meant for him to die, Shlomo. You've got to believe me."

Shlomo shook his head. His voice trembled as he spoke. "Had nothing to do with you, Apie. Nothing at all." Magistrate Tiller and the men from the quarry who had helped Shlomo lift the waterlogged bassinet out of the quarry sat at the far end of the long counter in silence, sometimes exchanging meaningful looks and even muted whispers. Tiller, who had long since abandoned his hopes of returning home by sunset, thought glumly about the prospect of another long drive with Apie.

"I never knew his family. I never knew your family. I didn't want them to die. I just wanted …"

Shlomo turned to Apie. "What did you want?" He was genuinely puzzled.

Apie's mouth worked soundlessly. He turned to Tiller, who quickly averted his eyes.

"He didn't mean it, did he? All those years ago? He wouldn't have shot me, would he?"

The babies had recovered some healthy pink color, and the tips of their noses, which had been ice-cold when they first came into the store, were now slightly warm and runny. Shlomo nodded as Luke greedily took more of the milk.

"Did Noah mean it?" Shlomo shook his head and stood, suddenly appearing extremely tall. His normal stoop-shouldered, limping appearance effectively hid his height, but now, in anger, he drew himself to his full stature. He leaned across the counter and pointed the dripping spoon angrily at Apie.

"Did you see him out there? Did you? In all the years I've known him, Apie, he's meant every word he said. He's with his God now, in his Kingdom, I guess. In his paradise. And you ask whether he meant it? Goddammit, Apie."

Apie lowered his head into his hands, covering his face. He might have been crying; it was hard to tell. Tiller, appalled by voices raised in anger, or any emotional scene, turned and looked out the front window. The quarrymen, used to Shlomo's normally smooth demeanor, stood gaping in quiet surprise. Some of them shuffled to the door.

Shlomo leaned further across the counter and cuffed Apie on the side of the head with an open hand, not hard enough to knock him down, but hard enough to get his attention. Apie looked up, surprised. Shlomo noticed one of the quarrymen, a born peacekeeper, take a few steps toward them, but Shlomo stopped him by shaking his head.

"He'd have shot you dead where you stood if you hadn't gotten out of there, Apie. And there's others, I'm sure, that'd do the same thing to you if they had a chance. They wouldn't care about your car, your money, or your judge. But there's damn few of them, aren't there, Apie? Damned few have got the backbone to take you on now you're rich."

Apie stared up at Shlomo, his eyes wide.

"And Noah might be dead, and his family, and," and here Shlomo choked slightly, "mine, but, damn you, don't you ask whether he meant it! Don't you ask me that!" Shlomo turned his back on Apie and looked to the cradle, where both babies were squirming; Amos had begun whimpering at the noise.

Apie, still staring up at Shlomo, said, "Your family, Shlomo. I'm sorry."

Shlomo seemed to wilt back into his grieving self. His shoulders rounded and his limp returned as he picked up the pot and returned it to the burner. He spoke to no one in particular as he stirred the milk absently.

"Two Nates, I've lost. Lost without a trace. And my beautiful Ruth." His shoulders began heaving, and he dropped the spoon onto the floor. One of the quarrymen came to his side and took him by the arm, walking him into the back room. The last time Apie saw him, Shlomo's face was twisted in pain, fighting back sobs. As the quarryman led Shlomo into the back, Apie looked at the babies, then turned toward the remaining quarrymen and Tiller.

"I hated him. Him and his righteousness. I was going to show him, I was. Guess I did." Apie took a deep breath and held it a long time. Finally, he looked over at the babies and exhaled. "What are their names?" he asked quietly. The voice of a defeated man.

One of the quarrymen cleared his throat. "Luke was Noah's. Amos there, that's Shlomo's."

Apie nodded and pointed to Tiller, suddenly animated. "Take a note of that, magistrate. And let's go. We've got work to do."

14.

The wind started deep below the surface of the sun when two atoms of hydrogen collided in a place of unthinkable heat and unimaginable pressure and in their collision left a legacy of even more heat and more pressure which formed itself into a stream of energy that bolted out from the sun's core and erupted into space at incalculable speed. Where it was struck by this solar wind, the earth was heated and the warm air rose. Waves of cold air waited patiently to replace the warm air, and at Black Rock Mesa, the cold air rushed in with an appalling swiftness known nowhere else in the world.

And on this morning as Amos walked into the kitchen where Sis and Tokyo were already sipping coffee, the wind sounded different to him, unusual in a way that had troubled his sleep and made him deeply uneasy. As he poured himself a cup of coffee, he cocked his head, listening. Tokyo noticed.

"Sounds like you're losing some planks off the store, Amos," she said.

Amos nodded. "Could be. Have to check it out this morning, I guess."

And he did, walking around his store twice, finding nothing out of place. On his second trip around the store, Tongate emerged from his house just as Amos was standing in the street shading his eyes, looking up at the flat surface of his roof.

"It would be easily construed to be a malformation of your habituation, Amos. But there is nothing wrong with your structural integrity. Nothing at all."

Not for the first time, Amos wished Tongate would lose some weight and be swept away with the wind. Tongate was correct, of course, there was no damage to his store. But the sound of the wind was puzzling, unlike anything Amos had heard before.

"Strange, isn't it?" Tongate yelled to be heard over the wind. His pink face barely visible under the hood of his heavy coat, Tongate took a few sideways steps, like a crab, carefully keeping his back to the wind. He leaned heavily against the side of the store, protected somewhat from the wind. Amos considered his choices: He could find something, somewhere to patch, or he could spend all morning listening to Tongate's blather. He stepped to the door. Tongate moved to block him.

"A tonal difference," he yelled. "It could be a harbinger of change. Big change."

Amos shook his head. "When was the last time anything changed around here, Barney?"

In answer, Tongate winked and smiled. "Everything's changing all the time, Amos. Here and everywhere."

Even though there was nothing to patch, Amos went inside the store to find his ladder and bucket. He'd be damned if he'd listen to Tongate's nonsense this morning.

15.

Shlomo did not spend a great deal of time contemplating the perils of raising two boys on his own; rather, he allowed his instincts to lead him where he otherwise would have relied on his wife. When instincts failed him, he tried to predict what actions Ruth would have taken in a particular circumstance. After a time, he stopped visiting the water-filled quarry to pay his respects, not because of the difficulty of the trip, nor because of the pain he felt while there, but rather because the boys required more and more attention and could not be trusted to be left alone in the store or even at the rim of the New Town quarry. Through the years, Shlomo limited his visits to the quarry to twice yearly, once on Thanksgiving Day and once on the spring day which marked the anniversary of the tragedy.

The boys grew up quietly, learning the chores of the store and taking on more and more of Shlomo's responsibilities as he grew older and his ankle more infirm. Despite the unwelcoming conditions, the town grew slightly, with other families occasionally trying to stay on the mesa and support themselves with earnings from working the quarry. In some cases the men had taken a strange liking to the town and had erected their own homes, at first periodically unattended and battered by the wind, but then, as the men's attraction grew stronger and they moved to the town full time, their homes became places of comfort where they could pride themselves on their ability to survive the conditions in Black Rock as Noah had before them. Proudfoot and Tongate were such men.

As one of the first to stay in the town, Tongate had taken to shuttling monthly back to the city to bring whatever provisions he could which were not carried by the trucks supplying Amos's store. Most particularly, he stopped at the post office and the bank in town, bringing cash for the others to buy from him at slightly inflated prices. He considered the modest premium he charged for cashing checks and the like to be easily defensible by virtue of the trouble he took in driving to town. He didn't

255

mention his personal enjoyment of certain massage parlors during his monthly visits in the city.

The boys learned about New Town early, since Shlomo spoke of it often as they grew. By the time they were in their teens, Luke and Amos felt as if they had actual memories of the doomed quarry. In the back room at night, surrounded by storage racks in the moonlight, the boys told each other details of the town, and Luke and Amos both secretly dreamed of rescuing their families from peril at the last moment.

Neither Luke nor Amos had photographs or drawings of their drowned family members, so they were forced to rely on the descriptions of Shlomo and the occasional quarrymen who regaled them with stories of the past. The boys were eager for details in a way older persons who had lived through such a disaster would not have been, for Amos and Luke knew only the pain of their mothers' absence, not the conscious pain of losing them.

Shlomo would describe Noah, Daisy, Prudence, Nate, and Ruth, and his voice would soften and sometimes his voice would catch and the boys would squint, not out of embarrassment, but in an effort to see the people Shlomo was describing. They learned of Ruth's intellect, of Prudence's temper, of Daisy's simple joys (Shlomo would edit some of the less savory details of her past), of Nate's mischievousness, and, towering over all of them, of Noah. Shlomo had a thing or two to say about Apie, whom the boys knew was the owner and absentee manager of the Johnson quarry.

Luke knew his father had been a religious man, and he often felt guilt at his lack of belief. Once, when Shlomo was recounting a particularly vicious verbal attack Noah had made on a quarryman who had dared to suggest Jesus didn't exist, Luke noticed that Shlomo did not judge the men involved.

"Was he wrong?" Luke had interrupted.

Shlomo, who in these later years enjoyed nothing more than talking about his many experiences on the mesa and otherwise, stopped and looked down at Luke. The boy had blond hair, like his mother's, but the cheekbones and piercing blue eyes of his father. Already, even at this early age, Shlomo could see Noah's drawn, white face in this young boy.

"I've thought a lot about this, boys. About whether Noah was right. Sure, I never believed in his God, not a bit, but I believed in Noah and believed in him so fully I stayed with him all those years. Told myself I couldn't live without the money I made here with him, even though I'd been poor my whole life." The boys were mute. Shlomo could see their lack of understanding. "Look at it this way, boys: I used to pretend I'd hurt my ankle, you know? And pretty soon I'll be damned if the ankle didn't start to hurt. And I couldn't get around anymore without limping for real. It hurt because I made it true. I did it to myself. Your daddy had that gift with other folks, Luke. He made things real for them. Made me think staying with him was the only way. Kept people by his side, he surely did."

"Your father could be wrong in the way he said things, the spirit he brought to things," Shlomo said, thinking particularly about the day Noah had threatened to shoot Apie. "But it's important you know he always was firm in what he believed. Right up to the end. Don't think you can really say whether he was wrong or right. Only his God could tell him whether he was wrong or right."

Luke shook his head. "No, I mean the quarryman. Was he right there was no such person as Jesus?"

Shlomo's eyebrows rose. He gestured to Amos, who, without words, understood his father's desire for more chewing tobacco. Shlomo watched Amos walk to the shelf on which the rough-cut tobacco was kept.

"Now, that's a big question, Luke." Shlomo paused as Amos handed him some dried tobacco leaves. He methodically smoothed the leaves between his thumb and forefinger, then folded them loosely and wedged them in his mouth. He looked down at his moist finger, stained from his recent years of tobacco use, then wiped the saliva off on his pants. Amos and Luke waited patiently, knowing Shlomo would answer virtually any question they asked.

"For the quarryman, I suppose it was right. I suppose he didn't believe there was any such person."

"What about you, Shlomo?"

Shlomo smiled and looked at Amos. "I come from a different place, Luke. Don't need to believe in Jesus. Not one of the requirements, you know? But I'm supposed to believe in other things, other folks that I guess I don't really believe in." His voice softened. "Don't believe in much, really, 'cept where I've been and what I know. That's the only thing's helped me along in my life. Remember that, boys. Remember where you've been and what you've done."

At the age of fourteen, the boys knew only the past Shlomo had taught them, and the history of what they had read in books. Shlomo hadn't read Ruth's books, but he remembered her talking about them, and had done all he could to reassemble a modest library of books for the boys to read. They spent their mornings at chores, working in the store, often work Shlomo invented, make-work projects like pulling cans and jars off the shelves, cleaning the shelves and replacing the goods. In the afternoons, after lunch, Shlomo would set the boys to reading, as he imagined Ruth would have, and he napped in his bedroom.

In later years, given Shlomo's impatience with numbers, Luke and Amos sought to help him with inventories and records of sales. Shlomo's impatience was apparently hereditary and Amos's interest in helping with the "fine details" of the business waned. Both father and son were grateful for Luke's interest in detail and left him to pore over books and records for hours as they talked lazily of the past.

Although most teenagers would have been lonely, Luke enjoyed his solitary afternoons, trying to find errant numbers to make accounts balance, occasionally getting up from his perch and walking to a shelf to count the number of canned peppers, or tomatoes, or boxes of hurricane hinges. He also learned woodwork and slate work on long afternoons when Shlomo taught him. In his memories of such times he could always hear Shlomo's voice, grown gravelly with age, recounting a story of the past, sometimes a story the boys had heard many times before. They silently did their chores as Shlomo's history filled the room around them.

It was on one such afternoon, a Wednesday, that Tongate arrived in the store, smiling more broadly than usual. Interrupted from his story, Shlomo regarded Tongate suspiciously, never having warmed to the younger man. The boys, who looked upon Tongate as a cross between the village idiot and a court jester, only glanced up as he entered. Luke could see Tongate had been to town and was carrying the normal batch of letters and cash for Shlomo's store. Luke reached out, expecting Tongate to hand over the pouch in the normal fashion, but Tongate held back, clutching the pouch to his chest.

"You boys have never had mail, have you?"

Luke and Amos exchanged looks. Tongate, who was spectacularly wrong in assuming any teenager to be only slightly above a dog's level of intelligence, smiled at them. Both Luke and Amos were too polite to demand he hand over whatever mail he had for them; instead, they waited, knowing Tongate would have to do it his way.

"I cannot recall," Tongate began, "when it was in my life that I received my first missive via the U.S. Postal Service. When could it have been?" Tongate put a finger to his temple, an exaggerated gesture. "Perhaps, if I think correctly on it ..."

Sitting in his chair, Shlomo uncrossed his legs suddenly, his massive boots crashing on the floor. Outside, the wind's howling ascended a note, moving from a piercing howl to a continued shriek. Tongate, still clutching the mail pouch to his chest, looked at Shlomo, who merely gestured, his forefinger upright, then curling toward himself. Tongate swallowed, about to resume his speech, when Shlomo stamped the floor again with both feet.

Amos and Luke stifled giggles as Tongate walked meekly to Shlomo and handed him the mail pouch. Shlomo rifled through the normal invoices and junk, then stopped when he found a large envelope addressed to both Luke and Amos. He examined the hard brown envelope, noting the return address.

"It's from a lawyer, it is. Back in Philadelphia," Tongate announced, pleased to salvage some part of the surprise for his own.

Luke and Amos stopped their work and leaned on the counter as Shlomo opened the envelope and reached for his glasses. After a few moments of reading, he shook his head and looked up at Luke and Amos. Then, as if disbelieving, he looked back at the documents in his hand and back up at Amos and Luke.

"Son of a bitch. That damned Apie. How about that?" Shlomo said to no one in particular, then took off his glasses and rubbed his eyes hard.

16.

Tokyo's foster father, a man named Cole, fancied himself to be clever, but he was not. He was educated, to be sure, and had a better-than-average grasp of history, particularly the history of World War II. Penn had talked to him in Boston as both men sat at a simple oak dining table in Cole's orderly home. Cole's wife moved quietly in the kitchen, preparing a dinner to which Penn was not invited.

Cole's father was a businessman, unsuccessful at first; then he overcame his string of failures with a massive triumph in the shipping business. He had meddled in shipping for a time, not able to work his way out of staggering debt. Then, almost by accident, Cole's father had contracted to carry a shipload of bananas from Central America to Boston. The owner of the bananas declared bankruptcy while the boat was in transit, leaving Cole's father with the unpleasant choice of allowing the bananas to go bad or selling them immediately upon arrival. He wisely chose the latter, and was stunned by the amount of cash the produce vendors in the North End were willing to pay upon delivery. As soon as he unloaded his ship, he sent it directly back to Honduras for more bananas.

Cole's family quickly leapt from lower middle class to Boston Brahmin, and his father's company reached its tentacles far into Central and South America, influencing both farmers and governors to send cheap bananas to the family's Central American Imports Company. Although a certain amount of exploitation was inevitable, Cole's father tended to view the bribes and intimidation necessary in Latin America as the normal cost of doing business. In any event, the people he dealt with in Central and South America were not usually white, so he felt no moral issue when cheating or bribing were required.

Ironically, the United Standard Import Company (which had changed hands several times since its creation) and the present owners marketed bananas with great fanfare about adherence to ethical standards. Cole was amused that years of dubious ethical practices apparently could be washed away with clever advertising promotions and protestations of heartfelt ethics.

Cole's father, who otherwise would have insisted his son follow a carefully scripted upbringing, ended up neglecting Cole due to his constant travel to Latin America. Left to his own devices, Cole pursued an academic life.

Cole became a high school teacher. He tried to instill in his foster daughter, Ayako, a curiosity about learning by quizzing her nightly on the books she was reading for school. Dinnertime was chosen as the most reasonable time for such impromptu tests, and Cole repeatedly ridiculed Ayako for her lack of interest in learning. He rarely raised his voice, more often relying on sarcasm and irony to drive his point home.

"I don't suppose," he would say to Ayako, "that it's important to you who was the fifth president of the United States." He would pause to sip coffee or to cut his meat, then continue in his reedy voice, "But some young women would probably believe it was a valuable piece of information."

Cole's only comment to Penn was that she had been a "difficult child." She was prone, Cole said, to long silences and stubborn behavior. She was repeatedly disciplined for her lack of responsiveness and for her defiance.

"Don't look at me like that, young lady," he would say to her after Ayako had dared to glance in his direction. She would look quickly down at her plate, immersed in anger, staring at her peas, or sweet potatoes or cod, seething with what she wanted to say, but afraid to even look up, for where would she go if these foster parents were to reject her?

"My wife, Meryl, and I, we believed it would be a good thing for us to take in a foster child, particularly one from a broken home." Cole raised his eyebrows, his probing insult hanging in the air. Penn remained expressionless. "My wife was unable to conceive, and we thought it would be a welcome broadening of our lives to raise an underprivileged child, particularly if we stayed true to her own culture. The double benefit, of course, was we," and here Cole had gestured again to his wife in the kitchen, "we would also learn about the Japanese culture, a culture which always fascinated me, the insistence on obedience, the reverence shown to one's ancestors …" He paused. "But you would have some familiarity with the culture, wouldn't you?"

Penn nodded.

"And so we took Ayako from the orphanage. You had vanished, and, as you know, her mother was a painful case, but we still insisted she learn about the Japanese culture of her mother and retain her original name, Ayako. She was stubborn, though, as I've said, and insisted on being called Mary one day, or Jane the next, buffeted by the latest name that struck her fancy, whether in a book, a movie, or even a name she heard in a passing conversation. Insufferably difficult to manage a child who can't even decide what she wants to be called."

Penn snorted as he remembered Cole's impatience, wondering what Cole would have said about Ayako today. Cole's wife was a clean woman, given to wearing neat wool dresses. Although both were now in their late sixties, Penn could see, simply by looking around their home, that not much had changed since Ayako had left on the day after her eighteenth birthday. Cole's wife had spoken only twice while Penn visited: once to say good-bye, the other to ask if he wanted more coffee. She had nodded her head in greeting, her eyes downcast, when he first arrived.

Cole was slow to ask why Penn was looking for her, but quick to guess they were related. His trained eye, he told Penn, noticed the family resemblance right away, even before Penn had told Cole.

"But what could you want after all this time?" Cole asked, widening his lips and showing his teeth in what he thought was a smile, but not smiling at all. It was a question of intellectual curiosity to Cole.

Penn, who tried to answer truthfully to most questions, even when he was not so inclined, nodded. "I want to see her. To talk to her."

Cole smiled his nonsmile again. "Of course, she won't be what you expect. Children so rarely are."

"That's why I'm talking to you. And others, along the way."

Cole sipped his coffee noisily and glanced into the kitchen, where he was sure his wife was listening, despite her apparent absorption in the preparation of dinner.

"I pride myself on knowing something about people, having dealt with them for quite some time. You, I think, Mr. Taylor," and Cole pointed with his little finger, "you want to go back and live your life again, differently this time, I think. Maybe this time with your daughter. Since you obviously cannot do so with your wife."

Penn's expression did not change, but he stood and looked into the kitchen.

"Good-bye, Mrs. Cole," he said. She came to the kitchen door hesitantly, like a shy child.

"Good-bye, Mr. Taylor." Her voice was barely audible.

Cole walked him to the door. "Good luck to you, sir," he said, somewhat formally, and the two men shook hands. Penn muttered his thanks and left the house.

17.

As Amos had expected, after a few minutes Tongate grew tired of watching him fiddle with the clapboard siding, and Amos was left alone to carefully caulk any cracks he saw where the slats of wood overlapped each other. Amos had seen the entire side of a house be taken by the wind in a single afternoon, plank by plank, stripped away. All the wind needed was a single toehold, and an entire house could disappear in a matter of a week.

Working on the front of the store, Amos kept his back to the wind by facing down the street, away from the mesa. The ladder he used was double-footed and well anchored to the side of the house by clips Amos kept for just this purpose.

Although the other townsfolk would think him mad to admit it, Amos enjoyed his time out in the wind, especially when he knew safety and stillness were nearby inside the store. Like his father before him, he was addicted to small comforts and usually unwilling to venture out onto the mesa unless there was a good reason. And the number of good reasons seemed to decrease as time went on. But here, ostensibly patching the side of a store devoid of any appreciable cracks, Amos reveled in the isolation from all other people, an isolation enforced by the maddening wind. With safety a few steps away, he could spend all day in the wind. On the mesa, he refused to do much more than roll down the window in his truck.

Standing on his ladder, propped firmly against the wind, he glanced back toward the mesa and saw the plume of dust approaching from the direction of the quarry ten minutes before Luke's truck parked in one of the diagonal spaces in front of Amos's store. He watched with some curiosity as the two men did not exit the truck immediately. From his perch he was unable to see their faces, but he watched as the driver—he knew it was Luke, since Luke, always wanting to be in control, insisted no one else drive his truck—held the passenger by the arm for a moment, then opened the door and walked into the store. The passenger—it could only have been Penn—slumped forward in the seat and held still for so long Amos wondered whether he might have fainted. Normally Amos would have waited until Penn moved, but outside in the wind such patience was foolhardy. He started down the ladder.

Penn looked up in time to see Amos walking toward the truck. Penn smiled a greeting, and Amos waved one big leather glove. Amos stuck one thumb up in the air, his fist clenched, and cocked his head. Penn nodded and returned the gesture, mouthing the words, "I'm okay." Satisfied, Amos pointed to the door of his store and walked back to his ladder to unlash it from its tight moorings.

Instead of following Amos's unspoken advice, Penn steeled himself for the wind and slid over to the driver's door, opening it carefully to avoid damage.

As Amos unleashed the ladder from the hooks built into the outside wall for that purpose, he briefly fought the wind's desire to seize the ladder and send it into a tumbling frenzy. With some difficulty he brought the ladder to the ground, then noticed another pair of hands, Penn's, pinning the ladder to the ground as well. Amos nodded his thanks and gestured. Penn returned the nod, understanding Amos would open the door and then they would carry the ladder into the store.

When they lifted, Amos was careful to keep the ladder no more than a foot or two off the surface of the ground, knowing the wind above such a height would be more threatening. Penn stooped, following Amos's lead.

Inside, Amos turned to Penn and nodded again. Penn released his grip on the ladder and watched as Amos propped it up against the wall near the door. Luke sat alone at the counter, his back to the two men. Tokyo and Sis were making lunch in the kitchen, and Penn shook his head at the prospect of another mealtime. He knew the uneasy truce among the five of them couldn't last, but the contest to see who would be first to break it was unnerving.

Soon, as they all sat at the table, only the sounds of clinking silverware, pouring coffee, and food being chewed broke the silence. Tokyo kept her eyes focused downward, as did Luke. Amos and Sis seemed impassive, eyes fixed ambiguously straight ahead, deviating from time to time to each other in some apparently shared understanding. In the corner, the handloom sat in a comfortable workplace. Several of Sis's weavings were stacked around her stool, forming a small, brightly colored nest in which Sis worked. Penn, like most people, assumed Sis might have preferred to locate her loom near a window with a view, but he came to understand that Sis was oblivious to the outside world while her hands flashed the shuttle back and forth on the loom. Indeed, after watching Sis's peaceful demeanor at the loom, Penn soon realized she might even have considered a view to be an unwelcome intrusion on the world she had created. When seized by a project, she sometimes worked all day, weaving with a dreamy, lost expression on her face, stopping late at night only in deference to Amos and Tokyo's desire for quiet sleep. Of course, she also stopped to prepare breakfast, lunch, and dinner.

Sis's meal was characteristically simple. In the oven, she had melted cheese over bread on which she had placed a spicy bean mixture. In an old, dented pot she had boiled rice, yellow from a pinch of saffron. Her meals were larger at lunch, smaller at dinner, but always appealing. Penn had been amused at first, noting most meals were self-contained and well-covered, like a piece of bread carefully sealed by melted cheese or tortillas wrapped around strands of chicken or beef. It was almost as though the Black Rockers feared the wind so much that they wouldn't allow anything, even the food they ate, to be unprotected.

Penn glanced over at Amos. "When did you say the next truck was coming through, Amos?"

Amos chewed thoughtfully. Since Tokyo had returned, he had willingly abandoned the inventory and ordering responsibilities to her. Finally, after swallowing loudly, he shrugged almost imperceptibly and raised his eyebrows in Tokyo's direction.

"Next week, probably. Tuesday, Wednesday, probably," she said without looking up.

Penn nodded. If nothing changed, he'd catch a ride with the driver, back into the city, abandoning this town and his daughter.

"You thinking of leaving?" Tokyo was looking directly at him now. Luke stopped eating for a moment. Penn could feel Luke's expectation, and, perhaps, even hope.

Penn nodded and returned her gaze. She immediately looked down at her plate, rearranging the yellow rice with her fork. Penn ate the last bite of bread and beans and leaned back in his chair.

"Amos, I never see too many people in here, and the ones that come in—Proudfoot, Tongate, the quarrymen—they don't buy all that much."

"Business could always be better," Amos replied.

"How do you pay for all this stuff?" Penn asked, gesturing to the shelves in the storeroom.

Amos looked at the storeroom shelves, at the jars and cans and hardware, at the items he bought on whim, out of some supplier's catalogue, items which, he knew, would never be used; items which would sit unnoticed on his shelves until their expiration dates came and went. His eye caught a particular shelf onto which he had recently emptied a carton of canned specialty meats. How they had managed to can liver pudding, Amos didn't know, but he had purchased a few boxes to see for himself. After he had opened one can, Sis had smartly refused to incorporate any of the foul-smelling concoction into a meal, so the cans were banished to the shelf.

"Tell him," Tokyo said. Her voice was angry. Perhaps if he exhausted his questions, he would make good on his threat to leave.

Luke and Amos exchanged looks. There was no predicting Tokyo's moods and why she would suddenly turn angry was beyond them. Only Sis kept eating. The others stared at Tokyo.

"Tell him about the money."

Amos rubbed the worn tablecloth with his large fingers, watching the indentations slowly fade as his fingers passed over the heavy material.

"I guess there's no secret about it," he said, but Luke's face looked pinched. "You never asked about the money, Tokyo. Never asked a thing about how things got to be the way they are around here. You always just let them be. Why are you asking now?"

Tokyo didn't look up from her plate. "He's asking, Amos. Not me."

Penn knew enough to let things run their course. He remained silent, sensing Amos's answer was somehow relevant to their strange stalemate.

"There was a man," Amos began. "A man who knew my father and Luke's. He came here one day with them, sort of like discovered this place. They stayed, he left. I guess he was the smart one."

Luke opened his mouth and made a noise like a cough, his version of a laugh. Tokyo could see Luke was relieved that Amos's story was vague.

"Well, he came back one day when things turned bad. Didn't stay long, just long enough to see my father be the only one left standing. Of both our families. Except Luke and me, but we were babies. He felt bad for us, I guess, and left money for us when he died. He was a rich man, you see. Left money in a foundation of some kind, they send us checks every month. Tongate brings them to us from the city. He brings us the cash, anyway. Well, most of the cash." Luke made his odd coughing sound again.

Tokyo, who had seen the cash coming in monthly, apparently from nowhere, and accounted for it in Amos's books more times than she could remember, tried to understand what she was hearing. She had always wondered about the source, but this story gave her no greater understanding of the mystery. If anything, it raised more questions, questions which, she saw, Penn was more willing to ask than she was.

"Who was he?"

Amos settled back into his chair. This time, Tokyo knew, the story would be longer.

"His name was Johnson. But my father always called him Apie. He was a rich man. And like most rich men, he had some peculiar traits." Amos sipped some coffee noisily. "Some downright peculiar traits."

18.

Apie's body arrived back in Black Rock in a lead coffin on the flatbed of a for-hire truck. The only sign of Apie's wealth was the fancy gold leaf on the edges of the coffin and the prepaid freight from Chicago to Black Rock. The gold leaf was visible even from inside the store. The boys had watched from the window as Shlomo limped out and spoke with the driver, then led him in to the store for a bite to eat. Shlomo was shaking his head when he walked into the store.

"I didn't believe the letter when I got it, boys. But damned if it wasn't true."

The driver, a man named McCoy, was accustomed to hauling loads of slate from Black Rock. When he had been offered three times the usual amount to take a shipment to Black Rock, he had leapt at the chance to augment his meager income by earning on what was normally a deadhead run, not realizing he would be carrying a dead body. As was normal for most truck drivers, McCoy was superstitious and thus anxious to rid his truck of the coffin quickly, for the longer the dead man stayed on his truck, the greater the chance there would be some curse that stayed with the truck.

"Where's the graveyard?" McCoy asked.

"There's no graveyard in Black Rock, friend," Shlomo answered.

"Then where the hell—sorry, boys—where the hell do you bury folks?"

Shlomo looked over at Amos and Luke, both of whom were trying their best to look busy with their chores.

"Apie out there on your truck, for some reason he wants to be buried with an old friend."

Luke and Amos dropped any pretense of chores and stood mutely nearby, staring at Shlomo. "What is it, boys?" Shlomo asked.

"The quarry?" Luke asked.

Shlomo nodded.

"But ..." Luke began.

"I know what I told you, about how special that place is, Luke. Amos. But come here." Shlomo reached under his counter and pulled out a letter. He read it, as if confirming again for himself what it said, then looked back to the boys.

"It's pretty simple. Apie died; that's sure enough true."

McCoy glanced out at his truck. If they needed help in confirming there was a dead man on the flatbed of his truck, he could provide it.

"And this here letter says that he wants to be buried in the quarry. With your dad, Luke. And with our families."

Growing up, Luke and Amos had known only what Shlomo had told them. And what he hadn't told them, which wasn't much, had allowed them to create their own myths about their families and, more importantly, about the quarry itself. The quarry was more than special; it was powerful and dreadful, mysterious and magical—so much so that neither boy had ever even considered throwing a piece of slate into the water to see it splash.

"Your dad, I guess he meant something to Apie after all," Shlomo said, mostly to himself. "Or maybe your family. And ours. Maybe that's what it was."

"We don't have to do it, do we? We could take him somewhere else, bury him?" Amos asked.

"Well, now, the letter asks this thing pretty particular. And there's something else. If we do it, you boys are gonna get money. Every month. For the rest of your lives. You won't have to work, you won't have to do nothing. There it is."

McCoy's eyes went from Shlomo to the boys. Teenagers in general are unable to grasp the concept of wealth, and Luke and Amos, even though isolated from most normal teenagers, were no exception. Money was nothing more than an abstract concept; more importantly, the concept of working every day for the rest of their lives to earn money was an abstract concept as well. To be told they could now be wealthy, if only they would dump a strange body into their special quarry, made no sense and was easy to ignore.

"We don't have to do it," Luke said, glancing at Amos for his approval. "And we won't. I don't care about working. I don't care about the money."

"You don't today, I see," Shlomo said. "But believe me, boys. You sure will."

Luke and Amos exchanged looks. Their resolve could be shaken and destroyed easily, Shlomo knew. They were young. But he wanted more than anything to be delicate and what he had to say next was anything but delicate. "There's something else, boys. The letter asks that you two be the ones who push Apie in."

Although they didn't agree and felt more than a little squeamish, Amos and Luke were not yet old enough that they couldn't be persuaded by Shlomo to do what he wanted them to do. Shlomo had long since grown out of any sentimentalism, and given the chance to take care of "his" boys for the rest of his life, he pushed hard. And so they crammed themselves into the front of McCoy's small truck and drove to the quarry. They struggled with the heavy coffin in the wind, moving it slowly over the jagged slate to the side of the water-filled quarry. After they had maneuvered the coffin to a perch from which it could be easily pushed, McCoy stood back and attempted to light a cigarette. Without speaking, Shlomo pointed to a small shelter carved from the slate, and McCoy nodded his thanks, lighting his cigarette with ease in the relatively windless cave.

Shlomo tapped each one of the boys on the shoulder and gestured to the coffin. As Amos looked up at his father, he realized that one day, maybe soon, he would be here performing the same grim task for Shlomo. Amos glanced at Luke and saw Luke thinking the same thing, as only brothers can see. And both boys saw in Shlomo's posture, in his eyes and in his limp, that he knew it too.

Shlomo took a few steps back and glanced into the wind toward McCoy, wondering what God's plan had been in creating a funeral. *It's not for the dead*, Shlomo thought. There isn't a person alive who's been to a funeral that doesn't put themselves in that box, lying there mute and stiff. No, God had made funerals for the living, and Apie was reaching out with his dead hand to finally take control of maybe the last situation he couldn't control with his wealth; he was controlling it finally, tearing at Shlomo's heart by a promise to care for the boys, a promise which Apie would have known Shlomo couldn't turn down, merging both Noah's and Shlomo's families, whether dead or alive, into Apie's own family.

Noah might have refused to come under Apie's control if he were living, he might have stood on his principles or his God and refused to smear the memory of his own family by adding Apie's body to the mix in the quarry, but Shlomo was not Noah. Apie and Noah would be together, and Apie's triumph over Noah would be eternal. Shlomo looked at the boys, wondering whether, if it were a year or so later, their respective principles would have developed to the point at which they would have refused the money and retained the quarry intact. No matter—it was today. And if they refused to spend the money in the future, it was of no concern to him.

Luke shook his head in resignation as Shlomo gestured for them to complete the task. He looked over at Amos, who seemed numb. The wind was searing across them from the west, as the two boys bent to the grim task. They were aware that this act would affect them for the rest of their lives, but the awareness was only dimly felt, and the task at hand was the only real thing in their lives at the moment. And so they pushed the lead coffin into the quarry without understanding, watching it splash and sink soundlessly. When they turned to walk back to the truck they saw McCoy stamping out his cigarette in the slate shelter and swiftly crossing himself in the Catholic manner.

19.

It was sometime after three o'clock in the afternoon when Amos had finished telling the whole story of Noah, Shlomo, and Apie to Penn. Luke had left the table and was sitting at the counter in the front of the store, and Sis had quietly cleared and cleaned the dishes. In deference to Amos's story, she spent the time rearranging her materials rather than using the noisy loom. Penn remained sitting at the table, fascinated by the past. Tokyo stood to help Sis at first and generally moved around the kitchen and the surrounding storeroom, but she was careful to stay close enough to hear the details of Noah, Shlomo, and their families. Despite the care she took to look disinterested, she was unable to ignore the amazing past recounted by Amos.

Luke could hear the muffled voices from the counter, but the words were inaudible. The wind, which had been noticeably temperamental over the past few days, gusted and calmed and gusted and calmed in irregular intervals. The pitch of the whistling ran up and down the octaves, and Luke listened to the wind with the same interest that Tokyo and Penn listened to Amos.

At the end, when Amos described Apie's coffin disappearing into the black water, Penn sat back in his chair and took a deep breath, and Amos nodded distractedly, his eyes fixed on a point a few feet behind Penn's head. Neither man spoke as Sis quietly took their coffee cups to the sink.

Tokyo stood still in the storeroom for a moment, contemplating what she had heard. Neither Penn nor Amos noticed as she left the room to find Luke. Sitting at the counter, Luke looked as if he had been whipped soundly. Tokyo's spontaneous reaction to his hangdog expression was anger, but she couldn't shake the feeling of sorrow, deep sorrow.

"You never told me any of this, Luke."

Luke shook his head slowly. He seemed close to tears. Tokyo walked past him and looked out the front window. The street was empty. The wind had scrubbed the wooden sides of the buildings clean and then had applied swirling patterns of slate dust to each and every dwelling, leaving the houses and storefronts dirty, like some coal mining town. Tokyo shook her head.

"I don't understand, Luke. Why would you stay here? After all that?"

Tokyo did not hear Luke stand and walk across the room toward her, but she felt him behind her; she could feel the warmth of his body even though he was careful not to touch her. She turned her head to look at him and saw he was staring out the window as well. He cleared his throat.

"The first thing a lot of people notice about Black Rock, there's not a lot of windows." He put one hand out and touched the thick plate glass in front of them. "No big windows like this one, for sure. Amos replaced this one, don't know how many times."

Tokyo nodded. At least five times in the past five years she knew of. "What the hell, he's got the money. You've got the money."

Luke looked at her for the first time. "It isn't a lot of money," he snapped. Embarrassed by his anger, he quickly looked back out the window and watched the wind. After a moment, he added, "It's enough, though."

"Enough to get the hell out of here?"

Luke looked at her angrily. "It's okay to say that if you've got no past, Tokyo. Or if you don't want one."

Tokyo turned to walk away, but Luke took her by the arm, firmly, but not firmly enough to keep her there if she didn't want to break away. She looked up at him, at the anger in his eyes, and realized once again that she had stayed too long. By the time the anger was strong enough for violence, she was normally another lifetime away, another five hundred miles and another name away, untraceable, like a gust of wind.

"I love you, Tokyo." Luke let her arm go and turned back to the window. He shook his head and twisted his lips, this time in pain. "I mean, I love you," he repeated.

Tokyo blinked and shuffled backward, stopping only when she bumped into the first shelf of dry goods. She looked past Luke, out the window at the wind howling down the street, imagining she could see the gust's tail still coiled on the mesa, waiting to catch up with its screaming head, imagining that this long snake of wind could see the things and feel the things she could. As the snake screamed past the window, she imagined it glancing over at Luke, standing there staring back out at it, and, further back, Tokyo, limp as a dishrag, leaning heavily against a shelf for support.

"You don't love me, Luke," she finally said.

Luke turned, his expression puzzled. Thinking he had not heard her over the suddenly louder wind, Tokyo repeated herself angrily. "You don't love me!"

Luke smiled thinly. He shook his head. "That's the thing with you, isn't it, Tokyo? You've got to look into everyone around you, know what they're thinking, how you're going to move your little piece on the game board. How you're going to stay out of the wind. How you're going to run out when it gets too strong for you. You telling me I don't love you isn't going to make it true."

Tokyo stood upright and stamped one foot on the wooden floorboards angrily, an almost childish gesture, it seemed to Luke. "You don't love me, Luke. You want your goddamned mother. You don't even fucking know me."

Luke took three steps toward Tokyo, one hand raised as if to strike her. When he was close enough, he clenched his fist tightly and slammed it down on the shelf behind her head, scattering cans and boxes of plastic cutlery and toothpicks.

"I didn't know my mother. Or my father. But I didn't have a goddamned choice in it either. Like you did. Like you do."

"You two all right?" It was Amos, standing at the counter looking at the mess in the front of the store. Penn stood behind him, as always full of questions.

"We ought to go, Penn," Luke said, and walked to the door and out without even glancing back at Tokyo. Penn walked by her, nodding a good-bye with a friendly smile.

"I'd like to talk to you once, before I go. Just you and me," he said.

Tokyo blinked and bit her bottom lip. After a pause, she nodded hesitantly and shrugged. "It's a free country," she said.

Penn smiled again and walked out the door. After she watched the truck pull away, she kneeled on the ground to pick up the cans and boxes. When Amos came across the front of the store to help her, she waved him off with one hand.

"No, I'll help you, Tokyo," he said, but stopped when she looked up at him. Her face was streaked with tears, and she held up a hand to ward him off. Since the day the flag salesman had walked out of his store he had not seen a tear from Tokyo, only hard silence, and he hesitated for a moment.

"Please," she sobbed, and Amos turned quietly and returned to the back room.

20.

"Her foster mother wrote me a letter a few months after I met her."

Luke glanced over at Penn. Moving west across the mesa, the truck lurched awkwardly in the buffeting wind.

"When she was a little girl, she made up her parents. She never told them about her real mother, or about me—of course, she wouldn't have remembered me. She made up her father, mostly. Mrs. Cole would hear her talking to herself while she played in the backyard. She'd be out there playing, I guess, with dolls or whatnot, and she'd be talking about how her father was a sea captain, or a pilot, or a general in some far-off army—always a guy in charge of things, important, you know?"

Luke nodded, and despite his inclination to turn inward, he listened intently as Penn spoke.

"She was a quiet girl, that's not too much of a shock, I guess. Anyway, this woman, this Mrs. Cole, she wrote this letter to me, told me all about how Ayako was as a little girl, all about how she imagined this whole world for herself, and when they'd ask her about who she was, or who her imaginary friends were, she'd clam up and not talk to them, just sort of look at them. Mrs. Cole said she thought the girl was just born angry and stayed that way."

Luke opened his mouth and laughed, a quick, short burst of air and sound. Penn smiled too.

"Well, this letter was the damnedest thing; it kept going on and on about how she made up her family, how she got more and more vicious, until she finally left home."

The two men drove in silence as Luke pulled up the long path to his home. He brought the truck to a stop and pressed hard on the emergency brake.

"What do you want out of her?" Luke asked.

Penn shook his head. Plans he had made, plans which had seemed to make so much sense, be so right—now he couldn't even grasp what he had been thinking. He sighed heavily. "She's all I have left. All that I'll leave."

Luke glanced over, surprised.

"Not like that man, Apie. He left you and Amos all of this." Penn laughed softly at his own bad joke.

"Why don't you stay? Get to know her?"

"How's that worked out for you?" Penn asked.

Luke let out a humorless laugh.

"All I can do is show up, ask questions, leave after a while," Penn continued. "I can't stay, it isn't in my nature." Penn mentally rifled through the places he had stayed in his life, the lack of any roots he had put down. At his age, he no longer blamed circumstances, luck (either bad or good), or other people for his endless wanderlust. Years ago, as a younger man, he had expected the inner restlessness to dissipate as he grew older, but it hadn't. And now, today, he sat in this pickup truck next to this odd man in this odd place and realized once again that he was the same man he had been forty years ago: restless and anxious, ready to move on.

"How come she wrote you that way? Her foster mother, I mean."

Penn shook his head. "I've thought about it a lot. Read the letter over and over again. And, you know, it didn't occur to me until just now, when I was telling you about it. I think Mrs. Cole was apologizing. Like she'd done something wrong. As if she had to apologize to me."

21.

Far away, in the mountains to the west, the end of winter was coming. The sun warmed the snowy mountains longer and longer each day, until the fine white powder grew thick and hard, sometimes in hard pellets the locals called corn snow, and sometimes congealed into an even harder sheet of ice.

High in the mountains, pieces of corn snow broke loose when they became too heavy, minor avalanches of snow for the most part, taking only snow and vegetation down the slopes of the mountains, but sometimes major ones, avalanches which threatened to change the shape and height of the mountains and valleys themselves.

The largest avalanches were those which occurred at the very end of the winter, when the greatest volume of snow had built upon itself, no longer able to hold itself together as a supportable mass. The snow and ice crashed downward, taking with it huge chunks of rock. The mountainside is changed, and the valleys below are changed, sometimes forever. Men and women in such areas rightly dread the suddenness of such an avalanche and the way it can rearrange whole lives. Houses, roads, even whole communities once living in peaceful valleys are sometimes uprooted, forced to move to another area undisturbed by the avalanche's sudden change.

22.

Early in the morning, Amos sat on the edge of his bed listening. Next to him, Sis was still asleep. She had been sleeping later and later each morning for the past month or so, and Amos did not begrudge her some rest. Sis seemed more tired in the evenings, prone now to finishing the dishes and retiring immediately to the bedroom to read but more often to sleep. Her loom sat silent. For the most part, Sis's interest in weaving had reached an unexpected lull. Amos could only conclude that Sis's sensitivity to people probably had tired her out, what with all the tension among Luke and Tokyo and Penn.

The wind had fooled Amos countless times, the latest example of which had just been the other day when he thought he had lost some siding and found the siding firmly in place when he struggled outside to check it. But this morning there had been a scratching noise, barely audible over the wind, a noise he couldn't place. Awake in bed, he had been staring at the ceiling. Today the truck would arrive, and Penn would leave. It was a good thing, he thought. Penn's reasons for being here had never been clear. It seemed as if he were cleaning up details, looking in the corners to find the dust of the past, and as he did so, Penn had managed to disturb the delicate atmosphere of life in Black Rock. Strange, he thought, that a place as harsh as Black Rock could be so fragile.

There it was again. A scratching noise. Maybe it was Tokyo, in the next room. No, the noise was too soft, and coming from the other corner of his room. Amos sat up, careful not to disturb Sis's sleep. He peered into the corner in the semidarkness but saw nothing. What had he expected? A hole in the wall, perhaps? The wind's actual fingers, prying their bony way into his safe house? He remembered the long nights with Luke when they were boys, the way they had made up stories to scare each other; there was a devil in the wind, they told each other, a devil who could howl through the slightest crack and gust his way into your lungs and your soul unless you kept the walls tight and your mouth closed firmly.

The boys would laugh and hold their breath as long as they could, seeing who would exhale first and expose himself to the devil in the wind.

Another tiny scratch. Amos quickly looked in the direction of the noise. He saw a quick movement across the floor. He shook his head and rubbed his eyes. There it was, running across the floor and suddenly stopping to explore some potential food—a mouse. A small, brown mouse. Amos's mouth hung open, and, despite himself, he said aloud, "Damn."

Next to him, Sis stirred and looked groggily up. Amos said nothing; he simply pointed. Sis propped herself up on one elbow and peered into the corner just as the mouse skittered across the floor and under a low-slung shelf.

"A mouse," Amos said. Sis said nothing. She nodded, then fell back against her pillow. Her eyes were slightly glassy, her breath coming hard as if she had been carrying something heavy. Amos leaned over her, and Sis smiled thinly, patting his arm, reassuring him. For the past month, the pain had been worst in the mornings, but then had faded as she got moving. It forced her to stay in bed longer each morning while she marshaled her strength to actually stand. There was no need to tell Amos, no need to tell anyone. It was her pain.

"In all my life, all my years, Sis, I've never seen a mouse," Amos said. "Not in here."

Sis smiled again. No, the only animals other than humans on the mesa were insects: cockroaches and such. They were a nuisance in the flour and the sugar packages, but never had they seen mice.

Amos rose from his bed and reached for his boots. Standing in the room, half dressed, he turned back to Sis, who coughed quietly a few times as she slung her own feet over the bed.

"I don't know what it could mean," Amos continued, excitement in his voice. "I have no idea. But a mouse! Damn, if it isn't strange. I thought most animals had the good sense not to be caught dead around here." He buttoned his flannel shirt thoughtfully. "Maybe he came in on one of the trucks, one of the delivery trucks. But he'd have to be a hardy little critter to make it all the way from the city on one of those refrigerated food trucks." Amos walked to the door of the bathroom, then stopped. "But the last truck was weeks ago. Why wouldn't we have seen the little guy? Or at least heard him?"

In the next room, Tokyo heard Amos's voice, heard Sis's quiet coughs. Unusual for them to talk so much in the morning. Hell, it was unusual for them to talk so much at any time of day. She rose and dressed slowly, dreading the moment when Penn would arrive but, oddly, dreading the moment he would leave. She would miss the distraction Penn supplied. Once he was gone, she would be forced to deal with her promise to Luke; she would be forced to tell him she would be leaving as well. Tokyo had always hated the way the past had surrounded everyone in the town, but she had welcomed their unwillingness to speak of it until Penn had complicated her life by arriving with his own cloud of the past swirling around his head, more irritating because it was the cloud of her past as well as his own. Why had she stayed in this place for so long? She listened to the wind for a moment before she pulled on a heavy sweater.

Even if she were unable to articulate it, she knew she had stayed for the wind. The wind which swept all the clouds of the past clean, the wind which let her start each day new, a struggle against nothing more than the wind itself, the past be damned. The wind swept the past of Amos, of Luke, of her, and of her father away, rendering it all meaningless in the battle for survival.

She knew her own past, knew it damned well, and Penn's arrival had made it difficult to evade, even in the strongest winds. There he was, a lurking reminder, willingly having explored where she had lived, like a detective, just to … to do what? He had already polluted Luke, she knew, and her determination to leave a man when he started asking questions was made that much stronger by Penn's interference. She sighed heavily as she heard the sounds of Amos and Sis in the kitchen. At least Penn would be gone soon. Today. The wind would take him and her past off the mesa, and she, too, would move on. She felt she should be happy, but a smile would not come to her face.

In the kitchen Tokyo was too distracted to notice Sis's face, pale and splotchy, as she prepared eggs and tortillas. The trucks usually came early in the morning, the driver having left his distribution center in the middle of the night to make better time out of the city. He would be here soon.

"I saw a mouse this morning," Amos said.

Tokyo looked up at him. A long, slow blink. She knew animals didn't survive in this place, the wind was like an exterminator of all things living. A mouse could never have made it across the great divide to the windswept plains and finally to Amos's store.

"Does he have a name?"

Amos smiled. "The mouse? We should call him Miracle, because that's what he is."

Sis moved stiffly toward the table, carrying two plates. Tortillas covered with eggs, covered with melted cheese. She put the plates down in the normal places, then turned back to the oven. Amos sat down at the table and began eating, still thoughtful. He chewed his eggs quickly and swallowed; the food was still too hot to taste.

"But a mouse, Tokyo. You have any idea how it could happen?"

Tokyo sat down in front of her plate and shook her head. She picked up a fork and stared at it. "You'd better kill him next time you see him, or you'll have more miracles than you'll know what to do with."

"Nah," Amos said, good-naturedly. "You think there's a chance two mice could've made the trip?"

The sound of the front door opening quieted the breakfast group. Footsteps came across the floor, then Penn's head poked through the doorway, smiling when he caught Amos's eye. He had come to like Amos: his easy way of loping through life, his lack of judgment, and, not the least, his willingness to tell a story. It made sense to him that his daughter had picked this man's household to hide in. Like a recluse who chooses to live in New York City, relying on the staggering population to provide cover, Ayako relied on the fury of the wind and the fog of Amos and Luke's shared history for her hiding place.

"Too bad you're leaving today, Penn," Amos greeted him. Penn cocked his head, waiting. "Saw a mouse. Right here in the store."

Penn hadn't been in town long enough to understand Amos's point.

"Not since they killed the last of the goats up here have we seen a live, furry animal. Been a long time."

Penn smiled and perused the people sitting at the table. There was Amos, eager to go on about the mouse, Ayako, who he knew, had done nearly everything she could to avoid this moment, and Sis, who seemed slumped in her seat, her eyes cloudy on the few occasions she looked up. Penn stood quietly, waiting.

"Can only mean one thing, you know?" Amos continued. "Means there's some kind of change coming, for sure. Maybe it means there's some kind of change already happened, and only the animals know it."

"He's leaving." Tokyo jerked a thumb over her shoulder toward Penn. "Maybe the mouse is taking his place."

She knew Penn wanted to say his good-byes, probably wanted to make some sort of half-assed apology, and maybe would even break down in tears, asking for some kind of absolution from her. Damn it, she wasn't a priest, and she couldn't make his problems go away by listening to him whine about how bad he felt about abandoning his daughter. And his wife. Her mother. The memory of the hot day on the woody path swirled back to her, and she bit her lip, fighting to suppress the memory. If he felt so bad about it, he should've done something different for her years ago. Her mother had died alone, Tokyo knew. Someone had told her, perhaps Cole, perhaps another man convincing himself that he was doing good by telling her. Penn couldn't go back and make her alive, and this thought more than anything caused her anger to turn white hot. He owed her nothing, not even an apology. And she owed him nothing.

Penn cleared his throat. "Ayako? Can we talk out front until the truck comes?"

"They call me Tokyo here," she seethed. It was a name given by chance, but she clung to it now, harder than she expected she might.

Penn nodded quickly; she couldn't see it, but she felt him doing it. "Sorry. But can we talk?"

Tokyo played idly with the remains of her breakfast. She was inclined to stay rooted firmly in her seat until Penn's patience dried up and the wind blew him out of town on the food purveyor's truck. Penn waited, then inhaled sharply. Tokyo smiled ruefully at her fork and eggs. She recognized the impatience, recognized it from her foster father Cole, from the men she had been with, from Luke, from bus drivers, from women too. She luxuriated in the feeling of triumph, knowing she needn't say anything further, knowing she had already won.

A touch on her arm startled her. The fingers were cold and dry. She looked questioningly at Sis. Sis's wrinkled and weatherbeaten face was pale, her lips chapped and flaking. It appeared as if she had some kind of sores at the bottom of her neck, hardly visible over the high-necked sweater she was wearing. Despite the anger Tokyo had built up to defend herself, she melted with concern for Sis. Sis saw the concern and smiled thinly, then shook her head. Sis gestured with her eyes toward Penn; Tokyo resisted, quickly staring down at her plate again. The grip on her arm tightened almost imperceptibly, and Tokyo looked back up. Despite the paleness and the appearance of weakness, Sis's gray eyes were intense.

Tokyo stared into Sis's eyes, realizing she had begun communicating with Sis in much the same way she had seen Amos and Sis communicate on so many occasions, without words or apparent language. Tokyo had sworn she would never get close enough to another person that they would be able to steal her thoughts, to steal her ability to use silence as a barrier, yet here she was, willingly communicating with nothing more than looks or nods, with a strange Indian descendant in the middle of nowhere. Tokyo jerked her arm away, repulsed with herself, involuntarily shaking her head.

"What's the matter, Sis? You look like you're sick or something." Tokyo turned to Amos. "She looks like she's sick or something, Amos."

Amos, aware of the struggle between Sis and Tokyo, and no less aware of the struggle within Tokyo, immediately saw what he had ignored for weeks: that Sis wasn't just tired, she wasn't just weak, but that some illness had crept into her while he had chosen to look elsewhere. He glanced over at her silent loom, then back at Sis. Amos opened his mouth to speak, but Sis waved one hand toward him, an unmistakable gesture to silence. She turned toward Tokyo, waiting. When Tokyo finally succumbed to Sis's gaze and looked up, Sis spoke quietly.

"Go with him, Tokyo. He might not tell you your song, but, listening to him, you might hear something of it."

Tokyo stared at Sis for a moment, blinking slowly. Then she glanced back at Penn. His expression was expectant but not hopeful to the point where he would be crushed with disappointment if she refused him. With a glance back at Sis, Tokyo inhaled sharply. *What could it hurt?* She stood up and walked past Penn to the front room, the invitation for him to follow left unspoken. She would be damned, she thought, if she had to say the words out loud; it was enough she would listen to him for a while.

23.

"A mouse, huh?" Penn settled himself into one of the seldom-used easy chairs at the front of the store. Tokyo sat on the arm of the other leather chair, studiously avoiding eye contact. Instead, she watched the wind swirling and dancing down the street. It seemed almost frivolous and playful today.

"There's no telling what old Amos is going to latch onto," she said. Looking out the window, she noticed, not without a great deal of satisfaction, the food purveyor's tractor-trailer wheeling slowly down the street toward the store. She recognized the driver through the dusty windshield. They called him Thad. He would pull the truck around back and bang loudly on the door. Amos would open the door and help him unload. Tokyo smiled and gestured with her head. "Looks like your ride's here. We done?"

Just then, Amos appeared at the counter. "Take your time, you two. We've got a big order to unload and I'll bet Thad is gonna want a free meal. Like usual." Amos waved and returned to the back room, leaving Tokyo to pout inwardly. Unloading and a late breakfast would take about an hour, she figured, maybe more. Surely Penn couldn't talk as long as an hour.

"I don't know where to start, Tokyo," he said.

Tokyo snorted. "At least you got the name right."

"From everything I've heard, everything I've seen, you've got a lot to be mad at. But I didn't come here to apologize to you, to tell you all the things I did wrong. I know what they are. And you know what they are, too. Hell, you probably know more things I did wrong to you than I do."

Tokyo shook her head. What the hell was he talking about?

"I don't mean I did them to you as if we were in the same room, or even in the same town," Penn continued. "Just that you probably have a lot of things you'd like to say to me, things you'd have wanted to say to me years ago."

286

"I don't have anything to say to you, mister." Why was she sitting here listening to this? *Probably because I have nowhere else to go.*

"I guess not," Penn said. During the ensuing silence, Tokyo wondered whether heading off his prerehearsed speech would be as simple a matter as venting a bit of anger. She waited, alert for signals of what would most effectively draw this potentially unpleasant conversation to a close.

"I just ask you to listen a bit; then I'll go."

Tokyo glanced at Penn, her eyes squinting. "Seems fair," she said. "So talk. I won't have a lot of questions." Penn nodded, smiling wryly. *I'll bet you won't*, he thought.

"I met your mother when I was in the Army. In Bangkok. She had come there from Japan to be with her aunt after her parents died. They died when she was young, she said. She didn't remember them, just thought of her aunt as her mother."

"So I'm in good company, not knowing my mother? Is that what you're saying? Is that what you wanted me to know?"

Penn shook his head. "You knew your mother. Until you were three, she raised you. I didn't stick around for you to be born. But you knew your mother."

Tokyo blinked. Flashes of her mother: the print dress, the sweat, the tears. Her mother always seemed to be crying in her memory. *Because of Penn*, she thought. *Because he left.*

"When I met her, she wanted two things: To come to America and to have children. I gave her both; then she was done with me. It'll sound like an excuse, but I left because I thought she wanted me to. I don't need you to believe me."

Long ago, Tokyo had learned to repress any memories of her mother. She had spent much of her youth creating images of what she wanted in a mother, until the images blurred with the reality and became even more painful. Tokyo had convinced herself that her lost mother had been a strong-willed, independent leader, a person others looked to for leadership. In her eyes, her mother had been a smart woman, a kind woman, a ruthless woman. Now, Penn was confirming Tokyo's created image. Her mother had used this weak, little man to come to America, to have her only child.

"Her name was Mari?" Tokyo asked. Surprised, Penn glanced up at Tokyo, who was still sitting on the arm of one of the chairs, staring out the window. Although her expression remained impassive, Penn imagined a slight easing in her anger. Outside, the wind shifted directions suddenly, blowing a gust directly toward Tokyo, kept away from her only by the thick plate window of Amos's store. The window bowed slightly, creaking ominously before the wind resumed its normal direction.

"Yes, Mari," and Tokyo could hear the sadness in Penn's voice. "You could say it was a marriage of convenience. Her aunt had taught her English, made sure she had the best education. She drove her to be the best."

"And she ended up with you?"

"A lot of Japanese girls in Bangkok did a lot worse. A lot of girls of all kinds did a lot worse in Bangkok," Penn said, remembering the abuse suffered by the Thai bar girls, abuse handed out by many of his compatriots in the Army, men who, in some cases, had only recently left the terror that Vietnam had become, but more often men without any such excuse. Penn seemed angry for a moment. "But not Mari. She wanted to come to America. A place she could raise children. A place you could see the horizon." Penn smiled and looked out the window toward the mesa. "What she'd have thought of this place, I don't know."

In the back room, Tokyo heard noises: Muted voices, shuffling boots moving heavy objects across the wooden floor. She silently willed them to move faster as Penn continued.

"We met, we fell in love. At least I did. We were both young. Her aunt wanted no part of her hooking up with an Army guy, tried a thousand ways to stop it, but we finally ran off, came to America, to Boston. Tried to settle down. But things moved faster in America than they did in Asia. Maybe not faster, but different. She stopped talking. First, to me. Then, when she got pregnant, she stopped talking to anyone, stopped even noticing things around her. Like she had lost contact."

"It's easy to say 'lost contact.' Hell, I was so young, I had no idea what was going on. Thought all kinds of things. That she had just used me to come to America, that she had another man, that she wanted to get rid of me."

"I can't see her wanting to get rid of you," Tokyo said dryly.

Penn sighed. Too old to respond to anger with anger, he was quiet for a moment. When he finally spoke again, he spoke quietly. "I'm not telling you this for me. And I'm not telling you because I feel like I owe you something. You need to know."

Tokyo laughed. "I know everything I want to know. I don't need to know anything else."

"Then why are you here?"

Something in Penn's tone, the lack of anger, or, more particularly, the lack of any sense of self in Penn's question—he wasn't asking for effect, he wasn't asking a question to win points in an argument, he was asking because he wanted to know. Tokyo found herself answering before she even knew what she was saying.

"I made a promise," she said.

Penn nodded. "Mari was slipping. Slipping toward some dark place inside. But I didn't know. I left her when she was pregnant with you. If I had known, I'd … hell, I don't know what I would have done. Maybe, back then, I'd have still left her. But then, all I knew was she didn't want me around, so I got out. Figured she'd be okay—always was. I was in Chicago when you were born. I didn't know what day you were born."

"December 28. If you wanted to get me a present, you missed your chance." Tokyo allowed herself a fast glare in Penn's direction.

"I wondered whether you'd be a New Year's baby," he said.

"I'd have been the life of the party."

"The Coles told me you hated your birthday," he continued. "Wouldn't let them make a cake, wouldn't let them have a party for you or have presents."

"What would you have done? Let these strangers pretend they liked you? Pretend they could be your parents when they didn't have any idea, any clue about you? Pretend it was okay that you knew your mother wasn't with you, would never be with you because she was dying alone in a hospital somewhere? They told me that, you know. It was like Cole was laughing at me, telling me she had died alone in a hospital." Tokyo was breathing quickly; she was angry. "I wasn't going to be some poor Asian kid in a birthday picture for those assholes. I wanted to be someone's kid. My mother's kid."

Penn was silent, nodding. "I called Mari a few times, trying to get her to ask me to come back and to bring you back, but talking to her over the phone didn't work. I drifted for a while, for a couple of years, until

I heard from a friend that you'd been placed in foster care and she had gone into a hospital."

Penn stopped and shook his head. Tokyo' breathing was now shallow, as if she were trying not to disturb the wind currents in the front room. Her expression remained impassive. In the back room, the sounds of heavy work had ceased, and Penn could hear dishes being moved out of the cabinet.

"I came back to help. I didn't know she was sick, not until I saw her in the hospital. It was terrible. They gave her drugs to keep her from being so depressed, but she didn't react well to them. Her hair, it was like yours, black and long. When I saw her in that place, her hair was dirty and stuck together. Her eyes were dull; she shuffled like an old woman."

"But when she saw me, she smiled. A sweet smile, the sweetest smile I've ever seen on her. It's what I remember when I think of her."

"'Penn,' was all she said to me. Just my name and she was my whole world again. She shuffled up and hugged me tight. I cried, cried hard, felt her body next to mine, felt how weak and frail she was, how stupid I had been not to see she was sick."

"I talked to one of the doctors, and he said it was depression, that she had tried to kill herself the first night she had been admitted, after they took you away. She talked about you constantly, about how she missed you. You should know that. The doctor thought the only way she'd make it was if she got out of the hospital and could somehow take care of you. But she couldn't even take care of herself, so it came down to me."

Tokyo felt her heart beating fast in her temples. She stayed completely still, the way she had seen hunted animals seeking to avoid capture.

"I took her out of there and we moved north into the country, trying to make a new start of it." Penn shook his head. "I thought I could do it, but it was so hard, taking care of her. I thought, if we could get to some normal level then we could send for you, and everything would work out."

"Looks like you fucked up," Tokyo said.

Penn looked at Tokyo. Waves of uncertainty and anger radiated from her, almost blurring her features. Her face and her intensity were so like Mari's. There were times when Mari would withdraw so far into herself that Penn couldn't stand to be in the same room, as if sparks were coming off her. Ayako had inherited that trait.

"I did. And I fucked up worse when Mari got pregnant again."

Penn stopped when he heard Tokyo's sharp intake of breath. So, it was possible to surprise her, to cut through the anger to something real. For a short time, he listened to the sounds of voices murmuring in the kitchen over the truck driver's breakfast, barely audible over the wind.

"Did she have the baby?"

Penn nodded. Tokyo bit her lip and looked down. Her anger had vanished as if by magic.

"It was another girl. Your sister, Kalyo." Penn added, although he hadn't needed to do so. "When she found out she was pregnant, she tried to kill herself again. Went crazy. Screaming, crying all the time. I had to call the doctor up, get more of the stuff they were giving her, just to calm her down. She said she couldn't abandon another child. She said she wouldn't." He shook his head again sadly.

Tokyo was looking directly at Penn now. She had slid into the other chair, her arms hanging loosely at her sides, palms upward as if she no longer possessed motor control. The sound of the wind filled the room for a few moments. Tokyo's eyes remained on Penn, who shifted uncomfortably a few times before he continued. He had imagined this scene differently, as he had traveled over endless roads toward Black Rock—imagined his daughter differently, imagined the ease with which he could tell her about his past, about hers. He imagined how grateful she would be to finally know. He had lied to himself, thinking that just telling her would be enough for things to work out.

But sitting here with his daughter, the simplicity of what he had to tell her became tangled, perhaps in the face of her anger, which he had anticipated, or perhaps in the face of his self-realization, which he hadn't. Their past—different but the same—was anything but simple. In fact, nobody's past was simple. Not his, not Mari's, not Ayako's. Certainly not Luke's or Amos's. Not even a person like Cole's wife, who seemed the caricature of a plain New England housewife even as her pinched face and odd letter revealed something much more complex. And certainly not for Tokyo, sitting limply in one of the seldom-used front chairs. Her past, an unbroken chain of attempts to simplify her life by withdrawal, by isolation, and by silence, would appear quiet and undisturbed to an outsider. She wanted it that way. She could keep her apparent impenetrability intact even in the face of the reality of her mother's sickness, even in the face of her father's sudden appearance. But a sister. This was someone she hadn't known even existed, someone who could be the same as herself, someone who could have shared, not only her anger, but also her fears, her desires. This was someone her mother had refused to abandon.

Penn sat with her a long time before either of them spoke. Tokyo shook her head a few times as if in disbelief. The only sound audible other than the omnipresent wind was the muted clinking of dishes in the back room. Dimly, Tokyo realized the late breakfast was drawing to a close. Time was short.

"Where is ..."

"*Kalyo.* It means 'forgiveness.'"

"Where is she now?" It seemed impossible to her that Penn wouldn't have found her sister as well.

Surprised, Penn swallowed hard and felt the film of dust on the back of his front teeth with his tongue. It had taken this long to wait her out, to finally reach her, and he knew he was about to lose her again. He looked at his daughter, into her eyes, for what he knew would be the last time. He saw her eyes, wide and brown, and luxuriated for a moment in her suddenly honest curiosity, unaffected by her anger or her defensiveness.

"She died." He watched Tokyo closely, hoping.

Tokyo blinked several times. Her hand went to her face. "How?" Her voice was a fierce whisper. *Like the wind*, Penn thought.

"Mari." Penn looked up at the ceiling. In the past, he had marveled at the collection of canes, at the cobwebs and dust in the rafters, mentally assigning them some vague importance. But now, they took on the meaninglessness of a stranger's past.

"She was only about two months old. Mari seemed better. I probably wanted her to seem better. I needed a break. I didn't know Mari hadn't stopped taking her pills. In the day, mood elevators; in the evening, sedatives. She took too many sedatives one night, didn't wake up the next morning. I was gone for three days. When I got back, they were both dead."

Tokyo stood up suddenly and took a few steps toward the plate-glass window. She put one hand up against the cool glass and felt the power of the wind. The vibration of the window and the sound of the wind were like a desperately needed anchor.

"Was it an accident?" she asked without looking at Penn.

Penn listened to the sound of footsteps behind him. He glanced back and saw Amos and the truck driver. The truck driver's patience had reached an end. He had more deliveries to make, a family to rejoin. Penn stood and held one finger in the air to Amos, who nodded and mumbled something to the truck driver. The driver, predisposed to giving Amos the benefit of the doubt, shuffled toward the back of the store.

Tokyo remained in front of the window staring out, waiting. She listened as Penn walked up behind her and stood silently for a moment, close to her. She could feel his breath on the back of her head. She smelled the coffee on this breath and fought back the almost instinctual repulsion she had for being in such close physical proximity to a stranger.

"Was it an accident?" she asked again, not turning.

Penn reached forward and squeezed her shoulder gently.

"It could have been," he said softly. She cocked her head, then nodded.

"Good-bye, Tokyo," he said, releasing her shoulder.

She turned, wiping the tears from her face with the sleeve of her sweater. It was an image Penn would remember forever: Tokyo's face, her eyes filled with tears for her past, for her mother, and for her infant sister, saying good-bye to him for the last time. Years of living, years of distance, were condensed into this one moment of connection.

"Good-bye, Penn Taylor," she sniffed and turned back to touch the thick glass of the front window again.

24.

"My parents, they called me Thaddeus, but they called me Tad growin' up, and it just stuck, 'cept now they call me Thad, mostly, I guess, 'cause of my wife."

Although the man seemed committed to repeating much of what he had told Penn on the trip in to Black Rock Mesa, Penn nodded as the truck rumbled up the interstate toward Salt Lake City. To leave Black Rock, the truck had traveled east for miles before it could link into a main artery which led to the interstate, which, in turn, looped back around to the west and north. Now, ten hours into the trip, Penn mused silently as Thad filled up the surprisingly spacious cab of his tractor with his life story. Penn was uncharacteristically uninterested in the man's history, but Thad pushed on, detailing grievances with his wife, with his two children, with his boss, with the government, and with the state troopers he believed were persecuting him.

"Just for being a truck driver, you know?" he said. Thad's motive was simple: he expected a tip from anyone to whom gave a ride—he was no bus service, and the more the rider thought his life was rough, the more money he was likely to get from him. And this fellow had made him wait, a fact that Thad underscored periodically in his monologue.

"The only good thing about this route here they gave me is old Amos; he always feeds me well, along with that squaw of his. Did you know she was an Injun? She cooks damn well, but simple, you know? Not simple like my wife. Hot dogs from a package, boiled in water. Now, that's simple. I tell her, take the hot dogs, fry them in a pan with a little butter or something, they'll taste better—I learned that at a diner just up the road a ways, they fry the buns in butter too—but she's got to do it her way, damn her."

Penn let him go on.

"I saw that little Chinese girl you was with back there," Thad said.

Penn nodded, staring out at the road in front of them. By and large, Thad drove faster than most of the other vehicles on the highway. He had already opined it was the only way to make real money.

"She something special?" Thad asked suggestively.

Penn shook his head. "Just a girl," he said, distracted.

Damn, Thad thought. *This son of a bitch was a lot more talkative when I brought him out here.*

"What happened up there? You sound like you been beaten up."

Penn considered. All these years, he had been free with his past, sharing it with anyone who had asked, exchanging stories of his past for stories of others' pasts, never reluctant to share. His willingness to talk of his past had led him naturally to assume that the best thing he could do for his life and for Ayako's was to find her and tell her, too. Now, sitting here in the cab of a truck speeding over a bland western highway, he realized that he had finally told the story of his past to the only person who mattered anymore. And having done so, he felt no need to talk further.

"I'll tell you what I think," Thad continued. "I think that girl up there put a whuppin' on you, eh?" He glanced over, leering. Penn smiled good-naturedly.

"Nah, nothing like that," Penn said. "You ever feel like you've got to say something to a person for their own good? Feel like it's the most important thing you can do?" Penn knew, from Thad's complaints, that he would understand.

"Sure as hell know what you're talking about, friend. Damned if I don't. When I see something, I just speak out."

Penn squinted out at the road. "But sometimes do you find you're not really telling them for them—you're telling them so you'll feel better, even though you tell yourself a thousand times it isn't about you, you're just trying to help them?"

Thad was silent. The truck roared across the highway, the tires slapping to the rhythm in the concrete cuts in the road surface. *Was this son of a bitch telling him to shut his damn mouth?* Thad glanced over at Penn, who seemed to be dreamily staring out the front window. *Nah, he's talking some kind of gibberish.*

"Well, I don't know about that," Thad continued. "But let me tell you something about this damn company I work for."

Penn settled back in his seat and listened to Thad's complaints for miles before he fell into a troubled sleep, not waking up until the truck pulled into the parking lot of Thad's favorite diner in Diamondville.

25.

When Tokyo returned to the back room, she was surprised to find the room in semidarkness, Amos sitting at the kitchen table sipping coffee, and Sis nowhere in sight. Tokyo moved to the sink and opened the tap, pouring some cold water into a coffee-stained mug. She could taste the coffee remnants embedded in the sides of the mug, bleeding into the water, giving it a slightly tannic taste, but she drank greedily anyway, then replaced the mug to the dish rack to dry. She turned to face Amos.

"Where's Sis?" Amos held a finger up to his lips and gestured to his bedroom. Tokyo walked over to the door and pushed it open slightly. Sis was lying in bed, asleep. Tokyo turned to Amos, who gestured for her to sit at the table. Tokyo walked slowly to the table and sat.

"She's sick, Tokyo. Don't know with what. Not a bad fever, really, not anything I've seen before. She said she's in pain."

"We should take her to town. To a doctor."

Amos smiled and shook his head. "You think she'd want that?"

"Who cares what she wants? Somebody who knows something ought to take a look at her."

They were quiet a long time, listening to the wind. Every so often, Amos cocked his head to listen, sometimes shaking his head. Finally Amos pointed at the ceiling.

"There, you hear it?"

"Your mouse back?"

Amos shook his head briskly, almost angrily. He wanted silence so he could listen. In the front of the store, the door banged open and Tongate's voice rang out.

"Amos? Luke? You hearing what I'm hearing?"

Inside the bedroom, Sis stirred. Amos turned toward Sis's room, but Tokyo put out a hand to stop him.

"Let me. I can't face *him* right now."

Amos looked guiltily into the bedroom and saw Sis's outline covered by the thick woolen blankets. He remembered when he had bought the blankets in a United States Army surplus catalogue. A gross of them, no more than five dollars a blanket. And still only 142 to sell.

"Amos?" Tongate's head appeared from the front room. He squinted through the darkness at Amos and Tokyo, then flicked on the light switch. "Where's Luke? His truck's outside."

Amos gestured Tongate to silence as he walked toward him. He flicked the light switch off, then turned to Tokyo. "Penn drove Luke's truck. Me and Barney'll take it back to him."   Tokyo's brow furrowed for a moment. "No. Leave it," she said.

"But Luke'll be wondering …"

"What's he going to think? Penn stole it? I'll take it back to him after I see to Sis, then Luke'll bring me back."

Amos considered while Tongate tried to put the pieces together into a coherent whole. Suddenly, Amos and Tongate stared at each other, their eyes wide, then, as if on signal, they looked up at the ceiling.

"Damn," Tongate whispered. Amos nodded.

By now Tokyo was standing at the bedroom door. "What the hell are you two doing?" she asked in a fierce whisper.

"The wind. It's acting crazy," Amos said.

"Unlike any heretofore experienced," Tongate spluttered.

Tokyo shook her head in disbelief. Back in Sioux Falls, Hingham had acted this way about football. He would name teams, recite statistics, all in the same fascinated tone these two were using to describe the wind. It had bored her then. It bored her now.

Tokyo waved Tongate and Amos into the next room with the back of her hand, much as a person would flick away an irritating fly. The two men shuffled away, murmuring softly to each other as they went.

26.

In all the months she had lived in the back room, Tokyo could count on one hand the number of times she had been in Amos's bedroom. She viewed the space as private, not to be invaded. Moreover, as she walked toward Sis, she felt uncomfortable entering a place in which other people bared their souls to each other. As she walked into the dark bedroom, she imagined the pain, the sex, the arguing, the rawness of it all—and, above it all, the wind roaring outside, shrieking and moaning like an insane woman.

To maintain control, Tokyo concentrated on the physical things in the room. As in most other rooms in Black Rock, the furniture in the bedroom was an odd mixture of slate and wood. The bed in which Sis rested was framed in red oak, but the wood frame was constructed so that all the panels were made of large black slate slabs. The mattress rested on such a slab, and on cold days buckets of hot coals could be placed under the bed to warm the slate, allowing the heat to radiate up through the mattress. Amos had placed such a bucket under the bed, but apparently he hadn't gotten it right. Tokyo could see Sis was drenched in sweat, her short hair matted in places from the moisture.

"Damn," Tokyo said. She pulled the bucket of coals out from under the bed, using the large prongs Amos had constructed for that purpose.

"No." Sis's voice was weak, cracking.

Still crouching at the foot of the bed, Tokyo looked up at Sis. Her gray eyes, slightly bloodshot, were fixed on the coal bucket. She gestured with her eyes. *Leave them there. I'm cold.*

In response, Tokyo moved to feel Sis's forehead with the back of her hand. She was feverish, but not alarmingly so. Getting her hotter wouldn't help matters. Tokyo shook her head and stood to retrieve a cool washcloth from the bathroom. Sis shivered as Tokyo wiped the sweat from her face and head. Close to Sis like this, she could see the sores on her neck and even on her scalp, sores like bruises. Mastering her reluctance, Tokyo pulled the blanket down slightly and hesitantly opened Sis's loose flannel shirt, exposing similar sores on Sis's neck and chest. Sis shook uncontrollably as Tokyo sponged.

"How long have you had these sores?"

Sis shook her head. Her lips were chapped and cracked. She looked up at the roof, thinking, moving her lips as if to speak. Tokyo shook her head. "It doesn't matter," Tokyo said. "Didn't Amos notice them?"

Sis smiled and shook her head. "I didn't show him."

"Can you sit up? We should change your shirt." Sis nodded, and Tokyo helped to pull her into a sitting position. Tokyo pulled off her damp flannel shirt, then the soaked undershirt. Sis's torso, splotchy and dotted with sores, was pale and surprisingly lumpy for such a skinny woman. As Tokyo returned from the slate-topped bureau in the corner with fresh clothes, she could see in Sis's naked body the former wiry strength, now degraded by some unknown sickness.

Tokyo helped Sis with the clothes, then tucked her firmly under the covers. Sis smiled when she finally rested against the pillows again and sipped hesitantly from a cup of cold water. Kneeling by the bed, Tokyo put her face close to Sis. Sis smiled weakly. With surprise Tokyo read the question in Sis's eye. *How did it go?* Sis had never expressed interest in Tokyo's life. Tokyo felt embarrassed.

"It wasn't what I expected," Tokyo said. "But we'll talk about it later. How can I help, Sis? Do you know?"

Sis closed her eyes, keeping them closed so long Tokyo thought she might be sleeping. Finally, just as Tokyo stood to leave the room, Sis opened her eyes and looked up at her. For the first time in weeks, Tokyo saw life in Sis's eyes.

"You asked me how I could walk in the wind like that, different from the others," she said. Sis waited as she caught her breath, then continued. "It's because I don't fight the wind."

Tokyo's head dropped for a moment, remembering. After a long pause, she looked up. Tears welled in her eyes, embarrassing her.

"Don't cry. There's lots I don't fight. Lots I don't have to fight any more. Neither do you."

Despite herself, Tokyo grew angry. "Now's not a time for riddles, Sis. You're sick. And there's nothing I know how to do. Understand? We've got to take you to see someone. A doctor."

Sis shook her head weakly and smiled. She cleared her throat before speaking, wincing slightly as if in pain. "I'll get over it, or I won't," she said.

Tokyo was unnerved by Sis's response, but could only blink repeatedly, rapid blinks as she turned her head.

"Don't cry, Tokyo. Don't cry." Her voice trailed off and her eyes closed.

"I don't cry," Tokyo said, but Sis had already drifted into sleep. When Tokyo saw Sis's breaths grow regular, she exhaled sharply and moved quietly out of the room.

In the front of the store, Tokyo found Amos and Tongate in their usual positions at the counter. Proudfoot had joined them. Ignoring the other men, Tokyo paused at the door, her hands defiantly on her hips.

"She's sick, Amos. She needs help."

Proudfoot and Tongate exchanged looks. Real news was hard to come by in Black Rock, yet today they had more than they had a right to expect.

Amos shuffled his feet and looked at the ground. It was amazing, Tokyo thought, how small a tall man could make himself look.

"What are you going to do?" she challenged.

Amos pursed his lips and looked directly at Tokyo. "Whatever Sis wants."

Exasperated, Tokyo shook her head. "She doesn't want anything. She wants to just lie there with her fever. That's not getting anything done!"

"It's the Indian way. The heathen way," Proudfoot said.

"Oh, Jesus," Tokyo said. "Is that what you think? You think she's trusting some great spirit or something?"

"That's what her people do," Proudfoot said. "They ain't Christians."

"Neither is he," Tokyo said, pointing to Amos.

There was a long silence. Amos finally spoke, his words soft. "She's a strong woman, Tokyo. Stronger than any one of us'll ever know. And she's gotten this far on her own, making her own calls on what she needs and what she don't. And I don't figure on getting between her and what she wants now. Just wouldn't make no sense. Even if she wants something I don't."

Tongate and Proudfoot nodded silently, neither one of them daring to look up at Tokyo.

"Damn you all," Tokyo said. "Where are Luke's keys, Amos?" Amos reached under the counter and handed the truck keys to Tokyo. She jammed them in her sweater pocket and reached for her coat. "Take care of her until I get back. And don't put the goddamn coals under the bed. She's already got a fever, you don't want to give her a worse one."

27.

Tokyo had spent long hours on the highways, driving or being driven. And she had read books written by young men and women, books which glorified the freedom of the highways—but Tokyo knew better. There was no freedom on the highways, only an illusion of freedom, an illusion crafted by the speed at which one traveled. At sixty or seventy miles per hour, the landscape screamed by one's windows in an unfocused blur, the lines of demarcation between one thing and another so indistinct they tended to blend together and render themselves indecipherable and unimportant. If a thing couldn't be seen, it couldn't be contemplated, and if it couldn't be contemplated, it certainly couldn't be important. It could be ignored, particularly by the young, as an unimportant detail. And at the highest speeds, nothing could be seen or contemplated, leaving the only important thing to be one's self. And, because of the lack of distinction at such high speeds, a person traveling felt herself becoming part of the blurred landscape, at one with the unknown, omnipotent.

Tokyo knew from experience that her internal speed could rival a car or truck moving down the highway, not in any absolute sense, but in the sense of ignoring everything but her own movement, and so she dismissed the false power others saw in highway travel. And Tokyo knew from experience that eventually the speed would stop, and all the details which had been blurred and ignored would snap into focus, and the power one felt would end rudely. There was no freedom and no power here, she reflected, as Luke's truck battled the wind toward the mesa; there was only an absence of reality—the truck seemed to remain in place while the wind roared by, until she came to a stop in Luke's driveway.

She sat in the driveway a long time with the engine idling. The soothing rocking motion of the truck in the strong wind was offset by the screaming sound the wind created as it bounced off the flat surfaces of the truck. Inside, she knew, Luke would be watching her from the window, safe inside the house he had crafted aerodynamically so it would slice through the wind and diminish the noise.

Luke was used to Tokyo's suddenness and her silence. In the past he had mistaken her silence for thoughtfulness, then for simplicity, but now he saw her silence as something more complex. He was surprised to see her. He had assumed Amos would drive his truck back out, or Sis, or, perhaps even Penn, though he knew the chances of Tokyo's father staying on the mesa even one day longer were remote. For Tokyo to have driven herself could mean many things, most of them bad.

In the truck, Tokyo smiled as she saw Luke's shape in the window. From here, of course, she couldn't see his face, but something about his posture made it clear he was uncomfortable. She shook her head and reached for the door. *He probably has no idea what I'm doing here.* She jumped down from the truck and muscled the door shut, hiding for a moment in the slight shelter the truck provided before walking the short, difficult distance to the door to the house. She smiled again. *I have no idea what I'm doing here.*

Luke met her at the inner door, grimacing a greeting when she entered. He backed uncertainly toward the kitchen table, bumping into it with uncharacteristic clumsiness. Tokyo took off her coat and dropped it on the bench next to the inner door. She heard the oversized buttons of the coat click against the slate top of the bench, then scrape loudly as the coat slid slowly to the floor. Tokyo stepped toward Luke, reaching him and without hesitation slipping her arms under his, locking her hands behind his back. She pressed her ear to his chest and closed her eyes for a moment, feeling the uncertainty in Luke's arms and his breathing. She shrugged her shoulders, prompting him to move his arms around her shoulders. He did so, holding her tightly. She kept her eyes closed and hugged him, enjoying the warmth for a moment. Outside, the wind moved up and down octaves at a frenetic pace. Tokyo kept her eyes closed and held Luke even tighter.

When she finally released her grip and took a step back, she held on to one of Luke's hands with both of hers, lifted it to her lips and kissed it, then pressed the back of his hand to the side of her cheek. Her breath was coming faster now, and she looked up into Luke's eyes with a directness he had rarely seen.

Tokyo's cheek was cool on the back of Luke's hand, her lips warm and soft. Luke had grown accustomed to Tokyo's aggressiveness when she wanted to make love, her almost frightening insistence. At such times, he felt himself to be some kind of fungible sexual tool, there for her pleasure, but interchangeable with any number of others. Her lovemaking was angry; she kept her eyes closed, clearly removing herself to some other place, some other time.

As he had so many times before, he allowed himself to be led to the bedroom. Tokyo paused at the side of the bed. She reached forward and stroked the slate inlay. Her eyes were fixed on the slate as she pulled her sweater and tee shirt off in one motion and dropped them on the floor. She leaned forward and pulled her gray cotton pants down to her ankles, then used her toes to pull off each of her socks along with the pants. Her face wore an odd expression, somewhat whimsical, still staring at the side of the bed.

When Tokyo lifted the blankets to lie on the bed, she looked at Luke and raised her eyebrows. "You coming in?" she asked.

Luke hesitated, rubbing his hands on the back of his jeans. "Tokyo …"

Tokyo smiled, a sad smile, direct and innocent. She lifted her chin toward the ceiling, listening to the wind for a moment. "Lie with me," she said, still listening to the marauding wind.

Luke sat on the end of the bed and removed his clothes. She could see the hesitation in his motions, the fear and desire in his arched back. His shoulder blades moved up and down as he worked his shoes off, then his jeans. He turned and looked at her. She smiled warmly at him, a foreign, but welcome, smile. He hesitated.

"I'm not going to bite," Tokyo said. She turned on her side.

Luke lay down behind Tokyo. He put one hand on her shoulder. His fingers were cool, nervous.

"Pull the blanket," she asked, and he did, covering them both. Tokyo moved her hips until she was pressed against Luke. She pulled his arms around her, clasping his hands across her breasts. Enjoying the warmth, she smiled and exhaled. To Luke's surprise, tears began rolling down her cheeks.

"Tokyo …" Luke began.

She let the tears come, saying, "I just want to be here, Luke. I just want to be here."

Luke lifted his chin and rested it on top of her head. Before, he had been attracted by her willingness to take control, but now, he felt bathed in a warmth he hadn't felt before—not with Tokyo, not with any woman. They rested for a long time, so long that Luke thought Tokyo might have fallen asleep. She finally moved, turning in his arms and looking directly into his eyes. Her gaze was steady, unblinking. She looked as if she might cry again. Not knowing what to do, he stroked her head and looked into her large brown eyes.

"I'm tired of running," she said, and she kissed him.

Luke responded, kissing Tokyo gently. "I'm sorry if I scared you, Tokyo. Telling you I loved you. But I thought I was out of time."

Tokyo nodded, a gesture of understanding and dismissal. She kissed him again, not hungrily. Luke, a man not inclined to see fine distinctions in people as he did in wood and slate, and even wind, knew something had turned in Tokyo, and he was glad to be with her as if for the first time.

28.

Luke stared up at the ceiling. Next to him, Tokyo nuzzled her head against his chest. She rubbed her feet rhymically, one against the other, the motion soothing and regular. Occasionally, Luke would start and squint at the roof as if it were speaking to him. From long experience, Tokyo knew he was listening to the wind, listening for nuances and changes only the long-timers could hear. She shifted in bed, still facing him and, bending at the waist, pressing her knees up against his thighs. He turned his head toward her without removing his gaze from the ceiling.

"You hear?"

Tokyo stopped rubbing her feet together and listened. "No."

He raised one hand and wagged his fingers. "There's something going on. Like this. I talked to Amos earlier. He heard it too."

"What?"

Luke shook his head, a gesture of helplessness. Tokyo smiled thinly. Of course. Who could understand this wind except someone who had lived in it his whole life? After another pause, Tokyo resumed rubbing her feet together and let Luke listen to the wind. After a time, he stroked her hair.

"Why'd Penn come here?"

Tokyo's feet stopped moving. She surprised herself by the lack of desire to answer cynically. "My mother died—and my sister. I didn't really know either of them; it shouldn't bother me, but knowing what they went through …"

Luke nodded.

Tokyo sighed heavily, "I guess he felt like it was the right thing to do. For him. For me."

After a silence, Luke spoke. "Most people know the 'who' of their father, but not the 'why.' You and me, we know the 'why,' but not the 'who.'"

In her life, Tokyo had valued her ability to tie up loose ends, to be in control. Those things that were uncontrollable or unexplainable she had held in contempt. When she had been unable to explain, her anger had comforted her like a warm blanket. But today, instead of her anger, she felt unexpected and unusual warm comfort and simplicity in Luke's bed. She couldn't explain Penn any more than she could have explained the wind, but at the moment she felt as if it didn't matter. Nothing really mattered as much as she had presumed.

"Can you drive me back to the store?"

Luke looked at her for the first time. She looked back unblinkingly. He was afraid, uncertain. Again, she surprised herself with the absence of revulsion, which was her usual reaction to his hangdog face.

"Sis is sick. Amos doesn't know what to do. I've got to help."

Luke nodded and sat up in bed, looking for his jeans. They dressed quietly, listening to the wind. When they were dressed, Tokyo stood at the bedroom doorway, slightly afraid of passing through, as if a spell would be broken. Luke stood behind her, aware of her reluctance, but unsure of its source. She turned to him, and he saw the expression of a girl of fourteen, filled with newness and enthusiasm, but frightened by the depth of her feeling.

"I'm coming back. I'm just going to take care of Sis," she said, at once surprised and scared by her promise.

Luke smiled, a rare, full smile, the cracks at the corners of his eyes stretching in unusual patterns. He leaned down and kissed her on the top of the head. She smiled back at him, and they walked into the kitchen arm in arm.

Changes are imperceptible at first. Some, like an avalanche in a faraway mountain in the middle of the night, are never noticed. Others simply begin small, creating a momentum which is unstoppable, finally noticeable, and, in some cases, ultimately overwhelming. In the truck, being pushed by the wind toward town, Tokyo was aware of changes in herself. When had they begun? When she had promised Luke she wouldn't leave? When she actually kept the promise? When she had discovered she had missed not only her own mother and father in her life, but a sister whom she could never hope to know? Just now, when she had sidled closer to Luke as they drove to town? Or sometime long ago, a time she couldn't remember? She smiled to herself, thinking of the boys in New England calling this position the "two-headed driver." So many years ago.

29.

As the succeeding weeks went by, Tokyo never abandoned hope of convincing Sis that she should see a doctor. Within days, Sis had been unable to get out of bed. By the end of three weeks, she could hardly speak. She always seemed feverish and had no appetite, but the fever was not high, nor would it break.

"You have to see a doctor, Sis," Tokyo tried repeatedly. "I don't know what to do for you."

Sis shook her head. "Nothing to do. Can't help it."

For the first time in a month, Tokyo felt anger, true anger. "You can't give up, Sis! I won't let you. I'll get Tongate to bring a doctor here. Pay him whatever he wants."

Sis smiled at Tokyo. She moved her chapped lips for a moment before a sound emerged. "Won't take what he gives me."

Frustrated, Tokyo angrily straightened the blanket under Sis's chin. She picked up the tray of uneaten lunch and looked at it. "Do you want to die?"

Sis closed her eyes and listened to the wind. In her earlier days she had been able to breathe like the wind, strong and full, but now she couldn't draw much of a breath without coughing. When she opened her eyes, she was surprised to find Tokyo still staring at her angrily. Sis moved one arm out from beneath the blankets and patted the side of the bed. Tokyo sat, still holding Sis's uneaten lunch.

"Nobody wants to die, Tokyo. Even them that kill themselves." Tokyo thought of her mother's tears and of Penn, returning to her home, finding her lifeless. Finding her sister lifeless. Tokyo shook her head.

"You're doing a pretty good job of convincing me otherwise," she said.

Tokyo watched as Sis tried unsuccessfully to avoid coughing, to avoid the pain which racked her body when she did. When Sis opened her eyes again, there were tears. Tokyo reached forward with her free hand and touched Sis's shoulder, a look of deep concern on her face. Sis patted her hand, then gestured, waving her hand weakly.

"I want to be a part of all these things. The wind, this place. Now, when I'm alive. And after I'm dead." Sis closed her eyes. Tokyo waited for a moment until the sound of Sis's breathing became regular. *A part of all these things.* Tokyo shook her head. Sis's calmness could be soothing, but sometimes, as now, it could be nothing short of maddening. Looking into her pale face, Tokyo feared Sis's death was close, but felt helpless to do a thing about it.

Tokyo lived in the back room as before, caring for Sis during the days and nights while Amos helplessly busied himself around the store. Luke visited frequently, talking with Tokyo in low tones, displaying a level of intimacy that surprised Tongate and Amos.

After lunch, made by Amos in Sis's fashion, Amos, Luke, and Tokyo would visit with Sis, to keep her spirits up, until Tokyo shepherded the men out of the room.

"Go on now," Tokyo admonished. "Let her sleep."

Luke would nod silently to Tokyo. Looking back at him, her eyes would shine and she would nod a farewell. They would be together later; no need to hurry now.

"No," Amos said. He was standing behind the counter in his usual position. "She doesn't want a doctor." Tongate and Proudfoot looked down at the counter, studying the slate top while they chewed peanuts. Tokyo ignored them, focusing instead on Amos.

"You've got to admire this slate. Look at this, no cracks after all these years," Proudfoot said to Tongate. Tongate nodded and moved one hand absently over the slate. Tokyo rolled her eyes and moved closer to Amos.

"I don't know what's wrong with her. She'll die." Tokyo's voice was a whisper, but she knew Proudfoot and Tongate could hear her.

Hunched over like an old man, Amos placed both hands on the side of the counter and leaned forward heavily. On the other side of the counter, the two men watched as Amos attempted to find words. "She may do just that, Tokyo. Never questioned her before. Seems like it'd be wrong to now."

"God's will," Proudfoot murmured. Tongate knew enough to keep his mouth shut.

"You can't speak for her," Tokyo barked. "Not on this. Go talk to her. Get her to see a doctor." Tokyo moved to one side, opening a path for Amos to enter the back room. Amos remained in place, staring at the counter. Unsure of what she was going to say, Tokyo strode over to Amos and tugged on his arm. Amos was much larger than Tokyo, and he was surprised at the strength of her hands. *Her grip is firm*, he thought. *Probably from living here in Black Rock so long. People get hard.*

"Look at me, Amos," Tokyo said. Amos turned toward her, but his eyes were downcast. *So this is what it's like to have children*, Tokyo thought. "How does it feel, Amos? Does it feel good?"

Amos looked at Tokyo, puzzled.

"How does it feel?" Tokyo repeated. "Making choices for other people, people you might love? How does it feel having those choices made for you, by people you didn't even know? By Luke's father? By the guy who sends you money? You sit here with these excuses, these men; you and Luke do your dance with this place, and you can blame it all on the past you didn't have control of, or what's down in that quarry, or 'God's will', but it isn't any of that, is it?"

Amos's normally imperturbable demeanor and ruddy complexion had grown pale. Tokyo continued, more gently.

"I don't want to hurt you, Amos. I don't. I want to help Sis."

"You don't understand ..." Amos began.

"Don't tell me I don't understand. Don't tell me about your suffering, your family's suffering, your goddamn cat's suffering. We all suffer, Amos. But we don't have to live with it forever. And, goddamnit, we don't have to let Sis suffer."

It seemed as if a long time passed before the energy in the room dissipated. Tokyo dimly became aware of the sound of the wind and the strange looks on the faces of Tongate and Proudfoot. Normally, the two men looked at Tokyo with a mixture of condescension and humor, but today there was something else entirely in their stares, something that caused Tokyo to look away quickly, embarrassed.

Finally, Amos stood upright and walked to the entrance to the back room. He paused for a moment, turning to look back at Tokyo. *Tokyo seems taller,* he thought. Then he turned and walked back to the bedroom.

30.

Tokyo sat on a stool looking through the inventory sheets which Amos kept in a large, old-fashioned ledger cover. The cover was black, but the faux-alligator quilting on the leather had allowed dust to highlight each of the cracks. Each time she picked up the ledger, before she opened it, Tokyo liked to wipe the cover with a hand, knowing the deeply ingrained dust would remain in place, but trying nonetheless. She silently checked off costs and sales, shaking her head on the many occasions when Amos had thoughtlessly sold inventory for lower prices than he had purchased it.

Amos had been in the back room a long time, over two hours. Tongate and Proudfoot, more uncomfortable than usual in her presence, had lasted only a half hour, despite their curiosity at what Amos might do. For what seemed like the first time in several days, Tokyo was alone, sitting at the counter, as if she were in her first months in Black Rock again.

On one such day, back when she had first acquainted herself with Amos's poor inventory and sales "systems," Sis had moved silently into the room behind Tokyo. In those days, it had been easy to sneak up on Tokyo, since she was new to the town and could still hear little over the violent sound of the wind. Sis, however, had no intention of surprising Tokyo; instead, she had come into the room to fetch several tablecloths she had woven. They were kept under the front counter, there being no room in the kitchen cabinets for them.

When she entered the front room, she saw Tokyo sitting at the counter, directly in front of the tablecloths. To reach them, she would have to disturb Tokyo, something which Tokyo clearly didn't seem to appreciate. Sure of what she wanted, but loathe to interfere, Sis stood silently a few feet behind Tokyo, looking down at the tablecloths as if Tokyo were not there. After a moment, Tokyo must have sensed something, because she turned her head and was startled to see Sis.

"Damn!" Tokyo said, rotating fully around on her stool to face Sis directly. Sis said nothing; she simply looked past Tokyo at the tablecloths. "Damn," Tokyo repeated. "You scared the hell out of me!"

Sis looked up. Her gray eyes pierced through Tokyo. "I did," she said. She was stating a fact. Her eyes remained fixed on Tokyo.

"What the hell do you want from me?" Tokyo asked.

In answer, Sis stepped toward Tokyo, who flinched reflexively. Sis reached smoothly past Tokyo and retrieved an indigo tablecloth from under the counter. Sis had reached one hand out and steadied herself on the counter, and her cool, dry hand had touched Tokyo's for an instant. Her touch was at once course like sandpaper and soothing like a cool hand on a hot forehead. Tokyo hadn't recognized the feeling at the time, but it struck her now: Sis's touch was like the touch of a mother.

Tokyo shook her head at the memory, wishing she could do the same for Sis now. Her reverie was disturbed when the front door opened and Luke entered.

"Hey," he said, waiting to speak until he was close enough to not have to raise his voice over the wind. "How is she?"

Tokyo shook her head. "Amos is back there with her." Luke squinted. "I told him we've got to take her to a doctor. He says she doesn't want to." She paused, then leaned across the counter and took Luke's hand, slipping her fingers between his. His hands were cold from the wind outside. They both looked at their intertwined hands and smiled nervously. The intimacy was frightening for them both, and Tokyo quickly broke her hand away, not quickly, but kindly, knowing that they would have to go slowly. Luke looked behind the counter with some concern.

"What do you think he'll do?"

"You know him better than I do," Tokyo answered. After a pause, she continued, "I was kind of hard on him."

Luke leaned against the counter the way a man might lean against a bar waiting for his first beer to be poured. He kept his coat on and looked up at Shlomo's canes.

"I don't know if I do, Tokyo. More like I know what he's been through, what he's seen. I guess it doesn't mean I know him."

Tokyo thought about the places she had been and how they might define her. All the places and people merged in her memory, until they swirled past and through her and felt like the wind: fast and cleansing at one moment, and dull and impeding the next. The combination of things she had done—some willingly, some unwillingly—was like a weight and wings all at once, and Tokyo nodded, knowing how right Luke was.

Luke suddenly looked up, behind Tokyo. She turned and saw Amos standing at the entrance. He was pale, shaken. In an instant, both Luke and Tokyo knew. His lips moved silently for a moment before he spoke.

"She's gone."

Tokyo felt herself wilt. She glanced briefly over at Luke, who was now standing straight. Vaguely surprised that neither man could hear the wail she felt in her heart, she stood and carefully closed the ledger book. She replaced it in the shelf behind the counter and walked a few steps toward Amos. He had been crying, she could see, but he wasn't now. He was in shock.

Tokyo stepped forward and hugged Amos. Then she backed away, tears pouring down her cheeks. "I'm sorry," was all she could say. Luke stepped forward and put one firm hand on Amos's shoulder. Luke's touch seemed to steady Amos and to bring him back to the present. He sighed deeply and reached forward, hugging Luke in a strong embrace, both of them sobbing.

In the bedroom, Tokyo entered quietly, moving toward Sis's still form almost on tiptoe. Tokyo had heard people speak of funerals— how nice they were, how the flowers were spectacular, how the family of the deceased had been strong—hedging their language around what they really wanted to speak about: death. Sometimes she had heard people, her foster father being one, say "He looked so peaceful," and she knew, looking at Sis, that such words weren't soothing; they weren't sympathetic—if anything, they were envious.

Tokyo wept as she moved Sis's cold body and wrapped it carefully in the sheets of the bed. She suddenly remembered something Sis had said one day while they were setting the table for lunch.

"You think it's the wind that mixes everything up. But it isn't the wind makes us all part of each other," she had said. "It isn't the wind makes us all part of everything," she said. "We just are." With that, Sis returned to the back room and made another simple lunch for another day.

31.

Luke and Amos stood next to Sis's body, which was wrapped in sheets weighted with black slate and covered with one of her tapestries. Tokyo, Proudfoot, and Tongate stood off to one side and watched the wind tug at the edges of the tapestry. Proudfoot had wanted to speak from the Bible, but Tokyo had forbidden it, telling him that if he said anything out loud, she'd throw him into the quarry right after Sis. He had had to be content with moving his lips silently to the Scriptures as Amos and Luke lifted Sis's body and swung it onto a wooden ramp they had built together back in the store for just this purpose. He watched with the others as her body hit the black water and quickly sank. Tokyo stood forward, next to Luke and Amos, who both stared down at the lazy ripples in the water for a long time until they calmed.

Amos turned to Tokyo. "You were right, Tokyo. I should've forced her."

Amos's sadness threatened to overwhelm Tokyo. She shook her head briskly, controlling the tears with difficulty. "No. She wanted to be a part of this place," Tokyo said. "You wouldn't have been able to stop her. Probably a doctor wouldn't have been able to stop her."

Luke took Amos by the arm, but Amos turned to him. "I don't want to go just yet. Let's sit over in the shelter for a minute, Luke. Like we used to when we were kids."

Tokyo stood next to the quarry lip as Luke and Amos walked to the shelter of the slate overhang. Tongate and Proudfoot had already retreated to their truck, despite the relative springtime warmth and high noon sun. Proudfoot had made the sign of the cross as he retreated, careful to wait until he was far enough from Tokyo. Glancing back at Amos and Luke in the shelter, Tokyo decided against joining them. She sat near the edge of the quarry and looked down at the water. The ripples had stilled, and Tokyo could clearly see the reflection of the sun and the fast-moving clouds on the surface of the black water. Somehow, the sight was more relaxing in the reflection than in the sky. She smiled to herself, thinking, *It's probably because I'm more comfortable looking down than up.*

In the shelter, Luke and Amos easily took the seats they had used so many years before while sitting at this windswept tomb. In prior years, when they were boys, they had talked about everything, but each year had brought a lessening of words and an increase in silence. Today, Amos felt as if everything had been said.

"I loved her, Luke. You know? I loved her."

Luke nodded and put his hand on Amos's arm kindly. "Sis was something."

Amos didn't seem to hear Luke. "I thought I loved her, anyway. Maybe you just get used to a person after so many years. You get to where you depend on them just being there. Maybe it lets you fill up a hole inside yourself with something familiar, every day having them there. Maybe."

Sitting at the edge of the quarry, looking down into the water, Tokyo saw the jagged edges and hard corners of the quarry walls reflected back at her. For a moment she resisted the impulse to move closer to the edge, knowing the wind could take advantage of her precarious position—a fall into the icy water would be fatal. But despite her better sense and her caution she inched closer to the edge, still sitting. Dimly, she was aware of nothing more than her desire to see her own reflection in the water. Somehow it seemed vitally important for her to see herself. The urge compelled her to move so close to the edge that Luke and Amos looked at each other with concern. Finally, she stopped and seemed rooted again, staring down into the water. The two men relaxed until she jerked upright and looked over at them, yelling something, then looked back into the water. Her voice wasn't audible, but her suddenly erect posture was. She squinted up at the sun, directly overhead, then down into the water again. Finally, her eyes fixed on the water, her body went rigid, and she gestured to Luke and Amos urgently.

The two men walked quickly but carefully over to Tokyo's perch and looked down into the quarry where Tokyo was pointing. At first, like Tokyo, they saw nothing but the reflections of sun, clouds, and quarry walls, but soon their eyes adjusted to the relative darkness of the water. Luke was the first to see it. The sight was like a blow to his chest.

Amos glanced over at Luke, his eyes wide, then looked down, wondering whether it was possible. Then he saw it too: past the reflections of the windswept sky, past the reflection of the jagged edges of the quarry, and past even the reflections of themselves looking down, he saw dim angular shapes, three of them visible, shapes forty feet below the water, which could only have been the roofs of houses.

Tokyo looked over at the two men, knowing only that she wouldn't want to feel what they were feeling. She didn't even know what *she* was feeling as she looked at them, awed in the face of their past, awed to silence in a way she had seldom seen men awed—without tears, anger, remorse, or jealousy—two men who cared at this instant about nothing more than what had been revealed. Tokyo looked at Amos and Luke as two brothers who had spent a lifetime trying to piece their joint histories together. And finally their history had been revealed, and it made less sense than ever before. She linked her arm through Luke's, and he held her arm tightly.

When she looked back down into the quarry, the wind had swept the sun behind a long line of clouds, and nothing was visible except the reflection of the windy sky.

32.

The final avalanche came at night. Weeks of minor slides had amounted to nothing, but suddenly, tons of snow, rocks, soil, and uprooted trees careened down the mountain, building more and more weight as the avalanche headed toward the vacant valley. At the bottom, the snow and soil crashed together in a fury, finally settling; the bottom of the valley was now some fifty feet higher than it had been.

A person standing in the valley, or safely nearby, would have been amazed by the sheer force of nature they had witnessed. But there were no witnesses.

The wind which had previously blown through the valley was directed upward instead, a minor difference unnoticed by the nearest homes, some fifty miles away. But in Black Rock, the change was profound.

33.

It was already dark by the time Tokyo and Luke drove back to Luke's home after Sis's burial. They had stayed with Amos for a long time, much longer than was comfortable for Tokyo, so long that Amos had said nothing for the last two hours. He had sat in one of the large chairs next to the window, listening to the wind, while Tokyo and Luke spoke in muted tones to several of the quarrymen who had already returned for the spring quarry season. Several of them had been on the mesa for years, had stayed in town at Proudfoot's bunkhouse, and were shocked and disappointed that the quiet Indian woman had died.

When the quarrymen left, Amos looked up at Tokyo and Luke and smiled briefly. "Thanks, you two," he said.

"That's okay, Amos. We'll see you tomorrow. Tokyo says she'll cook us lunch."

Amos curled his lips inside his mouth as far as possible and nodded. "That'd be nice. Thanks." He looked out the window again for a moment. "The wind's funny, isn't it Luke?"

Luke and Tokyo followed his gaze. "Been funny for a while. Don't know what to make of it. Well, see you tomorrow."

"What are you guys hearing in the wind?" Tokyo asked Luke. They had driven halfway across the mesa in silence, battling the wind as usual. Luke was about to answer when he stopped the truck suddenly. He peered out the front window, his mouth hanging open. Tokyo looked as well and was shocked to see a coyote standing in the road in front of them.

The coyote's hair was matted in some places and standing straight up in others, as if he had been tossed in an automatic clothes dryer when wet. His eyes reflected red from the headlamps of Luke's truck, and he stood as if frozen in place, staring at the truck.

"I think it's a coyote," Luke said. Tokyo nodded. "What on earth is he doing up here?"

As if in answer, the coyote turned his head toward the wind for a moment, closing its eyes and squinting, then looked back at the truck. He shambled off the road, walking slightly off-kilter, but in a relatively straight line. Luke didn't move the truck. Instead, he watched the darkness into which the coyote had vanished.

"The wind didn't seem to bother him," Tokyo said.

"Maybe he's got rabies. Went crazy."

A pause. The wind buffeted the truck lazily. "He didn't look crazy, did he?" Tokyo asked.

"But what would he eat up here?" Luke asked. "Even if he's the first coyote in a hundred years to come up here and survive, what would he eat?"

"Amos's mouse?" Tokyo smiled as she moved closer to Luke for warmth. He smiled and put the truck in gear.

"Maybe we're the crazy ones," he said.

⌒   ⌒   ⌒

Tokyo thought she might be dreaming when Luke shook her awake roughly in the middle of the night. He had tossed and turned for a long time before he had fallen asleep, so much that she had considered removing herself to the slate and wood couch in the living room, but the connection she had established with Luke was too new and frail for her to disturb quite yet. So she had waited patiently for his twitching to stop and then had inched next to him and fallen asleep.

In her dream, she stood alone on the mesa, the coyote's red eyes staring at her from only a few feet away. The eyes rose and grew larger; the rest of the coyote seemed to disappear from view. Tokyo suddenly felt hot, and in her dream reached for the eyes, but they blew away with a wind so fierce and strong she was knocked off her feet and blown backward onto the road. She tried to regain her feet, but the wind knocked her down again and again. She started to laugh at the comical scene she must have made, as if she were a first-time ice skater trying to stand on slippery ice.

Then Luke was shaking her awake, his voice uncharacteristically urgent. "Tokyo! Wake up! Tokyo!"

A woman known for unpleasantness can be doubly so upon a rude awakening. Tokyo shot what she hoped was a withering glare at Luke and stuck her head under her pillow. Luke, suddenly daring and aggressive, pulled the pillow back.

"What the hell time is it?" Tokyo asked.

Luke looked at the clock on the bedside table as if he were surprised to see it there. "Time?" Luke asked, incredulous. "C'mon, get your coat on." Tokyo, about to protest, was puzzled to see that Luke had brought her coat into the bedroom. She sat up and pulled the coat on, then shuffled after Luke into the kitchen. Only dimly regaining consciousness, she looked out into the sky and saw the distinctive purple-black sky which appeared only just before the dawn. The phone was ringing in the kitchen, but Luke ignored it.

"It's a special time of day," Sis had told her once. "A special color. Only happens once a day, for only a few minutes. Special."

Tokyo followed Luke out of the house, vaguely registering the fact that both the inner and outer doors to the house were hanging open. *That won't do,* Tokyo thought. *The wind will sweep the house clean.* She yawned and looked for Luke. He was outside, motionless on the pathway leading to the driveway and his truck. He turned and looked gleefully at Tokyo.

"It woke me up! It's what Amos's mouse was saying! It's what the coyote was telling us tonight! It's …" Luke stopped talking and turned his face to the cool springtime breeze coming out of the north.

The wind had stopped.

"I don't know how long it's gonna last. Shlomo told us about a day, here and there, when the wind calmed down, but not like this." Luke waved his hand. "This is almost calm! You couldn't sail a boat today! We have to get down to Amos's place. I'll call him!"

Tokyo turned as Luke ran inside and seemed to be surprised when he realized the phone was already ringing. She could see him through the kitchen window, talking excitedly to Amos, slapping his hand against the kitchen counter, amazed at the lack of wind and sharing the amazement with his friend, his brother.

Tokyo looked back into the sky and saw the purple color fading into a pink and blue. If the wind could stop, anything seemed possible. Her father had come and gone, her mother too, along with her sister.

Sis's time had come and gone as well. Tokyo felt the calm warmth of the spring dawn on her face, and she allowed herself to hope that the rough wind had disappeared from Black Rock Mesa forever.

Breinigsville, PA USA
04 April 2010
235500BV00001B/47/P